WORLD WITHOUT CATS

Bonham Richards

iUniverse, Inc.
Bloomington

World without Cats

iUniverse books may be ordered through booksellers or by contacting:

iUniverse
1663 Liberty Drive
Bloomington, IN 47403
www.iuniverse.com
1-800-Authors (1-800-288-4677)

ISBN: 978-1-4759-2601-9 (sc)
ISBN: 978-1-4759-2603-3 (e)
ISBN: 978-1-4759-2602-6 (dj)

Library of Congress Control Number: 2012908410

Printed in the United States of America

iUniverse rev. date: 10/31/2012

1

Associate Professor Noah Chamberlin donned his gray sweats for a morning jog. As he was beginning his warm-up routine, his pocket phone sounded the "Hallelujah Chorus." Noah directed an angry glare at the device. *Who the hell calls at six thirty in the morning?* He opened the phone to find Gary McKeever's agitated visage. Gary was his sole grad student. *Uh-oh, something's seriously wrong.*

"Hi, Gary, What's up?"

"Morning, Dr. C. Sorry to start your day on a negative note, but we've got a big problem."

Noah sighed. "You didn't prepare the culture."

"No, no, the culture is fine," Gary replied. "The problem is that the cats are gone."

"What are you talking about?" *Is Gary setting me up for some kind of joke?*

"Yup, someone broke into the lab during the night and snatched them. It was those animal-liberation nuts."

Noah was silent for several seconds. "They broke both locks?" he asked hoarsely.

"No, they must have had keys …"

"Is Alicia in yet?" Noah asked. He wondered if the laboratory technician might have seen anyone with the cats.

"No, she doesn't come in till nine."

1

Noah was silent. His heart raced. "Right," he rasped. "I'll get there as soon as I can. Go ahead and notify the campus police."

"Yeah, I already did. They should be here soon."

Noah had awakened fifteen minutes earlier, anticipating the clock's alarm by seconds. He'd lain, silently marveling at the precision of his own biological clock. Bastette had pursued her morning ritual, nudging his leg and then carefully negotiating her way toward the head of the bed. The cat's whiskers had tickled Noah's chin as she'd settled down on his chest.

Now Noah had a crisis to deal with—a big one. He mulled over what he'd planned for the morning. *Run, shower, breakfast, bike to the university, prepare lecture on protein synthesis ...* he heard the flap-flap of Bastette's private door as she went out to explore the backyard. Noah stared at the floor. *Always one step forward, two steps back ...* He considered skipping the run. Drawing back the bedroom drapes, Noah regarded a damp but quietly beautiful scene. Even the morning mist couldn't quite mask the vibrant reds, purples, and pinks of the bougainvilleas along the rear wall. He spied Bastette calmly grooming herself beneath a tall pine. A crow strutted across the yard, every now and then picking up a tidbit from the earth. The cat and crow eyed each other, but neither made a move. Noah smiled. The cat had learned long ago not to tangle with birds her size or larger. Noah laughed out loud. *Shit! I'm not going to let this get to me. It'll take time, but I'll replace the cats.*

He hurried out the front door and jogged at a comfortable pace. As he ran, he mulled over the experiment he had planned for the afternoon. *It's going to take several hours to set up so I better start right after the institute faculty meeting.* Gary had mentioned on the phone that the bacterial culture was ready, and therefore, everything was set—except, of course, all the cats were gone. *Well, cats aren't needed for today's experiment.*

When he stepped into the shower the needle spray drummed away all thoughts of world affairs, faculty meetings, experiments, and even the cat theft. For a few moments there was no universe outside the relaxing confines of the shower.

He fed Bastette and bolted a quick breakfast himself. Because of the drizzle, Noah decided against the Sirrus twelve-speed. He threw his attaché case into the old Ford Focus and climbed in.

Driving south toward the university, Noah's thoughts turned again to research. He recalled when, as a graduate student at Cal, he'd first read about macroerythrocytic feline anemia, or MEFA, a hereditary disease in cats that resulted from a mutation in a hemoglobin gene. He had immediately grasped that the mutation provided an ideal means to test the ability of recombinant DNA to cure a genetic disease.

His two-year post-doc with Jean-Paul Cuisance at the University of Massachusetts had prepared him well for his future research. The old Frenchman was not only a master at recombinant DNA technology but also a terrific teacher. Nevertheless, Cuisance urged Noah not to use cats as experimental animals.

"There are too many legal restrictions on use of cats for research," Professor Cuisance admonished one day as the two scientists fussed over a PCR apparatus.

"I know, I know," Noah had responded, "but the potential for saving lives and relieving suffering makes the challenge and the paperwork worth it."

Cuisance had pointed a micropipet at Noah as if it were a weapon, making jabbing motions as he spoke. "If the authorities don't stop you, the animal rights fanatics will."

"Those people break the law," Noah replied with a shrill tone. "Do you expect me to avoid worthwhile research because of the acts of a few criminals?"

Cuisance stared at Noah. Noah had seen that the old man was becoming frustrated. He'd resigned himself to the invective that was now to come. Cuisance was silent a moment. "Let's talk about that." He motioned Noah to sit on a lab stool and sat down next to him. Noah had been unprepared for the calm tone of the professor's voice.

"Back in 2001," Cuisance began, "a veterinarian at NYU was forced to quit his job because he was using cats to investigate AIDS in drug users."

Noah frowned. "Why should he have had to quit?"

"Ah, I'll tell you why. The animal-rights fanatics picketed the university and called him a cat-killer and other names. They threatened him and his family and performed acts of vandalism against the university. Finally, in order to protect his wife and children, he walked out, the research unfinished."

Noah shook his head. "Wow. That's incredible. I didn't realize those lunatics had such power."

"Well, they do. Other scientists have been attacked since then. Some have stopped using animals, others have defied the crazies. They're fanatics. Fanatics don't give up. Wouldn't you quit your job to protect your family if it came to that?"

Noah shrugged. "I don't know. I've never thought about it." They'd continued to argue, neither convincing the other.

As he neared the university, Noah spotted Alicia Diaz making her way on foot toward the campus. He pulled up beside her.

"Hop in. I think we're headed to the same place."

Alicia laughed. "I guess we are."

"How come you're on foot?"

"Car's in the shop. It should be ready this afternoon."

Noah turned to Alicia. "Gary phoned me a while ago. Apparently, all our cats have been stolen."

"What?" Alicia cried out. "You're kidding." She was silent a moment. "You're not kidding."

"Did you see anyone suspicious-looking in or around the lab yesterday?"

"No, not that I recall."

"Gary said that it was animal-liberation activists. They left their calling card."

"What are we going to do?"

"I don't know."

He steered the Focus into the University's main drive and headed for the institute.

"Could you let me out here, Dr. C?" Alicia asked. "I've got to run over to the personnel office. I'll see you up in the lab."

Noah spotted Gary's old, but well-preserved, Honda Civic in the parking lot. Gary had earned a BS with honors as a biology major at Stanford. Shortly after Noah had joined the institute's faculty, the tall, lanky young man had exploded into Noah's office, introduced himself, and exclaimed, "I've been reading your papers on feline hemoglobins, and I'd like to do graduate research in your lab if you have the room."

Noah remembered that he had laughed. "I certainly have room. You would be my first graduate student. I'm kind of new here myself."

Gary had enthusiastically repeated his desire to come to Camarillo and study at Cal State, Channel Islands under Noah's sponsorship. Now, three years later, the brilliant student was beginning his doctoral dissertation.

He walked toward the building with foreboding. Maybe today's experiment would succeed, but how could he then proceed without cats to experiment with? He caught sight of the quotation on the lintel over the glass doors.

> *There is nothing too little for so little a creature as man. It is by studying little things that we attain the great art of having as little misery and as much happiness as possible.*
>
> James Boswell
> The Life of Samuel Johnson

I hope so, he thought. He exited the elevator on the seventh floor and walked rapidly down the hallway toward his office. A group of undergraduate biochemistry students was clustered around his bulletin board where, the day before, he had posted their exam scores. They parted to let him through.

"Dr. Chamberlin, may I see you about my exam?" asked a teen who carried a stuffed backpack over one shoulder. Noah recognized the young man as a student near the bottom of the class. His stomach churned. He hated these post-exam sessions with students more concerned with grades than with biochemistry.

"Yes, of course," he answered. "Come in and make an appointment."

"Please, couldn't I just see you now while I'm here?"

"Well, I have some work to … oh, all right, come in."

The lad pleaded that he was a pre-med, and he absolutely had to pass this course or he wouldn't get into med school. Noah did not voice his thought—anyone who can't pass this course doesn't belong in med school. He handled the student as best he could, and the young man left the office only slightly mollified.

Noah headed down the hall to the lab. He greeted Gary, who awaited him at the door. The normally even-tempered youth looked uncharacteristically flushed and somewhat out of breath. His blond hair, usually neatly combed, was disheveled.

"This really sucks," Gary said. "How am I going to finish my project?"

Noah ignored the question. "We should probably disinfect the laboratory," he said. "The intruders may have brought in contamination." He fumbled nervously for his keys.

"Here, I've got it," Gary offered as he stretched out the retractable keychain clipped to his belt.

They entered the lab and donned the lab coats that were hanging by the door.

Noah made for the cat room. Inside, all the cage doors stood open, and not one of the thirty cats remained. The full implication of the theft now hit him. He felt dizzy. He went back into the outer lab, where Gary was already busy swabbing down the work tables with disinfectant. Noah looked up at the chalkboard and read the neatly printed message: "ANIMAL RESEARCH IS SCIENTIFIC FRAUD – CLAWS"

Noah was aware that the so-called Cat-Lovers Animal Welfare Society had been implicated in vandalism of research labs throughout the country. He grabbed a bottle of disinfectant and started to assist with the clean-up. Shortly afterward, two security officers in starched tan uniforms, one male and one female, made their appearance. After they entered the lab, Noah politely advised them not to touch anything.

"Oh … okay." replied the burly, dark-haired man whose badge identified him as Perkins.

The officers inspected the cat room and outer lab.

"No sign of forced entry," noted Perkins. "They must have had a key."

The woman with him, Officer Blount, took copious notes on a digital notepad. She informed Noah that there had been a rash of animal-liberation incidents at university laboratories around the state recently, and that rarely were any of the animals ever seen again. When they were finished, the inspectors departed, leaving Noah to ponder his immediate course of action.

"I have to get ready for biochem," Noah said. Crisis or not, his course had to go on. "We'll go ahead with our experiment this afternoon," he mentioned as he left the lab. "We may as well continue with our work until the cats are returned."

Noah scrubbed his hands at the sink and splashed cold water on his face. He wandered back to his office, sat down at his desk, and opened his notebook to protein synthesis. He tried to focus on the topic—ribosomal assembly—but couldn't stop obsessing about the theft of the cats. He put his head in his hands, and his thoughts returned to the student protests of the prior August— protests that had delayed his research by three months. Lost in thought, he remained thus until student voices in the hallway signaled that he was going to be late for his lecture.

2

Gary McKeever reclined on his sofa, analyzing a difficult paper on plasmid vectors. He was unaware of Jane's approach behind him until she slid her arms over his chest.

Gary flinched, dropping his e-reader. "Damn!"

"I'm sorry. Forgot how absorbed you get when you're studying," she whispered in his ear. "How about a hike up Sycamore Canyon tomorrow? It's Saturday, you know. I'll pack a lunch, and we can relax on the beach afterward."

Gary took off his glasses and rubbed his brow. "Sounds good." He turned and picked up the e-reader, kissing Jane on the cheek as he returned to it.

"We should leave early in the morning," she said, "so we'll be able to finish hiking before the heat of the day. I'll phone Dr. Barnett to make sure she doesn't need me tomorrow."

Gary turned and, with an amalgam of aesthetic and biological appreciation, watched Jane's shapely figure retreat to the kitchen. Her blond hair was uncharacteristically mussed. *That's my fault,* he figured, *probably happened when I kissed her after dinner.* He wished she didn't have to work part-time for the veterinarian. *Jane should concentrate on her courses,* he mused. *She barely has enough time to work on her English-lit term paper. Every time I ask her to move in with me, she says she isn't ready for such a big step.* Gary shook his head. *Why does she spend so much time driving to her parent's home in Ventura. What is it, fifteen miles one way?* He returned to his reading and began typing notes into his laptop.

"Gary," Jane called from the kitchen, "do you mind if I ask Anneke to join us tomorrow?"

"No, not at all." Anneke was Jane's closest female friend. Gary had met her just the previous week when the three of them had attended a Mozart concert at the university. All he knew about her was that she was a computer-science major, an animal lover, and a strict vegetarian. He got up and walked to the kitchen. "Tell her to get here early. I'll drive." He saw that Jane was assembling tuna sandwiches. "I thought Anneke was a vegan."

"She is," said Jane, "but she's not real strict. Anneke eats fish. She says fish aren't sentient creatures like mammals, and that it's important to consume omega-3 fatty acids."

Gary shrugged.

Anneke arrived at seven thirty the next morning, and, after coffee, juice, and muffins, the three set out in Gary's Honda. "Thanks for letting me tag along," Anneke said from the back seat.

"Hey, no problem," Gary replied. "Glad to have you."

Sycamore Canyon was located in the Santa Monica Mountains; the trailhead was near the ocean. Gary pulled the car into the parking area by the beach, and the three of them set out up the path in silence. Gary didn't find Anneke particularly attractive. *Too skinny for my taste. She should do something with her hair—a ponytail doesn't work for her; even her wire-frame glasses aren't stylish.*

"*Aooo,*" Jane cried out.

Gary stopped. "What?"

"Nothing," Jane said, "just a lizard that caught me by surprise."

Gary chuckled. "Forget the lizards and watch out for rattlesnakes instead. They're active at this time of year."

"There are rattlesnakes here?" asked Anneke. "If I had known that, I would have thought twice about coming."

Gary replied, "Just stay on the path, and you probably won't meet up with one. There are coyotes and mountain lions in these mountains too, but they aren't likely to approach a group of people." He wondered how a woman who's supposed to be an animal-lover could be so uneasy near wild animals.

"I'm from Chicago," said Anneke. "We don't have wild animals like that in Illinois."

"No, but you've got wolves, don't you?" said Gary. "And bears? I guess Californians have a different perspective than Midwesterners. You guys want to rest?" he asked as they came to a large, flat rock.

"Sure," said Jane.

Gary passed around a canteen of water.

Anneke took a swig, passed it to Jane, and turned to Gary. "I guess we're safe as long as we have a strong guy like you to protect us." She smiled.

"Hey!" Jane cried out. "Stop flirting with my boyfriend."

Although he knew Jane was joking, Gary felt a flush spread over his face.

"I was just kidding around," said Anneke. "I didn't mean anything by it."

They sat in silence for a minute, catching their breath. Anneke then said, "Say, Gary …"

"Yeah?"

"What kind of research are you doing at the U?"

"It's molecular biology. I'm working on a cat disease."

"What do you mean a cat disease? Do you infect cats with a virus or something?"

Although he knew Anneke was an animal-lover, Gary was startled by the tone of her voice. "Well, yes … no … it's a hereditary disease. It's called macroerythrocytic feline anemia—or MEFA for short."

"I've never heard of it."

"It's rather rare," Gary noted. "It's kind of like sickle-cell anemia in humans."

"I think we better get going," Jane interjected.

"Right," said Gary, grateful for the interruption. He certainly didn't want to get into a debate on the use of animals in research with Jane's best friend.

The trio resumed its trek up the canyon. Gary tried to think of a way to reach Anneke. *Should I tell her about all the advances in human disease prevention that have resulted from animal research? How about all the safety precautions we take?*

"Do you use real cats?" Anneke asked, breaking his thought train.

"Of course we do," he replied. "We hope to be able to make the cats better with recombinant DNA."

"You mean that you put foreign genes into the cats? Isn't that dangerous?" She stopped walking and brushed the dust off her pants. "Besides, I don't like the idea of using animals for research."

Gary turned to face her. He opened his mouth and started to speak, but Jane interrupted: "All right, you two, let's just enjoy the hike." As if to add emphasis, the sweet song of a finch came from nearby.

Gary ignored Jane's plea. "Look, Anneke," he declared, making an effort to keep his voice under control, "we treat the cats humanely. We keep them well-fed, we clean up after them, we take care of them if they get sick. I would say that our cats are a lot better off than feral cats."

Anneke asked, "Do you keep the cats in cages?"

"Yes, they're kept in stainless-steel cages that are cleaned every day."

"Shit! You think that cats in cages are better off than cats running wild? I don't think so."

Gary stared at Anneke's wrinkled brow. Her mouth was a thin line. He took a deep breath and changed the subject. "Hey!" he cried. "Look over there. There's still some water in the stream." The three of them left the path and climbed down to the almost-dry riverbed. "Watch out for the nettles," cautioned Gary, pointing to a plant with small, purple flowers. "They'll give you an itch you won't forget." A California jay squawked at the intruders from a tree on the opposite bank. It flew down and drank from the trickle of water a few yards upstream.

Anneke traced her initials in the dirt. She frowned. "Why do you have to use cats? Why can't you use computer modeling? A lot of medical research is being done that way."

Gary realized that Anneke was not about to be distracted. He noticed Jane staring angrily at him. Turning back to Anneke, he said, "I wouldn't know how to do that. A feline disease has to be studied in cats. We do use computers in the research, but they are an aid, not a substitute for the actual science."

They continued on up the path a short distance, but Gary was becoming overheated. Either the hot July sun or the confrontation with Anneke was beginning to make hiking unpleasant. "I think we ought to go back down to the beach and have lunch," he said.

After working their way down the canyon, they drove the car to a parking area by the sand and spread out a blanket. The surf was low, and, although it was a warm weekend day, there weren't many other people about. Jane unpacked the lunch while Gary passed out soft drinks.

Again, he tried to bridge the gap with Anneke. "Don't you agree that knowledge about animal diseases can ultimately be used to find the cure for human diseases?" He glimpsed Jane rolling her eyes.

Anneke responded, "Sure I do, but that doesn't justify the use of animals for human benefit. Animals have rights."

"I think humans come first," Gary replied, a trace of anger in his voice. *She won't give it up,* he thought.

"The animal-rights issue is like the slavery question during the nineteenth century," she said. "Today we look back on slavery and wonder how otherwise good, God-fearing white people could have justified it. But, of course, they did justify it, at least in the South, using any number of economic and pseudo-scientific arguments. I think, in fifty or a hundred years, we'll look back on animal experimentation in the same way."

"There's no comparison," grumbled Gary.

"You're too involved with it to see it." She shook her head and walked, alone, to the water's edge.

The remainder of the outing did not go well. Jane tried repeatedly to change the subject, but the two would not let go of the argument. Finally, they had to cut the trip short and return to Camarillo. Anneke departed in silence while Jane just glared at Gary.

"What?" said Gary. "It's not my fault that she's some kind of fanatic."

"You could've just not talked about the cats so we might have had a more pleasant day."

"But it was Anneke who wouldn't let it go," he grunted. "Aw, shit, never mind." Gary grabbed his music player and inserted the earbuds, ending further argument.

Leon and Rebecca Smith of Sweet Home, Oregon, did not have many possessions in their small cabin. They did have an old RCA phonograph and a collection of vintage 78-rpm jazz recordings. But what they loved most was their all-black mouser named Bib. Bib stood for "Black is Beautiful." The couple was asleep one evening when Bib, prowling in the nearby forest, came upon a rabid squirrel. The animals fought to the death. Bib, the survivor, sustained several injuries from the squirrel's claws, but had not been bitten.

In the morning Rebecca called, "Bib! Bib! Where are you you little rascal?" She went outside to discover Bib lying on the porch, licking his wounds.

"Oh my lands! What have you been up to?" She scooped up the injured cat, placed it in a carrier, and drove into town to the vet's clinic; it wouldn't open for twenty minutes. Rebecca sat outside with Bib in her lap.

When Dr. Healy arrived, he examined the wounds. "Looks like he was in a fight with some animal. See these scratches?" Rebecca nodded. "Could be from a squirrel, another cat ... possum ... I don't know."

"He's gonna be okay, right?"

"I think so. I don't see any serious wounds. I'll have his blood checked for rabies virus and write a prescription for amoxicillin. I think he'll be fine."

Rebecca started to sob.

"Hey, Rebecca, I think he's going to be okay."

"I know. I know. I just thought he might ..."

Neither Rebecca nor Dr. Healy would ever suspect that the squirrel had, in fact, carried rabies, but the virus had not been transferred to Bib.

3

One warm morning, shortly after fall classes had begun, Noah headed for the institute on his bike. *It's going to be a hot one,* he thought. He noticed a television news van headed along the campus road toward the institute. *What's that about?* he wondered. As he followed it, he heard an amplified female voice. Noah strained his ears and could make out the phrases "animal rights" and "defenseless cats." *Uh oh, this can't be good.*

Arriving at his building, he encountered a crowd of people carrying signs with the CLAWS logo. One read "NO PETS FOR RESEARCH!" Another read, "CLAW AWAY VIVISECTION."

Noah spotted the speaker, a young woman with glasses and dark hair collected in a ponytail, perched on a makeshift podium and addressing the throng with a wireless mike.

"… they keep the cats in small cages where the animals have limited room to move around. This sort of thing should not be allowed at CSUCI."

Noah felt a gnawing sensation in the pit of his stomach. He made his way to a rear entrance, where Gary was waiting in the lab.

"What's going on out there?" asked Noah.

"Anneke Weiss," Gary replied. "That's Jane's friend. You know, the woman I told you about, the one who believes we shouldn't be experimenting with cats."

"Oh brother, what next? How did she get so many people out there?"

"She's been posting fliers all over campus announcing a rally against animal research."

"I saw a TV news van. How did they know about it?"

"I guess she notified them," Gary said. "I bet there are newspaper reporters too. I'm sorry, Doc. This is kinda my fault. I guess I should have avoided arguing with her."

"It's not your fault at all. There's no way you could have anticipated what she'd do."

Noah's cell phone vibrated in his pocket. It was Dr. Stanaland, head of the institute.

"Noah," said Stanaland, "can you come up here right away? We have to talk."

Noah closed the phone. "I've got to run. Dr. Stanaland, wants to see me. He's not a guy you keep waiting."

"Oh crap!" Gary said. "You know it's about the crowd, right?"

Noah shrugged. "Gary, trust me. Dr. Stanaland is a fair man. He won't blame you ... us."

When Noah entered Lowell E. Stanaland's outer office, Mrs. Gonzalez motioned him to go right in. He stepped into an impeccably neat room whose darkly stained oak cabinets and rich, beige cowhide chairs and sofa conveyed the ambience of a four-hundred-dollar-an-hour attorney's office rather than that of a scientist. Noah always felt awestruck in Stanaland's presence. Here was a man who had worked with Nobel-Prize-winning molecular biologist, Francis Crick—first at Cambridge and later at the Salk Institute. He was amused that the institute's head wore a custom-tailored suit and tie, an anomaly in an environment where most of the scientists dressed informally. Of course, Noah was aware that this was not an affectation; it was a reflection of Stanaland's formal British upbringing. His father had been a high-level diplomat in the British foreign service.

Noah walked a few paces across the deep-piled maroon carpet. Stanaland rose and stepped to the large window, where he could observe the goings-on below.

"I take it you wanted to see me about what's going on outside," said Noah. He held Stanaland in high esteem both for his impressive scientific accomplishments and as a leader. He also looked up to the man literally, as Stanaland stood six foot three. Even his deep, modulated voice commanded respect.

"Noah, I'm quite familiar with your research, and I support it totally. So I think we should arrange an open meeting with students and faculty to address the issue of animal experimentation. I want you to explain to everyone why your work is important and why you need to use cats. Those students have the right to protest your research, but you have an equal right to defend it."

Noah stood there a moment, saying nothing. He resented that he'd have to defend himself to a bunch of students who were ignorant of the value of scientific investigation.

Stanaland had arranged a meeting with the protesters for a Friday afternoon. Noah entered the lecture hall fifteen minutes early and was surprised to see that the room was already half full. A few days earlier, Anneke Weiss had written an inflammatory article in the campus newspaper attacking not only the use of cats for research but gene-cloning as well. She had suggested a multitude of horrors that might result from the kind of work that Noah and Gary were engaged in. The next day, the article had been reprinted verbatim in the local newspaper. *That accounts for the crowd*, Noah thought. *My God, this room holds two hundred people. It's going to fill up.*

A large table had been placed at the front of the room. Noah nodded to Dr. Stanaland, who was already seated. At the same table, Noah identified Anneke Weiss, along with Andrea Vernon,

18

the university's biological safety officer, and Sanjay Krishnamurti, the campus veterinarian. Noah sat down at the table and looked around the hall. He spied Gary in the third row, holding one of their research cats, an orange male named George.

After Stanaland introduced him, Noah made his way to the microphone. There was scattered booing and a few shouts of, "No animal research!"

Noah slowly examined his audience. "Thank you, Dr. Stanaland. I am grateful for this opportunity to explain my work to the students and faculty of CSUCI and to citizens of Camarillo.

"First, let me assure you that recombinant DNA research has been carried out for over a quarter of a century without any problems." Noah glanced at an outline he had prepared.

"Get to the point!" shouted a voice from the audience.

Momentarily stunned by the outcry, Noah reddened.

Stanaland stood. He looked right at the offender and announced, "I must ask that you respect Dr. Chamberlin's right to speak. If there are further disruptions, in the interest of civility, I will have those responsible removed from the room." Aside from some isolated booing, the hall was quiet.

Noah regained his composure. "Do you realize that everybody here has recombinant DNA in his chromosomes at this very moment?" As Noah had expected, there were exclamations of disbelief. "Evolution of life on earth depends on it. That's right," he continued, "genetic recombination is a normal process occurring in all sexual species. It's simply the exchange of genes between the chromosomes of a pair; in animals this takes place when sperm and eggs are formed."

When Noah mentioned "sperm and eggs," he noticed a little blond girl in a light-blue pinafore being hustled out of the hall by a stern-faced woman. A low current of laughter followed. Noah stared, open-mouthed. *Unbelievable!*

"Uh, where—oh yes. Although DNA recombination is a natural process," Noah went on pedantically, "we can also do it in the laboratory." At this, the hall was again filled with laughter, but it took Noah a moment to get the joke. Disgusted, he shook his head. *Damn! This is turning into a circus.* "What I mean," he explained after the last titter had faded, "is that chemically we can fuse different kinds of DNA. We can even take a piece of DNA from one species and attach it to a chromosome from another species." The hall became suddenly quiet, but for the muted hiss of the air-conditioning.

Noah motioned to Gary, who came forward and handed over his furry charge. This brought forth a murmur from the audience.

"This is George," said Noah, cradling the scrawny feline in his arms. "George has a disease called macroerythrocytic feline anemia, MEFA for short." Gently stroking the gaunt animal, Noah explained the analogy between sickle cell anemia in humans and MEFA. He described how the red blood cells of cats afflicted with this disease would swell up like little balloons because their hemoglobin was defective. "Cats with MEFA are lethargic," he pointed out. "They lie around all day, panting pathetically, and they rarely live to maturity." He explained that the disease was the result of a naturally occurring mutation in the gene for one of the hemoglobin proteins called alpha-globin.

"What we hope to do is to isolate and clone the gene for normal alpha-globin from a healthy cat and then to attach this gene to a viral chromosome. The virus we use is called feline sarcoma virus and sometimes causes tumors in cats."

"Why don't you just say cancer?" yelled an angry male voice from the middle of the auditorium.

"All right, cancer," Noah acknowledged. He had to remind himself not to raise his voice. "However, the strain we use has been genetically altered so that it can no longer cause cancer. It is what we call a defective virus." Noah wiped his brow. "Anyway, after we attach the globin gene to this virus chromosome, we will allow the virus to infect certain immature blood cells from cats with MEFA. We hope that, as these cells mature, they will form normal alpha-globin in these sick animals."

Noah paused to let his words sink in and looked over the audience. They were quiet now, obviously interested in his proposed research. He noticed quite a few puzzled faces. "Before I go on, I would be happy to answer any questions."

Noah nodded toward a thirtyish, bearded man wearing blue jeans and a loose-fitting white shirt embroidered with birds and flowers.

"Dr. Chamberlin, my name is Norman Orgell. I teach biology at Camarillo High. I have several questions. First, what kind of bacteria do you use for cloning the alpha-globin gene?"

"We use a type of *Escherichia coli*, the common intestinal bacterium."

"Isn't that dangerous? Isn't there a chance that someone in the lab could ingest the bacteria, which could then multiply in the gut? Couldn't such a person carry the bacteria, with their recombinant DNA, everywhere he or she went?"

Noah was prepared for this one. "There are two reasons why there is no danger. First, we use a mutant of *E. coli* incapable of surviving in the gut of any animal, including humans. Our strain of *E. coli* has many, many mutations that prevent it from competing with normal bacteria in the intestine. It can only survive in the highly complex artificial media that we prepare for it.

"Secondly, the recombinant DNA itself is not dangerous. There is no way the gene for alpha-globin could be dangerous to anyone, even if, by some remote chance, it did manage to escape from the lab."

"Thank you. I think I understand," said Norman Orgell.

Noah spotted a blond woman with her hand raised. *She looks familiar,* Noah thought. *Quite a looker. She's been taking notes.*

"Dr. Chamberlin, my name is Vera Barnett. I'm a veterinarian. I'm embarrassed to admit it, but I've never heard of MEFA. Is it very widespread?"

21

"No, not at all," Noah replied. "As I mentioned, cats inheriting the disease rarely live to sexual maturity, so there is a strong natural selection against MEFA. The disease is what you might call a laboratory curiosity."

"Then where do you get cats with MEFA?" asked the veterinarian.

"The disease was discovered about ten years ago in the laboratory of Thomas Stambaugh at Harvard. Two kittens from a litter of five were scrawnier than the others and, when he examined the blood of these kittens, he noticed the abnormal red blood cells. He reasoned that by analogy with sickle cell anemia in humans, MEFA might be almost asymptomatic in the heterozygous state. Sure enough, in the next litter from the same parents, one kitten of the four had the disease. So, to answer your question, the disease has been perpetuated in the laboratory by breeding cats heterozygous for the MEFA gene."

Noah sensed that the listeners had become restive. "Look, I know this is kind of heavy stuff, but what I want to emphasize is that there really is little or no risk for people associated with this research.

"Many years ago, after several years of analyzing possible dangers involved in gene-cloning experiments, the National Institutes of Health established safety guidelines for the design of laboratories where recombinant DNA experiments were to be carried out. These guidelines specify four levels of possible risk. The lowest, or safest level, is the so-called Biosafety Level-1 lab. The next level is BSL-2 and so on up to BSL-4 for the really dangerous stuff like Ebola. Our research falls in the BSL-2 category and we follow the guidelines strictly."

"Why should we trust you?" yelled a voice from the rear. Several similar shouts followed. Stanaland stood. Immediately the hall was silent.

"Here's why," Noah responded. "The NIH requires all institutions where gene-cloning experiments are carried out to have a special committee called the Institutional Biosafety Committee, or IBC, that makes sure that the guidelines are followed. Dr. Vernon here is the biological safety officer for CSUCI. In addition, two members of the IBC are appointed from the community. One of them is the Ventura County health officer, Dr. Jerome Robinson.

"In addition, our animal facilities are inspected four times a year by members of the IACUC—that's the Institutional Animal Care and Use Committee. Dr. Krishnamurti here, the campus veterinarian, heads that committee.

"The IACUC is responsible for making sure that all animals used in research are treated humanely. In fact, no investigator can use experimental animals at all until his or her research proposal has been approved by the IACUC." Noah mopped his forehead with his handkerchief. "There are four other members of the committee, including two members of the clergy, Reverend Darius Shultz, of the First Methodist Church in Camarillo, and Sister Damien Nuñez."

Noah motioned to Dr. Stanaland, indicating that he was finished. "Thank you for allowing me the opportunity to describe my research to you," he concluded and, with George nestled in the crook of his arm, he returned to his seat.

"Ms. Weiss, do you wish to respond?" offered Stanaland.

Anneke rose. "Thank you, Professor Stanaland." She removed her glasses, paused, and looked out over the hall. With a strong voice, she read from a deck of note cards, carefully placing each at the bottom of the stack as she finished with it. "I wish to address two facets of Dr. Chamberlin's research—the immorality of using cats as research animals, and the danger of doing gene-cloning experiments." She spoke in a measured cadence. Noah discretely popped an antacid tablet into his mouth.

Anneke took a deep breath. "Since the beginnings of science, we have used animals as mere objects to be exploited, as if they weren't sentient creatures." She paused between sentences. "In fact, it wasn't too long ago that scientists thought nothing of cutting open live animals, without anesthesia, for experimentation."

This brought forth a murmur from the audience. "Toward the beginning of the last century, some courageous individuals began to question such vivisection, and, eventually, it became outlawed in civilized countries. It is heartening that, as we evolve as a society, we become more ethical—more moral." She stopped, transferred the top card to the bottom of the pile and again looked out over the audience.

At that moment, George the cat gave forth with a piercing yowl that began with a high note and gradually descended in pitch, but not volume. *Oh no,* thought Noah, *they're going to think George is in pain.* The audience responded in unison to the cry with a drawn-out, "Oooohhh." They then laughed heartily, seemingly at their own reaction. Noah was relieved that the crowd seemed to be amused.

Soon the merriment died down, and Anneke was able to continue. "For over a century, civilized nations have accepted the idea of racial equality and, for half a century, gender equality. Now it is time for us to adopt the moral equivalent—species equality, or at least mammalian equality."

This elicited scattered applause from the audience and a shout of "Bravo!"

She went on. "Peter Singer, the noted philosopher and former Princeton professor, has written: 'Dogs are conscious beings. They can feel pain, and they evidently enjoy many aspects of their lives. In that respect they are like you and me ...

"... the ethical principle on which human equality rests requires us to extend equal consideration to animals too.'"

At the mention of Peter Singer, Noah rolled his eyes. Noah had once read a book by Singer in which the philosopher had defended the animal liberation movement. He turned to Stanaland to respond, but Anneke continued.

"Now I'd like to turn to the question of gene-cloning and recombinant DNA. We live in a time when this kind of tinkering with the genomes of living things is taken for granted. We are told that it will help us solve all manner of problems. It will cure diseases, allow insect-resistant crops, even let us create plants that make plastic. However, many thinking people have raised serious questions about recombinant DNA technology." Another card made its journey to the underside.

"For example, Jeremy Rifkin, past president of the Foundation on Economic Trends in Washington, DC, wrote 'Most recombinant-DNA experiments are done with *E. coli* bacteria, which exists in the intestinal tracts of all human beings. The chief danger involved here is that a research accident could produce a particularly virulent virus that causes a disease for which there is no immunization. A lab technician who accidentally breathed or swallowed a few of its particles could then begin rapidly spreading the virus to others—perhaps eventually to a whole population."

When he heard the name Jeremy Rifkin, Noah groaned. Rifkin was widely known among molecular biologists as an arch enemy who had even gone to court to stop some forms of cloning research.

Anneke again looked out over the audience and said, "I apologize for presenting my argument against recombinant DNA research by reading the words of others, but I think that these great thinkers, on the basis of their much more extensive knowledge, are able to state the case much better than I could. In conclusion, because of the grave threat posed to the environment by the research going on at this university, speaking for the students of CSUCI, I urge that all experiments involving recombinant DNA, especially where cats are used, be banned."

As Anneke put down her cards, the audience again began applauding. Here and there a few individuals stood up and finally, almost all were giving her a standing ovation.

Lowell Stanaland waited for the applause to stop. "We have heard Dr. Chamberlin's description of his proposed research," he noted, "and we have listened to Ms. Weiss provide arguments against his investigation. I should point out that there are many other scientists here at the institute who are engaged in recombinant DNA work. If such research were stopped, it would effectively put us out of business. I will, however, be happy to entertain any discussion."

A bespectacled, lanky, dark-skinned young man in the center of the auditorium rose with a flourish. "Sir, my name is Jaime Leal. I'm president of the student body. May I say something?" The boy spoke with a confident voice. Without waiting for an answer, he continued, "In view of the real threat posed to the people of CSUCI by the DNA research going on here, as representative of the students at CSUCI, I urge that all experiments with recombinant DNA at the university be stopped." The young man nodded to the applause from the audience and seated himself.

"Thank you, Mr. Leal," said Stanaland. Noah turned and recognized the lad, whose picture frequently appeared in *The CI View*. "In order to ban such research, I think it would require an action by the president of the university or by the trustees or the chancellor."

There were a few shouts: "Stop the research!" It became a chant: "Stop the research! Stop the research!"

After Stanaland had again brought order to the hall, Andrea Vernon spoke up. "I'd like to offer a proposal. Instead of a total ban on Dr. Chamberlin's research, why don't we impose a temporary ban, a moratorium, for two or three months, during which we can investigate the risks more fully? We could form an investigative committee composed of students, faculty, and one or two citizens from the community and direct that the committee report in three months with a recommendation whether to ban the research permanently or let it proceed."

Noah was shocked. How could Andrea, with whom he thought he had a cordial, professional relationship, suggest banning his research? Anneke shrugged her shoulders and nodded her assent.

"Sounds like a good plan," Stanaland declared. "And I have a suggestion for a member of the proposed committee. Mr. Orgell, the science teacher, seems to know a lot about the subject. How about it, Mr. Orgell?"

"I'd be honored, sir," replied the teacher.

"Will you agree to abstain from doing experiments for three months, Dr. Chamberlin?" Noah caught Stanaland's determined gaze.

Noah was silent a moment. And then, his voice hoarse, he cried, "This is wrong. It's unprecedented. How can you ask me to give in to mob rule? Yes," he shouted, "I will stop my research, if you think it's necessary. I'll spend the time reading papers."

Stanaland addressed Anneke. "I trust you will consent to serve on the committee, Ms. Weiss."

"Yes, thank you," she replied.

"How about you, Mr. Leal, would you like to participate?" Stanaland motioned to the young man. The student body president said he would.

A woman's voice was heard. "I will volunteer."

"Who said that?" Stanaland peered about the hall.

"I did," replied Vera Barnett, the veterinarian.

"Thank you, Dr. Barnett. How about one more volunteer for a fifth committee member?"

A dark-skinned, gray-haired fellow stood up. "I'll volunteer," he said. "I have a cat of my own and see the merits of both sides on this issue."

"What is your name, sir?" asked Stanaland.

"Yousef Yazdani," replied the middle-aged man.

"Thank you Mr. Yazdani. Well, that should do it. We have two students and three people from the community. I suggest that we plan to meet again in about three months for the committee's findings."

Demoralized, Noah strode out of the assembly hall, carrying George the cat. There was now silence. Nobody said a word for several minutes. And finally, like a wave at a football game, a quiet buzz began to progress throughout the audience.

Beth Murphy operated a cattery in Coos Bay, Oregon. Over three decades, she had raised hundreds of purebred varieties of Siamese, Russian Blue, Persians and others. She kept all the important legal documents, pedigree papers, and such in a tempered steel safe in her office.

Beth, with two charming tiny kittens in her lap, chatted with Mr. and Mrs. Cozzens, a couple seeking a Maine Coon purebred.

"These two are just weaned," Beth said. "One's a male, the other female. If you can wait a week, that'll give me time to remove them from their mother and make sure they have all the required shots. You have your choice of either one."

While she explained the details, a Manx kitten wandering the compound entered the office and headed directly for the open safe, where she promptly lay down on a stack of papers and fell asleep. Neither Beth nor the couple saw it.

"Well, that's it then," said Mr. Cozzens. "We have a deal. We'll be back in a few days to pick up Mac."

"Oh, you've already picked a name!"

"Yes," said Mrs. Cozzens, "Mac the Maine Coon."

Beth smiled. "Perfect. Phone before you come; I'll have him ready."

After the couple left, Beth turned and noticed the open safe. "Damn.!" She shut and locked the door, not noticing the feline occupant.

As Beth prepared to leave the cattery for the day, an attendant came running down the hall. "Beth! Beth! Have you seen a kitten running loose?"

"I just put two Maine Coons back with their mama, but I haven't seen any escaped kittens. What breed?"

"Manx. We can't find one of the three kittens."

"Take it easy, Kim. Kittens get loose all the time. She'll show up."

"It's my responsibility. I'm not leaving until I find it."

"All right. I'll help you. Where did you see her last?"

"Him. It's a male. I saw him right outside your office."

"Really? Then let's search my office."

A half hour later they had gone over every square inch of the room twice. Kim was exhausted. She sat down in a chair by the safe.

"Let's go home," said Beth. We should leave it until tomorrow. The cat will get hungry and thirsty, and he'll damn sure let us know where he is."

Kim shrugged. "Wait! What was that?"

"I said, let's …"

"No. Listen!"

Beth, across the room, heard nothing.

Kim craned her neck and leaned toward the safe. The mewling got louder. "Open the safe!"

"What?" Beth paused. "You think …" She ran over to the steel box and carefully twiddled the dial back and forth a few times. She turned the handle, and it opened. The mewling was now very loud. Beth reached in and grabbed the tiny ball of fur, who was none the worse for the experience.

Kim stated the obvious. "If that kitten had stayed in the safe overnight, he would have run out of air and died."

4

Noah sat at his desk staring at, but not seeing the computer screen. Ostensibly, he was checking websites of scientific supply houses, evaluating equipment for the lab. Dr. Stanaland had encouraged him to do so, pointing out that, even if recombinant DNA research were banned permanently, the lab could be used for other types of biochemical research. That declaration hardly made Noah a happy man. *This is scut work,* he thought. *Anyone could do it … I don't even have Alicia here to help.*

He got up and paced around his office. *I just want to get on with the research, damn it. I could sneak in some simple experiment … no one's looking over my shoulder … no, I can't do that. I can't break my wo … they didn't tell me I couldn't think.*

It was time for his one o'clock lecture. He grabbed his notes and headed over to the classroom. When the period was over, Noah didn't wait to answer the many student questions; he was aware that the lecture had not been one of his better ones, and he didn't want to stay around, so he gathered up his notes and stomped out of the room. Glancing back, he noticed several students, open-mouthed, staring at him. Head down, he made for his office. *I've got to do better than that … I can't let my problems out on my students.*

A female voice interrupted his introspection. "Dr. Chamberlin." Noah looked up. It was Anneke Weiss. "Do you have a minute?" she said.

"What are you doing here?" Noah blurted, surprised she had the gall to enter the building after the job she'd done on him.

"May I speak with you, please?"

Noah was inclined to send her away. *No, she has the guts to come here, the least I can do is hear her out.* "What is it?"

"I … I came to apologize," Anneke said. "I know how much of a bother this ban is for you."

"Bother! You have no idea. You can't apologize. The damage is done."

"Dr. Chamberlin, please. We don't know how this is going to turn out. Our committee hasn't even had its first meeting. We're getting together this afternoon."

"I didn't know that. It seems that you're keeping an open mind, anyway."

"I'd like to think so. I've done some web research on these institutional biosafety committees and animal-care committees. I'll be honest, until last week's meeting, I didn't know they existed."

Noah was taken aback by her conciliatory tone. "I see," was all he could manage.

"Sir, I promise you that I'll maintain an objective attitude on our little committee. I'm sure the other members will do likewise."

Noah was left speechless by the woman's sincerity.

Vera Barnett had agreed to host the first meeting of the *ad hoc* committee at the clinic. She set out a ring of folding chairs, a box of donuts, and plenty of coffee. After all were seated, Vera spoke. "I think we should begin by electing a chair."

The others muttered assent and the group quickly elected the biology teacher, Norman Orgell, to head the committee.

"Vera," Orgell said, "how about you and I take on the responsibility of digesting the NIH guidelines for recombinant DNA research. We have the most biological expertise."

"Fine with me," answered the vet.

"Anneke, would you mind contacting state and federal health authorities about governmental guidelines?"

"Sure," she replied. "I think we should also request a tour of the lab facilities. You know, the scene of the crime ..."

"Let's try to keep an open mind," Orgell said.

"Sorry."

On the day of the tour, Vera Barnett, DVM, studied her reflection in the mirror and casually ran a comb through her short, blond hair. She paused to consider what appeared to be a new wrinkle at the corner of her mouth. "Damn!" she said aloud. Vera had always thought of herself as ordinary-looking. Now in her mid-thirties, she was becoming increasingly self-conscious about her appearance.

Vera looked forward to visiting the molecular biology institute. She had been to the university on more than one occasion to attend concerts, plays, and lectures, but had never been inside any of its laboratories. *Chamberlin seems likeable enough,* she mused. *Good-looking too.* Although she generally shunned makeup, she decided to apply a light shade of lip gloss.

She tucked the flaps of her blue shirt into her jeans and switched off the stereo. Vera rented an old, two-story clapboard house built during the early 1950s, when the post-war building boom was in full flower. The owner had agreed to convert the bottom floor to make it suitable for her veterinary practice, provided she agreed to a two-year lease. She co-owned the veterinary clinic with Dr. Kalman Forstner, who had graduated from the School of Veterinary Medicine at UC Davis just the previous year.

Vera hurried into the room she called "the ward" to check on the animals. They seemed calm and comfortable, except for Sparkles, a toy collie recovering from a urinary tract infection.

"Hey there, girl," murmured the vet, rubbing her finger alongside the animal's jaw. "They'll be coming tomorrow and you can go home." Sparkles responded with a whimper. "Kal, would you keep an eye on Sparkles?" she called out to her partner.

"Sure, no problem," he replied from the other room.

Vera left a note for Jane Brennan that she'd be back in a few hours. She carried her black leather vet's bag—it doubled as a handbag—upstairs to her living quarters, inserted a few personal items, and set off in her blue Porsche hybrid for the university. She drove the two blocks to Lewis Road and then south on Lewis to the campus. In the city, she generally ran the sports car on battery, but on Lewis Road, she opened it up, and the little car took off with a roar.

I just love the old Spanish-style architecture of these buildings, she thought. *It gives the campus a kind of romantic look.* She recalled reading that the older buildings were erected as a state mental hospital in the 1930s. The hospital closed in 1997 and was converted to a state university. Cal State Channel Islands admitted its first students in 2002. The more recent structures, including the library and the molecular biology institute, had been constructed within the last fifteen years.

Vera was the first to arrive. She was impressed by the conspicuous signs on the lab door.

BSL-2 LABORATORY

CAUTION

BIOHAZARD AREA   **RADIATION AREA**

NO SMOKING OR FOOD PERMITTED

No admittance except to authorized personnel
In case of emergency contact Dr. Noah Chamberlin, Room 506
Phone: 484-36744 or 388-36748

Vera's concentration was interrupted by a masculine voice. "Dr. Barnett, isn't it?"

She spun around. "Oh. Dr. Chamberlin. You took me by surprise."

"Sorry. Where are the others?"

"They should be … here they come." The rest of the committee members were heading down the hall.

The group entered the lab. Vera noticed that everything was literally gleaming—glossy black countertops, vinyl floor, stainless steel, and enameled machines with their scores of dials, LCD screens, switches, and buttons. In a corner near the door she saw a desk covered with notebooks, graphs, and technical books, as well as a small calculator and a laptop computer on whose screen was displayed a slowly rotating DNA molecule. Above the desk was a bulletin board on which were posted a number of technical papers, notes, and science-themed cartoons. A faint chemical odor pervaded the room.

Noah introduced Alicia Diaz to the visitors. Jaime Leal exchanged a few words in Spanish with the technician. She was running a chromatography column, delicately turning a small stopcock at the bottom.

Vera walked over to get a closer look. "What are you doing?" she asked.

Alicia closed the stopcock. "I'm trying to separate and identify proteins found in sera of MEFA cats, but not normals."

"Any luck?" asked the vet.

"I'll know within the next few days. It looks promising."

Noah explained the various pieces of equipment: incubators, PCR analyzers, analytical balance, pH meter, UV spectrophotometer, gel electrophoresis apparatus, and other devices.

"Must have cost a fortune, all this stuff," Yousef Yazdani observed.

"It certainly did," said Noah. "The institute was funded by a huge grant from Clonigen. The grant paid for constructing and outfitting the building on the condition that our grad students and post-docs focus their research on projects compatible with those of the company."

"Wait a minute," Vera interjected, "I thought the state universities couldn't offer PhD programs."

"Generally, that's true," replied Noah. "It's not an absolute, however. Originally, doctoral programs were confined to the UC schools. However, a state university can offer PhD degrees in conjunction with a University in the UC system. Ours is UC Santa Barbara."

"How long have you been on the faculty, Dr. Chamberlin?" asked Anneke Weiss.

"I came here in 2017, when the Institute of Molecular Biology was formed. In fact, my first job was to design the labs, both the biosafety level-two and -three labs.

Anneke pointed to the biological safety cabinet with ductwork connected to a port in the wall. "What's that used for? Radioactive stuff?"

"Sometimes," replied Noah, "but mostly that box is used for working with possibly dangerous biological materials. It uses high efficiency particulate air—HEPA filters for short—to keep any potentially harmful microbes out of the environment." He flipped a switch on the side of the cabinet. Vera heard the sound of a motor starting up and the steady whoosh of air flowing. "Air is forced down across the opening in the front," Noah continued, "then through the grill at the bottom. Any particles from the inside or outside are dragged by the airflow into the grill where they're trapped by the HEPA filter. That not only keeps anything suspended in the inside air from getting out, but also keeps outside microbes from getting in and contaminating the work being done inside."

There sure are quite a few safety precautions, Vera thought.

They went into the cat room, and Noah pointed out that the only entrance was through the laboratory. Even here, Vera noted, although the room was permeated by a faint odor of urine and feces, the stainless steel cages were spotless. Norman Orgell asked how many cats were kept in the room. "We have a capacity for fifty animals," Noah replied, "but right now we only have nine—two normals and seven with MEFA."

"Oh!" said Yazdani. "We won't catch it, will we?"

"No, no, not at all. MEFA is in no way contagious to humans—or even to other cats."

Vera walked over to the cages housing the ill animals. "Did you have any difficulty in getting a license to use domestic cats?" she asked.

"I thought it was going to be a long, hard battle, but it wasn't so tough after all. In the application, I pointed out the obvious similarity between MEFA and human sickle-cell anemia. I learned later that one of the peer reviewers was an African American MD engaged in sickle-cell research himself. He was so intrigued by the proposal that he not only recommended funding the full 1.9 million, but pulled strings to fast-track the approval of the licenses for the use of *Felis catus.*"

Noah unlatched a cage door and removed a beautiful but lethargic gray tabby.

"Why her fur looks like mink!" said Anneke.

"Yes, it does in a way," said Noah. "Her name is Ophelia. My students like to name our cats after Shakespearian characters."

"Like the cat you brought to the meeting the other day? George, I think his name was?" Vera said, sarcasm apparent in her tone.

Noah smiled apologetically. "I named that one. I'm not as imaginative as my students. Here's George right here." He pointed to one of the upper cages. "Come to think of it, though, I believe there may be a George in some of the history plays. Isn't one of the lords or dukes in *Henry VI* named George?"

Vera was abashed. "I … I don't know. Are you into Shakespeare?"

"Yes, very much so. You?"

"Yes, as a matter of fact, I am."

Vera's eyes widened. *The guy's a Shakespeare nut like me. Who would've thought?* "May I examine Ophelia?" she asked.

"Of course," said Noah, handing her the cat. "Here—a 'harmless, necessary cat.'"

Vera chuckled, delighted with the Shakespeare game. "Shylock, right? *Merchant of Venice?*" Noah nodded.

Vera placed the animal on a spotless countertop and probed here and there, all the while softly stroking the scrawny cat. She pried open Ophelia's mouth with her fingers and examined the teeth, gums, and tongue. "Well, there really is nothing distinctive, except possibly an enlarged spleen. The general condition is that of a dozen other feline diseases."

"Yes," Noah replied, "and you're right about the spleen. That's an invariant symptom of MEFA." Vera looked up from the cat and saw that Noah was eyeing her. His lips were parted as if he was going to say something else, but he didn't speak. The vet eyed him in return. Vera wondered if it would be a conflict of interest if she asked the Shakespeare-loving scientist out on a date.

After a few more questions, the group exited the cat room and thanked Noah for the tour. Vera felt that the tour had gone well and had worked toward Noah's credibility. Even Anneke acknowledged that the research animals were well cared for. As the five of them made their way down the hallway toward the elevator, Noah rushed after them, attempting to intercept Vera. "Dr. Barnett," he called.

"Yes?"

"Would you mind waiting a moment?" He paused until the others were out of earshot. "I … uh … wonder if …"

Vera, seeing at once what Noah was about, took the lead. "Dr. Chamberlin, would you have dinner with me some evening? I'd like to discuss with you the significance of this George fellow in *Henry VI.*"

Noah laughed heartily. "How about tonight? I know a pretty good steakhouse north of here on Lewis Road."

"I think I know the place. The Cock and Bull, isn't it? Yes, tonight would be fine. What time may I pick you up?"

"Oh, I'll drive, after all …"

"Dr. Chamberlin, it was I who asked you to dinner," Vera interjected.

Noah looked her in the eye. He acquiesced. "Okay, you drive. I live over on Agave Road, north of Las Posas, not far from the police station. Do you know where that is?"

"Yes, I think so. Okay, tonight then. Say, around seven?"

Noah wrote down his address and drew a simple map for Vera. She strolled out of the building, bemused. Who could have thought the day would turn out this way?

Vera eased into a dark booth opposite Noah. A single candle on one end of the resin-covered burl table cast ghostly shadows on his face.

Noah inhaled deeply. "There's nothing like the aroma of charbroiled steaks!"

They ordered drinks from the almost invisible waitress. Vera raised her glass. "To George." Noah smiled and touched his stemmed martini glass to Vera's scotch. "I looked it up, you know," Vera announced. "You were right. There is a George in *Henry VI*. The Duke of Clarence. He also appears in *Richard III*."

"Ahhh, the Duke of Clarence. 'Our hap is loss, our hope but sad despair …' George's opening line in *Henry VI*. The third part of the play, to be precise."

"I can't believe it! The Duke of Clarence is a relatively minor character, and you know an obscure line like that? That's incredible!"

Noah grinned sheepishly. "I looked it up too." They laughed.

"Drinking on an empty stomach is going to knock me for a loop," Noah remarked. "I think we'd better order." He signaled the waitress, and they ordered steaks and a carafe of California cabernet.

Conversation was suspended as they cut into the steaks. Finally, Vera stated through a mouthful, "Shakespeare was a male chauvinist."

Noah frowned. "Ah yes. Of course. *Taming of the Shrew*. That must be one of the most sexist plays ever written."

Vera nodded.

"But," continued Noah, "to be fair, you've got to consider Shakespeare's many strong and sympathetic female characters, Lady Macbeth, Portia, and Cordelia, for example. You can make any case for or against Shakespeare. Many Jews believe he was anti-Semitic."

Vera said nothing, but she looked into Noah's eyes with growing respect.

Noah returned her gaze and asked, "Tell me, how did you happen to become a veterinarian?"

"I grew up on a farm in the San Joaquin Valley. I always liked animals. In fact, until I was about eighteen, I preferred them to people. So naturally, I wanted to be a vet. However, my parents were very conservative, very traditional. They didn't even want me to go to college. I rebelled and broke with my family. But it's okay now. We're kind of in touch again. I majored in biology at Cal State Sacramento, got good grades, attended vet school at Davis. That's about it."

"How did you happen to come to Camarillo?"

"I started by interning with Dr. Graham Wu, a vet at Auburn, in the gold rush country, and then opened my own practice in Placerville. But I couldn't make a go of it."

Vera could see that Noah was an attentive listener. "Three years ago, I came across an ad from a vet here who wanted to retire and was looking for someone to take over his practice. So here I am." Vera shrugged. "I share the practice with another fellow whom I'm training. He's fresh out of vet school. How about you?"

"Yeah, here I am too."

"No, professor, your history. How did you get into your field? What's a nice guy like you doing creating Frankenstein monsters in the laboratory?"

"Well, let's see. Born in Los Angeles of mixed WASP and Jewish parentage. Followed a pre-med curriculum at UCLA. B.A in 2012 but couldn't get into med school—wrong race, wrong sex, wrong ethnic background. Maybe my B average had something to do with it too." Vera's incipient reproach dissolved into a smile.

Noah went on, "I wasn't really turned on academically until I got to grad school. Earned a PhD in molecular biology at Berkeley in 2015. Spent two years as a post-doc at the University of Massachusetts, honing my recombinant DNA techniques. Met my wife there and got married in 2016."

Vera was nonplussed. "Oh! I didn't … "

"Divorced," Noah droned on. "Final decree this February."

Vera smiled wanly. "Any kids?"

"No, thank God. That would have made it messier."

"Was it messy?"

"For a while. It's okay now."

Vera nodded. "What is she like?"

"Myra? Oh, intelligent, witty … like you, I guess. She wasn't content to live the rest of her life as a faculty wife."

"I don't blame her." Vera stared at Noah over her wine glass. "What did you mean, like me?"

"Huh?"

"You said your wife, Myra, was like me. You don't even know me."

"I don't know what I … forget it."

He changed the subject. "Have you been to the Ojai Shakespeare festival?"

"No. I've been meaning to go. It's in the summer, right?"

"Yes," Noah replied. "Late July and early August. Perhaps we can go together next summer."

"That would be wonderful," Vera exclaimed. "I went up to Ashland a year ago. They put on an unusual production of *Midsummer Night's Dream.* Sort of a surrealistic staging with a laser light show."

"Yeah, I read about that. How did you like it?"

"I didn't, really," Vera said. "I guess I'm too much of a traditionalist.

"There's another local festival in the summer," she continued, "I can't recall … oh, it's sponsored by Cal-Lutheran … The Kingsmen Shakespeare Festival."

"There must be many Shakespeare lovers in the area."

Vera raised her wineglass. "To Shakespeare."

Noah clinked his glass to hers. "To lovers," he said.

Vera smiled. "To lovers."

The waitress reappeared out of the gloom. "Care for dessert?"

"No thanks," said Vera. *Not anything on the menu, anyway.*

41

Noah shook his head. The woman scratched on her pad and deposited the check in front of Noah. He reached for it. "Wait a minute, Noah, I'll pay the check," Vera protested. "I asked you to dinner, remember?"

"Please let me. I don't mind."

"Dr. Chamberlin," she said feigning formality, "our incomes are probably comparable. Can you give me one good reason why, considering that it was I who initiated this evening, you should pay the check?"

"How about each of us paying our own?"

"Well, all right," Vera responded. "Look, Noah, I'm sorry I shot off like that. I don't want us to get off on the wrong foot. But I'm kind of sensitive about ... well ..."

"I understand, but I am a product of my upbringing." This was said with such obvious sincerity that Vera, in spite of herself, was suddenly overwhelmed by a feeling of affection. She reached out and silently touched his hand.

Noah let it linger. "I guess we should leave," he suggested at last.

As they departed the restaurant, Noah said, "Say, I just got a videochip of Branagh's *Much Ado About Nothing*. It was made back in 1993. Would you be interested in watching it with me?"

"Now there's an approach. What, no etchings?"

"Well, I do have some etchings. A book collection too. I just thought you might enjoy the movie."

Vera regarded Noah. *I think he's serious,* she thought. *Maybe he's gay.* "Is that the one with Keanu Reeves as Don John?"

"Yep, that's the one."

"Okay. Sounds appealing. Let's watch Shakespeare."

"How nice," said Vera as they arrived at Noah's house. "Quite a pretty area you live in."

"Yes, it is. Great neighbors too." When he opened the door, Vera was startled by a movement just inside. "What? ... Oh, you have a cat. I guess it didn't occur to me that a guy who uses cats in his research would have one as a pet. What a beautiful chocolate-point. What's her name?" Vera picked the animal up and stroked her.

"Bastette," said Noah. "I'll go whip up some popcorn."

"Ah, the Egyptian cat goddess." She let go of Bastette, who positioned herself on the back of the couch.

"That's right," Noah called from the kitchen. "Can I get you a drink or something?"

"Scotch, if you have it."

Vera surveyed the living room while Noah popped into the kitchen for ice. All was natural wood, red brick, and deep-pile carpet. An immense bookcase covered one entire wall. A large color photograph of a woman Vera assumed to be Myra was conspicuously displayed on one of the shelves. Klee, Picasso, and Braque prints adorned other walls. Several technical books and periodicals were scattered on and around the large blue-green sofa. Vera smiled when she spied a copy of *Shakespeare: The History Plays* on the walnut coffee table, opened to *Henry VI*.

Noah returned with the drinks. "Here you are. I'll load the chip." He took the one-inch square digital video chip out of its minibox and slipped it into the DVC slot.

As the movie began, Noah sat down on the sofa, leaving a large space between himself and Vera. *Hmm. What's with this guy?* she wondered.

After a half hour or so Noah remarked, "You know, we only met this morning, and yet I feel as if I've known you for a longer time."

"Yes, I know what you mean," answered Vera. She had been wondering what kind of advance he was going to use.

When the movie ended, they spent a half hour discussing it. "Wow. It's really late," Noah said. "You could stay here tonight if you like. You can sleep in the bedroom, and I'll sleep on the couch."

Vera was astonished, and then she was hurt. Did he find her so unattractive that he wasn't even going to make a pass? She said nothing, but put down her glass and slid over to Noah's side. She gazed wordlessly into his brown eyes. He returned the gaze. Vera put her hands around the back of his head and firmly pulled him to her. They kissed, and then they kissed again. She ran her fingers through his thick, black hair.

After they were both free of clothing, Noah exclaimed, "My God, you're beautiful!"

"You're not so bad yourself." Vera hadn't expected such an athletic body on a scientist. *So much for stereotypes,* she thought. "Do you work out?"

"Huh? Oh, mainly, I run."

"It shows." *God, he knows what he's doing.* Vera alternately sighed and moaned. She tried to return his lovemaking but was nearly incapacitated with ecstasy.

Vera gasped, "Do you have a condom?" She didn't want Noah to know that she had a few in her bag.

"Uh, yeah, in the nightstand." Hand in hand, they relocated to the bedroom.

In Salt Lake City, Leland Meredith, an autistic youth of sixteen, had made little progress since his diagnosis eleven years earlier. On the advice of his psychiatrist, Leland's parents acquired a pet cat. The doctor told them that animal companions often helped autistic patients to function, especially young ones. The all-black cat—Leland named it Darth Vader—was the boy's constant companion. His mental outlook improved dramatically. At times, his behavior was such that only an expert could suspect he was autistic. Sometimes, for as long as an hour, the boy would watch Darth's abdomen move slowly, in and out, as he slept. Mr. and Mrs. Meredith attended the First Baptist Church every Sunday and gave thanks to God for sending them the "miracle cat."

5

January 2020   1,099,700,000

Three months after Noah and Vera's memorable first date, Vera drove them to the campus in her Porsche. The ad hoc committee was ready to present its report. The protestors were out in force. Noah was greeted by a rhythmic chant: "Fe Fi Fo Fum, feline killers here we come!"

"Wow," exclaimed Noah, "there must be ten times as many as last time. They can't all be locals."

"No, they're not. Look," said Vera, pointing to a picket with a neatly lettered sign that read, "STOP SACRIFICING OUR PETS!" and, below that, "ANIMAL LIBERATION ARMY."

Noah spotted more signs. "TAXES PAY FOR TORTURE" was claimed by CLAWS, and another: "ANIMALS HAVE RIGHTS TOO."

"Look," he said. "They're picketing my research too." He pointed to a sign that read, "STOP RECOMBINANT DNA CLONING!"

By now, Noah had been recognized by the mob, not surprisingly, as his photograph had recently appeared in *The Ventura County Star*. Noah remembered how furious he'd been when he'd read a spurious op-ed piece dealing with the perils of gene cloning. The editor, Douglas Kohut, had stated that any research involving recombinant DNA was dangerous and should not be allowed near Camarillo. The editorial had made mention

46

of Dolly, the sheep that had been born as a clone back in 2002 and had died prematurely. Noah had exclaimed, "What the hell does that have to do with my research?"

Noah and Vera got out of the car. A thin-lipped, redheaded woman yelled louder than the chanters around her, "You Mengele! How would you like it if somebody used you for research?"

Shocked by the woman's hyperbole, Noah nevertheless kept silent. He was keenly aware of an irony the woman could not possibly imagine. Years ago, his mother had told him that his grandfather and grandmother had perished under the knife of the Angel of Death at Auschwitz.

The crowd pressed in; Noah and Vera had to force their way through to the building. Noah slid his arm around Vera protectively, but she pushed him off, hissing, "I can take care of myself!"

By the time they got inside the lecture hall, it was packed. Vera had already told Noah of the committee's conclusion, so that wasn't a concern, but he was apprehensive about how the students and the public would receive it. He pulled a tube of antacid tablets from his pocket. Vera and Noah made their way to the stage, where they joined Lowell Stanaland and the already-seated committee members.

With the help of ushers, Norman Orgell distributed copies of the committee's report to the audience. After Lowell Stanaland had brought order to the assembly with several sharp raps of a gavel, he introduced Orgell who then read from a prepared statement: "We have found that the controversy surrounding gene cloning research has been thoroughly chronicled in both technical literature and the lay press. We've learned that, in July of 1974, a committee of scientists engaged in recombinant DNA research had voted for a moratorium on such research until an assessment of the risks could be made."

Noah nodded. Until now, he hadn't realized the depth of the committee's research. There was a murmur from the hall. Orgell paused to survey the audience. He cleared his throat and continued, "Our committee was impressed by the fact that it was scientists themselves who voluntarily restricted their research and who publicly expressed concern about possible hazards. The guidelines established by the National Institutes of Health—Dr. Chamberlin mentioned these guidelines at the previous meeting—grew out of these early concerns. Furthermore, we have examined Dr. Chamberlin's facilities and found that all necessary safety precautions required for BSL-2 work are being observed."

Orgell paused. "That's Biosafety Level Two,"

Noah snuck a surreptitious glance to the rear. *Uh-oh,* he thought. *Lots of frowns.*

"However, we have also read articles by several scientists who believe that such research should not be performed at all, or if it must be done, should be confined to BSL-4 labs. These views comprise a small minority.

"The committee is divided on the issue of using cats for research. The two student members, Ms. Anneke Weiss and Mr. Jaime Leal, remain in conscientious opposition to their use. However, Dr. Barnett, Mr. Yazdani, and I feel that the overall benefits, both to cats and to humans, far outweigh the opposing arguments."

Yes! Noah almost shouted it out.

"Dr. Barnett, by virtue of her professional expertise as a veterinarian, was able to persuade our two student members to allow Dr. Chamberlin to continue his work on condition that his lab be subject to a monthly inspection by Dr. Barnett and one of the students. Also, as Dr. Chamberlin mentioned at the October meeting, his facilities continue to be inspected four times a year by the CSUCI Institutional Animal Care and Use committee. Accordingly, our committee has concluded that the potential benefits outweigh the risks, and therefore we recommend that Dr. Chamberlin be permitted to proceed with his research."

When Orgell finished his statement, there were shouts— "No! No!"— and an upwelling of murmured conversation. Stanaland rose and again waited for silence. "The committee has made its recommendation. Does anyone else care to comment before we conclude?"

There were scattered shouts from the audience. The time was now four forty-five p.m., and people were starting to leave. Lowell Stanaland stood and intoned, "As our ad hoc committee was fairly constituted and carried out its charge with due diligence, I believe it proper to accept its findings. The committee has recommended that the research be allowed to continue with the proviso that his facilities are to be inspected monthly by Dr. Vera Barnett and one of the student members. I presume, should either of the students leave the university, the responsibility will be passed on to another." He eyed Jaime Leal, who was sitting in the third row.

Leal nodded. "I'll bring that up before the student council at the next meeting."

"Good. I'll have the committee's report, along with a summary of this meeting typed up and sent to the university president's office and the Institutional Animal Care and Use Committee. I wish to thank the committee for its conscientious and thorough investigation. This meeting is adjourned."

It was all over. Noah was free to proceed with his experiments. He was surprised at the suddenness with which the meeting ended. *It's a good thing that the two students don't know that Vera and I are literally in bed with each other.* He squeezed Vera's hand.

Marty's was a tavern in Old Town Camarillo frequented by university students and faculty members. It was minimally furnished with redwood tables, had sawdust on the wooden floor, and was dimly lit, mainly by a large Budweiser lamp over the pool table. Vera, Noah and Gary eased into a booth.

"Vera, I really appreciate the part you played on that committee," said Noah sincerely.

"Noah, you understand that our friendship had nothing to do with what I did as a member of the committee. I voted the way I did because that's where our investigation led."

I wonder if she's really that objective, he thought. "I know. What I mean is, I appreciate that you took the time to really look into the matter—you and the other committee members. You people made a thorough investigation, and I'm grateful for that." Noah's face grew flushed. "You know, what we have witnessed here is democracy in action. A college community has become concerned about a scientific matter. A committee was formed to examine a highly technical subject. This committee educated and informed itself and ultimately reached the right decision. It really bolsters my faith in the reasonableness of people."

Gary emptied his glass and poured another. "Doc, would you have felt that way if the decision had gone against you?"

Noah studied a droplet that was making an erratic journey down the side of the cold pitcher. He looked up at his companions and confessed in a voice just above a whisper, "If the decision had gone against me, I would have left the institute and gone elsewhere to do MEFA research."

The next morning, after putting out fresh food for Bastette, Noah sat down at his laptop with a cup of fresh-brewed coffee. Vera was running a shower. He accessed *The Star* website, where he found a brief report of the meeting on the third page. On the op-ed page, he found an editorial Noah figured was written by Kohut. It expressed disappointment with the committee's decision and with Noah being allowed to continue to carry out recombinant DNA research. *The guy doesn't quit.* He read on. *Whoa!* Kohut expressed hope that no ill would result from the work and urged the citizens of Camarillo and the students at CSUCI to accept the committee's findings and let Noah get on with his work without harassment.

"Well, I'll be a sonovabitch," Noah uttered aloud.

Jake Moloney, a blackjack dealer at Harrah's, drove by the city animal shelter in Reno every day on his way to work. He was preoccupied on this day with his daughter Irene's fifth birthday four days hence. He had discussed a proper gift with Joan, but neither parent had any idea for anything appropriate. All they could think of were routine toys.

As he waited for a stop light to turn, Jake's eyes fell on the sign "City Pound." His brow wrinkled. *I wonder ...*

When he arrived home that evening, Joan asked, "Any ideas for a present? We've got to do something big. It's her fifth birthday, for crying out loud."

Jake smiled. "How about something very little that would make a big gift?"

"Oh Jake, she's too young for fancy jewelry," Joan objected.

"Not jewelry, a kitten."

Joan frowned. The frown turned to a smile. "And just who would take care of this kitten?"

"Okay, we would, at first. But this would be a great way to teach Irene about responsibility. We could start with showing her that the cat always has to have water, then how to feed the cat ... litter stuff, you know, all the chores we did with Tigerpaws before Irene was born."

"Honey, that's a marvelous idea. Do you know someone who's got a kitten to give away?"

"I was thinking we could stop by the pound and pick one up there. You know they don't cost much, and they've been given all the shots ... all that stuff. How about you meet me at the pound about four thirty tomorrow. Leave Irene with Mrs. Golter next door."

Joan put her arms around her husband and gave him a hug. "You have just won the most-thoughtful-father-of-the-year award."

"Oh? What's the award?"

Joan grinned. "You'll find out later tonight."

6

Three months after Noah had resumed his research, Vera and Kal at the clinic were examining the tender abdomen of a Rottweiler. When her phone sounded, Vera answered it with her customary, "Hello, Barnett the vet."

"Vera, this is Dottie. Vera, I need you. My cats are sick, real sick. I've lost four of the darlings already." Vera heard the agitation in her longtime friend's voice. Sixty-three-year-old Dorothy Knowland loved cats; her home was thick with them.

"Whoa, honey. Calm down. Do you have any of those tranquilizers you take?"

"Yes but ..."

"Well take one. I'll be right over." Vera shook her head. *Dottie and her cats,* Vera mused. *She must realize that with so many—I counted thirty once—there is a high probability that at any given time some will become ill or die.*

Vera asked Kal to take charge while she was away from the clinic. She hopped into the Porsche and headed for Lewis Road. *Poor Dottie. So many of her friends think she's a crackpot; she's just a lonely widow. It's her business if she wants to keep cats. I don't know anyone who's as kind, intelligent, and quick-witted. Sure, she's eccentric ...* Vera switched to gas and headed for the nearby community of Somis.

The two women had met shortly after Vera set up her practice in Camarillo. Several of Dorothy's cats had come down with enteritis. She'd driven into Camarillo, looking for a veterinarian who would make the trip to her home in Somis, north of the city. Vera, unlike many vets, often did make house calls. She agreed to drive over to Dottie's after the woman pleaded with her, contending that she had too many cats to transport to the clinic. Three other vets had declined to make the trip. Vera drove to Somis the very next day.

Over time, Dorothy and Vera had become good friends. Occasionally, Dottie would invite her to dinner, and the two women would converse at length on a variety of topics, from cats to casseroles. Vera valued her companionship. She enjoyed the tasteful, rustically furnished living room. Sometimes Dorothy would play the harpsichord after the meal, and Vera would lean back in an antique bentwood rocker, close her eyes, and lose herself in the music.

Turning into the driveway, Vera saw that Dottie was waiting in front. The chubby, middle-aged woman manifested a pathetic aspect, standing there in her cotton-print dress. Her hands hung by her sides, a kerchief clutched in the right one. Her graying hair was unkempt, and her usually smiling eyes were puffed and red. The two women hugged.

Dorothy immediately burst into tears. "Oh, Vera, I don't understand what's happening."

"Well, Dottie," Vera responded, assuming a brisk professional mien, "I'll just have to take a look at the cats, won't I?"

Accustomed to animals as she was, Vera nevertheless marveled at the profusion of felines as they went inside.. Vera made a quick, surreptitious count of twenty-two. She knew there were others in and around the house. The vet hardly noticed the musk-ammonia odor permeating the living room. Vera had once warned Dottie that she was probably in violation of laws prohibiting so many felines in one residence. Dottie had not seemed concerned.

They sat on the overstuffed sofa whose sides were frizzy from years of clawing. Beside Vera was a kitten pulling at the corner of an antimacassar while another looked on with interest. The once-fine handmade burl coffee table, legs scratched and clawed to bare wood, bore gilt-framed photographs of relatives. The largest was an eight-by-ten of Dorothy's late husband, who had died of prostate cancer over twenty years ago.

One item of furniture which, except for its legs, showed little evidence of cat damage was the exquisite hand-painted harpsichord by the front window. Vera knew that, although Dorothy allowed her *babies* the run of the house and never punished them much when they climbed on chairs, tables, sofas, and the like, no cats were allowed to venture onto the harpsichord. A squirt of water from a spray bottle that Dorothy kept within reach was enough to keep most of them off the instrument.

Her husband Dave had given her the harpsichord on her thirty-third birthday. She'd taken lessons for three years from Madame Lubitzovna, who'd maintained a studio in the nearby town of Ojai. Building on her years of playing the piano, Dorothy learned to play quite well for an amateur. Vera recalled that, once, when Dottie was playing for her, a thin mongrel tabby accompanied the delicate music with a discordant yowl that both women found hilarious, if cacophonous. Dottie had named the singer Dietrich, after the German baritone Dietrich Fischer-Dieskau.

Vera noticed at once that many of the animals appeared lethargic. "All right, hon, I want you to tell me everything that has happened since the first cat became ill."

"It started a couple of weeks ago," Dorothy began. "Three of the cats were just lying around. I could see they were sick. A few days later they were dead. I wasn't upset much at first. I've had cats get sick and die before. Why, just last July a calico named Quilt and an old tom that had no name died on the same day, within four hours of each other." Her voice wavered. "But now, four more cats are dead and about half of the others are ill. One of the dead ones is precious Lucy, the seal-point Siamese." Dorothy burst into tears.

Vera took Dorothy's hand. "Did you notice anything else?" she asked. "Anything at all in those cats before they died? Their appetite? Did they eat? Were they frothing at the mouth?"

"Well, yes. For the last week or so, quite a few of them haven't been eating much. Lucy and Aristotle weren't eating at all before they died. Even Martin there hasn't been eating." She pointed to a large tom sprawled on the carpet. "He usually eats the food left over by the others. And they haven't been as active as usual. Some of them have diarrhea, some have been vomiting, and I saw blood coming from the noses of two of them." Dorothy stopped speaking; the tears resumed.

Dorothy regained some composure and said, "Oh, and they seem to be very thirsty. At first, I didn't think too much of it because the cats often get sick with one thing or another. Maybe fleas are responsible."

Vera observed that some of the cats were showing their haws— the membranes under their eyelids that, in healthy animals, are generally hidden. She also noticed streaks of blood in their eyes. She took the rectal temperature of several of the sick pets. "They all have high fevers," she remarked. "No question that it's some kind of infection." The vet stroked the back of the animal she'd been examining. But the cat made an evasive movement and yowled loudly. *Hmmm. sensitive to touch.* She scratched her head. "Are there more fleas than usual right now?"

"No," Dorothy replied. "It's still early for fleas. They don't get real bad until summer." Dorothy had stopped crying. "I thought it might be distemper, but you gave most of them shots for that."

Vera nodded thoughtfully. "I think you should consider putting your cats on one of the long-lasting flea inhibitors." For years, she had urged Dottie to use an anti-flea regimen, but the woman refused to use any medications on her cats unless it was absolutely necessary.

Dorothy continued, "Most of the cats died at night. I found their dear little bodies when I got up in the morning. But one, a cat named Clyde that Pete Wingate brought over, was eating up a storm yesterday around ten in the morning … he purred so loud when I scratched him under the chin … then I found his furry body about two thirty in the afternoon."

Vera listened for possible clues to the illness. Her attention, however, was caught by the strange antics of a jet-black cat over by the grandfather clock. The cat, one Vera knew as Sabrina, was having trouble walking. She was making the same awkward movements that a kitten does when it first ventures to use its limbs. But Sabrina was fully grown. Vera rushed over and tenderly folded the animal in her arms. The cat protested weakly. Blood was dripping from her nose and mouth. Soon she was convulsing, her body jerking spasmodically. Within minutes Sabrina was dead. Dorothy and Vera exchanged horrified glances.

Vera shook her head. "You might swab down the floor around the food and water dishes with bleach," she suggested. "I don't know what we're dealing with, but bleach is a pretty good disinfectant."

Vera put the lifeless bodies of Sabrina and two other cats in a large plastic bag, and then gave Dorothy a hug. "I'll do my best to find out what this is."

The drive back to the clinic allowed her time to digest the afternoon's events. *What the hell is this? An epidemic? The symptoms point to a rapidly developing viral disease—maybe panleukopenia is involved.* But the speed with which the disease passed from animal to animal didn't jibe with any sickness she could think of.

Vera spent the rest of the afternoon performing necropsies on the three cats. The dead felines were quite emaciated and had enlarged spleens and lymph nodes. She noticed extensive internal bleeding, which she found both puzzling and alarming. Her pulse raced, and her hands started to shake. She closed her eyes, leaned back in the chair, and forced herself to relax. When she examined the blood of the deceased cats under the microscope, she saw that all three showed very high white-blood-cell counts. Panleukopenia would have shown low counts. Her preliminary diagnosis had to be wrong. She wondered if it might be a new disease with which she was unfamiliar. Kal Forstner was a recent graduate of vet school; Vera considered that he might have encountered this new affliction in one of his courses.

"Kal, would you come in here a minute, please?"

"What's up?" Kal said as he entered the lab.

Vera described the disease affecting the cats. "Does this sound like anything you studied at Davis?"

He put his fingertips to his forehead and closed his eyes. After a minute, he said, "No, I can't think of any infectious disease that spreads so fast."

"I was afraid you'd say that." She tried to dispel a growing feeling of unease. *Calm down, Vera,* she told herself. *This is probably some obvious sickness you haven't thought of.*

She called Noah at the institute. "Noah, it's Vera. I've got a problem." She told him of Dorothy's sick cats. "Is there someone at the institute who could do some diagnostic bacteriology on these cats? I'm not set up for that, and it's kind of urgent. My regular lab service would take too long."

"Sounds serious," Noah replied. "We don't do much of that here—wait a minute! They teach a course in medical microbiology in the biology department. I'll call Dr. Morton, the guy who teaches the course, and get back to you."

Vera thanked him and went back to her feline corpses. She went over to the bookshelf she called her reference library and pulled down a few books on infectious disease. After an hour, she still hadn't found any mention of an illness such as she'd seen at Dottie's.

On Saturday, Vera drove up to the campus with three small, chilled vials of clotted blood from the three dead cats. Arriving at the lab of Dr. P. Merrill Morton, Vera encountered a balding, ruddy man wearing a starched lab coat. He looked up from the microscope and greeted her with a concerned smile. "I understand you have some sort of epidemic on your hands." He took the samples and told her that it would take several days to isolate and identify any bacteria. "One suggestion, Dr. Barnett; you might call that woman—what's her name, Mrs. Knowland—and tell her to keep all her cats locked up in the house."

"You think it might be serious enough that a quarantine is called for?"

"I don't know. I just suggest we err on the side of safety."

Vera took a deep breath. "I have to admit, I've never seen such an aggressive set of symptoms in any animal."

As soon as Vera got back to the clinic, she telephoned Dorothy.

"But Vera," Dorothy protested, "even if I close all the windows and doors, there are ways the cats can get out of the house. There's an opening into the wall behind the kitchen stove."

Vera sighed inaudibly. "Well, do the best you can, hon. See if you can find a way to close up those holes."

That night, Vera and Noah took in a 3D movie, but Vera had trouble following the plot. Her mind kept wandering back to Dorothy's cats. Later, at Noah's, she settled down on the sofa while Noah fiddled with the stereo. Bastette jumped onto her lap and, in response to her caresses, began kneading the vet's tummy. Noah sat down beside Vera.

"She's smiling," she said.

"Cats can't smile."

"Sure they can. A purr is an audible smile."

"Oh. Right. Never thought of it that way."

Vera was silent. Distractedly, she ran her hands through her hair.

"Are you okay?' he asked Noah.

"Noah, I'm worried about Dorothy's cats."

He took her hand. "I would be too. Are you sure you can't identify it with one of the common feline diseases?"

"Yes," Vera replied. " I've gone over and over it in my mind and can't peg it to anything I'm familiar with."

"You don't suppose you could have picked up the infectious agent from the Knowland cats, do you? I wouldn't want Bastette to get sick."

"I guess that's a possibility. I did shower when I got home. Besides, most infectious feline diseases are transferred from cat to cat, not from cat to human to cat."

Noah frowned. "Are you sure it's not distemper?"

"It doesn't seem to be. I considered panleukopenia—that's what vets call distemper—but the white-cell count is up, not down. It looks more like a virulent bacterial infection of some sort."

Noah leaned over Bastette and planted a chaste kiss on Vera's cheek.

"What's that for?" asked Vera.

"I love it when you talk dirty like that."

"What, panleukopenia? Let me tell you about urolithiasis or calicivirus," she responded.

"Ooh! In some countries you could get arrested for using provocative words like that." Noah continued the game, and Vera leaned over the cat and kissed him.

"And what's that for?" he asked.

"Because you're you, that's all." For the rest of the night there was no more talk of feline diseases.

Sunday morning, they shared breakfast while Bastette fished with her paw for imaginary creatures in her water dish. Vera shook her head. "I'd better call Dorothy."

She learned that another cat had died during the night; Vera was bewildered. She looked up at Noah. "I better get back to Dorothy's and check her cats again." He shrugged.

When she arrived at the Knowland house, she put on latex gloves and a disposable paper smock. She wrinkled her nose. *Bleach and urine ... unpleasant mix ...* Vera looked around the house and saw that almost all of the pets were sick. Some could hardly move.

Vera examined over half the animals. She palpated their abdomens and listened to their hearts and lungs; she took their temperatures and noted their pulses. Without exception, they were feverish. Their gums were pallid, and their haws were showing. Some had blood trickling from their ears or noses or mouths. Several had diarrhea, making their examination a messy, difficult job. Vera was deeply disturbed. She couldn't recall a feline disease with such a high rate of transfer and mortality.

Dorothy sat silently in a corner, staring at nothing. Vera took more blood samples from some of the cats for additional examinations.

Back at the clinic, Vera asked Kal if he would assist. When they examined the blood samples, they again found a high white-blood-cell count. As with the earlier specimens, she again thought she saw bacteria. The telephone rang. Vera expected to hear Dorothy's voice and was surprised when it turned out to be Mrs. Amend, the wife of City Councilman Amend. Her cat was ill, and would Vera mind if she brought her in, even though it was Sunday? Of course, Vera could not deny her.

The blue Persian, whose mistress normally kept her carefully groomed, was a mess. Her hair was matted, and her hindquarters were soiled with diarrheic stool. The cat's eyes were dull. Vera realized that the symptoms were the same as those exhibited by Dorothy's cats. "You don't let Madame run loose, do you?" she asked.

"No, she is strictly a house cat," snapped Mrs. Amend. "We never let her out."

Vera's brow wrinkled. If Madame had the same illness that all of Dorothy's cats did, how did she contract it? "Have there been any other cats in your house in the past week or so?"

"Why no. Of course not," the woman answered. Her tone displayed resentment that Vera would even ask such a question.

"I have to tell you, Mrs. Amend, that the prognosis is very poor. I think your cat has a bacterial infection and ..."

"But you gave Madame a shot for enteritis in September!" Mrs. Amend accused.

"I know. But I don't think she has enteritis. It's something else. You'd better leave her with me and I'll do what I can."

Mrs. Amend frowned, eyeing Vera with suspicion. "All right."

By Monday morning, Madame was dead, the phone was ringing nonstop, and the two vets were exhausted. Cats were dying all over the city.

M. J. Pettit, professor of clinical microbiology in the UCLA medical school, ended his lecture on plague and tularemia. As his students bustled and chattered, he prepared to depart.

"Dr. Pettit, do you have a second? I have a question." The professor looked up. It was Marilyn Sturtevant, a studious blonde—one of the top achievers on exams.

"Sure, What is it?"

"Before today's lecture, I thought plague was a disease of the past like smallpox—wiped out. But you say it's still with us."

"That's right."

"You also said it's common in wild rodents in Southern California."

Pettit nodded.

The woman shook her head. "I guess I'm kind of shocked. I had no idea we had plague locally,"

"Most people don't … not until there's a case reported in the news or a campground is closed because plague bacteria are found in squirrels or other animals. Do a web search. You'll be amazed."

"I guess what I want to ask is, what is the probability of a black plague epidemic like that in Europe in the fourteenth century?"

"Excellent question, Marilyn. The odds are nearly zero. Why? Because the virulent genetic strain of *Yersinia pestis* responsible for the black death is thought to be extinct."

"Oohh. So there are different strains of plague bacteria that vary in their pathogenicity."

"Exactly. Remember, however, that under the right conditions, even a relatively benign strain can become virulent."

Sturtevant scribbled rapidly on her electronic pad. "Thank you, sir."

Pettit smiled. "You're quite welcome… and please, drop the *sir.*"

"Right." She headed out the door, turned, and gave him a wave.

7

Vera sat alone by a placid mountain tarn when suddenly she heard a man's voice crying "Help! Help me!" She peered out over the icy lake and saw the drowning man thrashing about. She could see no boat—no line to throw him. She dove into the chilly water and swam as fast as she could. Yet, no matter how hard she stroked, she made no headway. The man's head slipped below the water.

Vera woke with a start, her heart racing. *No lake. No drowning man.* She didn't need a shrink to decipher the dream. No way could she and Kal handle the work piling up without additional help. Her hand shook as she punched in Gary McKeever's number. "Gary, this is Dr. Barnett." Her voice wavered with fatigue and tension. "Is Jane there?"

"Just a minute, I'll put her on," Gary answered hoarsely. Vera realized that seven thirty in the morning was on the early side for a scientist who often worked hours past midnight.

When Jane came on the line, Vera said, "Jane, could you possibly put in some extra time for a while? There is some sort of epidemic affecting the cats in town and I have more work than I can handle. Kal and I could use your help in calming our clientele. I've been so busy answering questions, I haven't had enough time for the animals. I ..." Vera's voice broke. She sobbed.

"Take it easy, Dr. Bar ... Vera. I'll be over as soon as I get Gary some breakfast ... no, he can get his own breakfast. I'll come right over."

Jane arrived just as her boss was attempting to placate four agitated cat owners. Kal hadn't come in yet. Jane stepped right into the group, grabbed Vera's arm, and all but dragged her into the back room as Vera protested weakly. At Jane's urging, Vera lay down on the cot. Jane returned to the group out front. Vera heard her assure them that the vet was doing all she could, but that she had to get some rest or she wouldn't be able to work at all.

Before she dozed off, Vera thought how fortunate she was to have found Jane. Here was a helper who continually made herself useful, finding constructive things to do where others might find none. Vera knew that Jane would handle the cat owners with tact and courtesy. She slept soundly, but woke briefly when Kal arrived then fell back into slumber.

Jane roused Vera shortly after ten. "There's a Professor P. Merrill Morton on the line."

"Hello. Dr. Morton? This is Vera Barnett. What have you found?"

"Well, it's a bit of a puzzle, I'm afraid. We're not quite finished, but I can tell you that one blood sample has a Gram-negative bacillus we haven't yet identified; I think it's *Pseudomonas*. The other two samples appear to be sterile."

"But ... but ..." Vera was still groggy from her nap, but she then came fully awake. "I guess it's some kind of virus, then."

"Yes, it would seem so. However, I'm wondering about the one sample that shows bacteria. Is there any chance that you contaminated the blood with skin bacteria when you autopsied the cats?" Vera sensed that Morton was trying to be tactful.

"Yes, of course it's possible," Vera responded curtly, "but I do know how to take blood aseptically from a dead animal."

"Yes, I'm sure you do. I just ... well anyway, that's what we've got so far. I'd be happy to look at more samples. My wife told me that quite a few of her friends' cats are ill. I've got to tell you, my curiosity is piqued."

"Thank you, Dr. Morton. I'll bring more samples. And I will be very careful not to contaminate them. Perhaps I could bring up one or two of the sick cats and let you draw their blood yourself."

"That would be fine."

Vera gazed out the window. *So it's probably a virus after all ... but it can't be panleukopenia. What the hell is it?* Vera brewed a pot of coffee while she looked over the lengthy list of messages that had piled up while she slept. She checked all the animals in the ward, removing the bodies of two cats that had expired during her slumber. She consulted with Kal, but he had no new information. There was some terrible disease afflicting the cats of Camarillo, that's all they knew. Vera made a few calls to owners and then sat down and sipped coffee absently, while Jane continued taking calls and Kal dealt with walk-ins.

Vera and Kal drew a tiny amount of blood from several of the sick cats in the ward and prepared blood smears. "Look," Kal said, "those tiny needle sticks are still oozing blood."

"I see. Seems to be something wrong with their blood clotting. That's consistent with the internal hemorrhaging I saw in the dead cats. Vera diluted a small amount of blood in saline and placed it on a special slide called a hemacytometer. She examined it with her microscope. Her fingers clicked away at a counting device. "Ah hah!" was the only remark she uttered for twenty minutes.

When she was finished, she turned to Kal. "That's it! The lymphocyte count in all these cats is low, less than one tenth of the normal level. Also, I see lots of immature leukocytes. This is some mutant type of feline leukemia, and it develops much faster than any I have ever seen. It all fits. Swollen spleens, diarrhea, compromised immunity. Everything makes sense except the rapidity of the disease. Feline leukemia usually takes months or years to develop, not days."

As Vera was recording her results, the phone rang. It was Noah. Two of his new research cats were dead. He had slowly replenished his collection of felines after the break-in of the prior month. "I don't think they died of MEFA," he said, "because, for one thing, one of the cats didn't have MEFA. The other one did, but I didn't think he was that sick."

"Oh, I'm so sorry, Noah." Vera was silent a moment. "I'm coming up to your lab. I want to look at your cats, including the dead ones. I think this may be the same disease that killed Dorothy's cats. Besides I have to bring some cats up to Dr. Morton for more bacteriological tests. See you in a bit."

Vera placed three of the sick cats in carriers and asked Kal and Jane to take care of things while she was out. At the university, she dropped off the ailing cats at Morton's lab and headed for the institute.

She met Noah at his office, and they went down to the lab and entered the cat room. Vera went over to the cages and examined all of the animals. A few were obviously ill with the symptoms Vera was coming to associate with the feline leukemia—or whatever it was. Several had bloodshot eyes and were hypersensitive to any touch. Others appeared normal. She took blood samples from several of the ill cats. Acting on a hunch, she then drew additional samples from a few of the apparently healthy ones.

She asked, "Where are the dead ones?"

"In the lab."

Vera examined the two feline cadavers. She treated the blood samples with Wright's stain and examined them under Noah's microscope. It was as she expected—an abundance of white blood cells, but very few lymphocytes.

She then examined the blood from the cats that were not sick. For a moment she held her breath, and then she gasped. They all presented the same picture: a high granulocyte count and a paucity of lymphocytes. Vera shook her head. "One thing we can be sure of is that your cats have not had contact with any cats outside the institute. Of all the cats in Camarillo, I would have thought that yours would be the safest from an epidemic, unless …"

"Unless what?"

Vera regarded Noah, her face contorted with horror. "Unless," she exclaimed, "the disease started right here. Oh, my God!"

Noah frowned. "Vera, that's ridiculous. MEFA isn't contagious, and the symptoms of this disease aren't anything like those of MEFA."

"This isn't about MEFA. I'm talking about some kind of feline leukemia."

"What do you mean leukemia? My cats don't have leukemia."

Vera's tone was sharp. "I'll just bet they do. I did differential counts on some of the cats in my ward. They all showed a low lymphocyte count, but a high percentage of granulocytes. That's the same picture I just observed in the blood of your cats. I think it's some kind of accelerated leukemia."

"But what makes you think the epidemic started here and not someplace else?" Noah asked, his voice shaking.

Vera looked him in the eye. "I think your sarcoma virus could be involved."

"Sarcoma is not leukemia."

"No, but you know very well that all cats carry dormant viral leukemia genes in their chromosomes. Some also carry FIV, the feline AIDS virus. Maybe your sarcoma virus picked up leukemia genes or FIV genes."

Noah pulled a roll of antacid tablets from his pocket, popping one into his mouth. "But these cats are all new here," he said. "After my cats were stolen, I had to bring in others from the outside. So the epidemic couldn't have started here."

"The hell it couldn't. Before you brought these cats in, did you sterilize the cages?"

Noah frowned. "Well, of course we cleaned them."

"Are you absolutely sure that not one virus particle remained?" Vera walked over to the window and gazed out over the Spanish-tiled roofs of the campus buildings, too upset to speak. She whirled around and yelled, "You bastard! I think we made a big, big mistake in allowing you to screw around with cancer viruses and cat chromosomes. You better stop all research right now before you do more damage."

"No, dammit! I will not. You're trying and convicting me on circumstantial evidence. You're not being fair."

Vera realized that they were now shouting at each other. Alicia Diaz, working at the lab bench, looked over at the two, but said nothing. Vera stormed out of the lab and ran from the institute.

Ohio attorney Sam Neidleman helped a nurse ease his mother out of the wheelchair. "It's okay, Mom. You're in good hands." After watching Rebecca Neidleman's health decline for three years, Sam and Sarah had determined they could no longer care for her. They had discussed this for weeks. "I can handle the arthritis or the Alzheimer's," Sarah remarked, "but not both at the same time."

"She's my mother!" Sam shouted.

"Sam, I love her as if she were my own mother, but I can't do this anymore. Yes, she's your mother. I'm your wife. You've got to make a choice. We can afford to place her in one of the better care facilities."

Eventually, they settled on the Van Buren Home for the Aged in Cleveland. Although it was a half-hour drive from their suburban home and pricey, the facility had a good reputation.

Sarah asked the intake nurse, "Will Mrs. Neidleman be able to interact with the other patients?"

"Absolutely," replied the nurse. "We schedule social events every day. We've found it helps the Alzheimer's sufferers greatly. By the way, we don't use the term *patient* here. These elderly men and women are *residents* of the Van Buren Home. This is not a hospital."

"That nurse got her hackles up when I used the word *patient*," Sam noted.

Sarah smiled and reached over, placing her hand on her husband's shoulder. "That's a good thing, Sam," she said. "It reveals the philosophy of the home. I think we've made the right choice."

8

As he drove home, Noah's emotions ran the gamut from anger to guilt. Could Vera's theory be sound? Could the feline-sarcoma vector have acquired the ability to cause leukemia and gotten out of the lab? *Am I responsible for this disease? That's not possible ... or is it?*

When he arrived home, Bastette was not in sight. Noah found her in the living room, curled up in a corner. That morning, he'd noticed that she wasn't eating much. That night, she shunned her dinner entirely. She didn't act particularly sick, but, when Noah lifted her, she yowled. He froze. *Oh, no, no, no. Does she have the same disease?* Noah set her down gently on the sofa and started to telephone Vera. He held the phone in midair for several seconds and closed it without making the call.

An hour later, it rang. It was Lowell Stanaland. "Noah, I'm sorry to have to tell you this, but your friend Dr. Barnett has requested an emergency meeting of the biosafety and animal-care committees. It's tomorrow morning at nine thirty. You should be there."

All members of the Animal Care and Use Committee were present, but only four of the five biosafety committee members showed up. Noah, who had not slept a wink, sat tight-lipped and stared coldly at his accuser. He wondered if one could simultaneously love and hate the same person?

72

P. Merrill Morton brought everyone up to date on the latest bacteriological results. All of the samples were free of bacteria. The disease had to be viral.

Vera reviewed what was known about the epidemic and told them of her theory as to its origin. She urged the committees to prohibit Noah from continuing with experiments. "I see no other way to prevent further spread of the disease," she concluded.

Noah looked around the room to gauge how the committee members were reacting. Biological Safety Officer Andrea Vernon took notes as Vera spoke. Dr. Jerome Robinson, Ventura County's health officer, leaned back in his chair, his large, black hands held as if in prayer against his pursed lips. Dr. Stanaland, brow furrowed, drummed his fingertips on the tabletop as Vera spoke—a mannerism Noah found irritating.

"I feel somewhat guilty myself about this," Vera said. "I was a member of the committee that originally looked into the possible threats from Dr. Chamberlin's experiments." Noah saw that she was avoiding eye-contact with him. "I really think," Vera concluded, "that these experiments must stop until we are sure that the disease did not start at the institute. The evidence suggests that it did."

"Dr. Stanaland, do you have any comment?" asked Andrea Vernon.

"No, but I would … no, never mind."

Vernon turned to Noah. "Dr. Chamberlin?"

"There is absolutely no evidence that this epidemic started in my laboratory," said Noah, speaking in a monotone through clenched teeth.

Jerome Robinson spoke. "We should get an epidemiologist on this. I've never seen anything like it. Even though it's not a disease of humans—thank God for that—it seems to be so devastating to cats that we should seek outside help—someone from the UC Davis Vet School, or maybe even the CDC. I'll contact the State Board of Public Health and see if they can get the CDC involved."

"Getting back to our question," Vernon said, "are we ready for a vote?"

Nobody spoke.

"I'll take that as a yes. All in favor of implementing a ban on Dr. Chamberlin's research, effective immediately, and until further notice, raise your hand."

The vote was unanimous; it effectively put Noah out of business.

Noah went straight home without speaking to Vera. Bastette failed to greet him. He called her. "Bast! Bastette!" Noah looked through every room. *No cat.* He feared the worst. *Oh God, no.* Outside the back door he found her. She lay, not quite dead, eyes glazed, in a small pool of bloody vomit. Noah took her in his arms and went inside. Tears welled in his eyes. He grabbed a towel from the kitchen and gently wiped Bastette's mouth. He thought he felt a faint purr, but, moments later her chest heaved, and she was gone. Noah sat for a long time, his once-active, playful friend in his lap. He stared at the wall and pondered the intensity of the bond that develops between man and beast. Finally, he went into the kitchen for the first of what was going to be many bottles of beer.

Noah was not much of a drinker, and he awoke the next morning with a furious hangover. As usual, he felt around for Bastette, and then, as he remembered yesterday's events, he remained motionless for some minutes, unable to accept that Bastette was dead. Finally, he found the energy to get out of bed and unsteadily made his way to the bathroom.

Noah put on his jacket, went out the back door, and grabbed a spade. Without emotion, he dug a shallow grave for Bastette under a pine. Unmindful of the dirt he tracked through the house, he fetched the cold feline body, gently wrapped her in a pillowcase from the linen closet, and carried the enshrouded corpse outside and laid it gently in the grave.

Noah stood there for a moment, not knowing what to do next. What does one do when burying a cat? For people, there are rites, but what do you say for a cat? Though he made an effort to stifle the strong emotions that threatened to overwhelm him, a heaving sob forced its way out. He cried openly as he threw soil into the small hole. Shortly, he had covered the remains of his harmless, necessary companion.

Noah forced himself to go into work. He had a lecture at nine, and, short of complete incapacitation, he wouldn't think of missing a class. With difficulty, he reviewed his notes, but his mind wasn't on biochemistry. This morning's lecture on nucleic-acid structure would not be up to par. Prior to class, as Noah sat at his desk, attempting to go over the material, Gary and Alicia appeared at the office doorway in an agitated state.

"Doc, what the hell is going on?" Gary asked. "There's a note on the door of the lab saying the lab is quarantined. Nobody's allowed in."

Noah nodded. "They think that this cat epidemic started right here. Dr. Barnett does anyway. And I'm not so sure they're wrong. Alicia, I've arranged for you to work in Dr. Ivinson's lab until this blows over."

"I'm so sorry, Dr. Chamberlin," replied the technician. "I know this is a difficult time for you."

After Alicia left, Gary stood there, open-mouthed. Finally he said, "Jane told me about Dr. Barnett's leukemia theory, but she didn't tell me anything about us being implicated."

"Well, we are."

"How am I supposed to finish my work? Who'll feed the cats? Who's going to transfer the cell cultures. They'll die out if they're not transferred and fed."

"Gary, relax. This will pass. You can continue to work on your thesis. In fact, you've gotten a little behind in your writing, and this is a good opportunity to get caught up. As for the cats, I'm sure they will let us in to take care of them. I'll discuss it with Dr. Stanaland."

As if on cue, the head of the institute showed up at that moment. "Have you two seen the morning paper?" he asked. He tossed a printed copy of *The Star* onto Noah's desk. He and Gary stared at the paper blankly. "Kohut's grinding his axe today, and we've provided the whetstone."

Noah read the bold headline aloud: "CSUCI lab source of Camarillo cat epidemic." He looked up at Dr. Stanaland and exclaimed, "This can't be happening!" Noah read the body of the article in silence while Gary read over his shoulder. He quickly realized that the article was filled with misinformation and innuendo as well as opinion, which properly belonged on the op-ed page. Noah looked up. "This is outrageous!" he exclaimed. "It borders on slander."

"Libel," Stanaland corrected, "and I believe Kohut has crossed way over that border. I've got the university's legal department looking into it." He regarded the scientist and the graduate student somberly. "Noah, Gary, I want you two to keep level heads during this crisis. Most of your colleagues, myself included, think it unlikely that this feline leukemia started in your lab. We're simply the victims of a bizarre coincidence. On the other hand, we can't entirely rule out the possibility that the disease did originate here. Noah, go on with your teaching and use any extra time to catch up on your technical reading. And, Gary, you could work on your thesis. I understand you've fallen a bit behind."

Gary exchanged a glance with Noah and smiled wanly. He then said, "Dr. Stanaland, we've got to go into the lab to take care of the cats, and, if we don't keep up the cell cultures, they will all die out."

Stanaland nodded. "I don't think the IBC would object if you maintained the lab. Just don't do any cloning experiments." Without waiting for Noah to respond, he turned and strode out of the office.

"Let's take a look at the cats," Noah suggested.

A foul odor greeted them as they entered the cat room. Four more cats had died during the night. "If this keeps up, we can forget about doing any research, even if the ban is lifted," observed Gary.

"Bastette died yesterday," Noah blurted.

"What?"

"My cat Bastette died."

"Oh, uh, I'm sorry. I guess it's the same disease that's getting our cats."

"What if they're right?" Noah said dubiously. "Maybe we did start the epidemic, but I can't think how."

When Noah left for the day, he encountered a crowd of people milling about the entrance to the institute. He recognized some of them as animal-welfare supporters who had been present at the meetings of last year when he had been forced to suspend his research. He spied several T-shirts bearing slogans: "Stop research on sentient creatures," and "Vivisection is the work of the devil." *The Star* was also represented, and, when the photographer spotted Noah, flashes went off, one after the other.

When the demonstrators recognized Noah, they began yelling obscenities. Soon they were chanting in unison. "Cat-killer! Cat-killer!" A reporter from *The Star* pushed through to Noah. "Dr. Chamberlin, do you have any comments about what you've done?"

Noah glared at the young man and replied, "What have I done?" Without waiting for an answer, he turned back into the building and exited through a small service door at the rear, unseen. He asked himself, *What have I done?* He turned Vera's theory over and over in his mind. The more he thought about it, the more he became obsessed with the possibility that the cat sickness had actually started in his lab.

For what seemed to her the hundredth time that week, Vera drove out to the Knowland house. She did so, not because she thought she could be of any help to the remaining cats there—she fully expected all of them to die—but out of compassion for a dear friend. When she arrived at Dottie's, Vera sensed that her friend's mood had changed since yesterday—no crying this time. Rather, Dottie's inner strength had surfaced. Determination showed on her face; she was ready to brave the worst. Vera placed three more dead cats in a large plastic bag—for disposal, not examination. There was neither time nor need for performing necropsies on every dead cat. She did, however, make a cursory examination of some of the still-living felines. There were no surprises. "There is nothing I can do, Dorothy. I'm sorry."

"I know. It's not your fault. The newspaper says that it all got started up at the university. They think your Dr. Chamberlin had something to do with it."

"That's a possibility," said Vera. She was suddenly aware of how serious an effect this disease was going to have on Noah's career. "I've got to go now. I'll check back with you tomorrow."

Vera hastened out the door, fumbling with the sack of corpses, which impeded her retrieving the car keys. She wanted to cry. *Damn it! This is just horrible.* The bag slipped from her grip. A feline head protruded from the fallen plastic. Vera herself sank to the ground. "Oohhh … fuck." The tears came. She managed to get the door unlocked and sat in the Porsche, unable to turn the key, unable to think clearly. She sat quietly for a long time, her sorrow metamorphosing into anger and resolve.

At Vera's urging, Mayor Yoshino called an emergency meeting of the city council. It was a chilly Thursday evening, and the five council members sipped hot coffee in Vera's living quarters. "I'm sorry to call you here on such short notice," said the mayor, "but Dr. Barnett considers this an extreme emergency."

"You realize," noted Councilman Amend, "that this meeting violates the Brown Act."

"I know it does," responded the mayor, "but Dr. Barnett believes that time is of the essence. As soon as we're finished here,

I'll post a summary of the meeting on our TV channel and our website. In any case, the Brown Act has a provision for emergency meetings in the public interest. Mrs. Schubert, would you mind serving as recording secretary?"

"Not at all. I have a recorder here somewhere." She fumbled in her bag.

"Dr. Barnett," said Yoshino, indicating that the floor was hers.

Vera had no need to explain the situation. By now, almost everyone in the city knew about the illness sweeping so rapidly through the feline population. "I think we have a moral obligation to do what we can to keep the disease from spreading. I'd like to ask the council to impose a quarantine on the cats in Camarillo. Perhaps we could order all cat owners to keep their pets indoors."

"I don't think we have that authority," Councilman Amend pointed out. "Besides, how could we enforce such a decree?"

Yoshino countered, "We do have the authority to protect the health and safety of the citizenry, but I don't know about animals. It's a gray area. Much of the affected area doesn't lie within the city limits."

"We are dealing with an unprecedented situation," Vera said passionately. "Do we want Camarillo to be remembered as the place where began the Great Feline Epidemic of the Twenty-first Century? This disease, which I believe is a form of leukemia, has incredible destructive potential."

"We could probably pass a resolution," offered Councilwoman Schubert, "and have the mayor make a statement. Cat owners are usually nice people. I think they would voluntarily comply with the decree."

"I suppose we have nothing to lose," said the mayor. "Do I hear a motion?"

The motion to place the city's cats under quarantine passed unanimously. The next day, Mayor Yoshino appeared on television to urge compliance. As far as Vera knew, there was 100 percent cooperation by cat owners. But, when she read that a number of feline deaths had been reported in nearby Oxnard, Vera realized at once it was a futile effort. On Saturday, Vera came upon an article in *The Star* from the Associated Press reporting a highly contagious illness advancing rapidly through cats in Seattle, Washington. *Oh shit.* Vera stood up so suddenly, her chair fell over. *Seattle is more than a thousand miles away. This can't be.*

Ed Mason of Chattanooga, Tennessee, had loved wild birds since childhood. He enjoyed watching them eat the seeds he put out each morning. "Now there's a new one," he said to himself, leaning closer to the window. "What could it be?" It looked to Ed like a female house finch, but with a large, rounded crest—more like a cluster of small feathers. *The bird's rumpled, maybe molting. That's odd, she's picking up seeds with the side of her beak instead of the tip.* When the bird came closer, Ed saw that the "crest" was an injury. *The poor little thing must have crashed into a window,* he thought. *I bet she damaged her beak too and that's why she's eating that way.*

Just then the bossy Jays returned and the smaller birds scattered. *I hope the wee finch will be able to recover. At least she can still fly. If only she can get enough to eat with that damaged beak.*

The other birds came and went, but the lumpy injured bird lingered as she struggled to eat the seeds. He'd read that injured and sick birds were often worse off than they acted and looked. Their lives depended on their appearing normal to predators. Ed had rescued some wild birds over the years. *I hope this one's not worse than she looks. I could have helped her, but I wasn't there to pick her up when she crashed.*

The next morning, Ed watched Lumpy, as he'd begun to call her, struggle with the seeds. *She's not going to last long enough to get better if she can't eat,* he thought. He put out sunflower bits and bread crumbs and went back inside to watch. She arrived with the other small birds, and he was happy to see she had no trouble eating the new offering.

The following morning, Lumpy was eating, but looked more unkempt. *Can she groom her feathers with a damaged beak?* Ed knew that feather grooming was essential for flight. Days went by, and he worried that she wasn't getting any better, but she didn't appear to be getting worse. Was it healing under the lump? It looked the same.

In a day or two, he saw that poor little Lumpy was moving more slowly and ate and sat with her feathers puffed up. *Damn! She might not make it after all.* The next morning, the bird flew in slowly, low to the ground. As if that had taken the last of her strength, she sat where she landed, feathers puffed, and didn't move. She walked slowly forward, ate a few sunflower bits, and sat again for several minutes. *This doesn't look good at all,* he thought. *I hate this. That bird has suffered so long and tried so hard. She'd put up a fight but it didn't look like she was going to win this one.*

Ed didn't see her the next day. *I could have missed her,* he told himself. *She might still be alive.* She wasn't out there the following day either. *Well, it looks like she didn't make it,* he thought. He'd felt close to this little bird as he'd become involved in her daily struggle, watching her small victories and the stoic acceptance of her limitations. He sighed. *Well, at least she's not suffering any more.*

On the morning of the third day, a rumpled bird in the group caught his eye. It looked like Lumpy, but was fairly energetic and didn't have any bumps. He wasn't sure. *Could it be?* Surely not, she'd been so bad the last time he saw her. As he watched, the bird tipped her head and picked up a seed with the side of her beak. Ed sprang from his chair excitedly. *It is her! She's alive. How can that be? How did she do it?* She had not only survived, she seemed almost normal. Like other wild creatures she had the gift of a simple, innate resourcefulness. She never gave up. Ed Mason smiled to see little Lumpy recovering, looking neater, bright-eyed, and alert. And it pleased him to think that in some small way, he had helped her pull it off.

9

Few people are neutral when it comes to cats. Most of us are either ailurophiles or ailurophobes; Angelo Nils Kraakmo was, unquestionably, one of the phobes. That is why he was indignant when his boss at the Centers for Disease Control told him to put aside his investigation of Legionnaire's Disease in northern Minnesota to look into a problem with cats on the West Coast.

Angelo removed his horn-rimmed glasses and rubbed his brow. "But Warren," he protested, "I've narrowed down the focus of this Legionaire's to hot tubs in a couple of hotels in the lakeside town where the epidemic began. I just have to take scum samples from the hot-water pipes." He was proud of his detective work and was miffed when Warren Bronkowski, head of epidemiology at the CDC, wanted to remove him from the case.

"Sorry, Angelo," Bronkowski answered. "I'm reassigning the Legionnaire's case to Carlson. All that remains is dotting a few i's and crossing a few t's." Angelo recognized "dotting i's and crossing t's" as one of Bronkowski's favorite expressions.

One of Angelo Kraakmo's favorite expressions was "Scandaloose!" That is what he exclaimed on learning he was to be taken off the Legionnaire's study to investigate a cat disease. He tried to persuade Bronkowski that he was above this investigation. "I don't like cats," he uttered with his peculiar Norwegian-Italian accent, "and I suspect they do not like me. Besides, I am needed on the Legionnaire job."

"Actually, you aren't," retorted Bronkowski. "Carlson can finish it up. This feline disease is pretty serious. I want you on it, because you are one of the best people I've got." He played easily on Angelo's ego. "I've already arranged for your ticket to Los Angeles; it's a six thirty flight tomorrow morning. Here's all the information we've got." He handed a two-inch-thick manila folder to the perplexed epidemiologist. "You will be at the airport, won't you." It was not a question.

"Since when does the CDC investigate animal diseases?" Angelo demanded defiantly. "That's for the USDA."

"Ordinarily, we don't. However, there are some good reasons why we have to get involved with this thing. First, the disease may be a form of feline leukemia, but it seems to occur even in cats that have been immunized against FeLV.

"Normal cats carry provirus FeLV genes on their chromosomes," he continued, "and there are chromosomal genes in baboons that are quite similar to FeLV. Baboon DNA has lengthy regions with the same base sequence. Besides, the feline genome has more in common with the human genome than any other animal group except primates. You see where I'm going with this? There exists the potential for its transfer to humans.

"Second, it is universally fatal for cats that get it. This thing has a rapid onset and is fatal within days or even hours.

"Third, I recall that another cat virus, FIV, has been transferred to human cells in culture." Bronkowski paused while Angelo scribbled notes on his e-tablet. "Finally, it appears to have a hemorrhagic aspect; FeLV doesn't display such symptoms. What if it's some sort of feline Ebola?"

Angelo pondered all this while Bronkowski remained silent. "I will be at the airport," he finally grumbled. "I will be on the plane. I will do my job. I will solve the case. But I will not be happy working with cats instead of people." He turned and rapidly exited Bronkowski's office, muttering, "Scandaloose!" under his breath.

His coworkers might have thought it odd for Angelo to show such an interest in people; he was not a gregarious guy. Although he got along well enough with his colleagues, when off the job, he preferred his own company. Occasionally, he spent time socially with his coworkers, and, when he did, curiously, he was often the center of attention. None of his associates understood his preference for being alone. They would discuss Angelo behind his back.

Vince Carlson, Nickerson Brown, and other techs often lunched together at an outdoor table in the patio. "Did you know that Kraakmo invented the calculus?" asked Carlson.

Brown laughed. "Yeah, mon, right."

"I'm serious. Angelo told me that when he was nine, the idea came on him while he was completing an arithmetic homework assignment. He wrote it down over several days, then showed it to his father."

Brown shrugged. "So ..."

"Mr. Kraakmo looked over the math. It was the real deal. Angelo's old man had to tell his son that Newton and Leibniz had beaten him to it." Carlson took a bite of his sandwich. After a moment, he remarked, "I think Angelo's eccentricity stems from his upbringing by a strict Lutheran father. I understand the old guy was a successful Norwegian businessman in his day."

"On de other hand," replied Brown, a BSL-4 lab technician who, many a time, had processed samples sent in by Angelo, "his mother is a warm, outgoin' Italian lady. I met her a few years ago when she visit here."

"Perhaps that unusual pairing accounts for Angelo's idiosyncrasies," offered Carlson. "You know, he's in his mid-fifties and has never married. It looks to me like he's going to be a loner forever. Of course, he's not a very good-looking guy ... puffy face with those pockmarks. And where did he get those scars, anyway?" Nobody knew. Nor did they know how Angelo acquired his slight limp.

Brown was pensive. "Say what you will, mon, I tink the Epidemic Intelligence Service is fortunate to have him. We put up with him because, not only is he the Sherlock Holmes of epidemiology, he's a patient and effective teacher."

As Angelo repacked his travel case, he reflected on the agency he was so proud to serve. Originally called the Communicable Disease Center, the CDC had been established in 1946 as a subsidiary of the US Public Health Service. In those days, its mission was the study of malaria, typhus, and a few other infectious diseases.

During the great polio scare of the 1940s and 50s, the CDC took on the responsibility for control and surveillance of that viral menace. The work of the agency gradually expanded to other parts of the world. For example, it played a major role in the eradication of smallpox from African countries.

As the functions of the agency broadened to include the epidemiology of non-communicable diseases, the name was changed to the Center for Disease Control, conveniently allowing the same three-letter abbreviation.

In 1976, the CDC investigated a new epidemic involving attendees at an American Legion convention in Philadelphia. In due course, microbiologists at the center identified the bacteria responsible for what came to be known as Legionnaire's Disease. Later, the CDC opened an expanded, maximum-containment laboratory to handle viruses too dangerous for an ordinary laboratory.

The name of the agency was again expanded in the 1990s to the Centers for Disease Control and Prevention. Most people still referred to it as the CDC. It continued to participate in the worldwide search for the reservoir for Ebola.

Brilliant university student, Angelo Kråkmo—the spelling had been changed to Kraakmo for convenience after Angelo immigrated to the USA—had studied at the University of Oslo, where he majored in mathematics. There, he came across the book he later credited with altering his career course. After reading *The Coming Plague* by Laurie Garrett, Angelo decided to apply his mathematical training to the statistical analysis of diseases. He earned a doctorate from the department of medical epidemiology at the prestigious Karolinska Institute in Stockholm, where he specialized in mathematical epidemiology. His thesis on the origin of the AIDS virus in tropical rainforests of central Africa was widely heralded as a major contribution to the study of emerging viruses.

Angelo sat on the aisle and, after takeoff, began leafing through the file Bronkowski had given him. In spite of himself, he became intrigued with its contents. *So there are two foci of the disease, one in Western Washington State and the other in Southern California.* Angelo considered the unlikely possibility that the two areas were afflicted by different diseases and made a note to check that out as soon as possible. Years earlier, he had learned to question all aspects of a case, especially those others might take for granted.

"Excuse me," said the young woman in the seat beside him, breaking Angelo's train of thought. "I don't mean to be nosy, but I happened to notice that the file you're reading says 'Feline Epizootic-2020.'"

Angelo looked over and beheld a twenty-something, stunningly attractive redhead, dressed informally in a beige pantsuit. "Yes, so?"

"I'm a reporter for *The Journal/Constitution*," said the redhead, "and I'm on my way to Southern California to dig up information on the disease. Do you mind if I ask, what is your interest in it? Oh, My name is Sandra McNally."

"How do you do, Sandra McNally? I think I've seen your byline. It never occurred to me that the name was attached to such a beautiful woman."

Used to such flirtations, McNally tried to ignore it, but a slight blush gave her away. "Ah, you read *The AJC*. Good."

"Yes, on the Internet. My name is Angelo Kraakmo, and I am with the CDC. I too am heading to Southern California to dig up information on the feline disease. I don't know much about it yet. I would be happy to answer any questions."

"Oh, thank you so much. Do you mind if I record our conversation?"

Somewhat nonplussed by the sudden attention, Angelo wasn't sure what to say. "I ... I guess I don't mind."

The reporter switched on her tiny digital recorder and announced the day, time and location, which happened to be twenty-seven thousand feet above Alabama. She then asked, "Is it true, Mr. Kraakmo, that all cats that contract this disease die from it? Are there no survivors?"

"It's Dr. Kraakmo, but please call me Angelo. Yes, it is so. There is total mortality. This is fascinating, because usually an epidemic—or epizootic in the present case—leaves some percentage of the population alive. Even the terrible Black Death of the fourteenth century spared over half the European population. But this feline disease is apparently dispatching every one of the cats it touches. Excuse me a moment." He pulled out his e-tablet and scribbled a note.

When he looked up, McNally said, "I'm sorry, Dr. Kraakmo—Angelo. Do you have any idea of the origin of the disease? Is it a virus?"

Angelo noticed that the reporter asked the right questions. It was clear that she was good at her job. "It might be a variant of feline leukemia," he said. "My file here contains background information on the leukemia, as well as on feline AIDS. You're welcome to look over my shoulder while I read. There is nothing confidential."

"You are most kind. I didn't even know cats could get AIDS."

Angelo began to read while McNally leaned toward him. *Her cologne is pleasant,* he thought.

> *Feline leukemia virus, or FeLV, was first isolated in 1964 from cats with lymphosarcomas. Like HIV, as well as many other human and animal viruses, FeLV is a retrovirus.*

"Excuse me, Dr. Kraa ... Angelo, what is a retrovirus?" She switched on the recorder.

Angelo tried not to show irritation at the interruption. "A retrovirus is one whose genome, or chromosome, is made up of RNA rather than DNA, and which uses an enzyme called reverse transcriptase to make a DNA copy, which is then used to make RNA copies for more virus particles and messenger RNA for its proteins."

"Right. And Bob's your uncle."

"Oho! You have been to Australia?"

"Actually, no. But, I have an Aussie friend who is always saying that. I said it because what you just told me is over my head. When I get home, I'll read up on this stuff. Maybe I'll even drive over to the CDC and interview you again after you complete your investigation."

"Marveloose! That would be fine."

He read on, with McNally's head practically resting on his shoulder.

> *Cats normally carry one or more copies of the DNA code for the virus, so-called virogenes, in their chromosomes. Leukemia develops when a cat becomes infected with an exogenous FeLV that interacts with the DNA provirus. The antibiotic actinomycin D is somewhat effective in treating the leukemia.*

"Uh, pardon me again, Angelo, but what is meant by *provirus?*"

"That is the genome of the virus that has become incorporated into one of the host's chromosomes."

McNally pulled her head back. "You mean that the genes of the virus are actually right along side of cat genes in the cat's own chromosome? That's incredible!"

Angelo smiled. "Actually, Sandra, this is quite common. You and I have proviruses in our chromosomes too. This integration of viral genes into host chromosomes is found in all species, as far as I know. As a matter of fact, it was first observed in bacteria."

McNally scribbled on a PDA. "This antibiotic, actinomycin D, do you know if it has been tried on cats who have this new disease?"

"No, I don't," Angelo answered. "I was wondering about that myself."

McNally was silent a moment. She inhaled as if to speak. Angelo waited expectantly. Finally, she said, "I am so grateful for your patience in answering my questions. To show my appreciation, I'd like to treat you to lunch after we land."

Angelo reddened. "That is very kind of you, but I have to rent a car and then hurry to Ventura. I don't think I can spare the time."

"Well, maybe another time, perhaps when I visit the CDC." Angelo flipped through the file and found a summary of feline AIDS. He read aloud. McNally turned on her recorder.

FIV, was discovered in 1986 by Niels Pedersen and his colleagues at the University of California at Davis.

"Aha," Angelo exclaimed, "a Scandinavian."

"Oh," said McNally, "Are you Scandinavian?"

"Half-Norwegian and half-Italian."

"That explains it. I was having trouble placing your accent."

Angelo shrugged. He continued reading from the file.

> *Feline Immunodeficiency Virus or FIV, like FeLV,*
> *is a retrovirus; it shares some characteristics with*
> *HIV, although it is genetically dissimilar. There are*
> *FIV-like viruses found in other members of the cat*
> *family such as leopards, ocelots, and lions, but these*
> *wild cats do not seem to develop an AIDS-type of*
> *disease.*

McNally interrupted. "Do you know if any species other than domestic cats have been diagnosed with the new disease?"

"You ask good questions, Sandra McNally. I too would like to know the answer to that. I have not heard of any, but I have just been assigned to the case. At this point, you know almost as much about the disease as I do."

"I doubt that very much."

Angelo resumed reading about FIV.

> *The virus is most likely to be transmitted from one*
> *cat to another by a bite. Male cats, therefore, are*
> *twice as likely to become infected with FIV than*
> *females. Cats infected with FIV may take years to*
> *develop full-blown AIDS.*

Angelo put his head back and closed his eyes. "I don't think that fits with the new disease," he commented. "I haven't seen any mention of it transmitted by cats biting one another. Besides, female cats are being infected at the same rate as males."

For the rest of the flight, McNally and he shared the file, she taking oral notes and writing on her PDS while Angelo jotted his notes down on his tiny e-tablet.

At the airport, they headed for the same car rental booth. Angelo opted for a small Toyota hybrid.

"I hope very much to meet up with you again at the CDC," declared McNally. "When I write my copy, I will certainly acknowledge your help. Will that be all right?"

"Absolut! I will look for the article."

"If I gather enough information, I may make it into a series."

As they were about to go their separate ways, Angelo noticed McNally hesitate. She opened her mouth as if to say something.

"What?" asked Angelo.

"Um ... I hope you won't hesitate to say no, but ..."

"Yes, Sandra McNally, what is it?"

"Would you mind terribly if I kind of tagged along with you? I'm supposed to meet with a biologist at UCLA tomorrow morning, but I think I could learn so much more from your investigation, if you don't think I would be a burden ... *The AJC* would certainly split the cost of the car rental."

Angelo was silent a moment. "Well," he replied finally, "I can't think of any reason why not. I think I'd enjoy the company." Indeed, he rarely found himself in the presence of attractive, intelligent women like McNally.

"That's just wonderful."

After the reporter canceled her rental, the pair set off at once for Ventura. McNally phoned her contact at UCLA to reschedule the interview for two days hence.

Arriving in Camarillo, they drove right through town and continued on to the city of Ventura, where they made their way to the county department of public health. Without announcement, and over the protests of Dr. Jerome Robinson's receptionist, Angelo barged into the health officer's office, McNally in tow.

"I am Dr. Angelo Nils Kraakmo," he announced. "You may be familiar with my work on the epidemiology of Acquired Immune

Deficiency Syndrome." He proceeded to expound on his work to Robinson, who stared at Angelo, openmouthed.

Angelo paused. He sensed that Robinson wasn't following. "You understand? Is my accent a problem?"

"I didn't get all of that. You do speak rapidly. Please, have a seat," Robinson replied. "From what I understood, I think you might be interested in some papers I've been reading on the origin of AIDS." He held out his e-reader to Angelo and pointed to three papers written by the man opposite him.

Angelo glanced at the icons and bellowed, "Angelo Kraakmo, that's me!"

Robinson blinked. "You … you are Angelo Kraakmo?"

"Absolut! And this is Ms. Sandra McNally, reporter for the *Atlanta Journal-Constitution*."

McNally asked if she could record their conversation. Robinson brought them up to date on the feline disease, concluding with, "The person in this area who is most knowledgeable about the disease is a veterinarian in Camarillo, Dr. Vera Barnett. She's the one you want to talk to."

10

Vera eyed the dumpy man in the brown plaid shirt and sport coat. The guy's brush moustache eclipsed his large mouth. "May I help you?" she asked.

After Angelo introduced himself, he asked, "Are you Dr. Vera Barnett, the veterinarian?"

"Oh, you're the epidemiologist," Vera declared. "Dr. Robinson phoned me that you'd be coming." After all the introductions were made, McNally asked if she could record the conversation. "Sure," said Vera.

"Please," Angelo began, "I would like you to tell me everything you know about this cat disease. I understand that it started in the home of a woman who keeps cats, and that it has spread to some of the neighboring communities, but I would like to hear a more technical description from a person who has actually treated the cats."

"Certainly," Vera replied. "Well, first of all, I think that the epidemic started at—"

"Epizootic," interrupted Angelo.

"I beg your pardon?"

"Epizootic. An eruption of a disease in animal population is an epizootic, not an epidemic. Epidemics are for people … humans."

"Oh, right," Vera muttered, irritated at what seemed to her trivial pedantry. "The epizootic started at the university in—"

"There is university here?" Angelo broke in again.

"Yes, California State University, Channel Islands." Vera became increasingly annoyed at the man's continuing interruptions. Nevertheless, she went on to describe the disease. Vera related her belief that the disease was either a form of FeLV or FIV, and that the likely origin of the disease was in Noah's laboratory.

"Scandaloose!" exclaimed Angelo when Vera was finished. "So that's the theory." He pronounced the word as if it were spelled *teery*.

"That's my theory, yes," Vera replied.

"You think that sarcoma virus and *E. coli* plasmid DNA and FeLV or genes all got mixed up together in this laboratory at the university." Angelo stated this slowly, his brow furrowed.

"Exactly," replied Vera.

"But the report I read said that the epizootic started at the home of that cat woman."

"Dorothy," corrected Vera. "Dorothy Knowland. Yes, actually the first cases that came to my attention appeared in her cats. But there could be many reasons for that. Maybe her cats were more susceptible than the ones at the university. Maybe the cats in Dr. Chamberlin's lab had built up a partial immunity, because they were exposed to the sarcoma virus. I don't know."

"But there is no evidence of any immunity whatsoever," said Angelo.

Vera frowned. "Okay, you're the epide ... epizoologist; you come up with a better theory."

"I will try," said Angelo. "Actually, although I appreciate your attempt to use the correct word, I am, in fact, an epidemiologist. Most of the time I investigate human diseases. Anyway, the word *epizoologist* isn't used much, even by epizoologists."

Vera smiled, in spite of herself. "I'll try to watch my language."

Angelo sipped his coffee in silence. Suddenly, he looked up and demanded, "Show me one of the sick cats."

Vera eyed him for a moment and decided not to let his autocratic tone get to her. "Well, there aren't many left, I'll tell you that. I know of only three cats still alive in Camarillo, and all are sick. One of them is in back."

She took Angelo and McNally into the ward and had them put on disposable paper smocks and latex gloves. She did the same. Together, they examined the lethargic animal—a nondescript tortoiseshell. Angelo hurriedly recorded notes on his tablet.

"I would like to send some tissues for analysis to the CDC," he said, replacing the little book in his pocket.

"What sort of tissues?" Vera asked.

"Spleen, blood, lymph node, liver, and maybe some brain."

"All right, but I don't have any dead animals on hand right now. I incinerated the bodies."

"Hmmm. But couldn't we just sacrifice this one?"

Vera stared at him, tight-lipped. She glanced at Kal whose face expressed astonishment. McNally was equally aghast. Vera said, finally, "Dr. Kraakmo, I am in the business of caring for and trying to cure sick animals. I do not kill my patients."

"But it is just a cat!"

Vera glared at Angelo in silence for a moment. She then declared, "When, and if this animal should die, I will personally carry out a necropsy and provide you with the tissues you need. Until then, I shall try to maintain this cat, who is someone's friend and companion, in as comfortable a state as is humanely possible."

"Okay, okay," he said. "I want to talk to the cat lady. Is she close?"

"Well, it's only about a twenty-minute drive. Let me call her first."

Vera phoned, and, shortly, she, Angelo, and McNally had been invited to dinner. Dorothy's enthusiastic invitation made Vera realize that the widow would be happy for the company now that her feline companions were gone. McNally begged off, mentioning that she was exhausted, as she'd been up since midnight, Pacific time.

After dropping McNally off at a nearby motel, Vera turned her Porsche onto Lewis Road. She switched to gasoline and hit the accelerator. Angelo, who had a passion for fast cars, remarked, "This 999H handles well."

"Are you a sports-car aficionado?"

"Yes, but I've never owned one. Maybe after I retire ... It's amazing that batteries are so light they can be used in hybrid sports cars."

Vera nodded. "Right you are. Five years ago, it wouldn't have been possible." *Who'd have thought I'd have anything in common with this guy?*

It was late afternoon by the time they arrived at Dorothy's. As they approached the front door, Angelo suddenly stopped and grabbed Vera's arm. "Wait. What is that I hear?"

"A harpsichord. Dorothy plays the harpsichord."

They stood silently in the chill air, listening to the strident chords of a Bach toccata. Finally, Angelo whispered, "Marveloose." Vera cocked her head, eyeing the epidemiologist. She was suddenly aware that there was was more to Kraakmo than science and ego.

Inside, Angelo proclaimed, "You play very well, Madame Knowland. I would like to hear more, if you would be so kind. Perhaps after we discuss your cats ..."

"Do you enjoy Bach?" asked Dorothy, obviously flattered.

"Absolut!" said Angelo. "After 1750, there has been no reason for any composer to write a fugue or toccata or partita. Bach did all there was to do in these forms."

"Well, I don't know ..." said Dorothy, "you certainly have strong opinions about Bach."

"I am sorry," he replied. "I guess I do."

Dorothy smiled. "Dr. Kraakmo, I would be happy to play something after dinner."

Vera was becoming concerned that Kraakmo was behaving a little too genially toward Dorothy.

The three spent an hour going over the disease and its catastrophic effect on Dorothy's feline colony. All the while, Angelo assiduously took notes on his e-tablet.

Vera noted that Angelo's questions emphasized dates and facts. *He's good,* she thought. *If he just had a more agreeable demeanor ...*

"Did you ever receive any cats from the university?" he inquired.

Dorothy replied, "No, I don't think so. Most of my cats were strays or they were given to me by other people."

"Did you acquire any new ones in the month or two before your cats got sick?"

Dorothy closed her eyes and tilted her head back. "Just one, I think. Clyde, the tomcat that Pete Wingate brought over."

At this, Angelo let out a guffaw. "That is very funny name for a little cat. I never heard of a cat named Clyde." The two women glanced at each other. Vera shrugged. Angelo resumed his questioning. "Can you remember just when this Clyde cat came here?"

Dorothy thought a moment. "I think it was around the middle of February. Yes, I remember, it was a Saturday afternoon, and Pete brought me some pippin apples along with Clyde. I baked a pie the next day."

"Where does this Mr. Wingate live, please?"

"He has a small farm about ten miles from here."

Dorothy rarely had dinner guests, but when she did, she prepared an attractive table. After dinner, Angelo asked, "Will you play Bach now?" It was not quite a command, not quite a request.

Vera frowned. "Maybe we should be heading back."

"Oh, you can stay a while longer," said Dorothy. "I don't often have someone to play for."

"All right," Vera said. "Just for a while."

For over an hour, Dorothy played harpsichord music of Bach, punctuated from time to time by Angelo's "Marveloose!" Vera could see that the epidemiologist was enraptured. At one point, Dorothy began a sonata by Scarlatti, but Angelo interrupted, "Bach. Just Bach, please." Finally, she began "Toccata and Fugue in D minor." Angelo's eyes widened. When the piece finally ended, Angelo, eyes glistening, said, "Madame, I have never heard it played so skillfully on harpsichord. On organ, yes, but never on harpsichord."

Dorothy turned around to face him. Vera saw that her face was pink and beaming. Dorothy opened her mouth, but no words came. The lonely widow could only manage a smile of gratitude.

Angelo looked at his watch. "Well, it is getting late, and I don't have a room yet. I must find a hotel." Vera rose. "The motel where McNally checked in isn't far from my place."

Dorothy found her voice. "I won't hear of it. I have a spare bedroom. You will stay here tonight."

Vera, startled, was about to protest, but thought better of it.

Angelo eyed Dorothy slyly and asked, "You will play Bach tomorrow morning?"

Dorothy smiled. She pursed her lips and, affecting a parody of Angelo's accent, said, "Absolut! I would be happy to play Bach tomorrow morning."

"Marveloose," he said, and they laughed. "I will have to go to my rented car to get my things."

Vera wondered, "Will you be able to find your way back here in the dark?"

"Absolut! There's a fine GPS console in the car."

The next day, after collecting McNally from her motel, Angelo visited the institute. At the open doorway to Noah's office, he inquired, "You are Doctor Noah Chamberlin?"

Noah eyed the strange-looking man standing in the doorway. He surveyed the ruddy countenance of the mustachioed fellow, who reminded Noah of the character Mario from the video games he had played as a kid. "What can I do for you?"

"I am Dr. Angelo Nils Kraakmo, epidemiologist from the Centers for Disease Control. I am here to investigate the feline epizootic that has been occurring in this village."

Village? What kind of guy calls Camarillo a village? "Come in, come in," he said. Angelo removed books from the two Eames chairs in front of Noah's desk, introduced McNally, and sat down.

Noah said, "I suppose you've been told that the disease started here in my laboratory."

"Yes." He looked Noah straight in the eye. "But I would like you to understand that I, myself, have come to no conclusions."

"Thank you," replied Noah with a trace of sarcasm.

"Please describe to me your research and your facilities, if you will be so kind."

"May I record this discussion?" asked McNally. "I'm gathering material for a series on the disease."

Noah shrugged his shoulders. "I don't care. I have nothing to hide." Prohibited from doing any experiments, Noah was not particularly busy that day, so he patiently told Angelo of his plans to clone the feline alpha-globin gene. He soon realized that Angelo was conversant in the arcane language of molecular biology, and he described his work in some detail, leading McNally to shake her head from time to time. Later, he took the two of them on a tour of the lab and cat room. All the while, as McNally recorded the conversation, Angelo meticulously wrote his own notes on his e-tablet. He was particularly interested in the break-in and theft of the cats.

"Scandaloose!" Angelo exclaimed when Noah told him about the episode. "And there never was a sign of the cats after that?"

"Not a trace. I had to procure all-new cats, but now they are all dead from this new disease."

"I suspect the lady veterinarian has a good theory," commented the epidemiologist, "and I will proceed with it as my working hypothesis. But I will keep an open mind, Dr. Chamberlin. In epidemiology, the most likely theory does not always turn out to be the correct one."

After working the swing shift, Jake Moloney arrived home to find the lights still on in his white-frame bungalow. Joan greeted him at the door. Their six-year-old daughter, Irene, was asleep on the couch.

"What's wrong?" Jake asked.

"Slim died, and Irene's been crying all evening."

"Oh, hell." Slim, Irene's tabby, had been ill for a week. Their vet had warned them the cat might not survive. Jake went over to his sleeping daughter, her eyelids still red. He kissed her lightly on the forehead and whispered, "We'll get another cat soon, don't worry."

But that was not to be.

In Sweet Home, Oregon, Rebecca Smith called out for her cat. "Bib! Bib! Come here right now, you little devil!"

Bib had always raced to her call at mealtime.

"Lee," she cried, "have you seen Bib?"

Leon Smith put down his newspaper. "Not since yesterday. Isn't he showing up for breakfast?"

"No. Lee, I'm scared. What if he's got that virus thing you were telling me about?" She descended from the porch and walked the path into the woods. Shortly, she spied the cat's body twisted in an unnatural position. Ants and other insects were already at work on the remains. Rebecca screamed, *"Aaiioo!* No. No. No!"

Leon ran out. When he saw Bib's dead body, he took the grieving woman in his arms. They remained silent. They knew they'd never have another companion like Bib.

11

May 2020   1,050,000,000

Angelo continued to question cat owners—mostly former cat owners—in Camarillo and surrounding communities. When he arrived at the residence of Dr. Amend, city council member, Mrs. Amend invited him in. Angelo looked around at the opulent furnishings, parquet floor, deep-pile carpet, and, what looked to him like original artwork on the walls.

"Well," said Mrs. Amend, "what is it? I suppose you want to ask me about my cat." Angelo found her manner both condescending and rude.

"Yes, Mrs. Amend. That is correct. I am seeking clues to the origin of this feline epizootic."

"It certainly didn't start here," said Mrs. Amend coldly.

"No," Angelo replied. "I didn't think it did. However, I am trying to learn how the disease is transmitted from cat to cat. Anything you can tell me about the days before your cat—er, what was its name—became ill?"

"My cat was not an 'it.' *She* was named Madame."

Oops, thought Angelo, *that was a faux pas on my part. I've got to treat this lady with tact.* "Yes. I'm sorry. I had forgotten her name. I meant no offense. I know that you miss her very much. All the cat people I've spoken with are saddened by the loss of their pets. This is a difficult time."

Angelo saw that his words had the appropriate effect. Mrs. Amend's face softened noticeably. She said, "I don't know how I can help you. Madame was healthy. She got sick. A few days later, she died."

Angelo pulled out his e-tablet. "Did you let Madame outside or did you keep her inside all the time?"

"Madame was strictly an indoor cat," replied Mrs. Amend. Angelo wrote on his pad.

"Were there any cat visitors in the week or so before Madame fell ill?"

"No. Dr. Barnett asked me the same question."

Angelo asked a few more questions, thanked the woman, and said good-bye.

The next day, Angelo visited Noah at the institute. "I would like to take some swab samples from surfaces in your lab and the cat room," he said.

"Oh, now you really do think the disease originated here," said Noah in an angry tone of voice.

"Please, Dr. Chamberlin, as a scientist you surely understand that I am merely trying to be as thorough as possible. My taking samples from your lab does not implicate you in any way. I will also take swabs from Dr. Barnett's clinic and from Mrs. Knowland's house. I will have a complete picture of the disease only when all the data are analyzed."

"Of course," said Noah. "I'm sorry. I guess I'm on edge as a result of all the attention my lab has been getting."

"I understand." Angelo was silent a moment. "You know, it is possible that my investigation will exonerate you. Let us leave it to science, for better or worse."

Angelo sent all the swabs by express mail to the Atlanta headquarters of the CDC.

He even requested stool specimens from Noah, Gary, Vera, and Dorothy to have them checked for any unusual strains of *E. coli* that might have originated with Noah's research strains.

"Angelo, that's a nasty thing to ask," Dorothy complained.

"I'm sorry. I guess I should have explained why this is necessary." Angelo chose his words carefully. "Have you ever been asked by your doctor to furnish a stool specimen?"

"Yes," Dorothy replied, "several times when I had intestinal problems."

"Do you know why doctors need to examine stool?"

"I guess so. It's so they can look for germs that might be causing a disease."

"Exactly!" Angelo cried triumphantly. "That is the same reason I want the CDC to examine your feces. To see if you or Dr. Barnett or Dr. Chamberlin might be carrying some germ that is associated with the cat disease."

"Well, since you put it that way ... I guess sometimes there are unpleasant aspects to your job."

Angelo smiled. "Yes, my dear, that is correct. However, it is honorable work, no matter how disagreeable it is on occasion." He put his arms around Dorothy and hugged her. "Thank you for understanding."

His phone buzzed. It was the reporter McNally. Although she had spent three days running around Los Angeles, interviewing the biologist at UCLA and several veterinarians in the city, and even the vet at the Griffith Park Zoo, she had not obtained any information she hadn't already gotten while spending time with Angelo. She was planning to return to Atlanta that day.

"I wish you success with your article," said Angelo. "Perhaps we will meet again in Atlanta."

During his sojourn in Southern California, Angelo stayed in Dorothy's guest bedroom. One evening, while Angelo was typing notes into his laptop on the day's investigation, Dorothy was playing the harpsichord. Angelo looked up from his work. "Woman, I find it difficult to concentrate on my work while you play. Oh, that's not a criticism, it's a compliment."

Dorothy stopped playing and walked over to where Angelo was sitting. "You know, we have a lot in common—at least where music is involved."

"Yes, I guess we do." He stood and faced her. "I ... I think I am becoming very fond of you." Dorothy took his hands in hers and squeezed them gently.

Angelo was quiet. Finally, he pulled her close and gently stroked her face. He broke away and returned to his seat. Dorothy resumed her playing, but Angelo noticed it was a bit choppy. He refrained from commenting.

A few days later, after Angelo had spent the day investigating the disease in nearby Oxnard, he was relaxing as Dorothy played the "Goldberg Variations." Deeply moved by the beauty of the music and Dorothy's skillful rendering of it, he walked over to the harpsichord and put his hands gently on her shoulders. For a moment, the music faltered, and then continued. After she had finished the fourteenth variation, she turned and looked up at Angelo. His eyes were moist—the man was weeping. "What's wrong?" she asked, "Did I ..."

Angelo stifled her question with a chaste kiss. A little embarrassed, he backed away. "I am sorry, I don't know what came over me."

Dorothy gazed at him fondly. "It's all right. I thought for a moment that you didn't like the way I was playing."

Angelo smiled. "Scandaloose," he said quietly. He took Dorothy's hand and drew her from the bench. He brought his smile to hers. Now, without embarrassment, he kissed her with considerable passion. She responded in kind.

Angelo was in Ventura, interviewing a vet, when his phone buzzed. It was Vera. The tortoiseshell tabby had expired. The vet informed him that she'd dissected the furry corpse, placing small samples of the tissues Angelo had requested into small vials. She'd labeled each vial with the date and, in a notebook, recorded the gross and microscopic anatomy of the tissues. "The cat's spleen was much enlarged," she said, "and, as expected, there was considerable internal bleeding."

"Thank you," said Angelo. "I see you are thorough in your work."

Angelo went to Vera's clinic on the same day and sent the samples, frozen over dry ice, to his home base at the CDC for analysis. He included a lengthy note requesting a complete viral workup with special attention to feline leukemia, AIDS, and sarcoma viruses.

He had previously been providing a continuous flow of dust, skin scrapings, saliva, stool specimens, and other biological material to Atlanta. The technicians at the CDC were used to Angelo's donations. No other epidemiologist sent so many specimens for analysis. Angelo knew that some of the techs complained, but Bronkowski would always defend him; more than once it had been some obscure scraping or tissue sample Angelo had sent in that proved to be the breakthrough in tracing the origin of a particular epidemic.

However, this time, nothing had turned up. Even the stool samples contained only the normal intestinal flora one would expect in a cat or human. No recombinant plasmids or anything like that had been found. Angelo was mystified; the disease was like no other disease he'd encountered.

On Saturday morning, while Dorothy was tuning the harpsichord, Angelo browsed the local newspaper on his laptop. He came across a notice of Ibsen's play, *A Doll's House,* currently running in Ventura.

"Do you know this Tiber Theater?" he asked.

"Why yes," answered Dorothy, "Dave and I used to attend plays and musicals there."

"Ventura. Aha! That is not far. They are performing a fine play, *A Doll's House* by Norway's greatest playwright, Henrik Ibsen. Have you ever seen this play?"

Dorothy thought a moment. "No, I don't think so. Wasn't there a movie, though? With Jane Fonda, I think. There's a woman named Nora, isn't there?"

"Absolut. That is the one. We will go tonight."

"We may not be able to get tickets on such short notice."

"I will try."

As it happened, there had been a cancellation moments before Angelo phoned the ticket office. He was able to arrange for tickets provided he arrived early to pick them up.

"Well, that is certainly a feminist play," remarked Dorothy as they walked from the theater to Angelo's rented car under a star-flecked sky. "When was it written, anyway?"

"About 1880, before the word *feminist* had entered the language, I suspect, especially the Norwegian language. I think maybe Ibsen was ahead of his time."

"Do you consider yourself a feminist?"

Angelo remained silent for a moment. "I believe all people should be judged and rewarded on their accomplishments. Women are people. It follows, that, if I understand the meaning of the word *feminist,* I am guilty of being one."

"Oh, you're such a scientist, even when we're discussing a nineteenth century play." She gave him a peck on the cheek.

Angelo took her hand. "*A Doll's House* is more than a feminist play, you know. There are other levels of meaning. Some people find the last scene, where Nora walks out on her family, ambiguous. They see Nora as a villain, and not a heroine, because she abandons her children."

"Yes, I can see her that way. Maybe she's not such a feminist role model after all."

"Besides, throughout the play, Nora comes across as self-centered. She doesn't seem to be a very deep person. In the final scene, she complains to Torvald that they never have serious conversations. But whose fault is that, anyway? Torvald's or

Nora's? I once read an essay about the play where it was compared to a Greek tragedy and Nora to tragic figures like Oedipus."

"I don't know much about Greek plays," noted Dorothy. "Angelo, you know so much about drama and music. Sometimes, it's hard to believe you're a scientist."

"I suspect that is what you call, in this country, a backhanded compliment. Can't a scientist have interests outside his field? Oh, Oh—I should say, his or *her* field."

Dorothy laughed and squeezed his hand.

"My father was a lot like Torvald," Angelo offered.

"Really? That must have been unpleasant."

"It was not so bad. He was away on business much of the time, and my mother was everything my father wasn't. She made up for his coldness."

"But Torvald isn't what I would call a cold person. He's just very conservative and bound by society's rules."

"Yes. That is correct. My father resembled Torvald in just that sense. He was also very reserved, unlike Torvald Helmer."

In the car, Angelo mentioned, "I once saw a performance of the play in Norway where they had a living cat sitting on the sofa through most of the play. During one of Nora's conversations with Dr. Rank, the cat woke up and made a big yawn. It started clawing the sofa, the way cats do—you know, to stretch the claws. The audience laughed, and the actors had to wait before they could resume talking." He was quiet a moment. "I suspect we are not likely to see *A Doll's House* with a living cat anymore."

"How many times have you seen this play?"

"Mmmm. Maybe six. I'm not sure. I've seen most of Ibsen's other plays too. You know, Ibsen spent a good part of his life in Italy. I think of him as a kind of Norwegian-Italian like me—only with me it's genetic, with him it was cultural."

"You must be his biggest fan."

"Absolut!"

During the last two weeks of May, large numbers of cats in Tacoma, Yakima, Santa Barbara, Bakersfield, Vancouver, British Columbia, and other western cities came down with the rapidly developing, universally fatal disease. Newspapers across the nation reported new outbreaks on their front pages.

Beth Murphy, owner of the Coos Bay Cattery tearfully locked the doors of her breeding business. Without cats, she saw no point in keeping the business operating.

When he was seven years old, Juan Valenzuela's father had introduced him to the great outdoors on a hiking trip in the Grand Canyon. Juan's love of nature and open spaces had begun with that trip and was a dominant facet of his life. Now twenty-two, the native Chumash-American was hiking the John Muir Trail alone, through the high country, in Sequoia National Park. Much of the trail was still buried under snowpack. Resting by an ice-covered tarn, he noticed movement about a hundred yards away.

"*Madre de Dios!*" he gasped. The tan shape moved again, and Juan recognized it as a mountain lion. Juan's ancestors were Southern California mountain Chumash and had hunted pumas in the old days. His father had told him that the old hunters would use every part of the kill—the meat for food, the bones for tools, the hide for clothing; nothing was thrown away.

Juan drew his hunting knife and remained watchful. The cat also stayed where it was. After some twenty minutes, Juan realized that something was not right. By now, the beast should have made a move or slunk away. Juan slowly began inching toward it. The animal did not move. Shortly, the young man was within a stone's throw of the puma. He stared, and the cat stared back, but it still made no move. There was terror in the eyes of the animal.

He then saw why. The cat was sick—very sick. It was emaciated, and there was mucous stuff and blood around its eyes and nose. The young man stood in awe a long moment. Presently, Juan, having been imbued with a love of and respect for animals by his father and mother, quickly put the animal out of its misery with several well-placed thrusts.

12

As June approached, Angelo had run out of ideas. He'd uncovered nothing to bring him any closer to understanding the epidemiology of the feline disease. He prepared to fly to Seattle. But first he wanted to talk with Pete Wingate.

He drove ten miles east along Highway 118 to the Wingate farm. The red barn with its water tank and white-frame house, complete with chickens and ducks, reminded Angelo of picture books he'd read as a child in Norway. Irma Wingate set out home-baked rolls with coffee, making Angelo feeling welcome. He chatted with the couple about crops and weather, displaying a sincere interest in farming. This was not at all an affectation, as Angelo's interests were eclectic. Finally, he asked about the cat named Clyde.

"Yup," said the farmer, "I took a cat over to Dorothy Knowland in February. I remember, because it was Valentine's Day." He nodded toward an Irish Setter asleep on the rug. "Mike over there don't take too well with cats."

"How long had you had the cat?"

"Just a week. The wife and I had been up to Seattle visiting my sister—"

"Seattle? Did you say Seattle?" Angelo scrawled on his tablet.

112

"Right. She volunteers at the zoo there, and they had this cat they called Clyde that was sort of a mascot. Clyde was allowed to go wherever he pleased in the zoo. They finally had to get rid of him because he kept getting into the animal compounds. It's one of those zoos that don't have many cages, just a lot of open spaces with moats or pits around them. They were afraid one of the big animals would injure that cat. I figured I could give it a good home on the farm. The wife didn't mind, so we brought it back with us, but Mike wouldn't share the farm with no cat, and Clyde had to go."

"What is your sister's name, please?"

"Geraldine," answered Pete. "Geraldine Moore."

"Thank you," Angelo said, "you have been very helpful."

Driving back to Camarillo, he hardly noticed the scenic countryside. Angelo's mind was churning. *There it is,* he thought, *the connection I've been searching for … tenuous link to be sure, but a link nonetheless—a tie between the Camarillo and Seattle diseases.* Angelo figured that the cat known as Clyde would turn out to be the index case, the first instance of the disease, marking the beginning of the epizootic. *But what's the association with the university? Where do Chamberlin's plasmids fit in … or the sarcoma virus?*

At five thirty in the morning, on the first day of June, Angelo headed his rental car back to LAX, arriving two hours before his flight. He always took along a supply of reading material, so the interminable waiting wouldn't be wasted. Dorothy had been sad to see him go, but Angelo promised he would return. He had no professional reason to come back to Camarillo, but during the past few weeks, he had become very fond of the widow, and he was determined to see her again.

On the plane, he began to review his copious notes, but the flight was short, and soon they were landing at Sea-Tac airport. He rented a car identical to the one he had in California and drove

north in the rain to the city. He intended to go straight to the zoo
to see Wingate's sister even before he found a place to stay.

Angelo arrived just after the noon hour. The zoo was bustling
with excited schoolchildren and young couples, all seemingly
oblivious to the light rain. At the administration building, he
was told that Geraldine Moore was taking a group of Japanese
businessmen on a special tour and would be finished in an hour.

Angelo elected to go on a tour of his own. To get out of the
rain, he went into an exhibit building. He found it quite dark
inside; he could hardly see his way. He then noticed a sign with
the information that the room housed nocturnal animals. Indeed,
the only illumination came from the glass-enclosed cages, lit by a
dim, bluish light. As his eyes adapted, Angelo spied an anteater,
a sloth moving about slowly in a faux treetop, and, below them,
a porcupine.

A door at the end of the corridor led to the well-lit reptile
room. Here, he found slow-moving tortoises, gopher snakes,
lizards, and rattlers, as well as hairy tarantulas and various kinds
of insects.

He went through yet another door into a room identified as a
tropical forest display. A light rain was falling on the animals. A
flash of bright movement caught his eye, and he observed a couple
of golden tamarins. They were the most beautiful primates he had
ever seen. Their long, silky-golden hair would be the envy of many
a young woman—or young man for that matter, he thought.
Angelo passed some time observing a variety of tropical insects.
Just then, a group of noisy youngsters shepherded by their teacher
came in, and he figured it was time to leave the building. A bit of
rain was preferable to yelling kids.

Pete Wingate is right, he thought, *there aren't many cages.*
The large animals—lions, llamas, apes, and the like—were able
to roam in sizable open areas with few fences separating them
from the observers. Only the smaller animals, such as monkeys,
were caged. Angelo watched the gorillas for a while. Although
they were free to move about over a considerable area, they were

kept from the public by large, glass panels. In back of one of these panels was a mother with a watchful eye on her tiny baby frolicking a few feet away.

Angelo looked around him at the many open areas. *I suspect that viruses could easily be transferred from animal to animal in this zoo; insects could carry them—biting flies, maybe.*

Shortly, Angelo passed the bamboo-enclosed elephant compound where African and Indian elephants of various ages comprised a happy family, seemingly oblivious to species differences. He ambled past the polar-bear enclosure and meandered over to look at the big cats. He eyed the dozing lions in an area landscaped to resemble an African savannah, complete with flat-topped acacia trees. He walked around the perimeter, noticing at the back only a four-foot chain-link fence enclosing the area. Inside was a deep, water-filled moat, presumably large enough to keep the cats in. Angelo looked it over. Would it keep a small domestic cat like Clyde out? *I don't think so.*

The tigers were similarly enclosed. The lithe cougars, on the other hand, were in cages surrounded by a fine-mesh screen that a small cat would not be able to penetrate.

Angelo moseyed over to an imposing building, in front of which were two stone lions in the classic pose. This turned out to be the feline house. Inside, he came upon a sleeping lynx within a glass-fronted cage. Next to it was a flashy ocelot. Further on, there were quite a few species with which he was unfamiliar. *These creatures are in close proximity; it's not difficult to imagine viruses hopping from cat to cat.* He jotted down his thoughts.

He found fishing and Chinese desert cats, flat-headed and Pallas's cats. Stalking caracals and restless sand cats were in cages on the other side of the hall. There were, all in all, dozens of species new to him, ranging in size from smaller than a house pet to almost the size of a panther. *I should have brought Dorothy with me—she would have enjoyed seeing all these cats.* Angelo became so caught up with the animals, he returned to the administration building a half-hour later than he had planned.

Geraldine Moore, a slim, middle-aged woman, was waiting for him. She introduced herself and told Angelo that her brother had phoned to tell her of the investigation. She invited Angelo into a small meeting room festooned with a colorful collection of animal posters, photographs, and newspaper clippings about the zoo. In one corner Angelo glimpsed a few small bookcases housing a modest library. He noticed that the woman's uniform was a size too large for her. The two sat at a worktable and Angelo asked Moore about Clyde.

"Yes," said the woman, "we had to find a new home for him because he'd become a little too curious, even for a cat. He had gotten in the habit of going into various animal compounds looking for mice, and, one evening, he frightened one of the elephants. It took half the night for our people to calm the animal."

"Scandaloose."

"Another time, Clyde went down into the gorilla grotto and almost got mauled by Godzilla."

"Godzilla?"

"That's our largest male. Besides, there was always a danger that one of our animals could contract toxoplasmosis from a domestic cat. Anyway, that's when we decided we had to find a new home for the cat."

"You are aware of the feline epizootic in this city?" asked Angelo.

"Why yes, of course. It's terrible. But what has that got to do with Clyde? Is he okay?"

"I'm sorry. I assumed you knew. Clyde is dead. Maybe the epizootic has nothing to do with Clyde. I don't know. But in the city where he was taken, the city where your brother lives, there is also, as you know, a feline epizootic. It would be odd if the two diseases were not related."

"I see." Geraldine Moore pondered this a moment. "But Clyde wasn't ill. If he had been, I never would have given him to my brother."

"Possibly the cat was in the early stages of disease. Anyway, he is dead now. He died of the same disease that has killed all the domestic cats in Camarillo."

"All the cats? ... I ... I had no idea ... Oh, my God!"

"Absolut. All the cats." Angelo paused to let this sink in. He then asked, "Tell me, were any of the zoo animals sick in the month or so before your brother took the cat?"

"Why yes, as a matter of fact, we lost three cats. In September of last year, a lioness came down with a viral or bacterial disease, we're not sure which, and died three weeks later. Then, about the middle of October, we lost one of the two *Felis chaus*. Two days before Halloween, one of our European wildcats became ill and died after a couple of weeks." She frowned. "Wait a minute. There was another—a chimp we found dead one morning of an unknown cause."

At this, out came Angelo's e-tablet. "Please, what is common name of *Felis cha ... cha ...*"

Geraldine Moore smiled. "It is called the jungle cat. It comes from Southeast Asia, India, places like that. Ours came from Egypt."

"How many species of cats are there? Do you know?"

"Thirty-seven in all, I believe."

Angelo was trembling with excitement, but he asked in a calm voice, "What do you do with the body of an animal that dies in the zoo?"

"We usually incinerate them."

"These cats, were they incinerated?"

"Yes. Their bodies were incinerated."

"Scandaloose!"

"I am sorry. I suppose you wanted to examine them."

Angelo nodded. "It would have helped."

She continued, "Of course, our people always perform a necropsy on animals that die from causes other than old age, and we do have some frozen tissue specimens. Would they be of any use to you?"

"Absolut!" said Angelo. "I will need to arrange for keeping them frozen."

"No problem. We have insulated containers for that purpose. We do it all the time. All we need to do is order some dry ice."

"Marveloose!" Angelo thought a moment. "I noticed that many of the animals are out in the open, but others are in cages. Could Clyde have gotten into the glass cages like the ones in the feline house?"

"No, not likely." She stood up. "Come, I'll take you into the feline area."

"I have already been there."

"But I will take you behind the scenes," she responded with an air of mysterious playfulness, "the part the public never sees."

Inside the feline house, Moore unlocked a door marked "NO ADMITTANCE—EMPLOYEES ONLY" and, entering first, she stepped into a shallow tray containing spongy Astroturf saturated with a soapy-looking liquid. "What is that?" Angelo asked.

"It's disinfectant. It is supposed to kill viruses and bacteria that we might bring in from the outside."

"That's convincing." Angelo stepped into the tray. Inside he noticed a decidedly gamey, but not overpowering, animal odor. He followed the docent on a raised wooden walkway along a corridor, well lit by a skylight. They climbed a metal staircase to the roof, and Moore opened a door leading out.

The rain had stopped. The two made their way across a catwalk overlooking the lion compound. A large wall separated the lions from the tigers.

"Look down," Moore said. Immediately below, Angelo spied three lions sleeping on a rock platform.

The docent pointed to the rock above them, as tall as a house. "That rock is entirely man-made—sprayed concrete over a foundation. The platform is heated so the lions can keep warm in winter, and yet be in full view of the public. The entire compound is surrounded by a dry moat that keeps the lions in. The chain-link fence outside the moat serves a primarily psychological purpose.

It would keep neither the lions from getting out nor people from getting in if they wanted to."

"A cat could get over that fence, no?"

"I think it's a tad too high for a small cat to scale."

"Was Clyde ever inside the feline house? Inside the back part where we were?"

"Oh yes, quite often he would come begging for handouts. And he seemed to be quite interested in his various cousins."

"Cousins?"

"Yes. Some of these smaller cats, the sand cat for example, are thought to be closely related to the domestic cat."

Angelo stared, closed-mouthed, at the docent. He remained thus for fifteen seconds. Finally, he scribbled feverishly on the tablet.

He thanked Moore and left to find a place to stay. Once checked into a motel near the zoo, he drove down to the waterfront for a meal of fried clams. He studied his notes as he ate. *It's all coming together ... but I don't see where that Chamberlin fellow fits in. If the disease started here in Seattle, it can't also have started in Chamberlin's lab.* Suddenly he had an urge to talk with Dorothy. He wiped his hands and pulled out his vid-phone.

She answered immediately. "Angelo! Oh, I miss you so."

"You do?" He wasn't feigning surprise. Until that moment, Angelo hadn't realized that his affection for Dorothy was reciprocated in kind. "I ... miss you too. That's why I called."

She saw that Angelo's hair was unkempt. "You look tired," she said. "When are you coming back? Have you found out how the cat illness got from Camarillo to Seattle?"

"Aha! To the first question, I think I have another five or six days of work here. To the second, I have to unask your question."

"Angelo, that's silly. You can't unask a question. What do you mean, anyway?"

"Dorothy, suppose I told you that the disease didn't start in Camarillo at all, but entered your city from Seattle when the cat called Clyde brought it from the zoo here."

Dorothy was silent. She stared at her phone, open-mouthed. "Yes, I'm here," she said, finally. I ... are you telling me that the disease didn't get started at the university ... that it was brought to Camarillo from Seattle?"

"Yes, my dear, that is exactly what the evidence is pointing to. However, I ask that you not tell anyone just yet. I need to wait until I'm absolutely certain. There's no room for error here. Careers are at stake."

"I understand. This is really important, isn't it?"

"Yes, it definitely is ... Dorothy, I ... the first thing I'm going to do when I return to Camarillo is hold you in my arms." He closed the phone, preventing her from answering.

Before he returned to the motel, Angelo stopped by the zoo and learned that a dozen specimens from the three dead animals—spleen, liver, lymph nodes, and the like—were already on their way to the airport for their flight to the CDC.

During the week, while he waited impatiently for the results of the tissue analyses from the CDC, Angelo collected scrapings and soil from the zoo, as well as samples of nasal swabs, urine, and feces from zoo personnel. He traveled all over the city, talking with cat owners and veterinarians, collecting samples everywhere he went. He didn't obtain much information he hadn't already learned in Camarillo, so he ended his Seattle investigation and prepared to return to California. On Friday, June 5, the day before his departure, Angelo phoned Bronkowski in Atlanta, who boomed, "Congratulations, Angelo, it looks like you've cracked this case."

"Oh? What is it? I have heard nothing."

Bronkowski said, "Here, I'll let you talk with Carlson. He's been supervising the lab work."

Vince Carlson came on the line. "Hello, Angelo, good work."

"What? What did you find?" Angelo's heart was pounding.

"It's not like anything we've seen before. It's a retrovirus with multiple envelope genes derived from both FeLV and FIV. Nicky is rerunning the pyros just to be absolutely sure there wasn't a screw-up. Also, there are some sequences we haven't yet identified. We're running comparisons with genomic databases as we speak. We found the virus in both the Camarillo and Seattle tissue samples. However, there are quite a few mutations in the envelope sequences from sample to sample. It probably has a high mutation frequency like HIV."

"Well, that is interesting, indeed. Anything else?"

"Uhm ... oh, yes. The virus is extremely stable. We've dehydrated samples to a degree that would inactivate most other viruses, but this baby retains 95 percent infectivity. This may explain why the virus spreads so fast. It doesn't lose much activity in the environment. I don't know of any other virus so robust."

"I see," said Angelo quietly.

"And," continued Carlson, "it's unusually resistant to ultraviolet radiation, so sunlight isn't going to knock it out quickly. We found that full sun takes thirty-three hours to kill half the virus in clinical samples."

"Scandaloose! What have we got here?" Angelo shook his head. "Will you please send me a complete written report of the findings so far?"

"But aren't you coming back to Atlanta now?"

"No, there is some unfinished business here, or rather in Camarillo. There are still some pieces missing from the puzzle."

Angelo heard loud conversation in the background; Bronkowski then came on the line. "Angelo, I want you back here now," he demanded. "Your work is done there, and we've just learned of a possible Lyme outbreak in New England."

"No. I am not finished." He kept his voice low. "There is still a question about the molecular biology lab at the California University. I don't see where it fits in yet."

"Let it go, Angelo, please."

"Warren, I did not want to come here in the first place, remember? You put me on this case against my wishes. Now I am involved with this disease, and I am going to do just as thorough a job with it as with any other case. Please put Carlson back on the line."

Angelo could visualize Bronkowski throwing up his hands. Carlson came back, and Angelo asked, "Vince, will you please send the report to my e-mail address as soon as you're finished?"

Angelo arrived at LAX on Saturday evening. He drove straight to Dorothy's. When he arrived, it was still quite light, and she was sitting in front of the house in a deck chair. When Angelo's car pulled into the driveway, she rose and ran to the car. They enfolded each other, holding the embrace for a long time.

"Oof! You're crushing me," Dorothy cried finally.

"I'm sorry. I am so glad to see you again. I missed you very much."

Abruptly, they pushed each other to arms' length and gazed into each other's eyes. Angelo realized that there was only one future for them—a future in which they would spend the rest of their lives together.

Shortly, Angelo phoned Noah. "I think maybe Dr. Barnett's theory about the origin of the epizootic is not holding up so well," he offered.

"Oh?" said Noah.

"I would like to come and talk with you this evening. Are you busy?"

"Not at all. Do you know where I live?"

"No," replied Angelo, "but I am good at following directions."

What did Kraakmo find up there, Noah wondered. He'd been preparing a sandwich when Angelo phoned but now was too pent up to eat. He paced, and he tried to watch television but couldn't concentrate. Angelo and Dorothy arrived around eight. Noah invited them in and offered goblets of Chardonnay.

"How nice," Dorothy said.

"Marveloose," Angelo added.

Finally, Noah could hold his curiosity no longer. "Dr. Kraakmo, I'm very interested in what you found in Seattle. What did you mean when you said that Dr. Barnett's theory may not be valid?"

"Please, I think we know each other well enough to use first names, no?" Angelo then proceeded to detail the events of the last six months at the Seattle Zoo. He described some of the animals he had seen there, emphasizing, for Dorothy's benefit, the many different species of cats.

Noah listened intently, and, when the point of the chronology became clear—the disease had originated in Seattle—Noah could only say, "My God!" over and over.

"Your God," replied Angelo, "has nothing to do with it. The disease is caused by a virus related to FeLV and FIV, the common feline leukemia and feline AIDS viruses."

"Then Vera was right about it being leukemia."

"Partly, yes. She was in error only about the point of origin of the disease. She came to her theory based on circumstantial evidence. You have been the victim of a coincidence. Please understand that there are still some loose ends. We still don't know why the disease has such a devastating effect on the cats and why there is so much bleeding. We also do not understand how it spreads so very fast."

Noah experienced an immediate pang of anger when the conversation turned to Vera. She had sold him out. She was wrong. Noah doubted they'd ever be able to mend their torn relationship.

Angelo and Dorothy left around ten o'clock. Noah sat in silence for a long time, overwhelmed by Angelo's revelation. He started to sob. *What the hell is wrong with me? This is terrific news.* After a while, he realized that he'd been harboring a profound, suppressed guilt. Subconsciously, he had nursed a belief that he might have been responsible for the disease. Now it appeared that he was not.

13

When Angelo received the report from the CDC, he pored over it for over an hour, analyzing the data and considering their implications. In addition to the information Carlson had summarized by phone, there were over a dozen electron micrographs. These showed pictures of the virus in various feline tissue samples.

"Merda!" *The damned thing is a sphere. Aah! Carlson added a size marker. The inside seems to be about 125 nanometers across. Hmmm ... typical of many retroviruses. What are these things sticking out?* He saw that each viral sphere possessed one or more huge, partially curled filaments measuring about eighty nanometers in diameter and up to a micron in length. Some had as many as six such appendages, each of which appeared to Angelo like a tiny question mark attached to the sphere by its straight section. Angelo realized he'd never seen a virus like this, although the filaments remind him of Ebola virus.

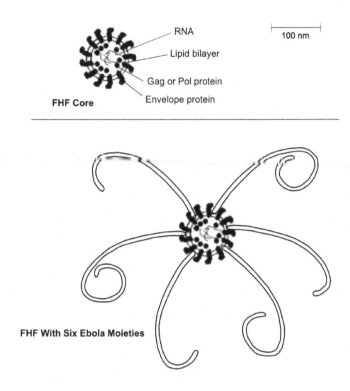

RNA

Lipid bilayer

Gag or Pol protein

Envelope protein

FHF Core

100 nm

FHF With Six Ebola Moieties

Feline Hemorrhagic Fever Virus

This resemblance had not escaped notice at the CDC. Carlson had compared the RNA base sequence of the feline disease with that of Ebola. Sure enough, the sequences that were not yet identified when Angelo had spoken with Carlson by phone were now determined to be Ebola genes. Several of them coded for a structural protein. Other genes determined the glycoprotein responsible for much of the pathology associated with Ebola. *Scandaloose! This is one scary virus.* This explains the hemorrhaging in the infected cats.

The technicians had separated a sample of the Ebola-like filaments from the rest of the virus and, using a BSL-4 animal lab, attempted to infect three cats and two chimpanzees with the preparation. Four days after the exposure, the five animals were still free of disease. *So the Ebola part by itself is not infectious; African chimpanzees often survive Ebola. It must be that either chimps or other apes at the Seattle Zoo were captured some time after they recovered from Ebola. Those apes could be carrying Ebola virus without showing symptoms of the disease.*

Angelo promptly telephoned Geraldine Moore at the Seattle Zoo. After he'd described the highlights of Carlson's report to her, Moore said, "That's incredible! You mean the disease is caused by a new virus that has pieces of three other viruses?"

"Yes, that's it exactly," replied Angelo. "I think the most likely source of the Ebola part is some kind of ape, probably a chimpanzee. I think it would be prudent if the zoo quarantined all the apes until they can be checked for Ebola."

"But we quarantine all new animals for two months before we let them mingle with the others. If any ape carried Ebola, it would have shown up during the initial quarantine."

Angelo countered, "Not necessarily. Some animals survive Ebola infection and become carriers."

"I see. I'll notify the director immediately. Thanks for the heads-up."

Angelo took time out around four in the afternoon to enjoy Dorothy's virtuosity on the harpsichord, and then he returned to the report until dinnertime. Later that evening, he phoned Vera. "I congratulate you, Dr. Barnett. Your theory of leukemia was partly correct. The epizootic is caused by a virus similar to FeLV, but it also carries FIV genes. It has surface envelope proteins of both viruses. And, as you know, it is much more virulent than normal FeLV or FIV. It appears also to contain portions of the Ebola virus. I must tell you, however, that your hypothesis that the disease started in Dr. Chamberlin's laboratory is no longer tenable. In fact, it looks like the epizootic started in a zoo in Seattle."

"Seattle? Ebola?" she mumbled. "Uh, thank you, Dr. Kraakmo. Thank you for calling."

"Wait, please. Do not hang up yet. I would like to meet with you and Dr. Chamberlin during the week if you have the time."

"Have the time?" Vera laughed sarcastically. "My practice has dropped off about a third since the cats died. Of course I have the time, but I'm not sure that Dr. Chamberlin will want to see me. Apparently, I've done him a terrible injustice."

"I will fix it. I'll let you know later when the meeting will be."

Vera poured a double scotch and threw herself down on the couch. She lay there, staring at the ceiling, sipping the amber liquid. She couldn't concentrate on a single train of thought. *How could a feline virus have incorporated Ebola genes? What could she do to make up to Noah? Could the Ebola jump to humans?* She had to apologize to Noah, but nothing she could say or do could possibly make up for the damage she had caused to his career and his psyche. She went over to her desk and started to write him a note. The words wouldn't come. She tried several times, each time hitting the delete button. She poured another double scotch, though she normally drank in moderation. Back on the couch, just before she passed out, her roving consciousness focused on the fragment: "Now is the winter of our discontent ..."

In the morning, her head spinning, she wrote those words on a floral e-mail template followed by:

> *I have wronged you*
> *I ask your forgiveness*
> *I will understand if it is not forthcoming*
> *I love you very much*

> *Vera*

Angelo had arranged the meeting with Noah and Vera for Wednesday afternoon in Noah's office. As it happened, Noah had received Vera's e-mail that morning. Vera arrived early and walked in the open door. Neither of them said a word. Vera felt her pulse racing. She moved haltingly toward Noah but feared he was through with her.

Finally, Noah glanced at the note on his computer screen and said with a smile, "'Now is the winter of our discontent'? It's almost summer!" He walked around the desk, faced Vera, and recited:

> *Doubt thou the stars are fire;*
> *Doubt that the sun doth move;*
> *Doubt truth to be a liar;*
> *But never doubt I love.*

Tears welled in her eyes. Vera and Noah enfolded each other tenderly. Eventually, Vera whispered, "I love you so much." She kissed him and said, "Leave it to you to find just the right quotation from Shakespeare. It's from Hamlet's letter to Ophelia, isn't it?"

"Uh huh."

At that moment, Angelo appeared, and, with his tactful clearing of throat, the two backed away from each other.

"I had to go through a picket line outside," noted Angelo. "They are picketing the institute because they think you started the disease?"

"That's right," Noah replied.

"Scandaloose! I will attend to that shortly, but first I want to talk about this disease. Here's the teery—the zoo woman told me that the three cats that died there had bacterial or viral infections. That may be, but the CDC lab has found the new viruses in the tissues from those cats. So the zoo cats had a disease much like the one in Camarillo, yes?"

Noah and Vera nodded.

"But the CDC lab did immunology analyses of the viruses, and they are not all the same. Interesting, no?

"I think the disease started when an endogenous leukemia virogene in the lion mutated and became virulent. This must have happened last summer. The lion then came down with leukemia. This virus could not be FeLV, as we find it in *Felis catus*, because FeLV is not found in lions."

"That's right," Vera agreed. "It's not found in any of the large cats."

"No. But did you know there are sequences in rat DNA that are identical to portions of FeLV? Perhaps rats are implicated … I don't know." Angelo jotted down something on his tablet and shook his head. "So what happened next? This lion virus infected a jungle cat, *Felis chaus*, in the same zoo. Maybe the virus was carried to the jungle cat by a zookeeper or a fly—who knows? Then the jungle cat came down with leukemia. Now the jungle cat is known to carry Type-C FeLV virogenes on its chromosomes. So I think that the lion leukemia chromosome combined with the FeLV in the jungle cat to form a virus chromosome with new properties.

"This new leukemia virus then infected the European wildcat, and maybe again recombination took place. The European wildcat is also known to carry Type-C genes, you see …"

Noah interrupted, "I don't understand why the disease seemed to originate in Camarillo."

"Aha! Now we bring into the story the famous cat called Clyde. The new virus, having undergone several genetic changes—first by mutation, and then recombination—now infected Clyde. I think Clyde was harboring an asymptomatic feline AIDS infection and the genome of the new FeLV virus, recombined with FIV, to make a virus with even more new properties.

"At some point, the virus also acquired some Ebola genes. The docent lady at the zoo told me that a chimpanzee had died there of unknown causes about the time this virus was jumping from cat to cat. I suspect that it died from Ebola."

Vera shook her head. "This is incredible—frightening!"

"Finally, Clyde was brought to Camarillo by the farmer Wingate. So what we have here is a new virus disease, a highly virulent form of leukemia/FIV/Ebola, whose primary effects are immunosuppression and bleeding. The cats die of bacterial infection and hemorrhage long before the effects of leukemia show themselves. I propose to name the new disease FHF," Angelo announced with a touch of self-congratulation, "Feline Hemorrhagic Fever."

Noah and Vera took a few minutes to absorb all this while Angelo sat, arms folded, self-satisfied grin on his face. Finally, Vera declared, "We must start a crash program to immunize cats with FeLV vaccine."

"I am sorry," said Angelo, "but that would be useless. FHF virus is not FeLV. The lab report says that there is very little cross reaction between the FHF virus and FeLV or FIV antibodies."

Noah offered, "Then a vaccine must be prepared from the new virus."

"That's convincing," said Angelo. "The CDC laboratory is now at work on this project. They are trying to find the best way to grow the virus in large quantity, using feline cell cultures. They are also examining the mode of transmission of FHF. We should have a report in about two weeks."

"Meanwhile," said Vera, "this FHF is spreading and spreading. I read that it's appeared in Louisiana and several cities in Mexico, including Mexico City. Half the cats in the country could be dead by the time we learn how to prepare a vaccine."

The epizootic spread rapidly. By June it had been spotted in San Francisco and San Diego, and was spreading eastward from Reno. On Monday, the eighth of June, the stock of Iams parent Proctor and Gamble was off nine points. It leveled off at thirteen a few days later. Stock prices of Mars Inc. and Nestle, both which owned cat-food subsidiaries, also plunged. As always, investors tended to overreact to negative news. Cat food accounted for less than 20 percent of these companies' revenues.

14

The Ventura County Star published an editorial entitled "Incrimination by Circumstantial Evidence." The piece described Angelo's theory of the origin of FHF. It explicitly exonerated Noah and included an apology. Noah sat at his laptop, openmouthed. *The nightmare is really over,* he realized.

At Angelo's suggestion, Dorothy hosted a small weekend party to celebrate Noah's public vindication. Angelo tended the barbeque, and Lowell Stanaland made sure that everyone had a drink. Noah and Gary enthusiastically discussed the resumption of their experiments.

"What's the point of working with MEFA if there are no cats to experiment on?" Vera asked. "Why don't you two work on FHF? You have a state-of-the-art laboratory, and you're already set up to do that kind of research. Why not see if you can develop an immunizing agent?"

"I don't know anything about infectious diseases," said Noah. "We can't just stop everything we're doing and start a new project."

"You've already stopped everything," Vera cried, "even if it was against your will. Anyway, you don't have any cats, and you aren't likely to get any for a long time."

Noah felt his stomach do a flip. He took a long swig of beer. "There are quite a few things we can do without cats, you know.

Right now, we're just trying to get the globin gene to function in *E. coli*. We don't need cats until we get that gene to work. Besides, there are qualified people at the CDC working on a vaccine. Why should I butt in?"

Lowell Stanaland had been standing nearby. "Excuse me, Noah, I couldn't help overhearing. I think Dr. Barnett has a point. Shouldn't you use your skills where they are most needed at the moment? I think the institute could come up with funds to support such a diversion in your research."

"You too?" cried Noah.

"Well, it's something to think about," said Stanaland.

To Noah's relief, the conversation was interrupted by Dorothy's announcement that the food was ready. Talk turned to Angelo's upcoming trip back to Atlanta and Dorothy's attempt to sell her home.

"You mean you're going to leave Camarillo?" asked Vera.

"Of course," replied Dorothy, "unless the government agrees to move the CDC to Camarillo." She turned to Angelo and gave him a playful wink. "At our age," she added, "we don't want to lose what remains of our time together."

"One thing I don't understand:" Noah stated, changing the subject; "why does this FHF virus spread so rapidly and so devastatingly compared to, say, ordinary FeLV or FIV?"

"Ah," said Angelo, "I have a theory about that."

"You have a 'teery' about everything," said Dorothy teasingly.

"Absolut!" agreed Angelo. "First, to understand how the FHF virus is different from the feline leukemia virus, you have to realize that the normal FeLV actually requires two viruses for the infection to be successful. It needs virus genes carried on the cat chromosomes—we call that the endogenous virus—and it needs an …"

Dorothy interrupted. "Are you saying that all normal cats carry genes of the leukemia virus?"

"That is correct. The domestic cat carries these genes. So do several species of wild cats. But, in addition to those endogenous virogenes, a successful infection requires introduction of an infecting virus from an external source such as another infected cat. I believe that FHF, either by mutation or recombination with virus genes in the Seattle Zoo cats, has lost the need for the endogenous virus genes. So all the infecting viruses are now able to invade and start the disease by themselves. We don't know how the virogenes interact with the exogenous virus. I think that if this interaction were no longer necessary, the exogenous FHF would be more likely to mount a successful infection."

"Yeah, that would make sense," Noah remarked.

"Then," Angelo continued, "somehow the altered FeLV picked up genes from FIV, the feline AIDS virus. My guess is that FIV and FeLV have some base sequences in common that make recombination between the two possible."

"That all seems plausible," said Vera, "but there must have been still another step in the evolution of FHF. It could have picked up some Ebola genes at the zoo. That would explain the bleeding as well as the strange morphology, right?"

"Yes, that is how I see it," Angelo replied.

Angelo hated leaving Dorothy behind, but he had a job to do. The gray walls of the CDC offered him little comfort. He tried to concentrate on the FHF report, but it seemed anticlimactic. When Carlson appeared at his office door to tell him that Bronkowski wanted to see him, Angelo welcomed the distraction.

They chatted about his experiences on the west coast and Angelo told Bronkowski of his marriage plans.

"Congratulations, Angelo. That's great. By the way, are you aware that your name is all over the major web news sites and in magazines?"

"What? Why? Where ...?"

Bronkowski burst out laughing. "You taking a journalism course or something? You left out when and who." He pulled a print copy of *The Journal-Constitution* from under a pile of papers. "Look at the front page."

Angelo first saw his photo, followed by the headline "CDC epidemiologist discovers cause of cat disease." The byline was that of Sandra McNally. Below was a lengthy article with a continuation. He looked up at Bronkowski, open-mouthed.

"What's the matter, Angelo? Cat got your tongue?" Bronkowski laughed at his own choice of words. "Seriously, how would you like to go on television?"

"Television? Why do you ask?"

"We've had a request from the producers of Rita Kenyon's show for an expert to discuss FHF."

"Rita Kenyon? I watch her show sometimes at night. She's a very funny lady. She wants someone from the CDC to be on her show? She usually has people like the Secretary of State, or Ryan Gosling, or Dakota Fanning. You want me to go on Rita Kenyon's show?" Angelo could not conceal his uneasiness.

"Sure," answered Bronkowski. "Of all the people here, you are the most knowledgeable about the disease. You're not afraid are you?"

"Afraid? Scandaloose! I … well … maybe a little."

When he arrived at the studio, Angelo was met by an officious assistant director who briefed him on on-air protocols—no profanity, don't interrupt Ms. Kenyon when she is speaking, and so forth. Angelo was a bit put off by the fellow, but he was enchanted by Rita Kenyon herself. She was even more attractive in person than she appeared on TV. Tonight, she was wearing white slacks topped by a white, silk blouse. Her auburn hair was cut short as usual. Kenyon quickly put Angelo at ease.

"I'm just going to let you do the talking," she said. "I'm sure our viewers want to hear what you've learned about this terrible disease."

Angelo was not Kenyon's first guest. He was preceded by a buxom young actress he had never heard of. He waited patiently off camera while the overly made-up blonde in an orange jumpsuit touted her latest movie. As he waited in the green room, Angelo became increasingly nervous. The longer he had to wait, the more anxious he became. When Angelo was finally led on camera, his throat was dry. He was introduced as the epidemiologist who had discovered the cause of feline hemorrhagic fever. He sat down between Kenyon and the well-filled orange jumpsuit.

"Thank you very much," said Angelo in a hoarse voice.

Rita Kenyon, cradling a white Persian cat with a light-blue ribbon around its neck, began matter-of-factly. "Dr. Kraakmo, would you tell us how you came to the conclusion that the disease started at the zoo in Seattle?"

Angelo made an effort to overcome his anxiety. He described his detective work in some detail—more detail than was appropriate for a general television audience. Kenyon interrupted him. "Is there a possibility that no cats will survive?"

"That is not usually the case with epidemics," replied Angelo. "Most epidemics, or epizootics, leave survivors. AIDS was an exception for a while, but with the development of the new chemotherapeutic cocktails, there are now many survivors."

Speaking of the disease helped Angelo to calm down. "So far, however, FHF seems to be unique. We know of no cat that has remained alive once it has definitively been diagnosed with the disease. The prognosis is as poor as I have ever seen in any disease. None of the known antiviral drugs, such as acyclovir or ribavirin, has been effective against it. As you know, it has been less than three months since FHF was detected on the West Coast, and it has now swept all over the North American continent, invaded well into South America, and has been detected in several areas of Europe and Asia, in spite of strict embargos against the import of cats from the USA. So I'm afraid that it is very possible that there will be no survivors this time—no survivors unless we manage to develop a vaccine. The CDC is working on this, but we have not been successful so far."

"Why, that is just horrible!" Kenyon proclaimed. "Does that mean that even Scheherazade here will come down with FHF?" She stroked the dozing cat affectionately.

"Yes. I am sorry. As a matter of fact, your cat could be incubating the disease right now." A murmur passed through the studio audience. "I am curious. Why does your cat not show symptoms of the disease? Has she been isolated from other cats?"

Kenyon replied, "I … I keep her indoors most of the time. Maybe I shouldn't have brought her here tonight."

"Just how does the disease get from cat to cat anyway?" asked the orange jumpsuit.

Angelo turned toward the young woman. "Well, uh … er …" Angelo was overwhelmed by her perfume and ivory smile.

The starlet attempted to set him at ease. "Do fleas carry the disease from cat to cat?"

"Yes," answered Angelo, suddenly aware that she was not only beautiful, but intelligent. "We have found that fleas can carry the virus. They don't even have to bite the cat. The virus just takes a ride on the fleas. There are many other ways the disease is transmitted. This virus is very stable. It resists drying, which would inactivate most viruses, and it can survive in the environment for weeks. Therefore, it is easily transmitted from one cat to another by objects and by humans. It can enter the cat through the mouth, the nose, or even through the smallest cuts in the skin of the cat."

The woman's eyes opened wide. "You mean if I handle a cat that has FHF, and then pet an uninfected cat, I can give the disease to the second cat?"

"Absolut!"

"That's awful!" She faced the audience. "Isn't this terrible?" There was a murmur of assent.

"Also, the virus may be transmitted to the female by the male during copulation, and vice versa."

"Oh, I wouldn't call it vice when cats do it," quipped the starlet, drawing laughter from the studio audience.

Angelo, not getting the pun, stared at her blankly.

Rita Kenyon broke in, "So that's why the epidemic is spreading so rapidly—the virus is exceptionally strong."

"We refer to such viruses as *stable* or *robust*. Yes, that is one of the reasons for the quick spreading of FHF," said Angelo. "By the way, we call it an epizootic, not an epidemic. Animals have epizootics; people have epidemics." Angelo uttered this with such earnestness, that the audience laughed at his pedantry. Angelo, seeing that he was the object of their laughter, played the good sport and flashed a big smile.

"I would think that kittens could get the virus from their mother as well," offered Kenyon.

Angelo nodded. "Yes, they can get it directly from the mother or even from her milk. We have found the virus in the milk of mother cats that have the disease. At the CDC, we have seen that newborn kittens from mothers with FHF always have the virus. So we cannot simply take the kittens away from the mother to keep them free of virus. It either infects the embryos, or else the kittens contract it during the birth process. We're not sure. It could be both.

"We are presently experimenting to see if the placenta acts as a barrier to the virus. If it does, we might be able to develop a colony of virus-free cats if the kittens were removed from the mothers by cesarean section. If we succeed, we could buy time so that we could develop a vaccine before all the cats are gone."

"Isn't there anything we can do to help?" asked the starlet with anguish. "I have a cat at home."

Tears formed in her eyes and, in the booth at the rear of the studio, the director ordered, "Camera three, close-up on Josette."

Angelo continued, "We are currently following three strategies at the CDC. First are the experiments with cesarean section. Second, we are trying a treatment with a drug called Actinomycin

D. This is known to have some success with ordinary feline leukemia. Unfortunately, it often kills the cats before it cures the disease. Finally, we're trying to develop a vaccine. This is tedious work, and I must confess that we have not been successful yet. Anyway, the disease is spreading throughout the world so fast that, even if we are able to produce a decent vaccine, we might be too late."

The interview went on a few more minutes, during which Kenyon asked the audience how many had pet cats and how many of those had come down with FHF. It turned out that of a hundred and twenty-seven people, forty-seven owned cats, and twenty-eight of those pets had come down with FHF. Twenty-two of the sick cats had already died.

Later, in his hotel room, Angelo reflected on his television debut. *I guess it went okay,* he thought. *Maybe I could have been less technical. Oh well ...*

A sizeable army of scientists and technicians labored at the Communicable Disease Center in Atlanta and the National Institutes of Health at Bethesda, Maryland, to develop an immunizing agent effective against FHF. They made no progress. Technicians could not grow the virus in cell cultures—a prerequisite to creating a vaccine. The CDC began a crash program to develop a cell-culture system for the FHF virus. The small quantity of virus available from cats that had died of FHF was purified and tested as an immunizing agent. It failed to elicit a protective immune response in cats. The investigators surmised that the failure was due to the FHF virus possessing three classes of envelope proteins—one derived from FIV, one from FeLV, and a third from Ebola.

Darth Vader, Leland Meredith's companion animal, died suddenly of FHF. The autistic boy fell into a deep depression and became totally uncommunicative. After trying their best to cope, Mr. and Mrs. Meredith admitted defeat and had Leland institutionalized.

15

On a Thursday morning near the end of June, Angelo arrived at Bronkowski's office, ostensibly to discuss the progress of the FHF research at the CDC. He had a second motive—to wangle another trip to Camarillo.

"Good morning," Angelo said.

"An arguable observation," said Bronkowski without looking up. "Zero progress. That's what we've made with the FHF antigen. Zero. Zilch. Zip. Did you see the paper this morning? Look!" He turned his laptop around so Angelo could see. "Twenty-two percent. It's on the front page. They're estimating that 22 percent of the domestic cats in the US have died of FHF, and 4 percent in Europe, 11 percent in Mexico, 5 percent in South America. I see, also, that the Russians have announced that they're beginning an all-out program to develop an immunizing antigen. So now it's us, the French, and the Russians." He looked Angelo in the eye. "Angelo, I don't know where we go from here. Our lab people have reached a dead end."

"I know. That is why I am here," Angelo replied. "I have an idea."

Bronkowski looked up. "So?"

"I would like to get Chamberlin to work on the project."

"Chamberlin? That molecular biologist in California?"

"Yes. I think he is one sharp fellow. He has a laboratory setup ideally suited for the work. His lab has state-of-the-art cell-culture facilities, and he is experienced with virus techniques."

Bronkowski scowled at Angelo for several seconds. The frown changed to an expression of inquisitiveness. "Go on."

"I suspect maybe Chamberlin could find a way to culture the FHF virus or perhaps clone its RNA. I would like to fly to Camarillo to discuss it with him."

"You want to go back to Camarillo? Oh hell, Angelo, you just want to see your woman. When are you two getting married, anyway?"

"Soon. When Dorothy sells her house, she will move to Atlanta, and we will get married. And yes, of course I want to visit her, but I have a sound reason for going there."

Bronkowski chewed on a pencil for a long moment. "Why Chamberlin? Why not some of the people at NIH?"

"Well, Chamberlin is not too busy now," Angelo explained, "because, without cats, his research is not progressing. If we can get him to work on FHF, we would be increasing, even if slightly, the possibility of a breakthrough."

Bronkowski nodded. "Okay, go to Camarillo. I must be crazy to let you talk me into these jaunts."

"Scandaloose," Angelo replied with humor.

As Angelo drove to Camarillo from the airport, he pondered how much he had missed Dorothy. *Amazing how much has changed in my life in only two months ... and it's all because of cats.*

Dorothy was not in sight as he drove up, but, when he cut the motor, Angelo could hear the harpsichord. The front door was unlocked, and Angelo entered quietly. He stood listening for many minutes. Finally, in a soft voice, he said, "That is very nice; have you been playing long?"

Dorothy froze and, recognizing the voice, turned. "Angelo! You scared me half to death!"

"Scandaloose."

"Oh, Angelo, I missed you so much." They held each other closely and kissed. Unable or unwilling to postpone his physical need, Angelo placed his hand on her breast. "Angelo, not now. Not in the middle of the day."

"Why not? Is there a rule I should know about?" He continued stroking her. Dorothy finally responded and kissed him passionately; Angelo's call to Noah would have to wait.

On that same day, Noah and Vera took in a movie. During the drive back to Noah's house—Vera was now practically living there—their conversation turned to the epizootic. "Did you hear that a panther at the San Diego Zoo has FHF?" Vera asked.

"No. Look, could we talk about something else for a change?" The movie had been a depressing and violent one, putting Noah in a sour mood.

"I'm sorry. I guess we do spend a lot of time talking about FHF."

They drove in silence for a while. Noah finally said, "I didn't mean to snap at you. I'm just tired of FHF. FHF, FHF, FHF. That's all anyone hears about these days. You'd think the world was coming to an end."

She turned to face Noah. "For *Felis catus*, it just may be."

Noah glared at her. His gaze softened as he thought about what she'd said. As he pulled into the garage, he asked, "Do you really think the domestic cat could become extinct?"

"Who can say? You know, don't you, that yesterday the EPA placed *Felis catus* on the endangered species list?"

"I'll be dammed."

At Noah's, they relaxed on the sofa. Vera nestled in his arms. Neither spoke for several minutes. Vera arched her head back so she could see Noah's face. "At the risk of putting you off again," she said, "do you mind if I bring up the subject of you-know-what?"

"What?"

"FHF," she whispered.

"Oh, shit."

"Sorry. Forget it."

They sat in silence for a while—a silence Noah finally broke. "Well, what is it?"

Vera pulled herself away and picked up her drink. She sipped the scotch, eyeing Noah over the glass. "Have you … Have you given any more thought to the FHF virus antigens?"

Noah rose up from the couch. "No I have not. Why should I, Vera? I don't want to alter the subject of my research in mid-course. It is not efficient to keep changing projects."

"Is that what this is about, efficiency?"

"No, I didn't mean it that way."

"Sure you did, Noah. That's all that matters to you, isn't it? Publish those papers. Win that Nobel Prize. To hell with the cats! What does it matter if one more species becomes extinct? It's ridiculous that you continue to study MEFA, a feline disease, while all the cats are dying off day by day."

"Why me?" protested Noah. "There are dozens of capable scientists working on FHF right now. What makes you think that I would succeed where others have failed?"

"Because you're good, Noah," Vera responded firmly. "Because you're considered by your colleagues to be one damned good molecular biologist. Maybe you won't succeed, but, if the cats disappear, how will you feel ten years from now? Will you be asking yourself, 'Could I have done something? Could I have saved the cats?'"

"That, lady, is a cheap shot."

"Yes, I suppose it is—" Vera's apology was interrupted by the chirrup of the telephone.

Noah looked at the mantle clock. "Eleven o'clock. Who the hell is calling at this hour?" He grabbed his phone. "Hello, Noah Chamberlin speaking." Vera saw him start with surprise. Noah put his hand over the phone. "It's that epidemiologist, Angelo Kraakmo. He's in town and wants to have lunch with us tomorrow." Vera shrugged and nodded her okay.

Angelo arrived at the café before Noah and Vera. *I hate it when people come late,* he thought, unmindful of the fact that he was several minutes early. When the couple did show up, on time, Angelo greeted them warmly.

"Thank you for coming," he said. "Let's go inside."

"Have you heard about the fleas?" asked Angelo, after they had settled into a booth.

"What fleas?" asked Vera and Noah in unison.

"In Los Angeles," Angelo replied, casually hiding his burrito under a dome of salsa. "The fleas are attacking people and dogs."

"Cat fleas?" asked Vera.

"Yes, all over the city. In fact all over Southern California. It's on *The Los Angeles Times* website."

"I'm not surprised," said Vera, "Cat fleas aren't too particular anyway. Most of the fleas found on dogs are actually cat fleas, *Ctenocephalides felis*, even in normal times. Some flea species are particular about their hosts, but not cat fleas. If they can't find a cat, they go for what's available—dogs, humans, whatever. With the cat population so decimated, we can expect a pretty awful flea problem everywhere. It's strange that we are just hearing about it now. Oh, I know; it must be that the winter weather kept the fleas dormant. Now, with the temperatures warming up, I'm sure there will be more flea problems."

"Oh, brother," muttered Noah.

"I did not know that about cat fleas," said Angelo. "I guess that shows once and for all that I am not an epizoologist." He grinned. "I suppose you are wondering why I asked to meet with you today."

Noah nodded.

Angelo looked Noah in the eye. "I would like to know if you have thought any more about possibly working on the FHF problem."

Noah stopped chewing and, mouth open, scowled at Angelo, and then at Vera. "Did you two cook this up together?"

"Noah, I swear I had no inkling—" Vera began. She then stopped, and, like an opening fan, a grin spread over her face.

"What's so damned funny?"

"It's not funny at all," she countered, "ironic maybe, but not funny. It seems that I'm not the only one who believes you could make a contribution to the FHF problem."

"Absolut!" said Angelo. "Am I to understand that you two have, ah, discussed the prospect of Noah working on the virus?"

"Yes, we have," Noah responded, "and I have told Vera that I am not interested."

"Scandaloose," said Angelo soberly. "Well, I am not one to try to pressure you into doing something you don't want to do."

They ate in silence awhile before Angelo remarked, "I read in the paper yesterday that the Pope is holding a weekly cat-blessing in the piazza of San Pietro."

"Why are you telling us this?" Noah asked sharply.

"Just making conversation," replied Angelo innocently.

"There must be something else that three intelligent people can find to discuss besides FHF and cats."

"No, Noah," Vera said. "These days intelligent, caring people can talk of little else."

"That is correct," agreed Angelo. "Perhaps, Noah, you underestimate the magnitude of the disaster. Do you think it is just cats that are affected? Man has been living with cats for at least ten thousand years, you know. Do you think that such a stable, intimate association can be broken quickly without having a major effect on mankind? *Homo sapiens* does not live in isolation. We say that no man is an island, yes? But no species is either. We humans depend on our cattle, our pigs, fowl, and yes, on our cats and dogs. And I say this even though I do not care for cats." As he spoke, Angelo's voice rose in pitch and volume.

Noah glared at Angelo. "I'm sure glad you are not one to try to pressure me into doing something I don't want to do," he grumbled. Noah rose and stormed out of the restaurant, leaving Angelo and Vera staring at each other in astonishment.

At the institute, Noah stared at the vinyl tiles of the elevator floor. *Everybody I'm close to is pressuring me to work on FHF. Why don't they mind their own business?* When the elevator stopped at the fourth floor Noah headed for his office. *I wonder if, somehow ... What could I do, anyway?* Noah was halfway down the corridor before he looked up and realized he had gotten out on the wrong floor. He threw up his hands and moaned under his breath.

When he finally arrived at his office, Gary was waiting. "Doc, I've got some news."

Noah looked up questioningly. "Yeah, what is it?"

"Guess who's making alpha-globin RNA?"

Noah's eyes widened. "You don't mean *E. coli* WC1953?"

"Yep. No doubt about it. It hybridizes quantitatively with alpha-globin DNA."

"So that altered promoter was the key."

"Yes. We're on track now. Tomorrow I'm going to try inserting the RNA into the FeSV chromosome."

Noah stared at the enthusiastic, bespectacled youth. "Gary, sit down a moment. Let's talk." Gary deposited his lanky frame in a chair too small and regarded Noah expectantly. Noah pursed his lips. "Gary, what are you going to do with the FeSV once you get the globin RNA integrated?"

Gary shrugged. "You mean what will I do if there are no cats to test it on?"

Noah nodded.

"I don't know. I've been proceeding one step at a time."

"You know," Noah commented, "one mark of a good scientist is to look forward. Good science is like good chess. You've got to look beyond the next move to the next and the next."

"Hell, what can I do about FHF? That's way outside my field."

Noah said nothing for a moment. "Maybe not. Maybe the two of us could do something. You know that epidemiologist, Kraakmo, is in town. He came to ask me to work on FHF."

"Really! But, Doc, you're not a vet."

"No, but I think the disease might be attacked with the help of the techniques and concepts we've been using with MEFA."

"Where do I come in?" asked Gary.

"I don't know. I'm not even sure that I should start on FHF. But if I do, I may ask for your help from time to time. For now, go ahead and continue with the MEFA project. If you have to stop, you can work on your thesis—at least up to the work you've completed."

Gary grinned. "Doc, you've made up your mind, haven't you? You're going tackle FHF."

Noah displayed a worried smile. "God help me. I guess I am."

Reprinted from *The Bakersfield Californian*, June 27, 2020

Taft overrun with mice

The central valley town of Taft is battling a massive infestation of mice that began on Sunday, and has been worsening in spite of efforts to trap and poison the rodents. According to residents, mice are running thick in the streets and seem to be unafraid of people or dogs. They enter homes and commercial buildings through any available opening. Homeowners have been kept busy searching their exterior walls for access points. The mice are active mainly at night but are quite noticeable in the daytime also. Annie Vishay awoke in the middle of the night to find two mice scurrying across her bedspread. Townspeople have discovered mice in their linen closets, clothing drawers and beds. Of course the rodents are also routinely detected in kitchens and pantries.

Dr. Judith Manishevsky, field biologist at Cal State Bakersfield, estimates the average density of mice in the fields north and east of Taft at seventeen mice per square yard, or about eighty-two thousand mice per acre. Several species of Hawks have been seen feasting on the mice in the area. Farmers have also noticed increasing numbers of barn owls and ravens, but no cats. Some locals have been shooting the predatory birds, fearing that they are apt to do more harm than good. Many farmers have set zinc phosphate traps but have been unable to control the hordes of mice. Jim Pfeffer of Taft reports that his barley and alfalfa crops are total losses. He sets several dozen traps each night, but by the next morning, the traps are so full of the dead mice that no more mice could possibly gain access to the poison. Several corpses of predatory birds have been found, apparently dead from eating poisoned mice.

Dr. Carmine Petrucci, population biologist at Cal State Sacramento, notes that such population explosions of mice in the valley are not uncommon, especially in the area around Buena Vista Lake near Taft. "However, the numbers are generally not of the magnitude we are seeing at this time," he said. "The unusually wet winter and warm spring have resulted in abundant vegetation on which the mice are able to feed. As they use up the available food, the mice migrate until they find new forage." Indeed, farmers in the area have reported them entering granaries and consuming or fouling large quantities of feed and seed grains.

The stench of mice, living and dead, as well as their excrement, is said to be overpowering, and many residents of Taft have taken to wearing cloth masks, a strategy that is not very effective, say the locals. Jamie Gunderson, age 12, a youngster with a keen business sense, has been buying up all the aerosol deodorant he can find in Taft stores and going from door to door selling the cans at a handsome profit.

Petrucci reports that the mouse explosion (mainly the common house mouse Mus musculus*) began* *at Buena Vista Lake in February. The mice began migrating from the lake when available food in the area ran out. The rodents then migrated southwest in the general direction of Taft. Bands of mice have also been seen moving north and east and are expected to reach Bakersfield by Friday. Engineers at the Department of Water Resources contacted by The Californian have expressed alarm at the potential for damage to the California Aqueduct.*

Public Health authorities have issued an alert to all communities in the area, advising residents to seal up all openings greater than a half-inch wide. However, Petrucci points out that such precautionary measures may be fruitless as the mice are quite capable of gnawing through wooden walls."

Two people were killed late last night when their SUV skidded on Interstate 5, forty miles south of Bakersfield. The car hit the center divider and overturned, crushing the occupants. The fatalities were a mother, 44, and daughter, 23, returning to Bakersfield from an overnight stay in Los Angeles. Names of the deceased are being withheld pending notification of next of kin. Witnesses reported that the highway was slick from the crushed bodies of mice that had been run over. The California Highway Patrol has posted signs limiting the speed on I-5 to 25 mph from Buena Vista Lake to Highway 58.

Biologist Petrucci notes that, although house mice are primarily vegetarians, when food is in short supply, they will eat anything, plant or animal. Mice that are killed on a freeway attract others who then come out at night to feed on the bodies of the dead ones. This, of course, increases the probability that more mice will be crushed by automobiles.

Petrucci believes that the mouse boom is probably not a direct result of the recent decimation of domestic and feral cats by the FHF virus, although their absence has probably aggravated the problem. Cats are only one of several environmental factors that tend to keep mouse populations in check. According to Petrucci, coyotes, in years past, also tended to help control such mouse explosions, but sheep farmers have long since killed off these animals."

16

Noah paced the floor. "In order to design a protective immunizing agent, we absolutely have to be able to grow FHF in cell cultures."

Gary threw up his hands. "Doc, people are trying to grow this son-of-a-bitch all over the world. What can we do that others haven't tried?"

Because of its high infectivity and because the FHF virus harbored Ebola genes, the two scientists now carried out their experiments in the institute's only BSL-3 facility. The lab had an anteroom that served as an air lock. All air leaving the lab was filtered by a HEPA system, and all manipulations were carried out within biological safety cabinets.

"I suspect," said Noah, "that the inability of the FHF virus to grow in cell culture is because it can't penetrate the cellular membranes."

"You sound like that guy Kraakmo," Gary noted. "He's always saying 'I suspect this … I suspect that …'"

"Absolut!" Noah responded, getting a laugh from Gary. "Why," asked Noah, "can't the virus make it into cells in culture?"

He and Gary performed a number of experiments with a variety of chemical agents designed to alter the cells' outer membranes in the hope that this would allow the virus to penetrate. They tried mixing the virus with dimethylsulfoxide, mercaptoethanol,

Tween-80, and a chemist's trove of other polysyllabic reagents, but they were not successful.

On a Sunday afternoon in early July, when summer announced its onset with a sudden rise in temperature, Noah and Vera invited Gary and Jane to go for a walk at Point Mugu State Park.

"There used to be feral cats in this meadow!" shouted Vera as she ran ahead of the rest.

"There used to be all kinds of cats in all kinds of places," answered Noah. *Here she goes again,* he thought.

Jane called out, "They must have lived on field mice."

"Yes, and birds," said Vera.

"Did you hear about the baboons?" Gary asked.

Noah looked up from the path. "What baboons?"

"I read on *The New York Times* site that the London, Chicago, and a few other zoos have experienced fatal FHF diseases in baboons, but no other primates."

Vera stopped in her tracks. "What? FHF in baboons? Are you sure?"

"It's on their website—but it's kind of sporadic. There are many zoos where baboons are just fine."

Vera scratched her head. "You know, it must have to do with the FeLV genes in baboons. That might allow the FHF, which also has FeLV genes, to mount an infection. Let's hope it stays in baboons and doesn't mutate to a form that can cross to other primates … *Homo sapiens,* for example."

No one spoke.

As the day grew warmer, Noah took off his sweater and tied it around his waist. Spying a large oak whose canopy created an inviting shadow, he called out to the others, and they settled down to eat. Vera poured iced punch into plastic cups while Jane distributed sandwiches.

"Did you hear that Dorothy sold her house?" asked Vera.

"No kidding," said Noah. "Good for her. I suppose she'll be moving to Atlanta now."

Vera nodded. "I wonder if we'll ever see her or Angelo again after she moves."

Gary munched on a carrot strip. "He's quite a character, that Kraakmo. One day, I ran into him in the hall, and he was humming—or rather singing—some tune from Bach or something. He seemed to be oblivious of me, just striding down the hall going 'Gdum gdump gdum dummm, gdum gdump gdum—'" Gary's attempt at an imitation brought forth guffaws from the other picnickers.

"I can just picture him doing that," Vera remarked. "He really is a unique individual."

"Say what you will," said Noah, "but he is one sharp fellow. "The way he put the information about the cats that died in the Seattle Zoo together with the epizootic in Camarillo was a brilliant piece of deduction."

"You wouldn't be saying that because his theory exonerated you, would you?" Vera teased.

"There are still mountain lions in these hills, aren't there?" asked Jane.

"I think so," answered Vera. "I've read that mountain lions occasionally contract FHF, but most of them survive."

Gary, with one arm around Jane and the other balancing a cup of punch, was pensive. "Hey, Doc," he said, "Maybe we should try infecting tissue from some other kind of cat."

"What?"

"You know, Kraakmo said that he thought that FHF, or at least a precursor of it, started in a lion or some kind of wild cat. Then the virus mutated or recombined in another kind of cat and so on until it got into that domestic zoo cat, Clyde."

"So?"

"Well, perhaps we'd have more success with growing the FHF virus in lion tissue or jungle-cat tissue or ..." Gary let his thought trail off.

"And just where do you suppose we are going to get lion tissue or jungle-cat tissue?" Noah asked. Gary shrugged.

They ate in silence for a while, and then Vera stated, "The Santa Barbara Zoo, The Los Angeles Zoo ... there are lots of places where they have lions and other cats."

"The Santa Barbara Zoo is less than an hour's drive," Jane offered.

Noah stared at her, and at Gary and Vera. He smiled bemusedly. *Other species ... why didn't I think of that? Gary is turning into a hell of a scientist.*

Later that day, Vera contacted the zoo's vet and made the necessary arrangements.

Noah and Vera drove to Santa Barbara in her Porsche, ostensibly to collect lion tissue samples, but also to enjoy a one-day vacation. They spent the night at a quaint B&B. The next day, they met with the zoo's vet, Jake O'Hara. Noah looked on with interest and amusement as O'Hara assisted Vera in examining two lionesses. She then checked an old, lazy male lion and a couple of frisky cubs. Vera called out to Noah, "These cats are quite docile. They seem to be in good health. I can't find any sign of FHF or any other illness."

With O'Hara's help, she anesthetized one of the lionesses and, with a very long, sharp needle and syringe, took a small sample of lymph-node tissue from under the right-front shoulder joint. She also drew 50cc of blood and placed everything on ice in a small camp cooler. She and Noah immediately climbed into the Porsche and headed back to Camarillo.

By Tuesday, Gary had isolated T-lymphocytes from both the lion's lymph-node and blood tissues. The cells were thriving in their transparent plastic bottles.

Noah examined the cultures. "Looking good. You know, just a few years ago it would have been almost impossible to grow T-cells in culture."

"Really?" said Gary. "Why?"

"You know that amino-acid mix you add to the medium? That was developed by Josephine Beay at Stanford. Before that, it was a rare lab that succeeded in growing T-cells."

Two days later, Gary opened up the ultra-cold deep freezer and withdrew a sample of spleen tissue taken from one of the many Camarillo cats that had died of FHF. When the tissue had thawed, he filtered it and added a portion of the filtrate to the T-cell cultures

Noah and Gary examined the cell cultures every day for evidence of FHF activity, but they showed no evidence of infection. In fact, they were flourishing. "It looks like these lion cells do better in culture than housecat cells," Noah observed.

They tried several more times by exposing them to different samples of FHF tissue from the freezer. Each time, the lion cells remained vital. There was no disintegration, no interference with cell division—nothing at all to indicate that the most lethal feline virus known to man was present in the bottles along with the cultures. By the end of July, Noah had to admit that the experiment was a failure. Lion T-cells—least these lion T-cells—were absolutely resistant to FHF.

Noah sat, slouched at his desk, flipping paper clips with a ballpoint pen. Gary paced back and forth. Neither spoke. So absorbed were they with their failure they barely noticed when Vera appeared. "Did you guys hear what's going on in the San Joaquin Valley?"

"What?" questioned Noah and Gary simultaneously.

"Mice are invading the town of Taft."

"Where's Taft?" Noah asked.

"It's in the San Joaquin Valley," replied Gary. "I have a cousin who lives in Bakersfield who's mentioned it."

Vera nodded. "That's right. There's a complete report on the Bakersfield newspaper's website. She ran her hands through her hair. "I recall reading about a hantavirus epidemic in the early 1990s among Navajos living in the four corners area of the Southwest."

Noah shrugged. "So?"

"Well, the virus had been endemic in deer mice. Right before the human epidemic, there was a population explosion of deer mice in the area."

"Oh, great. Can you think of anything more pessimistic to bring up? By the way, we're giving up on the lion experiments."

"Yes, I thought so. Actually, I didn't come up here just to mention the mice. I had a thought about the lion cells. Maybe the virus is unable to infect adult lymphocytes, but might be able to infect immature, undifferentiated cells, say, those from a lion cub."

Noah raised his eyebrows. "Why?"

"Well, I'm not sure," replied Vera, "but lymph cells change a lot as an animal matures. In young animals, the thymus gland, where the T-lymphocytes develop, is large and active, but it shrinks as the animal grows up. I was thinking that we could go back to Santa Barbara and take thymus samples from the cubs. We have nothing to lose."

Although there was no way an actual count could be made, statisticians later estimated that, by early July, over one third of the cats in the contiguous United States had perished. In Seattle, three veterinarians operating their practices as limited liability corporations declared bankruptcy. In many cities, however, pet stores were thriving. Former cat owners were buying up puppies, and, to a lesser extent, rabbits, to fill their need for companionship.

Feline Hemorrhagic Fever spread rapidly across the Western Hemisphere. On the seventh of July, it was detected in Buenos Aires, Argentina, Ciudad Juarez in Mexico, and Juneau, Alaska. In Arles, France, veterinarian Alain Severins was puzzled by the large number of ill cats brought in during the past week and had not yet related this to the news from *Les États-Unis*. Scientists expressed concern that the domestic cat might soon disappear from the Western hemisphere.

At the Harvard Business School, the noted economist Ching Kwo Ren predicted that the revenue loss related to FHF at the federal, state, and local level would prove to have a significant effect on the economy. The governments would experience a considerable loss of income taxes from veterinarians and other professionals involved with the care, boarding, and feeding of cats. Ching also foresaw a loss of sales taxes at the state and local level from lower cat-food sales and from diminished purchases of cat paraphernalia.

17

On Sunday, Noah and Vera returned from their second trip to Santa Barbara with small samples of thymus tissue from the zoo's two lion cubs. As they drove south along the coast, Vera turned on the car's radio to hear the latest reports from Bakersfield. The migrating mice had reached the city and were entering buildings as they had in Taft. The US Army was furnishing helicopters to aid in the spraying of poison over the bands of mice, but such tactics could not be used in inhabited areas. One little girl had already died in Taft from eating poisoned grain.

As he had done with the adult lion thymus sample, Gary isolated T-cells from the cub tissue and set them up in cell-culture dishes inside the biological safety cabinet. By the end of the week, the cells were thriving. Gary and Noah were ready to expose them to FHF-infected tissue. Gary opened the freezer and drew out a vial containing a piece of lymph node from a cat Vera had autopsied several months earlier. He thawed the sample and quickly pulverized it in a sterile glass tissue grinder. He then filtered the coral-colored soup and added small amounts to some of the lion-cub thymus-cell cultures.

A few days later, Gary thought he saw evidence of cell degeneration. By Friday, there was no doubt; the cells were dying.

He transferred a small portion of liquid from one of the infected cultures to a fresh, uninfected one. He removed his protective clothing and ran down the hall to Noah's office. Noah took one look at the glow in Gary's face and did not have to be told the news.

He accompanied Gary to the lab. They put on the paper garments and entered. As he looked over the petri dishes, he didn't need a microscope to see the degeneration of T-cells. "Well," he said, "we've got to make sure it really is FHF."

"What else could it be?" Gary asked.

"It's probably FHF, Gary, but we can't take a chance of a screw-up. This is just too important."

A week later, they had prepared a large quantity of the new FHF virus and had demonstrated that, although its chemical composition was similar to the common FHF virus, it was not identical. Where *Felis catus* FHF contained 68 percent protein, the lion virus had 71 percent. However, they looked alike under the electron microscope. The lion virus displayed the peculiar cartwheel appearance earlier characteristic of FHF that had been isolated from domestic cats. Noah speculated that the FHF viral genome had recombined with an endogenous lion virogene, a reversal of the process that Kraakmo had said was the origin of the FHF virus.

The question remained whether the new virus, which could be grown in cell culture so easily, would act as an immunizing agent protecting cats against FHF. The odds were not good, considering the failure of FHF virus isolated from *Felis catus* to serve as an effective antigen.

"Now just where are we going to get some cats with which to test this vaccine?" asked Noah.

"There are some areas of the country where the epizootic hasn't yet been reported," Vera replied. "Northern New England, parts of Texas, Florida, in fact the southern US seems to be relatively free of FHF so far. Also, I hear that the CDC is maintaining a colony of virus-free cats in a kind of bubble room. No humans are allowed in, and all the air is filtered, food sterilized, that sort of thing."

"Well then," Noah declared, "I think I'll put a call in to Kraakmo."

Angelo confirmed that there was a fairly large, germ-free colony at the CDC, numbering about a hundred cats. He arranged for Noah to send a batch of the virus grown in lion cells, now called the FHF-L strain, to Atlanta for a trial immunization of twelve cats. They were transferred to separate quarters and injected with heat-inactivated virus at two-week intervals. By the second week of September, it was time to challenge them with virus, designated FHF-C, from domestic cats. The immunized cats were removed from their special quarters and placed in a colony of infected cats.

Within a week, all the test cats had become infected with FHF, and, by mid-September, several of them had died. The scientists at the CDC then carried out a second trial, this time with living FHF-L virus. Like the first trial, it did not prove effective. Although the test cats did not become infected with FHF-L, the live lion virus vaccine failed to protect the cats against FHF-C. The lab technicians soon discovered why—antibodies to FHF-L cross-reacted only weakly with FHF-C.

On a day in mid-September, Camarillo became superheated by Santa Ana winds rushing to the sea from the Mojave Desert. The fall semester had begun, and Noah, perusing his lecture notes, needed a break. He wandered down the hall to the lab. Alicia was preparing reagents, while Gary was hunched over his desk, writing. "Working on your thesis?" asked Noah.

Gary, who had been engrossed, looked up, startled. "Yeah, what there is to work on."

"It's okay, you know. Your work is sound. It's not your fault that you can't bring it to completion."

"Yeah," said Gary without conviction. He leaned back, yawned audibly, and stretched. "If only there was some way to make a vaccine without that damned FHF virus …"

Noah noticed an envelope on the desk addressed to the Molecular Biology Institute at UCLA. He picked it up and asked, "What's this?"

"Oh, I've been thinking of applying for a post-doc with Fudderman."

"Good idea. Might I recommend that you use one of the institute's envelopes rather than this one? It will make a better impression. The first thing Fudderman is going to see is the envelope, right?"

"Yeah, I suppose so."

Noah moved about the lab in a desultory fashion, putting glassware away in the cabinet, chatting with Alicia, and twiddling with various pieces of equipment. He reached up to adjust the temperature of an incubator. Gary continued writing. Suddenly Noah shouted, "The envelope!"

Gary, startled again, said "Okay. I'll use an institute one."

"No, I mean the FHF envelope. We don't need the purified virus—all we need is purified envelope proteins."

Gary stared at him. *Obviously, the outer proteins of the virus—the envelope—were the important ones needed for immunization. But how can you get purified envelope protein without isolating it from pure virus,* he wondered. Immediately, he too saw the answer. All they had to do was to isolate the envelope genes from a sample of FHF-C virus, make DNA copies, and clone them in *E. coli*. With the system he and Noah had already developed for the MEFA work, they could get the bacteria to make all the envelope protein they needed. It was no problem at all to grow large quantities of *E. coli*. The CDC had enormous vats for that purpose.

"Of course!" cried Gary, "We clone the envelope genes!"

The two young scientists, mentor and student, gaped at one another. Neither was ready to admit the simplicity of the idea.

After a long moment, Noah wondered aloud, "How could we have been so dense?"

It was too late in the day to phone Atlanta, so Noah, overly stimulated and disinclined to continue with his lecture notes, phoned Vera to tell her of the plan. He explained to Vera how they would isolate and clone FHF-C envelope genes.

"Sounds promising," she said.

"It just seems so obvious," Noah remarked. "I don't know why we didn't think of this before."

"Will this really do the trick, Noah? We're running out of time—or cats are, anyway."

"I don't know. I hope so. If the envelope antigens don't succeed, maybe one of the other labs will come up with something. The CDC people are still working on it. So are the Russians and a group with the special pathogens branch of the Pasteur Institute."

Noah phoned Angelo at the CDC. After Noah described his plan, Angelo replied with a hearty, "Marveloose! I will speak with Dr. Bronkowski about having some purified virus sent to you, and I will call you back in a little while. Will you stay by the phone please?"

"You've got my cell phone number. I'll have it with me." *This is great,* he thought, *Vera was right to get me involved with FHF. To think, I resisted.*

Angelo did, indeed, telephone back within the hour. "I am very sorry, Noah, Dr. Bronkowski will not allow the FHF-C virus to leave the laboratory. All work with it must be done in a BSL-4 lab. Your lab is not adequate. I am sorry. If you could come to Atlanta, we could have the work done here."

Noah's euphoria vanished. "Oh, for God's sake, Angelo, what's the point of restricting FHF to BSL-4 conditions? There are so few cats left."

"Well, we are afraid that the virus could change again. What if it acquired the ability to infect humans? A virus related to feline leukemia is found endogenously in baboons, you know. And, don't forget the Ebola part of FHF. We want to make sure that if the virus mutates into something even more dangerous, it doesn't get out of the lab. I think the boss is being reasonable."

"But I have samples of the virus in my lab already!" Noah realized he was shouting into the phone. He lowered his voice. "We have a great many samples of infected tissue."

"Yes, but that is not purified virus," replied Angelo in measured tones. "As you know, the purified virus is millions of times more concentrated than that in infected tissue. We cannot take any chances."

"Angelo, the techniques required to clone the genes are complicated and need all sorts of specialized equipment."

"So you think our labs are primitive? We have state-of-the-art facilities here, Noah. If there is some specialized equipment you need that we don't have, you can bring it with you. You write up the detailed protocols and what materials and equipment you need, and we'll work out the details by e-mail or telephone."

Noah felt sick to his stomach at the new complication. "All right, all right," he said in a low voice, "I'll get started on it."

In zoos across the USA, many species of felines were becoming ill with a FHF-like disease, but rarely did they succumb. The larger cats—pumas, leopards, lions, and the like—seemed to have a much greater resistance to the virus than domestic cats. There was no question that the bigger cats were, in fact, infected with FHF. The CDC had demonstrated that by isolating the virus from the animals.

At the Toronto Zoo, a baboon named Tarzan showed symptoms of hemorrhagic fever. Aware of the possibility of Ebola, Ian Beswick, the primate-keeper, immediately quarantined the animal by placing it in a cage within a larger cage. He put up cautionary warnings to alert the other keepers that the primate should not be handled. When Tarzan died, the corpse was autopsied. The organs displayed evidence of severe hemorrhaging. Blood and tissue samples were tested for Ebola, but the results were equivocal. Beswick, who had been avidly following the news about FHF, sent samples to the CDC in the States to have them tested. The results were positive. It was now clear that primates could acquire FHF.

It had been over three months since Angelo Kraakmo had described FHF to the public on Rita Kenyon's talk show. At that time Scheherazade, Kenyon's Persian, had been in good health. In the months that followed, Kenyon had taken pains to keep her feline friend indoors at all times. She made a ritual of washing her hands before preparing the cat's meals and showered several times a day to wash away any of the virus she might have brought in. Kenyon also sent her clothes to the laundry much more frequently than she had before FHF. She was determined that Scheherazade was not going to become another victim.

Kenyon no longer welcomed her many male friends to her apartment. Instead she either accompanied them to their homes, or they met in hotels. When she explained to them why, most accepted her reason—although a few thought she was a bit eccentric.

One night, an obstreperous fellow named Jason, whom she had been dating for a few months, remarked, "You're loony, Rita. It's just a cat, for God's sake." Jason slept alone that night; Kenyon told him to take her home and never to call her again.

All these precautions notwithstanding, it was evident to Kenyon that her beloved companion had now become quite ill. It started without warning; the once-beautiful white Persian had become disheveled. She was no longer grooming herself and had lost her appetite. Rita sat on a sofa, the cat on her lap, and gently stroked the animal. She was too smart to deceive herself, and she realized that she was about to lose her friend. Most who knew her thought her stone-hearted. Certainly, that was the image she projected on television. Now she cried openly. Would she have done so if others had been present? Who knows?

Scheherazade died during the night. The next day Rita Kenyon drove to the studio as usual, assuming the persona that was expected of her.

18

322,600,000

Noah finally allowed that the CDC labs were fully equipped to isolate RNA from the FHF virus; all he needed to bring to Atlanta were his notes. He meticulously worked out all the procedural details with Gary and arranged for a substitute biochem lecturer. By the time he was ready to depart, his e-tablet was loaded with over a hundred pages of detailed protocols for every step of the work.

Angelo, smiling broadly, was waiting for him and they headed from Hartsfield-Jackson Airport to the CDC campus. Without delay, they proceeded to Bronkowski's office. Noah beheld a large desk with papers and books scattered in seeming disorder, which reminded him of his own office. Behind the desk sat the director, coatless, with his sleeves neatly rolled up to his elbows.

After Angelo had introduced the two to each other, Bronkowski asked, "Would you like to see the Centers?"

Noah was anxious to get started on the work, but he figured it was better to be diplomatic. "Um, yes, that would be nice," he replied.

As they walked toward the research buildings, Bronkowski remarked, "You know, we've been getting dozens of letters, e-mails, and even phone calls from people all over the country offering theories as to how or why FHF got started. Some of them are bizarre. One lady in Kansas believes the disease is God's revenge on witches. I guess it's the association of witches with cats. Several other people proposed religious or mythological origins."

Noah shook his head. "Maybe you can make them into a book someday."

Bronkowski nodded. "Not a bad idea." Though heavyset, he was a fast walker, and Noah, despite the fact that he was several inches taller, had to double-step from time to time to keep up with the man. A moment later, Bronkowski said, "The lab building I want to show you is just ahead. We have seven BSL-4 buildings now," he noted. "After 9/11 and the anthrax scare, the government spent millions of dollars upgrading our facilities, out of fear that terrorists might resort to biological weapons: anthrax, Ebola— who knows what. As a result, we now have the most hot-lab space of any facility in the world."

They visited three BSL-3 labs, including one in which several technicians were in the process of sequencing FHF virus proteins. Next, Bronkowski showed Noah the large library and the vivarium. Finally, they arrived at the door to the enormous building that housed the BSL-4 labs. The sign read "ADMITTANCE TO AUTHORIZED PERSONNEL ONLY." Above it was displayed the single word "BIOHAZARD" with the bright orange-and-black circlet of the universal biohazard symbol.

Bronkowski took a plastic card from his shirt pocket and slipped it into the slot. The sliding door opened with a high-pitched whine, and they went inside to an anteroom, where they encountered another door. Noah heard a hiss of flowing air as negative pressure was re-established. Bronkowski explained that the BSL-4 labs lay deep in the interior of the building, surrounded by a series of thick, concrete walls. To pass through each wall to the next inner level, one had to make one's way through a double-air-lock chamber, such as the one they were now in.

Bronkowski stepped up to a device that reminded Noah of a monocular microscope. With his left eye, Bronkowski peered into the lens. The scanner emitted a three-note chord. The director put his other eye to the ocular—another chord, several notes higher. "You guys don't take chances," Noah remarked.

"Yes," said Angelo, "each entry portal has one or more identification criteria. The one outside was the magnetic card. This one's retina and fingerprint." As he said that, a green light flashed on the scanner, and Bronkowski placed his hands flat over two windows. Noah saw a light go on inside the machine.

In a moment, a second green light came on. They passed through another door, headed down a hall, and turned a corner to encounter a second air lock. Here were additional requirements, the main one being voice recognition. Bronkowski articulated, "Warren Bronkowski. The trees of Atlanta bloom in the spring."

Noah glanced at Angelo, a questioning look on his face.

"That's today's password. This step employs both voice recognition and a password. Each day, the password is changed. Yesterday, it was, 'There's no business like show business.'"

A dull rumble emanated from the powerful air-conditioning system. The entire building was constructed so that all airflow was directed inward and was HEPA-filtered at each level to remove bacteria, viruses, and even large molecules. The whole setup seemed to Noah like a huge, concrete maze. After the group had moved through two more airlock chambers, they arrived at an observation room containing several closed-circuit television monitors. Each monitor displayed a different laboratory; only one showed activity.

Noah, who had often seen diagrams of hot labs but had never viewed one in person, observed a row of Class-III biological safety cabinets in one of them. These were larger and more substantial-looking than those with which Noah was familiar. Each cabinet was outfitted with sturdy gloves that extended into the box. At one end of the line of glove boxes he observed a large autoclave mounted in the wall, while a door to another one was visible at the other end of the lab. All exposed surfaces were either enameled or stainless steel, giving the BSL-4 lab a hard, cold, bright appearance. At the top of the video image, Noah noticed a complex system of ducts and pipes crisscrossing the ceiling within. Some of the ducts extended down to the safety cabinets.

Two people were at work in the lab, but Noah was hard-pressed to determine the gender of either. Each wore a one-piece protective blue suit with gloves and a helmet. Flexible, yellow air hoses hung down from the ceiling and were attached to the helmets. Noah thought the workers looked more like astronauts than lab technicians. He could see from the forehead of one that he or she was dark-skinned. That person happened to look up and nod to the camera. Noah sensed that the person was smiling at him, though the mask concealed the mouth.

"Who is that?" he asked.

"Ah, that's Nicky Brown," Bronkowski replied. "He's the technician who's going to do your procedures."

Noah turned abruptly to face Bronkowski. "What? What procedures?"

"Why, the experiments you came here for. The isolation of FHF RNA, the synthesis of cDNA, and so on."

Noah replied, "I'll do my own work, if you don't mind." A knot formed in his gut. Noah trusted only one technician, Alicia Diaz. The reason was simple—he had trained her himself.

"But, Dr. Chamberlin," said Bronkowski, "we can't let an untrained person use the BSL-4 lab. Each of our ..."

Noah felt helpless and deeply angry. "What do you think I am, a hack?"

Angelo remained silent.

"As I was saying," continued Bronkowski, the warmth gone from his voice, "each of our technicians goes through months of training in the proper safety procedures for the hot lab. Nicky has years of experience in recombinant DNA technology as well."

At that moment, Nicky Brown pointed to the airlock door and gestured with his forefinger.

"Looks like he's coming out now," observed Bronkowski. "It'll take him about fifteen minutes."

"I suppose he has to take off that space suit and put on civilian clothes," Noah remarked.

"Yes," said Bronkowski, "but first he has to pass through a Lysol shower. Then, after he rinses off the Lysol and removes the space suit, he takes a regular body shower. It's all quite time-consuming, but necessary."

Back in Bronkowski's office, Noah continued to voice objections to a technician doing the lab work. "I'll have to train him from scratch; that could take weeks."

"I doubt that," Bronkowski countered. "Perhaps a day or two. Believe me, you are underestimating him. You'll see." The men were silent a moment, each appraising the other. The chief rubbed his brow and said, "You know Noah, you really are naive. I am surprised you even entertained the thought that you would be allowed to work inside a level-four lab without training. You know, don't you, that even experienced technicians have occasionally allowed dangerous viruses to escape hot labs?"

Noah raised his eyebrows. "That's right," said Bronkowski. "In 1978, for example, foot-and-mouth virus got out of the BSL-4 lab at the Plum Island Agricultural Station and infected a herd of cattle on the island. It could have spread from there to Long Island and then to the whole Eastern Seaboard. Fortunately, it didn't. As it is, they had to slaughter all the cattle on Plum Island to prevent any spread of the virus. We don't know how that virus escaped the lab, but you must understand that I am obliged to enforce the regulations here."

"But FHF is already all over the country. All over the world, in fact. What's the point of trying to keep it contained?"

Angelo responded, "I can answer that. You and Nicky will be performing genetic manipulations on the viral genome. You'll be cloning and copying into cDNA. It is possible during these manipulations that you could change the virus in such a way that it might expand its host range. That would be scandaloose."

Bronkowski nodded. "That's it in a nutshell. You know, Dr. Chamberlin, we're fortunate to be starting on this project at all."

"Why's that," asked Noah.

"Two days ago, I received an emergency call from the head of the OMB. He told me not to start any new projects. The budget crisis is worsening, and even previously approved research is being halted. I managed to convince the guy that saving a species warranted breaking a rule."

"Oh, I hadn't heard this. But …" Noah tried to think of an argument that would allow him to work in the BSL-4 lab, but he could not. At last, the intercom buzzed, and the secretary reported that Nickerson Brown was at the door.

Bronkowski made the introductions. Noah rose and shook the hand of the technician, but said nothing. He was distracted by the man's appearance. From one earlobe hung a small golden earring. His hair fell in dreadlocks that, to Noah, seemed unkempt. The fellow was lean and appeared taller than he actually was. He wore a loose-fitting, starchy-white shirt, which contrasted sharply with his shiny ebony skin. He was smiling, his eyes more so than his mouth.

"Pleased to meet you, mon," said Nicky Brown with a noticeable Caribbean lilt.

"Nicky is from Kingston," said Angelo. "He's been in this country about ten years now. He has a BS from the University of Florida and a master's from CUNY Stony Brook."

Noah nodded. "How do you do?" he said, his voice strained. Nickerson Brown's smile vanished.

Angelo had invited Noah to stay with him and Dorothy. Noah could see at once that she was a very happy woman. He couldn't help but recall her melancholy when he'd met her shortly after she'd lost all her cats. The harpsichord, moved across the country at no little expense, occupied a corner of the living room of the white clapboard house. A large, brick fireplace faced the instrument at the opposite end of the room.

"How long have you lived here?" asked Noah as they sat down to eat.

"Not quite a month," answered Dorothy. "We haven't even finished unpacking."

"So I see," Noah said, eyeing several unopened cartons at the side of the dining room. "Did the harpsichord make the trip okay?"

"Oh, yes," replied Dorothy, "but the humidity here makes it go out of tune too often, even with air conditioning. I have to tune it almost every day."

"Absolut," replied Angelo. "Bach tuned his every day. So if Bach could do it, you can too."

Dorothy pursed her lips and gave Angelo a mock look of irritation. She turned to Noah. "How is Vera?"

"Oh just fine. By the way, she asked me to tell you that the family that bought your home has two small dogs. She's been out to the house once. They have fixed it up some, knocked out the wall between the dining room and the living room."

Dorothy became quiet, distracted. A tear formed at the corner of her eye.

Later, after Dorothy, at Angelo's request, played several melodies from Handel's *Water Music*, Noah and Angelo sat in the living room, sipping cognac. Following a long silence, during which each man sat, absorbed in his own thoughts, Angelo regarded Noah and said, "You know, Aaron, Nicky Brown is one of the most competent and respected CDC technicians."

Noah frowned. "I just need time to accept that I'm not allowed to carry out my own lab work."

Angelo nodded. "I understand."

The following day, in the patio of the center, Noah met with Nickerson Brown to go over the RNA extraction procedures. They sat at a picnic table under a huge magnolia, a table that soon was carpeted with notebooks, papers, tablet computers, and large thick leaves that occasionally dropped from the branches above. Noah described his methods for isolation of FHF RNA and learned that Brown had considerable experience with such operations. Noah realized early on that he'd underestimated the guy. He saw that Brown behaved coolly toward him, but that did not compromise the tech's professionalism. Both men became absorbed in the work and were oblivious to the passage of time. Eventually, Noah felt hungry and glanced at his watch.

"Whoa! I had no idea it was so late. You interested in breaking for lunch?"

"Sure, mon. Angelo plans to meet us in the cafeteria."

"So how's it going?" asked Angelo as he tucked a paper napkin, bib fashion, into his shirt.

"Okay, okay," Nicky responded, looking Noah straight in the eye. "Don' you agree, Dr. Chamberlin?"

"Yes, I do. We made a good start this morning and should be able to start the work tomorrow, right, Mr. Brown?"

"Yah, it look to be so." He took a sip from his orange soda. He furrowed his brow. "I am curious about something. Why don't you just use killed virus for an immunizing agent?"

"Actually," said Noah, "that has been tried several times here at the CDC. It doesn't seem to work. And so far, no one has succeeded in attenuating the virus so that a live vaccine can be developed. Our only hope is to use viral envelope proteins as the immunizing agent."

"At the rate the cats are dying off, we better work pretty damn fast," Nicky offered. "My sister, she write from Kingston that there are no more cats on de whole Jamaica island. They're all gone."

"Scandaloose," Angelo declared. "I didn't know that. I guess there must be some places like that where the entire cat population has disappeared."

Nicky said, "She say people are using dogs as rat-catchers. They pay good money for trained dogs. The best ones are Manchester Terriers; we call them black-and-tans in Jamaica. Actually, I don't care much for cats. But it would be a damn shame if the whole species became extinct."

Angelo finished consuming a chicken wing, wiped his mouth, and remarked, "I do not like cats either, but I agree with you. He crumpled his napkin. "I must get back to work. There's been an outbreak of encephalitis in Omaha, and I may have to go there for a few days. Good luck with your vaccine."

After lunch, Noah and Nicky Brown went over the procedures for the work to be carried out during the first week.

"There's one thing that's been bothering me," Noah said. "In order to identify the bacterial cells containing the cloned envelope genes, we'll need some anti-envelope antibody. Yet that's the very antibody we hope to make antigens for—a Catch-22 situation if there ever was one. Perhaps there is some anti-FHF antibody left from the attempts to immunize cats with whole virus. Could you check into that?"

"Sure thing. Angelo might know if we have some."

After an hour, during which he interrupted Brown frequently with questions, Noah asked, "Are you sure you have all the necessary reagents and enough of the phage?"

"Absolut, mon. Absolut."

Noah laughed at Brown's parody of Angelo and then, after a brief silence, "Look, I … I owe you an apology. Yesterday I guess I was rather unsociable. I …"

"I did notice that you were. It's cool, mon," he said softly, without spite. "We don't need to speak of it further." Without warning, Nicky got up and declared, "I would like to start to work in de lab tomorrow mornin' at eight thirty sharp. Can you be in the observation room by then?" He walked away without waiting for an answer, leaving Noah alone with his thoughts.

Noah gathered his papers and sauntered over to the administration building, where he was fingerprinted, retina-scanned, and given a plastic admittance card for the hot-lab building. He was given a sheet of instructions on the precise steps to gain access to the observation chamber he'd been taken to earlier.

The next morning, Noah arrived early and entered. He made his way to the observation room, using the information sheet he'd been given the day before. The password for the day was "Go west, young man, go west." By the time he arrived in the chamber, Nickerson Brown and another technician were already at work inside the hot lab.

"Good mornin', Dr. Chamberlin," said Nicky without a hint of unfriendliness. The voice came through a speaker located above the monitors.

"Oh, good morning," Noah answered. "Can you hear me okay?" Noah couldn't see a microphone.

"Perfectly, mon. Let's get started." He walked over to one of the Class-III safety cabinets and stuck his arms into the stout but flexible gloves within. The walls of the cabinet were of transparent plastic, and Noah could see reasonably well into the interior.

"Do you have the concentrated virus there now?" Noah asked.

"Yes. It's sitting here on ice." With a micropipette, the technician began transferring reagents from small, conical plastic centrifuge tubes into other tubes. Noah couldn't tell what they were, but he could see that Nicky was adept with the devices. After a few minutes, Brown took his arms from the gloves and said, "Well, that's it for now. We have to wait for the digestion."

"More 'hurry up and wait,'" muttered Noah.

The isolation of FHF-C RNA took over a week and resulted in an ample yield of the purified viral genome. The two scientists were now ready to begin the synthesis of the complementary viral DNA. Noah wanted to continue working through the weekend, but Nicky Brown balked.

"Hey, mon," he declared, "this is a civil-service job. We get weekends off."

"How about half a day tomorrow at least?" Noah asked. "We've got a good start. I'd like to press on."

"I was plannin' to drive over to Gainesville with me woman to visit her brother."

"You're driving all the way to Florida tomorrow?" Noah asked with astonishment.

"No, no. We got a Gainesville right here in Georgia, Noah. It's about forty or fifty miles up the Chattahoochee."

"Oh. Well, damn! I wish I could work in the lab. I feel useless."

Nicky nodded sympathetically. "How about Sunday afternoon? I could come in for a few a hours."

"Okay. Good," Noah responded, "How about one thirty? Is that all right?"

"That's fine. We can put in three hours."

Noah looked him in the eye. "Thank you, Nicky. I really appreciate it."

Saturday, Angelo and Dorothy took Noah to Stone Mountain, where they hiked for an hour and ate a picnic lunch. In the evening, the three of them watched a televised documentary on cats and their history. Noah became caught up in the program, in spite of himself. The domestic cat apparently originated about ten thousand years ago in the fertile crescent of Mesopotamia when farmers encouraged wildcats to take up residence around their stores of grain. It was the cats' ability to keep the rodent population under control that endeared the felines to their human hosts.

As the narrator continued, mention of the Egyptians and their feline goddess Bastet reminded Noah of his dead cat, and he suppressed a pang of sorrow. It was the Egyptians, he learned, who had endowed the felines with nine lives. They revered the domestic cat for thousands of years. For a time, Bastet was the supreme goddess, higher in the Egyptian pantheon than Osiris, Isis, or any of the others. Ailing cats were taken care of in the manner of sick children. When a cat died of natural causes, the animal was mourned in the same way a deceased human would be, complete with wailing and mummification.

"Why," the narrator asked, "is the cat not mentioned in the Bible, though other domestic animals are? The Jews, while they were held as slaves in Egypt during the time of Moses, certainly must have been exposed to domesticated cats. Perhaps the Hebrews, after fleeing Egypt, and aware that the Egyptians had deified the animals, shunned them in fear of violating their first two commandments.

"The Romans brought domestic cats into the British Isles during the invasion of England by Julius Caesar. Cats eventually spread throughout the world, primarily by sailing ships, which almost always harbored cats in their holds as rodent-catchers."

Noah turned to Angelo. "This is pretty good. I wasn't aware of a lot of the history."

"I still don't like cats," Angelo remarked.

The commentator added that the Japanese, from at least the tenth century, also revered cats, probably because of their prowess as mouse-catchers. Mice, relishing tasty cocoons, were the bane of silkworm growers.

The program went on to discuss the biology of cats. Noah, who had begun to doze, perked up when the narrator mentioned that in only three years a fertile female might produce as many as four hundred descendants. He looked over at Angelo, who also had turned to study Noah. It was apparent to both men that, owing to the enormous fecundity of the domestic cat, if just a few fertile individuals of both sexes were to survive, there was a decent chance that the species *Felis catus* could be saved from extinction.

On Sunday Nicky began the process of making DNA from FHF RNA, with Noah offering suggestions from the observation room.

"Damn!" shouted Nicky. "The reverse transcriptase is inactive. I'll have to get a fresh lot. Sorry, Noah, we won't be able to continue till tomorrow."

Noah threw up his hands. *Just like working in my own lab.* The next day, they made progress. By Thursday they had prepared a usable preparation of viral complementary DNA and were preparing to insert it into the lambda GT114 vector.

They would mix the FHF DNA with lambda DNA so that the two molecules would be able to genetically combine. "With any luck," said Noah through the intercom, "some of the lambda DNA will pick up envelope genes from the FHF virus." He articulated this, not so much to edify Nicky, but to cement the concept in his own mind. Nicky nodded. "Then," Noah continued, "when we infect *E. coli* cells with the altered lambda DNA, we can only pray that some of the bacterial cells will pick up the FHF envelope genes."

"Are you a prayin' man?" asked Nicky.

"It's a figure of speech. I didn't mean it literally." Nicky looked up at Noah through the port but said nothing. "Anyway," Noah went on, "we'll then have to find those few bacterial cells containing the desired genes—definitely a needle-in-a-haystack problem."

Noah now had even less to contribute than before; he was in unfamiliar territory. He could only watch as Nicky deftly manipulated pipettes and vials inside the glove box. Noah no longer felt the need to watch Nicky work every second and spent part of the time reading research articles on his iPad. Fortunately, as Noah had surmised, there was some anti-FHF antibody left over from earlier attempts to immunize cats. Nicky was to tag this antibody with a fluorescent dye. After the lambda virus had lysed the bacterial cells, any envelope proteins contained in the bacteria would then be released and could be detected by specific FHF antibody.

Noah and Nicky labored for two weeks, at the end of which they had succeeded in isolating not one, but three strains of *E. coli* capable of manufacturing FHF-C envelope proteins. On their last day of work, when Nicky Brown emerged from the airlock, Noah held out his hand. Brown paused a moment, and then he shook Noah's hand vigorously, following with a high five. Noah returned the gesture.

Lunching for the last time with Angelo and Nicky, Noah thanked the technician and declared, "Well, it's up to you guys at the CDC now. With your giant vats, you can grow two-hundred-liter cultures of *E. coli* and make all of the FHF envelope antigen you need—for all immunizations the whole world needs, for that matter."

Angelo nodded. "We have a task force gearing up for a crash program to locate and immunize cats all over the world."

At that moment, Bronkowski dashed in, breathless, carrying a sheaf of papers. "Oh, am I glad I caught you before you left," he said to Noah. "We have a problem. OMB has stopped funding all work on FHF."

The three men, incredulous, stared at him. "That's impossible!" Noah cried.

"It is quite possible, even certain," Bronkowski declared, handing the papers to Noah. "Remember, when you arrived here, I mentioned that I'd had to persuade the OMB to fund the work you've just completed? For some time, the bean-counters have been sending me memos to the effect that we should not be squandering—that's what they call it—our resources on a disease that does not affect human beings. Now they've turned off the tap. No more FHF work. They will not fund the preparation of the FHF vaccine, let alone the immunization program. I'm sorry I didn't tell you of the correspondence earlier, but I didn't want to discourage you while the work was ongoing."

Nicky shook his head. "Dat's crazy, mon."

Bronkowski shrugged. "Noah, you will have to seek private funding. Perhaps you can get a grant from Nestlé or some such company."

"I'm a scientist, not a goddamn fundraiser. Shit!"

"Noah, I think the best scientists are also good fundraisers," said Angelo. "This has been building for a long time," he noted. "The OMB has been interfering with CDC projects for over a decade. It's not just FHF. They even rejected proposals to investigate human birth defects, STDs, effects of toxic wastes, all kinds of important projects. It's this damned recession. The federal deficit is supposed to increase by over twenty-two trillion this year."

"Yes," said Bronkowski, "with 15-percent unemployment, bankruptcies at an all-time high, the stock market tanking … I don't know why they don't come right out and call it a depression."

"Maybe we could enlist public support," Nicky commented. "Public outcry. Letters to senators and congressmen, dat sort of thing."

"I don't think so," Angelo said. "It would take weeks or months. We need to get started now. Right now."

Noah closed his eyes, lowered his head to his chest, and ran his fingers through his hair. "Couldn't you grow the bacteria on the sly, so to speak? Does OMB have to know about it?"

Bronkowski shook his head. "It would never pass audit, Noah. We have to account for every pound of nutrient medium … every watt of power. There is no way we could hide a project of such magnitude. Besides, how would we explain where the vaccine came from?" The director extracted a handkerchief and wiped his brow. "It's over, Noah," he said softly. "Take your envelope-producing bacteria and go home. It's up to you now."

On the plane, Noah was too demoralized to look out the window at the scenery below. He perused the news on his laptop. It seemed to him that most of the articles were devoted to cats, or

183

rather the consequences of the absence of cats. Apparently, rodent infestations were increasing throughout the world.

Noah questioned the wisdom of the OMB withdrawing funding for the FHF vaccine. The worldwide impact on human health resulting from the loss of cats should be sufficient reason, deficit or not. He figured that the president, whose campaign had been fiscal responsibility and a balanced budget, was probably behind the OMB's action. Noah closed the laptop and shut his eyes. A knot had formed in his stomach; it wasn't airsickness.

No one knew how many cats had perished, but biological statisticians estimated that 52 percent of North American cats had died. For Europe, the estimate was 19 percent. In South America and Asia, an undetermined number of cats had died. Russian newspapers reported that over a fourth of the cats in the Russian Federation were gone.

In the US, cat owners were resorting to desperate measures. Veterinarians and holistic practitioners who espoused "alternative" therapies were thriving. Rosemary Hughes of Marin County, California, treated FHF-infected cats with flower essences—alcohol extracts of various flowers which she placed under the tongues of the cats at a hundred dollars a treatment. There was no evidence that treated cats survived FHF infection. Hughes made out well ... for a while.

Homeotherapy, deep massage and aromatherapy were also put to the test. Herbs such as garlic, goldenseal, cats claw, essiac tea, and a pharmacopeia of exotic botanical products were tried. None of these treatments had the slightest effect. The cats died as if they had received no treatment at all.

The Taft mouse infestation was partially controlled after the city's department of public health offered ten cents for each rodent, dead or alive, delivered to the authorities. Adults and children alike caught and killed hundreds of thousands. The program was to be funded by a special bond issue provided voters approved it, as they were expected to do.

In Cleveland, ninety-year-old Rebecca Neidleman, a resident at the Van Buren Home for the Aged, was mauled by mice while lying in her bed. Both her ears were shredded, as was part of her nose. She was expected to live. Governor Terrence Houghton called for an investigation.

In San Francisco, large numbers of rats were migrating into the city from Pacific-facing beaches. Several residential neighborhoods were badly infested. Hardware stores could not keep rattraps in stock. Rats had been a problem on the west side in the past, but now, owing to the absence of their natural enemy, the common house cat, the rodents were moving into the city without hindrance. Public-health authorities were reluctant to use poisons, because of the many dogs and young children in the area.

New York City was also battling a huge population explosion of rats. Ever a problem in lower-income areas, the rodents were now so numerous that residents were fleeing their homes. Central Park was overrun with squatters who staked out areas for themselves and their families. To date, four people had been killed—two by gunshots, two by knifings—when they encroached on territory claimed by others.

19

Noah briefed Stanaland on his work in Atlanta. "Bollocks," the director cried out on learning the CDC would not be making the vaccine.

Noah was startled. Until then, he had never heard the director raise his voice.

The two scientists considered producing the vaccine right there at CSUCI, but they lacked a fermentor of sufficient capacity. The largest one on campus held up to one hundred liters but they needed at least a five hundred liter vat, the sort used for industrial processes such as the manufacture of antibiotics.

"Why don't you look into the possibility of industrial participation," Stanaland suggested. "There would be money in it if they could get a vaccine out fast enough to do any good. Meanwhile, I'll phone my contacts at the NIH to see if we can get federal funding."

Noah phoned Clonigen, the biotechnology giant located up the hill from the institute. He arranged to meet with the vice president for research the next day. Noah stayed up all night preparing his presentation. He would emphasize the humanitarian and public-relations benefit to the company of manufacturing a vaccine against FHF. Noah had once met the VP at a seminar on cloning vectors held at CSUCI. He recalled Evelyn Parker as a no-nonsense professional.

When he was shown into her office, Parker waited until after they had exchanged pleasantries to say, "We last met—what was it—about a year and half ago?"

Noah nodded.

"So you have an idea for an FHF vaccine?"

"It's more than an idea," he said. "I've just returned from the CDC in Atlanta where I had several strains of *E. coli* constructed that synthesize FHF envelope proteins." He explained that the CDC was unable to produce the vaccine, owing to budgetary constraints. It would take a large commercial company such as Clonigen to do the job. He played up the publicity angle. *I hope she's buying it,* he thought.

"We do have the capability, but, you realize, don't you, that the workup of a project of that magnitude would take at least a year? It wouldn't be a profitable venture for the company."

"But ..."

She didn't allow Noah to voice his argument. "By the time significant quantities of an FHF vaccine were produced, checked and then shipped to various parts of the world for use, there wouldn't be many cats left to immunize. I'm sorry, Noah. Clonigen is hurting from the recession just as everyone else is. It would be imprudent for us to take on a project like this with so little probability of a positive result. You don't even know if the vaccine will be effective."

As he drove down the hill back to the university, Noah pondered his predicament. *Catch-22 in spades. To get them to manufacture the vaccine, I have to show that it will work. To show that it'll work, I need vaccine. This is crazy!*

With Vera's help, Noah began contacting other major pharmaceutical companies. One after another, they declined to take on the task.

Stanaland failed in his attempt to get funding from the NIH. He was told that there was no way to provide funding outside the formal procedure of grant-application and approval, a process that could take up to a year. Besides, the current recession, signaled two years earlier with a 920-point drop in the Dow, showed no sign of remission. The NIH was operating on a budget down 30 percent from the prior year and had no funds to spare.

Stanaland phoned both California senators in Washington. Anita Hernandez, the senator from Salinas, whose political claim to fame was that she was an aggressive animal rights advocate, would not even speak to him because the institute had received so much negative media coverage of its use of animals in experimentation. Furthermore, there was still a suspicion that FHF had somehow been generated there, even though the CDC had shown beyond doubt that this wasn't so. The other senator, Francis Prentice, could not be reached; he was in the hospital, recovering from an emergency appendectomy.

Vera couldn't sleep. She poked Noah and said, "Okay, the fermentor at the institute isn't large enough. But wouldn't it be better to start making some vaccine, even if it's just a little at a time?"

"Hmmph?"

Vera shook him. "Hey, don't fall asleep on me! I said, why can't you start making vaccine a little at a time at the university? I'd think that even a small amount would be better than none at all. We could start immunizing a few cats."

Noah rubbed his eyes. Now awake, he said, "Yeah, I suppose so." He turned to face Vera. "But here's the problem. From one fermentor run, we would get less than a gram of FHF envelope proteins. In order to use it on cats, it would have to be freed of bacterial proteins. Otherwise, the cats inoculated with it could die from endotoxin poisoning. By the time the vaccine was purified, there would be only about two tenths of a gram left. That would be enough to inoculate only two or three cats, and that does not take into account any booster shots. A single fermentor run costs about three hundred dollars. We simply cannot afford to run it to immunize a few cats, not even knowing if the vaccine will work."

"It's got to work," Vera responded, more in hope than conviction. She was silent a moment. "It's always money … the root of all evil, but the *sine qua non*. All those big companies care about is profits. It's enough to make one turn to socialism. Those giant companies—whoa, wait a minute. I wonder if a smaller company might get involved."

"What smaller company?" asked Noah.

"I recall a small one in Davis, near the university. They manufacture vitamin B-12 by growing *E. coli* in large fermentors. The bacteria make the vitamin, and then it's purified by chemical procedures. Why didn't I think of it before?"

Noah, now fully awake, asked, "What's the name of the company?"

"Uh … oh, hell. I'll think of it in a minute. It's on the tip of my tongue."

Noah turned toward her. "Well, stick out your tongue. Let me see."

Vera did and let forth with a loud, sloppy raspberry. Noah grabbed her and they wrestled playfully. In a moment they were making love in earnest.

Shortly after they had climaxed, Vera gasped, "Ferm—"

"Hungh?" Noah grunted.

"Fe … Ferma … Fermi … Fermentacorp!" Vera shouted. She cried out again, "Fermentacorp! Fermentacorp!"

A quiet while later, after Noah had disengaged himself, Vera glanced over and saw that he was gazing at her expectantly. She tried to stifle a laugh, but it came out anyway. "Fermentacorp," she blurted between giggles. "That's the company in Davis that has the large fermentors."

"Oh. I thought it was some sort of sexual incantation. Maybe a fertility rite or something."

She grinned, a glint in her eye. "Oh, I'm sufficiently fertile without any help, thank you."

"How do you know? Have you ever been pregnant?"

"I am pregnant." *Oh my God! I wasn't ready to tell him. How's he going to react?*

Noah got up on one elbow and gazed at Vera open-mouthed. "You ... you ... why didn't you tell me?"

Vera took his free hand in hers. "I ... I was waiting for the right moment. I guess this is it. I was afraid it might upset you."

Noah shook his head slowly from side to side. "Upset me?" he said at last. "My God! I'm delighted. Well, I guess I'm delighted. I'm more in shock. Good shock. Uh, when? Did you miss a period? Do you ..."

Vera put a finger to his lips to shush him. "I missed a period, so I did a home test. It was positive. Then I went out and got a different brand and did a second test. I am undeniably, absolutely, without any doubt whatsoever, incontrovertibly, with child, gravid and pregnant."

Noah cocked his head. "I thought you were on the pill."

"I ran out. I thought I was close to my period. I thought it was safe. I'm sorry."

"No, it's okay, really." Noah smiled. "Some medical professional you are. You're supposed to know better than that."

Vera nodded. "Yeah, I know. Does that mean you would rather not have a child? We need to talk about this. If you think having a baby would complicate our lives, we can have it aborted." She put her two hands on his cheeks and looked him in the eye. "For my part, I would like to have a child ... raise a child ... be a mother. You know, all that conventional motherhood stuff."

"Abortion is out of the question. I look forward to being a father." He smiled sheepishly. "Well, I suppose we should get married."

Vera took a deep breath and again looked into Noah's eyes. "We don't have to, just because I'm pregnant. I am perfectly capable of raising a child alone. Many single women do, you know."

Noah declared, "If I were pressured to marry, I probably wouldn't. I want to marry you because I love you. I would have asked you eventually anyway. Will you marry me? Now? Tomorrow? That is, if your schedule permits."

"Oh, you … Dr. Chamberlin, I would be very happy to become your wife."

The next day Vera telephoned Fermentacorp and spoke with the company's president, a man named Brock P. Osborne. At first he was as cool to the idea of producing a vaccine for feline hemorrhagic fever, as had been the officers of the larger companies. But Vera pointed out the publicity benefit and persuaded him to meet with her and Noah.

On a Friday early in November, Noah and Vera left Camarillo before dawn and drove to Davis, where they met with Brock Osborne. Not at all like Noah's preconceived image of a company president, Osborne—"Call me Brock, please"—was thirty-something, tieless, jean-clad, and quite open and friendly with them. After showing them around the plant where several of the giant fermentors were in operation, Osborne expressed reservations about Fermentacorp's ability to make the vaccine.

Osborne sat facing Noah and Vera. "Tell me," he said, "when *E. coli* synthesizes these envelope proteins, do they get secreted into the growth medium, or do they stay inside the cells?"

"They remain with the cells," Noah answered. "We will have to harvest the bacteria, break open the cells, and purify the envelope proteins from the cell extracts."

Osborne shook his head. "Whew, that's a big job. I guess we could handle most of it here but we would have to shut down some of our other operations for a time. I suppose we have enough B-12 to last until spring. But we'd have to hire personnel familiar with vaccine production. There's quality control, sterility checks, assays. It seems like a real long shot. This is not a big enough company that we can afford to gamble on R&D like, say, an Abbott Laboratories."

"I understand, Brock," said Vera, "but couldn't you prepare one fermentor batch of vaccine? That should provide enough to test on about twenty or so cats. If it works, well, then we would have demonstrated a market and you could sell all the vaccine you can make."

"But, Vera," Noah protested, "it might take months before we knew whether the vaccine was effective or not."

Vera glared at Noah, her eyes saying, *Shut up, will you?*

Osborne caught the glance and chuckled. "It's all right, Vera. I'm not naive, you know. I'm well aware of the time frame of FHF infections and of vaccine testing. My own cat died of FHF about three months ago. If I weren't a cat guy, I suppose I'd have turned you down when you phoned me. But, damn, my wife and I miss that cat. I would like to have another some day. So, let's go for it."

By late November, the first batch of vaccine was ready. There was enough to immunize about twenty-five cats. Vera, despite bouts of morning sickness, assumed responsibility for the injections. She placed classified ads in several Southern California newspapers soliciting cats for the test. The ads emphasized that there would be no charge, but that success was not guaranteed.

She received four hundred and thirty calls within a week. Jane Brennan took most of the calls and dutifully recorded all relevant information about each cat—its location, the name and address of its owner, state of health, and when it could be brought in for immunization. Vera turned down about three hundred of the applicants whose cats were already in advanced stages of FHF. At random, she then selected thirty in various regions of Southern California, Arizona, and one in Western Nevada for the trial.

On the last day of the month, anxious owners formed a line outside the clinic. Some held small animal carriers, others had their pets nestled in their arms. They engaged in spirited conversation; the common theme was one of hope and, for some, prayer. Vera had each owner sign a release absolving Fermentacorp and the molecular-biology institute at CSUCI from responsibility in the event that the cat died after exposure to FHF.

"Okay, let's do it," said Vera. "Kal, you do the injections."

"No problem," Kal replied. Before he injected the cats, Kal took a small sample of blood from each and smeared it on a microscope slide for Vera to examine. They noticed that one of the animals was obviously ill, but immunized it anyway. Vera hadn't the heart to turn down the young redheaded girl who cradled the skinny tortoiseshell in her arms. After they had been inoculated, the cats were kept at Vera's clinic, where they could be cared for and watched for any signs of illness.

Vera treated the blood smears with Wright's stain. When she examined the slides, without exception, they all showed the typical picture of FHF—high numbers of leukocytes but a low proportion of lymphocytes.

"The question now," she said to Noah later that day, "is whether the vaccine can work after a cat is already infected with the virus."

"I suppose, if the animal can make antibodies faster than its immune system is compromised by the virus, the answer is yes. Otherwise, no. It may depend on how long ago the cats became infected. It's a lot like AIDS. There is no way of knowing when the infection occurred."

During the second week in December, the tortoiseshell was the first of the injected cats to die. Vera phoned the little redheaded girl, the cat's mistress, to break the news. The child did not blame Vera, who had explained to her that it might not work. Vera had suspected that it was too late for the pet, anyway.

By early January, three more of the inoculated cats had died. Vera now became deeply disquieted. She suggested to Noah that they start preparing another batch of vaccine, but he felt they should wait. "What's the use of making more of the stuff if we don't even know if it's any good?" he said. "If it does work, it won't take long for Fermentacorp to gear up and turn out the vaccine."

It was eight months since feline hemorrhagic fever had appeared on the West Coast. The disease was now as familiar as the common cold. The number of domestic cats that had perished was not known. However, veterinary epidemiologist Darnall Rengis at the University of Michigan estimated that 80 to 90 percent of the animals in North America had died. Cats in Europe and Asia were becoming ill at an alarming rate. Spot-checks indicated that worldwide, three-fourths of all domestic cats on Earth were wiped out.

On the Australian continent, plagues of mice were invading homes, clogging machinery, and destroying cereal crops. Farmers were poisoning thousands of mice each night and scooping up their carcasses with skip loaders the next day. In New South Wales, a pilot was killed when his small plane skidded on a runway swarming with mice. Australia's minister of agriculture pointed out that the murine population explosion was not simply due to the absence of cats, but to bountiful crops following an exceptionally wet winter and spring.

In Los Angeles County, after a thirty-four-year-old woman was diagnosed as the thirteenth victim of plague in four months, public-health officials declared that plague, both pneumonic and bubonic, had reached epidemic status. Emergency measures would be taken to eradicate infected rodents. It was the largest outbreak of the disease since 1924, when pneumonic plague killed thirty-three people in the county.

Baboons in zoos all over the world were coming down with FHF-like illnesses. Some died, but most survived. The primates proved to be considerably more resistant to FHF than domestic cats. Ruth Schau, senior zoologist at the National Zoo in Washington, pointed out that no primates other than baboons had developed the illness. The NIH and the USDA worked with the CDC to monitor all viral infections in zoo animals. They stood ready to impose strict quarantines at the first sign of FHF in primates other than baboons.

Throughout North America, veterinarians were inoculating any cats brought to their clinics with all the common FIV and FeLV vaccines. They and the cats' owners hoped that one or more of these might protect the animals against FHF. None of the vaccines demonstrated any benefit.

20

All the test cats at the institute were dead. The vaccine had failed. Vera phoned Brock Osborne to break the news.

"Oh no! What a blow!" cried Osborne. "I had such hopes for it."

"We all did."

"I guess that's it, then. I don't see how domestic cats can survive."

"Yes. I have to agree. Thanks for daring to take a risk. It took courage." Vera ended the call. And then the tears began.

Valentine's Day fell on a Sunday. Noah and Vera were not in a loving mood. The scourge of FHF was all they could think about. Noah nursed a beer, but Vera, out of deference to her pregnancy, sipped club soda. They sat, deep in thought, listening to an old Miles Davis album whose mournful trumpet blues closely matched their spirit. Vera fell into Noah's lap and sobbed in his arms.

"We'll think of something," he said, stroking her hair.

Vera raised her head. "You don't believe that, do you? It's really over. The domestic cat is about to become extinct."

"Maybe we should contact Kraakmo before we give up," Noah said without conviction. "I wish we could test the vaccine on cats that hadn't been exposed to the virus." Without warning, Vera grunted loudly.

"What's that for?" asked Noah.

Vera responded with another guttural noise.

"What's the matter with you?"

"It's the baby," she replied. "It's kicking me."

Noah pulled up Vera's top and placed his hand gently on her slightly rounded belly. On cue, the fetus moved again "I felt it! I felt it!" Noah shouted.

"Right on schedule," Vera remarked. "The mean time for the quickening is about twenty-one weeks. I'm right in there, I think."

"Quickening? I haven't heard that term in a long time. They still call it that?"

"In some circles. Wow! I guess this creature inside me is developing the way it should." The fetal movement had, for the moment, completely taken her mind off the vaccine's failure.

The following day, Vera's mood had improved. At Noah's suggestion, she phoned Angelo. "We really have only one chance left," she explained. "We have to test the vaccine on cats that have never been exposed to FHF. Do you think we can find any cats like that? My God, are there any to be found?"

"Hmm ... well, you know in most epidemics and epizootics, there are always some members of the population that escape the disease. Some survive low-grade infections; others never come in contact with the agent. But with FHF, I don't know. We've never met with a disease like this. I think we might advertise in the papers and on television for unexposed cats."

"Advertise? Who would pay for that?"

"Nobody. We need only call a press conference and get the media interested."

"Ah, yes. I see what you mean. Get the public involved."

After a brief silence, Angelo said, "You know, there are still about seventy germ-free cats here at the CDC. I think several colonies are maintained for research in other institutions, as well. I know Cornell University has one, and there is a colony at one of the universities in Louisiana."

"Why that's perfect! That should be our first approach. Why am I just hearing about this now?"

"Not so fast," Angelo said. "Germ-free cats have been raised that way from birth. They've never been exposed to the routine microorganisms that normal kittens are. Therefore, their immune system is undeveloped. Even if they could be immunized against FHF successfully, they might succumb to other, more mundane microbes if released into the environment."

"Oh ... I see. Well, it might be worth exploring."

"Yes. I'll make some phone calls."

Angelo's misgivings concerning the fragility of germ-free cats were validated. Somehow, FHF had gained access to the colony at Cornell, destroying it before the staff even knew they had a problem. In Louisiana, scientists had tried to immunize the cats with various FHF fractions. None was effective; all the cats were lost.

Another germ-free colony was housed at the Washington State vet school at Pullman. Aware of the need to keep some cats alive in case FHF wiped out all the cats in the outside world, the biologists there refused to release any of the animals for experimental purposes. Their plan was, if an effective vaccine were developed, to immunize all cats in the colony and then breed them. In this way, there would be a population that might be able to re-establish the species. Angelo immediately saw the wisdom of the plan and ended his attempts to locate germ-free cat colonies. Because the cats' immune systems were undeveloped, the animals couldn't be used as research subjects anyway. They would almost certainly succumb to any of the dozens of viral or bacterial pathogens in the environment.

Vera received an e-mail from Angelo. The special pathogens scientists at the Pasteur Institute had also failed to protect cats with the envelope vaccine. He wrote of rumors circulating on the web, hinting that a group of Russian scientists working at the Moscow Institute for Veterinary Medicine had succeeded, but there had been no public announcement.

She phoned Brock Osborne again. He told her that he'd suspected from the start that the FHF envelope vaccine might not protect cats previously infected with FHF. "Can you afford to cook up another batch to test with cats free of the virus?" she asked, diffidently.

"I think so. I'll get back to you."

With Lowell Stanaland's backing, Noah and Vera called a press conference to announce the need for unexposed cats. On Friday afternoon, a crowd of newspaper and television reporters gathered in the institute's auditorium. All the major networks were represented as well as reporters from other parts of the world.

"As you are all aware," Noah began, "the FHF crisis is reaching a point of no return. According to the best estimates, all but about 15 percent of domestic cats on the North American continent have perished, and most, if not all, of the remaining cats are presumed to be infected with the virus. Also, two thirds or more of cats outside North America have died. The chances are slim that the species will survive." A murmur arose from the audience as reporters scribbled on their PDAs. "Other species are involved," Noah continued, "including mountain lions and caracals."

"Would you spell that?" asked a woman from *The Los Angeles Times*.

Noah did, and added, "It's an Asian cat. Something like a lynx, I think. It is quite possible that the virus could mutate in these species too, placing them in the same danger of extinction as *Felis catus*. We just don't know." Noah wiped his brow. "Over the past year," he continued, "we've seen increasing evidence that the demise of cats has serious economic consequences as well as proving to be a threat to public health. Is it too late to do anything? We think not."

A hush came over the reporters; they looked up expectantly. Noah paused to let the suspense build.

"We have a plan to immunize cats against the disease." Noah waited for the commotion to die. "Since the middle of last year, scientists at the CDC and others here at the institute have worked to develop a vaccine against FHF. So far, all the tests have failed. Now, however, we may have a vaccine that will work. It was developed here at the Institute in collaboration with the CDC and is being manufactured by Fermentacorp in Davis, California.

"As some of you know," continued Noah, "the first trial of this vaccine was a failure. Dr. Vera Barnett has inoculated twenty-seven cats brought to her from various places in the western United States. Unfortunately, none of these has survived. Why? We believe that all the cats were infected with FHF before they were brought to us, and that the vaccine is not likely to be effective unless it is given to cats before they become infected.

"That's why we are asking representatives of the media for help. We want to put out a call for cats that have never been exposed. We believe that there must be some cats, perhaps in isolated environments, that have not had contact with the FHF virus."

"What kind of environments?" asked a voice from the crowd.

"Oh, small towns where there might be someone keeping a cat and living alone ... Any place where cats might have had no contact with other cats or with people who have been anywhere near cats. If we can locate such pets, with their owners' permission, we will test the vaccine on them. We'll immunize any cats that are volunteered, without cost to the owner. We'll continue that policy until the vaccine has been tested sufficiently and shown to be effective.

"Of course there are no guarantees. The vaccine may have no protective effect. You'll find all the necessary information on our website. We've also prepared handouts summarizing the details."

The three sheets given to the media explained how to apply for the vaccine, and how to report possible FHF-free cats to the institute. Vera's clinic would serve as the clearinghouse. Each application for the vaccine required a statement from a licensed veterinarian certifying that the cat in question appeared to be free of FHF. The vet's address and telephone number had to be included.

That evening, the unprecedented appeal was announced nationwide by the broadcast media. By the next day, it had appeared in all the world's largest newspapers and was being broadcast several times a day on radio and television. Countless websites and blogs were devoted to the search for unexposed cats.

Noah and Vera were married at the Unitarian Universalist Church in Ventura. It was a small, unpretentious wedding, with only Gary and Jane present to act as witnesses and Dr. Stanaland to give away the bride. Vera wore turquoise; she was five months along.

"It isn't often I've seen you wearing a dress," Noah observed, "let alone a maternity dress doubling as a wedding gown."

"I'm not the dressy-feminine type," Vera replied.

"No, you're not. That's one of the many qualities I love about you, soon-to-be Mrs. Chamberlin." Her smile was luminous; she wasn't the least bit self-conscious. Noah, however, manifested his usual nervousness.

They traveled south for a short honeymoon in La Jolla and spent one full day at the San Diego Zoo. "Busman's holiday," mumbled Noah as they went through the turnstile.

"We both like animals. What's the problem?"

"I didn't say it was a problem. It was just an observation."

"Okay," said Vera. She took his hand. "One of the critters I most want to see is the giant panda. It's on semi-permanent loan from China."

"Good," Noah replied. "I don't think I've ever seen a panda— just pictures. I do want to see the big cats. I haven't seen a living feline of any kind in a while."

However, a sign was posted on the door of the feline house. All the cats, including the large ones, were off-limits to the public. The same notice was posted on the fences of all the outdoor compounds.

By the time Vera and Noah returned to Camarillo, requests for the vaccine had begun arriving at the veterinary clinic. Vera noticed envelopes from the USA, Canada, Mexico and, in smaller numbers, from elsewhere in the world.

Vera and Jane sorted through the forty-odd envelopes.

"Look," said Vera, "these two don't have the required note from a vet."

"I have one of those," said Jane. "And here's one with a vet's note, but I think it's forged."

"Forged? Let's see." Vera nodded. "Good catch, Jane. 'Hemorrhagic' is misspelled, and there's no DVM after the signature."

On five of the applications, vets wrote that they could not be sure that the cats were free of FHF because the animals had high white-blood-cell counts.

In the end, Vera had identified two rather good possibilities— one a farm cat from eastern Iowa that apparently had had no contact with any other cat for over a year, the other from St. John's Newfoundland. The latter was a cat owned by a woman who never let it out of the house and, because she was an invalid, did not go out herself. Her daughter brought her groceries but did not like cats and so avoided contact with the animal. In both cases the accompanying vets' letters stated that the cats appeared to be free of FHF, and the owners were earnestly pleading for the vaccine.

Vera telephoned the vet in Iowa, a Dr. Parsons. He explained that the Wilson couple had a small farm near Grinnell where they raised corn and soybeans. The nearest farm to the Wilson's was four miles away, and, as far as the vet knew, there were no cats in proximity.

"I took the obvious precautions before handling the cat," noted the vet. "I scrubbed myself down with rubbing alcohol and put on Jim Wilson's overalls."

"Good thinking," Vera replied.

"I also took a sample of the cat's blood," he continued. "With Wright's stain, it appeared normal—no overabundance of leukocytes, nothing out of the ordinary. The cat certainly seems to be healthy."

Vera said, "I'd like to meet you at the Wilson Farm. I could fly out, say, next Monday and bring the vaccine. Would that work for you?"

"Let me check ... yep, that's good. As you might guess, my practice has fallen off quite a bit because of this FHF thing. Fortunately, I've been able to make a living with farm animals."

"Okay, then," Vera said, "I'm going to book the flight."

"Would you like me to pick you up at DSM? That's the closest large airport."

"Oh, that would be terrific. Thank you so much. I'll send you an e-mail when I know my flight number." She wrote down his e-mail address and sat back in her chair. She clasped her hands behind her head and closed her eyes. *If this vaccine doesn't work, I'm going to fall apart ... at least this Parsons guy seems to be competent ... thank God for that.*

"What do you mean?" Noah shouted when Vera told him of her planned trip. "You're five months pregnant, you can't go running all over the country!"

"Iowa, is not 'all over the country.' It's one part of it, near the middle."

"Don't be facetious. This is serious."

"Noah, my dear husband, pregnancy is not a pathological condition. I am perfectly fine. The morning sickness has stopped, and, apart from a little more fatigue than usual, I'm okay. I will not behave like a prissy, helpless, nineteenth-century female."

Noah couldn't come up with a response.

On February 22nd, about thirty-two-hundred cat lovers assembled in a Tokyo park to celebrate Japan's annual Cat Day and to mourn the passing of so many adored felines. Ironically, the celebration—or, what used to be a celebration—had begun in 1987 when hundreds of cat owners had gathered in an auditorium to offer prayers for the longevity of their animals. They had also honored a famous cat that had traveled 222 miles to find its owner after having been accidentally left in the countryside. The date of February 22 had been chosen because two-twenty-two is pronounced *ni-ni-ni*, resembling *nya-nya-nya,* meow-meow-meow in Japanese.

Researchers at the National Institutes of Health and the CDC attempted, unsuccessfully, to produce virus-free kittens from FHF-infected mother cats by cesarean section. Unfortunately, the placenta failed to act as a barrier to the virus; all newborn kittens of infected mother cats harbored the virus at birth.

In many labs, both in North America and abroad, scientists attempted to grow the FHF virus in cell culture. They tested feline T-cells, B-cells, mixed spleen cells, liver, kidney, lung, and even cancerous muscle cells. The FHF virus refused to grow outside a cat's body. None of the scientists could explain why.

At the CDC, biochemist Larraine Sakai purified the virus using high-performance liquid chromatography. She was able to produce only minute quantities of the highly purified agent. Much greater amounts would be necessary for the immunization of large numbers of cats, even if a way could be found to make FHF virus an effective immunizing agent.

Public-health authorities on all continents expressed concern about the increasing incidence of rodent-borne diseases. In Long Beach, California, an epidemic of rat-bite fever broke out near the docks. One hundred forty-seven cases of typhus were identified in Northern Germany near Hamburg, and another thirty-six cases in Copenhagen. At Tabriz in Northern Iran, yellow jaundice, commonly transmitted by rat urine, was traced to contamination of a local water supply by *Leptospira* bacteria.

Chinese authorities attempted to deal with the booming rat population. Increasingly, rodents were making their way into factories, warehouses, granaries, and even tourist hotels. Spot-food shortages occurred in Northeast China and in Japan. Government officials considered a crash program to breed rat-killing snakes and weasels. Meanwhile, large quantities of zinc phosphide and sodium diphacinone were used to poison the rats.

Especially ominous was an outbreak of thirteen human plague cases in the Korean city of Musan on the Chinese border. In addition, forty-seven people had died of bubonic plague in northern Uganda's West Nile region, and another four hundred and eighty were under treatment for the disease. The World Health Organization dispatched a five-member medical team to the area.

21

Larry Parsons was waiting in the airport lobby. Vera figured he was in his mid-fifties. A circle of gray-brown hair surrounded his smooth round pate, and he was dressed in blue jeans and red plaid flannel shirt. She supposed she'd be unable to tell him from a local farmer if she met him on the street. Parsons drove them east on Interstate 80 to Grinnell.

It rained heavily for most of the forty-mile trip through heartland cornfields and other crops Vera was unable to identify. To reach the Wilson farm, they had to travel a gravel road pocked with muddy chuckholes. Vera felt her swollen abdomen bounce in synchrony with the movement of the pickup. Whenever she saw a mud-hole ahead, she clenched her teeth and grabbed the sides of the seat.

"When's the baby due?" asked Parsons.

"Late June, I think."

He nodded. "Sorry about the bumpy ride. You must be feeling every jolt."

"I'll be okay." She glanced at the man. *He seems like a nice enough fellow, she thought.* "I want to handle the cat as little as possible," Vera said. "Because of my pregnancy, I don't want to risk a cat scratch or bite. There's also the possibility that I could be carrying FHF virus on me, and even though I'll scrub with

208

alcohol and Betadine, I think it'd be best if you hold the cat while I do the injection."

"Sure," replied Parsons. "In fact, I have a portable decontamination chamber complete with air pump in the back of the van. I thought we could set that up outside the house, decontaminate the chamber, and then have Mr. or Mrs. Wilson bring the cat to me after I've scrubbed and disinfected myself."

It was obvious to Vera that the guy had really thought this through. "That's great, Larry. Thanks for thinking ahead."

By the time they reached the farmhouse, Vera was feeling tense. *Am I nervous because of the prospect of failure*, she wondered, *or of success?* As they drove up, Mrs. Wilson emerged from the house and waved. Red-cheeked, chubby, and middle-aged, she reminded Vera of Dottie.

Protected from the rain by a large awning over the porch, the vets stayed outside, while Parsons explained the procedure to Mrs. Wilson. Vera glanced inside. She saw that the home was spic-and-span. A hooked rug lay over the hardwood floor, and she noticed a well-worn family Bible on the coffee table. A stitched sampler on the wall read, "God Bless our Home." And there, sleeping by the warm hearth was the cat. *God, right out of a Norman Rockwell painting.*

At that moment, wearing a dripping yellow slicker, a John Deere Cap, and smelling faintly of fertilizer and motor oil, Jim Wilson made his appearance. He removed the slicker and laid it over the porch swing. He smiled out from a two-day growth of beard and offered his hand. Vera looked him in the eye and shook it.

"What are the odds, Dr. Barnett?" he asked.

"What? Oh you mean of success with the vaccine? I think they're pretty good. It better work, because it may be our last hope to save the cat species."

The Wilsons read over the release form and signed it without ceremony. It was obvious to Vera that they had already given the matter careful thought and simply wanted to get on with the injection.

"I think there's room for the decontamination chamber right here on the porch," Parsons observed. He turned toward the van. "I'm going to get started."

It took a half-hour for them to set up the equipment and start the gasoline-powered air pump. Once started, the motor made a racket. "It's time for us to disinfect ourselves," Parsons shouted over the din. "How about you go first. In the back of the van are bottles of Betadine and alcohol, cotton, and sterile protective gowns, caps, and booties."

"You've thought of everything, haven't you?"

"I try."

Vera climbed into the van. She took off her clothes, except for underwear, thankful that the van was windowless. First, she swabbed her entire body with the Betadine. *I look like a pumpkin,* Vera mused as she glimpsed the amber tone it had colored her slightly swollen belly. She removed most of the Betadine with alcohol. Vera figured that there was no way FHF could survive the stuff. She finished her preparation by donning the sterile, white, plastic-coated paper jumpsuit, mask, and latex gloves left by Parsons.

When she emerged from the van, he prepped himself in the same manner. Vera reentered the van and loaded a syringe with the FHF vaccine.

"Okay, Joanne, you can bring Sugar over," Parsons yelled.

The woman approached her pet, but the cat, frightened by the noise of the pump motor, squirmed and fought for release. The vet clasped the animal tightly and took her into the van, where Vera waited with the syringe. While Parsons held the cat still, Vera deftly shot 3 cc of the vaccine under the loose skin in back of the neck, avoiding contact with the cat. "An hour to prepare," she uttered, "and thirty seconds for the injection. Hope it's worth it."

"God bless you," said Mrs. Wilson when Larry handed Sugar back to her. "We never had no kids, you know. Jim had a war injury. Sugar is like a child to us."

Vera replied, "Well, let's hope for the best. But, you know there is no guarantee of success."

"We read the news on the computer and watch TV," said Joanne Wilson. "We know how it is. If the cats are dying, someone has to take a chance. I don't think I'd want the world to be without cats."

Vera was suddenly overcome, and she felt like crying. She stepped forward and hugged Joanne Wilson. She then shook Jim Wilson's hand.

After she changed back into her travel clothes, Vera handed a booster dose of the vaccine to Parsons and noted, "The second shot should be given to Sugar in about a month. By the way, how old is she?"

"'Bout nine years, I'd say," answered Jim Wilson.

"Spayed?"

"Yup."

I would have been amazed if it wasn't, Vera thought. *We're just testing the vaccine at this point. If it's effective, we'll have to face the problem of locating fertile cats that haven't had contact with FHF.*

She prepared to leave. Joanne said, "We'll pray for your success."

Vera looked back and waved. She knew she was going to cry, and she hurriedly made for the van. Parsons gunned the motor and headed back down the muddy gravel road. When he heard Vera's sobs, Parsons reached over and gently clasped her hand, but said nothing. By the time they had plowed through a dozen deep chuckholes and reached the main highway, she had stopped weeping. Vera reflected on her new tendency to cry. She had never understood what people meant when they talked about the emotional effects of pregnancy hormones, but now she got it.

On Friday, Vera flew to St. John's, Newfoundland, and, with the assistance of a local veterinarian, injected the vaccine into a black male cat named Simon belonging to the McNaughton woman.

While Vera was away, more than fifty new applications for the vaccine had come in, some from as far away as Europe. There was one from Santiago, another from Osaka. Half the requests lacked the required vet's letter; Vera removed them from consideration.

One evening, Vera read a vituperative letter from Mobile, Alabama castigating, not only her, but Fermentacorp, the institute, and the worldwide secular humanist conspiracy for meddling with God's Creation. It ended with "May you rot in hell!" Vera groaned. "Secular humanist conspiracy …?"

Noah looked up from his reading. "What?"

Vera showed him the letter. Noah shook his head. "Didn't you tell me that the Wilson woman blessed you?" he asked.

"Uh-huh."

"Well then, it's a wash, isn't it?"

Vera smiled, kissed him on the forehead, and sat down next to him. "I made an appointment for an ultrasound."

Noah set down the e-reader. He gazed at Vera in silence for a moment. "You know, we don't need to know whether it's a boy or a girl. Healthy would be fine with me." He smiled.

"I know, but ultrasound is for more than just learning the sex of the baby. If there is anything grossly wrong—two heads, that kind of thing—it would show up."

"I hadn't really considered the idea of anything going wrong. I don't want to think about it."

Vera took his hands in hers and looked him in the eye. "Noah, sometimes things do go wrong, especially with pregnancies in women my age. Let's not be ostriches."

Noah was silent for a moment. "You're right … as always."

The sonogram revealed a healthy female fetus. Vera's eyes welled with tears—tears of joy, tears of relief. Until that moment, she hadn't realized that she'd been harboring a suppressed fear of some nameless problem.

When she told Noah, he hugged her. "Oof!" she cried.

"Oops. Sorry, I forgot. Gotta be careful from here on. What shall we name her?"

"We could check the Internet or get one of those baby-naming books from the library. Do you have any favorite names?"

"How about Bastette, in honor of my dead cat?"

Vera gave him a hard smack on the shoulder. "Hey! Watch it!" he yelled.

"You know," she said, "maybe some kind of feline name isn't a bad idea. How about Lilith?"

"Lilith? Is that a feline name?"

"Yes, I think so," Vera replied. "Lilith is a quasi-cat goddess. She's a recurring mythological figure. In one myth, she's Adam's twin sister. In another, she's Adam's first wife."

"First wife!" Noah was unbelieving. "I don't recall anything in Genesis about any wife other than Eve."

"I think it's from the Jewish Kabbalah. There's more to Judeo-Christian mythology than the Old and New Testaments, you know. Besides, there are Lilith-type myths, not only in Jewish folklore, but in Persian, Babylonian, Greek, Arab, early English, Gothic, Oriental, Native American, and even Mexican legends."

Noah was incredulous. "How the hell do you know all this stuff?"

"I've read a lot about cats in mythology. It's something of a hobby of mine."

Noah shrugged. "Lilith it is, then. It's a pleasing name."

"There's just one thing," added Vera. "Most of the Lilith myths are rather negative. They paint her as a kind of witch."

"You're not superstitious, and I'm not either, right?"

"Right. And I agree, Lilith is a pleasing name."

Near the end of April, the CDC sent a hazmat team to sterilize Noah's cat room with ethylene oxide gas. The entire building had to be evacuated for two days, but FHF-free cats could now be brought to the lab without risk of exposure to the virus. Three apparently healthy cats, all spayed females, were the first to be housed in the room. Vera, who was dividing her time between her clinic and Noah's lab, tested the cats for FHF by using the sensitive ELISA test.

"Damn!" she cried when she examined the test plate.

"What is it?" asked Noah.

"One of the new cats has the virus."

Noah looked over the ELISA plate. "We'd better get that cat out of here, fast." He removed the diseased animal from its cage and placed it in a sterile carrier outfitted with fiber filters over the openings. He dashed out of the lab with the risky package.

Vera watched, open-mouthed. *That boy can move!*

By the middle of May, four cats were under test at the institute. The Pasteur Institute in Paris had immunized seven more.

"That's it, then," said Vera. "Including the Wilson's cat and the one in Newfoundland, we're testing thirteen cats with the envelope prep."

"I wish we had a larger sample size," said Noah.

Near the end of the month, all the test cats had been challenged with FHF virus. When Vera received blood samples drawn from Sugar and Simon, she and Noah performed ELISA tests on the sera. To their dismay, both came up positive for FHF antigens.

Vera moved away from the lab bench. She stared at the floor. "Maybe ..."

Noah put his arms around her. "There's no maybe, Vera. The envelope prep isn't effective."

A few weeks later, Vera received e-mails from Grinnell and Newfoundland, Sugar and Simon were dying. Three of the cats housed at the institute were similarly ailing.

"I just can't believe it," sobbed Vera. "I just can't believe it," she said over and over. Noah could say nothing to comfort her. The depth of their despair was measured by the extent to which they had allowed their hopes to soar, and by their empathy with the owners of these previously healthy pets.

Most zoos in North America kept their patrons at some distance from the cats. This policy was put into effect across the US and Canada after several large felines contracted FHF. Fortunately the virus was not universally fatal for big cats. Nevertheless, zookeepers were not taking chances, and, until the course of the disease became better understood, parents were going to have to show their children videos of lions and tigers, pumas and leopards. The only way to view the tigers at the San Diego Zoo was to climb up to a large platform, erected for the purpose, hundreds of feet from the animals and to use field glasses to peer into their compound.

In San Francisco, Minneapolis, and quite a few other American cities, large and small, support groups were launched for helping those who had lost cats cope with their grief. Many who did not feel comfortable in the group milieu visited their own counselors. Psychiatry and clinical psychology were two professions actually benefitting from the crisis.

Three new charities had formed whose purpose was to raise funds for research into a cure for FHF. One of these, Citizens Against The Sickness, had already raised four million dollars, although it had not yet received tax-deductible status from the IRS.

A spokeswoman from CLAWS, an organization notoriously opposed to any use of cats for research, was featured on the CBS evening news. She acknowledged that it might be permissible to test vaccines on cats if this could save the species from extinction.

22

The test cats were dead. Vera was quiet as she lay with her head in Noah's lap. Gary gazed out the window silently. The injections had failed. The three would-be cat saviors languished in the living room of the Chamberlin home.

"It's over, isn't it?" Vera remarked.

"It looks like it," Noah answered. "We've run out of ideas. It's hard to believe, but I think the domestic cat is on the way out. Odd, isn't it? With all the species extinctions brought about by humans during recent years, this one doesn't seem to be the fault of *Homo sapiens.*"

Vera frowned. "I don't know, Noah. If we hadn't collected those different species of wild cats at the Seattle Zoo, gene exchange among species would not have occurred, and the recombinant FHF virus wouldn't have found its way into that cat, Clyde. In fact, it makes me wonder why such viral diseases are relatively rare in zoo animals."

Noah nodded reflectively. "I hadn't thought of it that way."

Gary, who had remained silent, said, "I wish there was some way we could exploit RNA interference."

"We discussed that months ago," said Noah. "You know it hasn't proved effective in mammals. Besides, the group at the Pasteur Institute looked into RNA interference for FHF last year and gave up on it."

"What's RNA interference?" asked Vera.

Noah turned to Gary. "You want to explain it?"

"Sure. You know that most of the RNA in a cell is single-stranded, right?" Vera nodded. "Well, in the late 1990s, someone found that cells also carry a small amount of double-stranded RNA. This dsRNA blocks genes that aren't supposed to be expressed in a particular cell by destroying any messenger RNA that the gene makes. This destruction is called RNA interference, or RNAi for short."

"Good explanation," said Noah. "In fact, the effect was first identified in a nematode worm ... earned the guys who discovered it a Nobel Prize. Later RNAi was found in cells of most higher organisms."

"I see," said Vera. "But why would this RNA interference be considered a cure for a virus?"

Gary paused. "Consider the retroviruses—those that make DNA copies of their RNA genomes ..."

Vera laughed. "I'm sorry, Gary. You were so intent. Please continue."

Gary shrugged. "I get that way. Anyway, the genome of a retrovirus is often identical to its messenger RNA. If the right kind of RNA could be introduced into infected cells, it might be able to shut down viral multiplication. When RNAi was discovered, virologists thought that it might be a cure for any number of retroviral infections ..."

"That's right," Noah interrupted. "In fact some early experiments were encouraging. Several labs reported success in inhibiting hepatitis B and HIV viruses in human cell cultures. However, getting RNAi to work as a viral cure in whole animals proved to be a challenge. How do you get the interfering RNA into the infected cells? So far, no one has found a way to do it."

Gary continued, "Some researchers tried using DNA viruses to insert sequences carrying interfering RNA genes into cells. Once inside, the DNA was supposed to allow the cells to synthesize

RNA that would then interfere with whatever gene was under investigation."

"I see," said Vera. "So one could insert into a cell ... genes for interfering RNA ... complementary to certain FHF genes." She spoke with a slow, measured cadence as her gray matter absorbed the concept. "If the introduced genes functioned properly, they would cause the cell to make interfering RNA." Her expression brightened. "This would lead to the destruction of messenger RNA specified by those FHF genes."

"Couldn't have put it better," offered Noah. "The problem is, how do you get the vector DNA into the cells where it is needed? You can't just inject a virus vector into a cat and hope that all the proper cells will get infected."

Vera stared at the rug, brow knotted, as Noah and Gary also pondered the question. Suddenly, she looked up. "Hmmm ... if a way could be found to use feline leukemia virus as a vector for interfering RNA genes, those genes might become part of the feline chromosome and act continually to make the interfering RNA."

Noah's jaw dropped, and his eyes opened wide. Gary, who had been gazing out the window, wrenched his head around and stared at Vera. "But FeLV is an RNA retrovirus itself," he said.

"Sure it is," she responded, "but most cats, maybe all of them, have FeLV DNA integrated in their chromosomes. That's the way the virus reproduces. Feline lymphoid cells become infected with exogenous FeLV virus. Then, DNA from the incoming virus recombines with viral genes in the cat's genome. That way new genes enter the genome. The vector would have to be altered in some way so it couldn't cause disease. Isn't that the kind of thing you genetic engineers do for a living?"

"That's just amazing," said Noah. He turned to Gary, "Why didn't we think of that?"

Gary shrugged.

"I ... I was just thinking out loud," said Vera. "You think this could actually work?"

"You are theorizing like a seasoned molecular biologist," said Noah. "Good sentences, and well-pronounced."

Vera blushed, then frowned. "What did you say?"

"I said you are theor—"

"No, after that."

"Oh. I said, 'Good sentences, and well-pronounced.'"

Vera nodded. "Yes. That. Why does that sound so familiar? What is it?"

Noah grinned. "It's a line from *The Merchant of Venice*. Portia speaks it in response to something her maid says."

Vera laughed. "It's always Shakespeare with you, isn't it?"

"Actually," Gary interjected, "many retroviruses, maybe all of them, recombine with host chromosomes and get integrated into the host genome."

"That's true," Noah agreed.

"There's still the problem of getting this hypothetical genetically engineered FeLV into all the FHF-infected cells," said Gary. "It's not just lymphoid cells that harbor FHF. I understand that epithelial cells of the capillaries and arterioles are also infected. That's why the cats hemorrhage to death. It's obviously the Ebola part of the virus that's responsible."

Vera began pacing back and forth across the living room. "What if one could get the FeLV vector with its interfering genes into fertilized eggs of cats? Then the DNA copy of the FeLV might recombine with the native FeLV genes in the zygote. As the cells of the embryo multiplied, all the cells of the kitten would possess the engineered genes for interfering RNA."

Noah and Gary regarded Vera, their eyes and mouths agape. Vera giggled. "You guys look like cartoon characters." For a moment both men remained silent, staring. Noah then asked, "Just how would you go about injecting something into a fertilized egg?"

"Aha!" said Vera. "It just so happens that I have some experience in that area. I carried out a graduate research project in vet school on artificial insemination of cats. It's really not all that hard. You make a small incision in the abdomen of a female and, with a laparoscope, remove some of the ova. You check for mature eggs under the microscope, and then you add semen from a fertile male. Finally, again using a laparoscope, you deposit the fertilized eggs in the uterine horns of a female. It can be the same female or a different one. In our case, using microsurgery apparatus and a micropipet, we could inject the FeLV vector before implanting the ova."

"And you could do all this if we were able to manufacture an appropriately altered FeLV?" asked Noah.

"I think I could … sure. We would have to get hold of a microsurgery apparatus. And, of course, there's the matter of finding cats."

"I read that there are still sizable numbers of cats in Europe, Latin America, and Africa," said Noah, "but they're all thought to be infected with FHF."

"If you boys will prepare the altered FeLV, I'll work on getting cats," said Vera. "I had an idea yesterday that I'd like to explore."

"What's that?" Noah and Gary said in unison.

"Well, up to now we've been focusing on domestic cats. In other words, cats that are owned by people. All over the world, however, there are populations of ferals—cats that may once have been domestic but have either been abandoned or have escaped. Some of these wild cats live in colonies, others are in remote places so they don't have a lot of contact with domestic *Felis catus*."

Gary said, "So, if you could locate some of these colonies and capture some of the cats, you might find that they are free of FHF."

"That's the idea," she said. "Right now, however, I'm exhausted, and it's past my bedtime. I'll be glad when I lose this load," she said, pointing to her protruding belly. "Do you two mind if I stretch out on the couch for a while?"

"Sure, go ahead," said Noah. "I'll download the genomes of FeLV and FHF." He sat down at his laptop and opened the

NCBI website. Gary looked over Noah's shoulder as he worked. The National Center for Biotechnology Information was Noah's preferred source of genomic data. He quickly located the complete genomes of FeLV, FIV, as well as that of Ebola, and downloaded them. Noah printed out several copies of each and of FHF so he and Gary could work with them independently.

Vera lay down on the sofa and soon dropped off. Noah and Gary sat in the kitchen. Soon they had papers and books spread all over the table, floor, and kitchen counter. Vera slept fitfully. She was awakened from time to time by the animated voices of the two men.

Once she heard Gary say, "We can take twenty-one nucleotides from *gag* and another twenty-one from *pol.*"

She then thought Noah said something like, "We've got to include hairpins, of course." Later: "We'll use TT in the three prime overhangs" It was all gibberish to her, and it contributed to several bizarre dreams, one of which featured a senatorial candidate she'd once met in Sacramento. In the dream, the politician was vomiting.

By morning, Noah and Gary had mapped out what they hoped would serve as a workable FeLV vector. "Now there's an all-nighter I won't forget," Noah remarked.

Gary nodded and gave a high five, which Noah matched. "Now," noted Gary, "all we need to do is synthesize it."

Noah massaged his eyes. "We've already developed procedures for most of the steps from the MEFA research. It should be a snap to put together this FeLV vector."

Gary frowned. "Doc, you know if we succeed, there'll be a permanent change in the feline genome."

Noah took his hands from his eyes and regarded the young man. "Yes, that's right. So be it." He suggested that Gary lie down on the sofa and get some sleep.

"Works for me," Gary replied wearily.

Although Noah was just as tired, he brewed a pot of extra-strong coffee and went over the night's work, making minor adjustments in the base sequence. Vera awoke around six and shuffled into the kitchen, where Noah was scrutinizing his notes.

"You didn't sleep much, did you?" she asked, her voice husky with the dawn.

"Actually, I never went to bed. Too keyed up about this FeLV thing." He nodded toward the living room. "Gary's asleep on the couch."

"Oh. I hope I didn't wake him." She pulled her robe tight.

Noah smiled. "He's dead to the world, I'm sure." Noah stood and took her hands in his. "I think we have a plan for a workable interfering vector. It should recombine with the FeLV region in the feline genome and ... well, you know, this was really your idea."

Now fully awake, Vera whispered, "Noah, that's terrific! You really did it?"

"I think so. Now we have to construct it in the lab, but I don't see any technical problems."

After she had showered and downed glasses of orange and vegetable juice, Vera drove back to the clinic. She looked over several dogs she'd been boarding, but was too preoccupied with FHF to give them more than a cursory glance.

"Kal, I can't tell you how grateful I am that you're here to take care of the practice while I'm working on this FHF thing."

"No thanks necessary. I just hope you come up with something."

Vera smiled. "Yeah, it's make or break for cats." She turned to Jane. "You too. Thanks for handling the business matters. I think I'll change your title to 'anxiety-reducer.'"

Jane smiled. "I appreciate being appreciated."

Vera described the FeLV vector plan.

"Wow!" said Jane.

"Yeah, wow!" Kal echoed.

Vera went on, "There are some unanswered questions. Where are we going to find cats that haven't been exposed to FHF? Could we locate feral cat colonies somewhere? And, money … how will we pay for the expensive microsurgery equipment? The apparatus and accessories could run to fifty thousand dollars or more." She sat down at her desk and began a budget estimate. They should probably offer a reward to anyone locating cats that had not been exposed to the epizootic. After a half-hour of work, Vera figured they required a minimum of a hundred thousand dollars. She started to prepare a pot of coffee.

Suddenly, her hand jerked, dumping coffee grounds on the table. "Of course! Dottie!" When her first husband died, Dorothy had inherited a large estate, and she wasn't a big spender. Most likely, she still had most of the inheritance. Vera had no doubt that Dottie loved cats. Anyone who had kept as many furry friends as Dottie merited a spot in the cat-lovers hall of fame.

She called into the reception room, "Jane, would you phone Dorothy Kraakmo in Atlanta, please. It's about twelve-thirty there. She should be home."

When Jane had Dorothy on the line, Vera picked up the phone.

They traded small talk. Angelo was away on one of his investigations, and Vera realized that Dorothy welcomed the chat with an old friend. Vera finally broached the subject of money. "Dottie, I think Noah may have a new strategy for preventing FHF."

"That's wonderful!" Dorothy exclaimed. "Is it a new vaccine?"

"No, it's not a vaccine at all. It involves injecting some protective genes into fertilized eggs. When the eggs develop into kittens, the cats are protected for their whole lives."

"I see," said Dorothy, although Vera sensed she didn't.

"The thing is, the procedure is rather expensive, and we have no money. Because of the recession, there's no hope of any federal funding. Noah's institute is also tapped out." Vera rushed through the pitch. "That's why I'm calling you. I know you love cats, and I thought you might be willing to help out financially." Suddenly, Vera felt embarrassed and regretted making the call. *How could I take advantage of such a dear friend …*

"How much do you need?" asked Dorothy.

"Well, I figure about a hundred thousand dollars," she answered, her voice weak.

"Did you say a hundred thousand?"

"Dottie, I'm really sorry. I shouldn't have asked you. I have no right to take advantage of our friendship."

"But Vera, it's not for you personally, it's for the cats! I donate hundreds of thousands of dollars to charities every year. How should I make out the check?"

Vera was stunned. *Is that all I need to do—just make a phone call?* She hadn't given any thought to how the monies would be handled. She didn't even know what regulations had to be followed. "I … I … Dottie, don't write the check yet. I'm going to have my attorney create a non-profit charity for the project so that any donation you, or anyone else contributes, is tax-deductible."

"Oh, yes. That's a good idea. Let me know when it's all set up, and I'll get a check out to you. Vera, this may be the last chance for cats. Good luck to you and Noah." The phone went silent. Vera felt a lump form in her throat. She decided not to phone Noah, figuring he might be asleep after last night's toil.

Just then, Vera felt a warm, wet sensation on her leg. "What the hell?" she gasped. *My water broke!* Almost simultaneously, she felt a pang in her lower abdomen. *Oh, my God! It's time.* "Jane," she called, "would you mind phoning Noah to tell him I'm having our baby and to meet me at the hospital? Then I'd like you to drive me there."

Jane dashed into the room, Kal close behind. "Did you say what I thought you said?" When she spied the wet floor, she said, "Right. I'll phone him."

"Don't worry about the practice," Kal said. "I'll handle everything."

"Thanks, Kal. I know you will ... Aaagh! ... contraction ..."

Vera had Jane go upstairs for the hospital bag she had prepared weeks before, and they set off for Pleasant Valley Hospital.

Vera sat in a wheelchair, filling out forms, Jane standing at her side, when Noah arrived. He kissed Vera lightly on the cheek. "Can I help with the paperwork?" he asked.

Vera shook her head. "I'm fine." She turned to Jane. "Now that Noah's here, I think you should go back to the clinic and help Kal handle things there."

"Will do. Call me if you need anything."

"Have you seen a doctor yet?" Noah asked.

Vera smiled wanly. "No. In a hospital, documents have priority over medical matters. My OB-GYN is en route, however. She'll be here soon."

"My God! You mean she's not even here? What if the baby comes before she gets here?"

Vera took his hand. "Will you relax? Haven't you ever heard of 'labor'? A baby isn't born instantaneously."

"Oh. Right."

"You are the archetype of an anxious father, you know. It's a good thing I had Jane drive me here and not you ... Aaagghh!"

"What is it?"

"Another contraction. It's okay. Everything is proceeding the way it's supposed to."

At that moment, Dr. Kingsley walked in. She took Vera's hands in hers and asked for details of her labor. She had Vera taken to the birthing ward while a nurse tossed Noah a set of scrubs. "You can come in when you've put these on," she said, pointing to a changing room.

Anneke Weiss was working through the complex syntax of HTML for a summer course in advanced web programming. She welcomed the distraction of Jane's ringtone.

"C'mon over and keep me company," said her friend.

"Sure," Anneke replied eagerly. "I can get more studying done there than at home." Anneke arrived before noon. The two women walked to a Thai restaurant not far from the clinic. Jane told Anneke of the new idea for attacking FHF.

Anneke shook her head. "I've got to tell you, I'm surprised that Dr. Chamberlin is so involved with finding a cure. I know, I know—he wasn't the source of the epizootic ... I guess I have a lingering prejudice against him. It's my problem, not his."

"Deal with it," said Jane. She smiled at her friend. "He's really an okay guy." She twirled a forkful of Pad Thai. "Getting back to FHF—the big stumbling block is finding cats that haven't been exposed. That's becoming just about impossible. Vera had this idea to try to find feral cats that might not have had contact with the virus."

"That's a pretty good idea. I could help."

"What idea? Oh, you mean the feral cats?"

"Yeah. There are ferals all over. Some live in out-of-the-way places and have no contact with other cats or with humans."

"How do you know so much about feral cats?"

"You know how I feel about animals ... and animal rights. Well, I belong to a group called the Feral Cat Coalition. They're headquartered in San Diego. Before FHF, they used to locate feral cats, capture them, and immunize them against enteritis, rabies—the usual viruses. The FCC would often pay to have ferals spayed or neutered, so they wouldn't spawn even more feral cats."

Jane laughed. "What's the Federal Com ... oh ... FCC is Feral Cat Coalition."

"Sorry. Members just call it the FCC. Anyway, when the cats recovered from the operation, they'd be released in the area where they were captured.

"There are chapters in the USA and in Canada—other countries too. I'll bet members would do anything they could to help beat FHF. Let me look into it."

"Anneke, that's great! I'll tell Vera as soon as she rejoins the human race."

Anneke chuckled. "You mean giving birth makes a woman inhuman? That sounds like something a man might say."

Vera's labor lasted seven hours. By day's end, she and Noah were the parents of a healthy six-pound-three-ounce baby girl named Lilith. Noah kept moving about the bed snapping mother-and-child pictures. "Will you stop that?" cried Vera. "You're driving me crazy."

Noah put the phone in his pocket. "Years from now, you'll treasure those photos," Noah protested.

Vera nodded. "Yeah, I guess I will." She stroked Lilith's tiny cheek. "Isn't she beautiful?"

"You're both beautiful. I think this may be the happiest day of my life."

Vera took his hand. "Me too. I love you both so much."

They remained thus, utterly at peace for a time as Lilith took her nourishment.

Later, after the nurse had taken the infant, Vera told Noah about Dorothy's pledge of funds for the microsurgery equipment. "Now we have to locate some cats. That's apt to be the biggest hurdle of all."

"You've just given birth to our child, and all you have on your mind are the damned cats?"

Without humor, Vera looked him in the eye. "Lilith is not a problem. The extinction of domestic cats is unthinkable."

As spring pushed winter out of the way, sparrows, wrens, finches, and other migratory birds returned to their summer quarters. In cities all over North America, men, women, and children had to cope with huge flocks. Nora Saunders of Boise, Idaho, loved the melodious call of the swarms of finches. But soon, the cacophonous chatter of sparrows in the thousands drowned out the finches.

It wasn't long before birds became a nuisance—and then a menace. Sparrows, starlings, and finches nested everywhere, as did other species. Using a broom, Sam Landesman removed the twenty or so nests from under the eaves of his home in Newark. A few days later, they had been rebuilt. He counted at least ten different types of avians, several of which he didn't recognize.

Of course, trees were another favorite nesting venue. Beth and Lonnie Rodman could only manage five hours of sleep a night as the feathered creatures fought into the late hours over prime nesting sites. The noise was intolerable to the Wisconsin couple. They tried earplugs, white noise generators, pillows—nothing helped.

In Chattanooga, Ed Mason, a man who had always had an affinity for wild birds, was awakened in the middle of the night by a noise in his attic. Carrying a flashlight, he climbed up, opened the hatch, and beamed the light in. Suddenly, there was a flurry of wings and feathers and screeching. Ed quickly closed the wood panel. *What the hell is going on?* He brushed feathers and dust from his pajamas and hair. *Reminds me of that old Hitchcock movie,* The

Birds. He could still hear the fluttering and screeching noises from the attic. *Jeez, I hope those damn birds don't start attacking people like in the movie.* The next day, he phoned a pest-control company. He was told that, owing to huge demand, he'd have to wait a week before they could send someone out. Ed moved to a hotel in town for the duration. When the exterminator finally came, he said that all over town, wherever attic vent openings weren't properly screened, birds were getting in and building nests.

Rob Lichtman, violinist with the Santa Rosa Chamber Ensemble, was now in his seventh year of AIDS. The newest antiviral cocktail had proved to be a miracle drug for patients infected with HIV. While his partner, Zane, folded laundry in the dining room of their home in the Northern California town, Rob practiced his bowing for an upcoming performance of Beethoven's third string quartet. All at once he gave out a guttural sound, fell to the floor, and began writhing uncontrollably.

"Robby! Robby!" cried Zane. He knelt and cupped Rob's head in his hands. He grabbed a towel from the table and forced it between Rob's teeth; he then dialed 911. When the EMTs arrived, they checked for vitals and transported Rob and Zane to the hospital. Later, the attending physician told the frightened Zane that he'd been encountering more and more cases of relatively rare bird-transmitted diseases such as psittacosis and cryptococcosis.

"Has Mr. Lichtman been diagnosed with AIDS, or is he under radiation treatment for cancer?" asked the doctor.

"Why, yes," replied Zane. "Robby has AIDS. But it's under control with vironixal."

The doctor nodded. "I'm pretty certain Rob has a case of cryptococcosis. We'll know for sure after the lab work. It's a fungal disease that we find mostly in patients whose immune systems have been compromised. The fungus, actually a yeast, attacks the brain."

"Oh my gosh!" Zane cried.

The physician put his hands on Zane's shoulders. "With treatment, Rob will probably come out of this just fine." He explained, "This isn't an isolated case. The fungus is found in bird droppings, and, as you know, this is a big problem everywhere. We're seeing epidemics of avian-transmitted diseases in major cities like Milwaukee, Providence, Portland, Knoxville and many others."

23

June 2021   10,250,000

Jane arrived, just as a nurse was taking Lilith from Vera after a feeding. "Wait," said Jane. "May I see the baby?"

"Why, of course," answered the nurse, uncovering Lilith's face.

"She's got Dr. Chamberlin's dark hair," Jane noted good-naturedly, "but your face, Vera."

"Yes, she's got the Barnett high cheekbones. With the black hair, she looks Asian, doesn't she?"

"Uh huh, I see that. Are you sure Noah's the father?" Jane teased.

"Keep that up, and you'll be out of a job," Vera responded with humor.

"Where's Dr. Chamberlin?"

"He went out for a bite in the hospital cafeteria."

Jane pulled up a chair by the bed. "Do you remember Anneke Weiss, the computer science major? She was involved with those demonstrations against Dr. Chamberlin's research a couple of years ago."

"Of course I do," Vera answered. "How could I forget her? Why?"

"I had lunch with her today and told her of your idea to locate feral cats. It turns out that Anneke is a member of a feral-cat rescue group. She's going to try to get such groups to help with locating cats."

"That's wonderful, Jane, just wonderful! Thank you so much. And please thank Anneke for me. I was aware of the feral-cat organizations and was planning to contact some of them after Lilith was born. Of course, we'll be looking for cats that haven't had human contact or association with domestic cats."

"Yes, I discussed that with Anneke. She understands and will emphasize the fact when she contacts the members. When you're up to it, Anneke wants to talk with you about how to proceed further."

For her part, Anneke sent e-mails to feral-cat activists on her mailing list, one hundred twenty-three in all. She explained the new strategy and wrote that the scientists sought feral cats that had never had contact FHF virus. Anneke suggested looking for cat colonies in out-of-the-way places, away from human habitations. She made it clear that no one was to approach the cats, let alone try to capture them. It was essential that the animals not have any exposure to FHF.

The next day, replies were arriving in Anneke's inbox by the hundreds. She read each one and prepared a table that listed locations, number of cats in the colony, and any remarks offered by the sender.

Her mail described feral-cat colonies all over the planet. Some flourished on farmland in the central United States and Canada, some on islands in the Great Lakes. There were ferals throughout Australia and on many of its islands. Others nested in the foothills of the Alps, on uninhabited islands in the Pacific, on Catalina Island off the Southern California coast, and on the fringes of the Gobi Desert. Many of the communications mentioned feral-cat populations that clearly had had human or other feline contact, such as the wild cats inhabiting the London Dockyards in the UK. However, most of those populations had already succumbed to FHF. Anneke did not include the survivors in her catalog, because the cats were likely already infected with the virus. Not all of the e-mail was supportive. A man in Toronto knew of several feral-cat colonies in rural areas of Ontario but had no intention of telling the world where they were. He didn't want to have them exposed to FHF.

"I'd like to hire a nanny," Vera declared. "I've got to get started locating cats for our test. I need someone to take on as much of Lilith's care as possible."

"I'll be here," said Noah. "Not to worry."

"No, I want to hire a nanny, Noah. We can afford it."

Doris, a nanny-cum-housekeeper, arrived a few days later. *Finally, I can relax,* Vera thought. *Jane's looking after the clinic business. Kal can handle any emergencies ...* "I'm going to take a nap," she said to Doris.

"You go right ahead, ma'am; Lilith will be fine."

Vera was awakened by the ring of her phone; it was Jane informing the vet that Anneke wanted to discuss her search for feral cat populations. "Sure, tell her to come over," Vera replied. "I want to keep the momentum. Every day, more cats are dying."

Anneke arrived late that afternoon and showed Vera the list she had compiled, now displaying 237 annotated entries. "That's just wonderful!" cried the vet.

Lilith was so startled by the outburst that she separated herself from her source of nourishment and began to cry loudly. "Oops," Vera said. "I guess I need to keep my emotions under control." She quickly quieted the infant, and Lilith resumed nursing. The two women went over the list and highlighted the most promising colonies. Vera shook her head with concern. "Now we have to find a way to capture cats without contaminating them, and we need to set up a lab where we can house cats and perform the surgery. I don't see how we're going to accomplish all that." She put her head in her hands. "And the money. My God! This is going to cost a fortune."

"You know, don't you," offered Anneke, "there are thousands of people who would contribute money to bring the cats back." Vera raised her head and stared open-mouthed at the young woman. "That's right," continued Anneke, "there are already several charities collecting donations for cats. Perhaps you could start one too."

Vera rose, set Lilith down and hugged Anneke. "You are so helpful, I ..."

Money ... it's always about money. She phoned her accountant who, when he learned of the new baby, agreed to come out to the house that evening.

Lyle Kane, rosy-cheeked and plump, toted a laptop in one hand and an attaché case in the other. Vera welcomed him in.

"I've got Form 1023 right here," said Kane. "I'll enter the information while we talk. By the time I leave, it'll be ready to print out. Let's start with the name of the charity. What do you want to call it?"

Vera pondered a moment. "How about 'Feline Phoenix'?"

Kane nodded. "Sounds good. It's easy on the ear. But the phoenix is a bird, isn't it?"

"Yes, but it's a symbol of resurrection. It's appropriate."

"So be it. Feline Phoenix it is."

"You'll need a board of directors. Have you given that any thought?"

Vera shook her head. "Oh, heavens! I really don't want to be bothered with that stuff."

"Look, Vera, that's part of the process of establishing a nonprofit. Can't you get some of your friends involved? Then you can get them to prepare bylaws and choose officers. Think about it. If there weren't standards, anyone could declare themselves a tax-free corporation. Fraud would be rampant."

"Yes, I guess you're right."

"Will Feline Phoenix pass funds or services to any other organizations?"

Vera shrugged. "What kind of organizations?"

"Other charities, vet schools ... think a moment."

"Oh. I could do that?"

"Sure," Kane replied, "as long as such organizations advance your stated purpose."

"Even an entity of the federal government?"

Kane frowned. "For example ..."

"Don't laugh," Vera replied, "but I was thinking the CDC, should they get involved."

It took Kane only an hour to gather the information. "I'll have my secretary prepare the necessary papers. You should be good to go by Thursday."

When Angelo returned to Atlanta from his latest investigative trek, Dorothy told him of the new baby. She popped open her phone. "Marveloose!" he exclaimed when she displayed the photos. "Are mother and daughter both well?"

"Yes, they're doing fine." She told him of the plan to save the domestic cat and mentioned her donation to the effort.

"That's convincing," said Angelo. "Do you know what they have in mind?"

"Not really. Vera said that it wasn't a vaccine, and that it had to do with injecting something into eggs."

Angelo frowned. "Perhaps they are growing a virus in chicken eggs."

"No, I think she was talking about cat eggs."

Angelo laughed. "Cats don't lay ... oh." He raised his eyebrows. "I think I'll give Dr. Chamberlin a phone call."

Ten minutes later, after Angelo and Noah had exchanged amenities, Angelo said, "I hear that you have a new theory for treating the FHF virus. Is that right?"

"Wow! Word travels fast. Oh, you heard about it from Mrs. Kraakmo. I understand that she's going to contribute money for the experiment."

"Absolut. So you are calling it an experiment. That is the proper way for a scientist to approach the question. Would you mind telling me the plan?"

"Of course," replied Noah. He proceeded to describe in some detail the idea to use FeLV as a vector for carrying interfering FHF RNA genes.

"That is quite a clever plan, especially the idea to inject the vector into fertilized eggs."

"That's Vera's suggestion," Noah stated with pride. "In fact, she has some experience with injecting into fertilized eggs, and we plan to have her carry out that step."

"That's convincing ... There is the matter of finding uncontaminated cats to experiment with, however."

"Yes, that is a hurdle. Vera is thinking of looking for feral cats in out-of-the-way places."

"Feral? That means wild, yes?"

"That's right. Feral cats are cats that once belonged to someone and have either run away or been abandoned, or which have been born in the wild and never been domesticated."

Angelo was silent a moment. "But how will you capture these feral cats if you find them? Unless precautions are taken, they will immediately become exposed to FHF carried by the capturers."

"Right. I don't think our planning has gotten that far. We do have a place here in the BSL-3 lab where we can house them and keep them free from contamination."

"Hmmm. Uh, Noah, I'd like you to take your time on that part of the planning. I will have a talk with Dr. Bronkowski. Maybe I can get him to help with trained personnel."

"Sure. That's great! I'll tell Vera you called."

"Good. Please relay my congratulations to Dr. Barnett."

" Angelo! Her name is Vera!"

"Aha. Of course. Tell her I send my best wishes. I will talk to you again soon."

Although Bronkowski had enormous respect for Angelo's investigative acumen, he was ever wary of the star epidemiologist's manipulative ways, and was apprehensive when Angelo asked to speak with him.

"I have a request," Angelo said as he breezed into the chief's office. He was never one to waste time with small talk.

"I'm sure you do," responded Bronkowski.

"You don't have to be so hostile."

"Well, what is it, Angelo?"

"It's about the cats …"

Bronkowski interrupted, "Come on, Angelo. You know we exhausted all the funds for such projects. If the cats are to be saved, funding will have to come from the private sector."

"I didn't come here to ask for money … well, not really. Do you remember Noah Chamberlin, the molecular biologist?"

"Yes, of course," Bronkowski replied warily. "What about him?"

"He has a new idea for protecting cats against FHF virus. He and his wife, the veterinarian, have what I think is a sound approach." Angelo described the plan.

"That does sound like a plausible attack," admitted Bronkowski, "but, as I said, we have no money."

"No, we don't," said Angelo, "but we do have personnel." Before Bronkowski could interrupt, Angelo drove on. "Chamberlin's plan requires cats that haven't had contact with the virus. Dr. Barnett believes such cats might be found among feral populations. The problem is that the very act of capturing the cats is apt to infect them. That's where the CDC could help. We have trained field workers who could wear sterilized jumpsuits to keep from exposing the cats to the virus. They could spray the cats with disinfectant and transport them in disinfected cages to the labs where the procedures are to be performed."

Bronkowski frowned. "It's not like supplying personnel and equipment wouldn't cost anything, you know."

"True, but it would not require any new money. It could be funded by the present budget."

Bronkowski put his head in his hands and remained that way, mumbling to himself for over a minute. Angelo remained silent. Finally, Bronkowski raised his head and said, hoarsely, "Okay, I'll arrange it. Perhaps, if the plan actually works, we'll get some good PR out of the effort."

Angelo fired off a flurry of e-mails. First, he sent a message to Noah informing him that the CDC would be assisting with locating and capturing FHF-free feral cats. Next, he contacted his friend André Fidèle, the team leader for France's effort to preserve *Felis catus* at Paris's Pasteur Institute. He apprised the Frenchman of the plan and urged Fidèle to have the institute prepare a clean facility where feral cats could be isolated from the virus.

Fidèle replied within the hour, noting that he and his colleagues were excited by the news and that they were already preparing their BSL-3 labs to house and operate on any FHF-free cats they could find. He requested details of the surgical procedure to be carried out on the cats.

After returning home, Anneke assembled a set of instructions she downloaded from several websites for capturing feral cats. *This is a waste of time; nobody's going to read it.* She described so-called "live traps" available from several vendors. These were small, metal cages that allowed the cats to be captured without harming them. She advised setting them at night when cats were likely to feed. Newspaper was to be placed on the bottom of the cages to absorb waste and to allow the cats a surface on which to rest. It was important not to use too much newspaper, as it could interfere with the trap mechanism. Canned mackerel was an effective bait and should be placed at the back of the trap so the cat wouldn't get hurt when door of the trap closes. She suggested that trappers conceal the trapdoor with a towel. After ferals are caught, they should be fed and watered as needed.

Anneke printed her cat-trapping manual and read it over. Not satisfied, she made a number of changes. Perfectionist that she was, Anneke prepared four drafts before she was pleased with the text.

The next day, Jane accompanied Anneke to Vera's clinic.

"I think you're amazing," Anneke remarked. "You just had a baby, and you're back at work already."

"Just a few hours a day, for now. I understand you've prepared some instructions for trapping feral cats." Anneke handed Vera the trapping procedure. Vera examined it in silence, nodding from time to time. "This is terrific, Anneke. I'll fax it over to the CDC, along with the list of likely locations of feral cats you gave me the other day."

"The CDC! How did they get involved?" After Vera filled her in, Anneke said, "I never met the Kraakmo guy, but I know of him. He's the scientist who discovered that FHF started in a Seattle zoo, right?"

"That's right, and now he's helping with the search for ferals. It's a team effort. There are the trappers from the CDC, and Noah and Gary, who are synthesizing the vector to inject into cat's ova. Mrs. Kraakmo is paying for some specialized equipment—it's all going to take a lot of money. I've formed a non-profit corporation I call the Feline Phoenix to receive donations."

Jane added, "Dr. Barnett is going to remove fertilized eggs from female cats and inject the stuff that Gary and Dr. Chamberlin are making."

"Yes," Vera acknowledged, "and let's not forget you, Anneke. The research you've done to identify likely feral-cat locations will prove invaluable, as will the instructions for trapping."

"Thanks, Vera. I'm glad to be of help." Anneke was pensive for a moment. "I guess I owe Dr. Chamberlin an apology. I used to think that his experimenting on cats had no justification. Now I …"

Vera gently placed her hands on Anneke's shoulders. "Thank you. Noah will appreciate that."

Anneke made ready to leave. "Say, Vera, I'm interested in this Feline Phoenix. Is it already functioning?"

"It will be in a few days."

"You know, I belong to several animal-rights groups that have been taking donations for the cats, but they don't know how to put the money to work. I think it would be great if they simply turned it over to you. This vector thing you and Dr. Chamberlin are doing may be the last chance the cats have. I'll contact the groups. What should I give as the address of Feline Phoenix?"

Vera was speechless.

By mid-July, three specially equipped vans were ready to depart from the CDC for areas Anneke Weiss had pegged as possible sites of FHF-free feral cats. The first three were an abandoned farmstead in Nebraska, the outskirts of a town called Wheatland on the Platte River in Wyoming, and several abandoned farms in California's San Joaquin Valley, near Fairmead. The vans, each with two technicians, set out caravan style from Atlanta.

One van parted from the others at Nashville and headed for California on I-40. The other two continued north toward Nebraska and Wyoming.

Richard Sitwell, a veteran CDC tech, woke from a short nap. "I don't know why they didn't just send a van from a California office," he remarked.

"C'mon, Rick," replied Sanjay Singh. "Look behind you. These three cat vans are unique."

"Right." Sitwell shrugged. He glanced at a GPS map. "Hey, you want to spend a couple of hours in Vegas?"

"Nah," answered Singh. "I don't gamble. It's a no-no in my religion."

Sitwell looked over at his partner but kept his tongue.

After three hours, Singh said, "You ready to spell me? I'm getting sleepy."

"Sure. Pull out at the next rest stop. Shall we stop for the night or head straight through?"

"As long as one of us can drive, I'd like to get to California as soon as possible. The sooner we fill this crate with cats, the sooner we can get back home."

Sitwell frowned. "That's three days of driving."

"Yeah, I guess that is a bit much," acknowledged Singh. "Let's stop in Oklahoma City for the night."

"Can you imagine this trip without air conditioning?" Sitwell asked rhetorically as the van sped across the Mojave Desert.

"You're such a wimp," replied Singh. "At least it's not humid, like Atlanta."

"Hey! Highway 58 coming up."

"Right. Then we hit the 99 at Bakersfield."

The van arrived at Fairmead at two in the afternoon.

The techs had been given approximate locations of the farms and had no trouble locating the first one. They got out of the van and donned disposable sterile outfits, consisting of reinforced paper jumpsuits, masks, goggles, disposable booties over their shoes, and latex gloves.

"Let's look in there first," Sitwell said, pointing to a decaying two-story farmhouse, its once-white clapboard siding now mostly gray. The front door swayed on one hinge. The techs pushed it aside and went in.

"Look," said Singh, "there's still furniture here. I figured the place would be empty."

"Maybe the people left in a hurry," Sitwell offered.

Singh frowned. "Or someone died … The carpet seems to be in good shape." He walked over to a wall where a group picture was hanging. "This must be the family that lived here," he observed. "I'll look around down here. You take the upstairs. Watch out for those stairs. They don't look very secure."

"Yeah. I take the risks, and you get the cushy jobs," Sitwell answered good-naturedly. Although there were a few loose boards,

Sitwell negotiated the stairs without mishap. He went from room to room, shining his LED flashlight into every corner. This must have been one grand mansion in its day, he mused, noting that there were four bedrooms upstairs and a huge living room below. Mounds of termite dross were everywhere. Sitwell gingerly stepped over clumps of plaster fallen from the ceiling.

Downstairs, Singh was equally thorough. He even descended rickety steps to a large cellar. He noted plenty of spiders and old mouse droppings, but no cats. After examining every part of the house, they had found no evidence suggesting any feral cats were in the dwelling.

"Let's try the barn," Sitwell suggested.

The huge doors of the once-red barn lay on the ground, their hinges long since rusted away. Inside, the two men spied an old horse bridle hanging on a nail. Singh ran his hand over the leather straps, but it crumbled when touched. The roof was missing several boards, allowing rectangular beams of sunlight to penetrate.

"Look over there," said Singh.

Sitwell looked in the direction indicated by his colleague. "Aahh," he said. "We've come to the right place." At the end of the barn away from the main entrance, he made out scattered bird feathers and rodent bones. "Those tamped-down areas look like they might be birthing nests," he said.

Singh whispered, "Rick! Here."

Sitwell's gaze followed Singh's pointing finger. There, in the dark corner, he spied a mound of sleeping kittens—no mother cat. "Looks like three or four," he said, softly. "Can't be more than a week old."

Singh nodded. "Let's get out of here."

Back at the van, the men agreed to wait until nightfall. Singh read a magazine. Sitwell perused Anneke's trapping guide on his PDA. Sitwell grunted, "Hmmmph."

"What?"

"Says here that we should put some closed traps in places where the cats are likely to pass and then wait a few days."

"Yeah," Singh said, "I remember. We're supposed to let the cats get used to the cages for several days before we set the traps."

"It doesn't say if we should put bait in the traps during the wait."

Singh eyed the page. "No, but the woman's cell number is right there. Why don't you phone her?"

"Right." Sitwell tapped the phone number. "This is Rick Sitwell with the CDC," he said. "I'm calling from central California. My colleague and I have located some feral cats at a site on your list …"

"CDC?" Anneke interrupted. "You're calling from the CDC? You're actually using the list?"

Sitwell laughed at her reaction. "Isn't that why you collected the information?" He asked.

"Well, yes, of course … I … I'm really glad that it's helping."

"And, no," Sitwell added, "we work for the CDC. We're calling from an abandoned farm near Madera." He explained that two other groups were heading for areas on Anneke's list. He heard sobs. "Are you okay?"

"Yes, I'm fine. It's just that nobody told me that you guys were actually using the list."

Sitwell said, "Then I'm happy to be the one to tell you. I have a question about the trapping guide …"

"You're using the guide too? Oh my God!"

Singh shook his head. Sitwell shrugged. "Isn't that why you prepared it? To assist us with finding and trapping feral cats?"

"Yes, of course! Yes!"

"I've got to tell you it's well-written. I've read manuals written by CDC professionals that aren't as clear."

"Thank you. Oh, thank you—so, what's your question?" she asked between sobs.

"As I said, we found a litter of newborn kittens. Haven't seen the mother yet."

"You didn't touch the kittens, did you?" Sitwell sensed that she was now all business. "If you handle the kittens, the mother might abandon them … what's your question again?"

Sitwell rolled his eyes. "We plan to set up trapping cages without setting them, as directed in the guide. Should we place bait in the trap?"

"I left that out? I'm really sorry. Yes. Absolutely. Put a small amount of mackerel near the cage. It doesn't even have to be inside."

"Got it. Thanks for the info. I'll pass it on to the other groups."

After they positioned the traps, the two techs drove into Madera to grab a meal and secure a motel room.

On Saturday, the techs drove back to the farm from Madera and, after sunset, laid sterile absorbent paper in the bottoms of the traps and a chunk of canned mackerel at the back. After propping up each trap's door, they placed a sterile towel over the trap, leaving just the opening uncovered. Again, they drove back to town.

When they returned the next day, two of the traps held hissing, spitting, angry felines. The techs lugged them to the van, where they sprayed the cages and their furious occupants with a disinfectant known to kill all bacteria and viruses. This, of course, enraged the cats even more.

"My God," said Singh, "I'd hate to meet up with one of those in a dark alley in the middle of the night."

"Yeah," answered Sitwell, "I see why some people hate cats."

The van had been outfitted with a total of twelve enclosures, six on each side. Each of these boxes was separated from those adjacent by a plastic barrier. When the cage door was shut, the interior was effectively sealed off from the cab of the van. A closed, forced-air blower, powered by the van's electrical system, provided ventilation. The air passed through two HEPA filters before it reached the cat boxes.

After a half-hour, Sitwell said, "That's long enough. There can't be any infectious virus particles left on the fur." They held each of the traps in its turn up to the door of a cage and pulled up the trap's door. Singh prodded the snarling animals with a sterile stick, forcing them out of the traps and into the boxes.

That night, Singh and Sitwell disinfected the traps and reset them. The next day three more trapped ferals had been caught. By Tuesday, the van had its full complement of twelve. Sitwell and Singh prepared to head for Camarillo with their feline cargo.

Singh asked, "What about those kittens in the barn?"

"Oh shit! I forgot about them," said Sitwell. "They're probably dead already. Without milk from the mother, they can't last long."

"Let's go check," Singh suggested.

When they entered the barn, Singh was the first to see the queen with her litter. "Look, over there. Looks like Mama escaped our traps." The mother cat growled and hissed at the intruders, her hair standing up and ears flattened.

Sitwell started walking backward. "I think we'll just leave her and her family alone," he suggested.

"Right. Let's get out of here!" They turned and tore out of the barn.

Shortly, the van was headed to Camarillo. As they already had filled their cages, the two technicians would not need to visit the other two abandoned farms. Perhaps they would on another trip. The two other vans were en route back to the CDC with twenty-two ferals—just two shy of their full complement.

For decades, feral cats, called bush cats in the land down under, had proved to be an ecological disaster throughout Australia, including Tasmania and the smaller islands. Many native species of birds and small marsupials had been driven to extinction, owing to predation by feral cats and by several other non-indigenous species imported by the early Europeans.

The Aussies were evenly divided on whether to kill all the cats or to use other means to keep them from further harming the native fauna. When the call for feral cats arrived, many Australians felt that it wouldn't be such a disaster if the species became extinct. One vocal group in Western Australia wanted to pass legislation making it a crime to assist with the perpetuation of the species *Felis catus.* They failed.

In any case, quite a few Australians mourned the loss of their pet cats and chose to help with the project. As in other countries, there were feral cat societies, and, when Anneke's e-mail message reached them, members of these groups were able to identify areas throughout the continent where FHF-free feral cats might be found. Ultimately, the Aussies rounded up forty-seven cats free of the virus. These were all sent to the Moscow Institute of Veterinary Medicine, where a special facility had been erected to house and experiment with feral cats, using Vera's procedure and Noah's vector.

24

Noah was eager to show Vera around the revamped BSL-3 lab. "You're going to love it," he said as he unlocked the first of two locks on the reinforced door.

"I've looked at the plans, honey. I don't expect to be surprised."

"Just wait." He opened the door, flipped a red switch just inside, and took Vera's hand.

"What's that switch?" Vera asked.

"It turns off the UV germicidal lamps. They're kept on all the time, except when there are personnel or cats in the lab."

Vera looked unhurriedly around the room. "Well, it's certainly more crowded than I had expected."

"Yes," Noah agreed. "Probably too congested. You know, it almost qualifies as a BSL-4 hot lab."

Vera pointed to a separate windowed chamber at the far end. "What's that?"

"That's where the incoming cats will be held in isolation cages until they can be checked for FHF."

Vera nodded. "And I see that the operating area is also enclosed within its own inner room—oh! There's the laparoscope."

"That's what you asked for, isn't it? The computer and monitor are below the table. You raise them to working height with a foot pedal."

"Noah, I'm scared … seeing all this stuff …"

Noah put his hands on Vera's shoulders and faced her. "I know," he said. "Me too." He was silent a moment, and then he took her hand. "We're going to do it. We're going to win the war against this FHF virus."

A single tear plunged from Vera's right eye to the floor. She moved forward and hugged Noah. "I know we will," she whispered. "I know."

Facilities similar to those in Camarillo had been constructed at the CDC, the Pasteur Institute, and the Moscow Institute for Veterinary Medicine. These centers had engaged veterinarians who were proficient, not only in routine feline surgery, but in microsurgery as well. Each had been put through a crash course in Vera's planned methodology. All the labs had received a plentiful supply of Noah's FeLV-FHF vector. The vets and their support technicians waited anxiously for feral cats to arrive from the hinterlands.

"Oh, crap!" Vera muttered when she spied the small crowd behind the thirty-foot circle of yellow tape around the loading dock at the rear of the institute. She had hoped to keep the date of the van's arrival confidential. A cadre of campus police stood guard over the area.

"Here they come," said Vera, pointing to the CDC van pulling into the parking area at the rear of the institute. She and Kal wore disinfected jumpsuits—not to protect themselves from the cats, but to shield the animals from any FHF the vets might be carrying on their persons.

Kal picked up two of the special transport boxes. The containers had been constructed at the CDC; each was large enough to house a trapping cage. They had been disinfected with ethylene oxide gas and sealed in sterile plastic wrap.

The two vets proceeded to the van, where the two CDC techs were donning their disinfected outfits. Vera was to supervise the transfer of the feral cats to the lab.

"Kal," she called.

He turned. "What? Is something wrong?"

"No mistakes. This has to be perfect. No FHF gets near the cats."

Kal nodded. "Vera, we've rehearsed the transfer for a week. It'll be okay."

"Sorry. I didn't mean to badger you."

At the van, Kal held a box while Vera removed the plastic bag. Although she had examined diagrams, this was her first look inside a trapping van. *My God, they really did a great job ... everything's so white.*

Inside, Sitwell released the retaining latches of the first cage and disconnected its air hose. He withdrew a sterile HEPA filter from its container and screwed it into the air port. "You have about three minutes until this cat runs out of oxygen."

Vera took a deep breath. "Kal, you take this one in. I'll start on the next."

Kal and Vera took turns moving each of the twelve hissing, spitting, feral cats—six females and six males—into the BSL-3 lab. Vera recorded any details she thought might be relevant. "It's up to us now," Vera remarked. "Let's get to work."

After a lengthy routine of decontamination, Vera and Kal took several hours to complete preliminary workups. The animals were unruly. "Here, Kal," she said, "try this." She handed him a small bag of catnip.

"No good," he replied. "They won't touch it. They just cower at the back of the cage."

Vera sighed. "All right. Put on the canvas gloves and hold the cats down. I'll inject ketamine. That'll knock them out for an hour or two."

When the first of the cats was under, the two vets drew blood, after which they declawed its front paws. Vera knew that the wild cats could be unpredictable and were likely to scratch or rip the gloves or garments of anyone handling them. She had decided declawing was the prudent strategy. Finally, before the cats recovered from the anesthetic, Kal injected them with vaccines against feline enteritis and calicivirus.

"Damn!" said Vera when she looked over the serological test results. "Two of these cats test positive for FHF—one male, the other female." She gazed at the tiny wells, trying to think of another interpretation. "And then there were ten … Kal, would you see that the two infected cats are taken to the clinic? They can spend the rest of their short lives there."

"Sure … uh, there's something else," he said as he handed Vera a stack of data sheets.

"What?"

"One of the other females has been spayed."

Vera shook her head. "Well, it's not surprising. Remember, those organizations that capture feral cats and immunize them often have the animals spayed or neutered. Nine out of twelve … I guess it could have been worse."

The remaining cats were housed in special cages inside the BSL-3 area. Each of the spacious chambers was equipped with sterilized bedding, food, and water, self-emptying litter boxes, and a variety of playthings for the cats.

Vera divided her time between baby Lilith and the Feline Phoenix project.

A few days after the first load of cats, a second van arrived with seven more. Three were removed immediately when they showed symptoms of FHF. "Now we're up to thirteen," said Vera as she deftly transferred a soiled diaper into a laundry hamper.

"Yep," Noah replied. "I'm keeping score, you know."

Vera looked up. "What do you mean, 'keeping score?'"

"Here," said Noah, "look." He turned his e-reader toward her. "Angelo e-mails me updates almost every day."

Vera looked over the list. "Thirteen cats here at the institute … that's right. Five test cats at the CDC, eight cats at the Pasteur Institute, and eight at the Moscow lab. So as far as we know, there are thirty-four fertile cats available for testing with the vector."

On the appointed day, Vera and Kal drove to the institute with the materials and equipment they needed for semen collection. Jane remained at the clinic in case she was needed to bring anything they'd forgotten.

When they arrived at Noah's office, Vera declared, "It's showtime."

"What happens now?" Noah asked.

"Today, we do three procedures. First we'll inject three of the females with gonadotropin to stimulate superovulation. That way, we should have plenty of oocytes ready to harvest tomorrow. Second, we'll inject four other females—the ones that will receive the embryos later—with FSH to induce estrus."

"What's FSH, and why do the mother cats have to be in estrus? They're not going to be mating, are they?"

Vera explained, "FSH stands for follicle-stimulating hormone. We shoot it into muscle tissue every day, until the queen shows signs of estrus. This should take three or four days. The reason we want the donor queens in estrus is that the embryo transplants are only likely to take if the recipient cat is in the same physiological state as the mother cat would be if the ovum had been fertilized naturally."

"Whew! I had no idea there was so much to this."

"Yeah, it's almost as complicated as molecular biology." Vera smiled wryly. "Anyway, once the mother-to-be is in estrus, we inject gonadotropin, just as we'll do with the egg donors. Also, today, we plan to collect semen from the toms."

Noah wondered, "How do you do that? Masturbation?"

"No. That's one way—some vets use an artificial vagina—but it's much easier to use electroejaculation."

"Aaghh! Doesn't sound humane."

Vera grinned. "Actually, it is. The male is anaesthetized and has no awareness of the procedure. When he wakes up, he's normal and in no pain. Who knows, maybe he has an erotic dream during the process."

Noah chuckled. "Is there anything I can do to help?" he asked.

"Not with the semen collection. We'll extract the oocytes from three of the queens tomorrow. After we do the IVF, I'll need your magic bullet prep. You can thaw it and hold it on ice until we're ready." They were now referring to the FeLV vector with its attached FHF genes as the "magic bullet," an expression popularized over a century earlier by the German chemist Paul Ehrlich to refer to chemicals that fight microbial infections without harming the patients.

"What's IVF?" asked Noah.

"In-vitro fertilization."

"Oh, right. You guys use as much jargon as molecular biologists, don't you? I've got a dozen vials of the vector in the ultra-cold freezer. I'll thaw a couple of them as soon as I get in tomorrow morning."

"Fine. I'll have Jane and Kal with me to help with the surgery. Jane will act as surgical nurse and Kal as an assistant surgeon." She frowned. "Sounds pretentious, doesn't it?"

Noah smiled. "I think you're entitled to any pretentions you fancy."

She squeezed his hand. "One thing you can do," she said, "is help Doris look after Lilith. I'm going to be spending more time here for the next few days than I have recently."

"No problem. I can run home in the middle of the day."

Vera made use of the shower adjacent to the lab, washing down thoroughly with hexachlorophene soap. Kal did the same. The two vets donned sterile surgical scrubs, complete with facemasks, hoods, and paper booties over their shoes. They scrubbed their arms a second time with surgical soap and Betadine. No way were they going to introduce any FHF into the lab. Before entering, Vera switched off the UV lamps.

"Okay, that's it," Kal remarked, after he'd injected the three females with gonadotropin. "Let's go collect the semen. Romeo's first, right?"

In keeping with the tradition set in Noah's lab, the thirteen feral cats had been named after Shakespearian characters. After several days in captivity, the first donor, Romeo, had become somewhat conditioned to his cage and to the lab environment. Kal, with the help of a pinch of catnip, met little resistance when he opened the sliding door and reached in. With a small electric clipper, he shaved Romeo's right forepaw to expose the cubital vein, while Vera readied a syringe containing ketamine mixed with diazepam. While Kal held the tom steady, Vera injected the mix.

"He's under," Vera said. Kal took the teflon-coated electrode and inserted it in the cat's rectum. He switched on the power supply and applied a succession of rapid-fire stimuli. Vera collected the resulting semen in a small vial containing a holding buffer. When they were done, Kal gently placed Romeo back in his cage. The vets collected specimens from two other toms, Polonius and Lear, in the same manner. The semen would be used the next day, so Vera decided simply to keep the vials unfrozen in an ice bath overnight.

Later, when Kal examined the first of the semen samples with Noah's microscope, he raised a fist in the air and shouted, "Yes! Good sperm count with excellent motility."

Vera let out a lungful of breath she'd unconsciously held in. "Ah, good," she sighed.

The other two specimens showed favorable sperm counts also. Before they left for the day, Vera and Kal removed the food dishes from the two gonadotropin-treated females. Tomorrow, the queens would be egg donors.

Vera, Kal, and Jane arrived at six the next morning, carrying several large cases of surgical supplies—instruments, a small tank containing compressed carbon-dioxide gas, anesthetics, buffers, and the like. As soon as she had showered and put on sterile garments, Vera took the semen samples out of the ice bath to warm them. They would sit at room temperature for several hours to allow capacitation of the spermatozoa. She then removed the water dishes from the two females that were to serve as egg donors.

Kal and Jane soon joined Vera and prepared for the surgery. "All right, team," Vera pronounced officiously, "let's review. The procedure is to extract egg cells from the donor queens, fertilize the ova *in vitro* with semen collected yesterday, and, after fertilization occurs, to inject the bullet vector into the nuclei of the cells. Kal, continue."

"Testing me, are you? Okay, then. We'll incubate the fertilized eggs for four or five days, until the cells divide a few times. Finally, we'll transplant the embryos into the four recipient females. With luck, they'll develop into FHF-resistant kittens."

"Good, Kal." Vera shook his hand. She hugged him, and Jane joined. They remained in a tri-part huddle for almost a minute.

After several hours, everything was ready. "I think we should eat something before we start," Vera suggested. None of them had eaten breakfast, and it was now approaching nine o'clock.

After removing their special clothing, they took a quick meal at the campus cafeteria, with Noah along to offer what encouragement he could. When they returned, the three again went through the tedious process of showering, disinfecting, and donning the scrubs.

While Noah watched through a window, Vera anaesthetized Ophelia, the first of the queens to donate her eggs. When she was sure that the cat was unconscious, Vera positioned her on the surgical table.

"Tie her limbs, will you, Kal?"

He quickly tied Ophelia's four legs to hooks at the sides of the table. Jane grasped electric shears and shaved the skin of the cat's lower abdomen, after which Vera swabbed the area with Betadine and surgical soap. Kal then draped sterile cloths over most of the animal, leaving only a small rectangle of skin exposed.

"Okay, Kal, inject the carbon dioxide."

Kal picked up a sterile needle attached to a long, flexible length of tubing that extended from the small tank. He inserted it through the exposed skin of the cat into the abdomen. He nodded to Jane, who twisted the valve on the tank through a small arc. The trio could see the abdomen begin to expand.

"It's like blowing up a balloon," Jane remarked. "Why are we doing this? I forgot."

"It makes it much easier to work inside. If all the organs were sitting on top of one another, it would be difficult to get around with these delicate instruments."

When all was ready, Vera made small cuts with a scalpel, first through the dermis, and then through the abdominal wall. With a grabber, she pulled the cat's left ovary toward the opening and handed the instrument over to Jane as she said, "I want you to hold this as steady as you can."

"Right."

Vera nodded. "Kal, would you position the laparoscope, please?"

She took hold of the probe with her right hand and the aspirating needle with her left. Jane held the collecting tube with her other hand.

Vera checked the computer screen as she moved the probe. "Hah!" she announced after a few seconds. "Several oocytes to choose from. Suction, please." Kal turned on the aspirator, and Vera maneuvered the needle over the ovary, where she could see the oocytes. Each time she lowered the needle, she heard a faint *sshloop* as small bits of ovary were sucked into the collecting tube.

"All right, that's three so far. Let's get some from the other side." Vera took the grabber from Jane and allowed the ovary to settle back into its natural position. "Now pull up the right ovary," she said, handing the grabber back to Jane. Vera then carefully guided the probe to the organ and harvested four more oocytes from the right side.

When they were done with Ophelia, Kal carefully closed the small incision. Gently, he carried Ophelia to her cage to recover. Vera waved to Noah through the window and held up her thumb in an okay sign. Noah pointed to his watch and indicated that he had to get to work. By mid-afternoon, the three surgeons had finished collecting oocytes from the other two females, Portia and Goneril.

"There," said Vera, pointing to the three small plastic culture dishes, "rest twenty-four microscopic cells that might provide the only hope for the survival of the domestic cat."

Vera and Kal now proceeded to carry out in vitro fertilization with feline semen collected the previous day. Vera sat down at the stereomicroscope and, with the help of the micromanipulator, carefully teased oocytes away from the tissue, transferring them to dishes containing buffered nutrients and antibiotics to inhibit bacteria and molds. For the next five hours, she and Kal took turns at the stereomicroscope, examining the dishes for signs of successful IVF.

Near the end of the first hour, Kal shouted, "Got one!"

"Let's see." Vera peered through the oculars and immediately spotted the thickened outer membrane on one of the oocytes, characteristic of fertilization. She could barely make out the two pronuclei—one from the egg and one from the sperm—until she cranked up the magnification. "Well, here we go. One small step for a vet, one giant leap for catkind … or so we hope."

As Kal and Jane looked on, Vera removed the fertilized egg to its own tiny transparent plastic dish. She loaded a small amount of the FeLV-FHF vector constructed by Noah and Gary into an extremely thin glass pipette attached to the micromanipulator.

Abruptly, Vera stood up and, eyes on the floor, paced around the room.

"What's the matter?" asked Kal.

"I'm just nervous, I guess. There's so much riding on this … we can't fail this time. We just can't."

Jane reached for Vera's latex-gloved hands and took them in her own. She said nothing, but looked into Vera's eyes, an expression of empathy on her face.

Vera regarded Jane and looked over at Kal. "Well, then," she sighed, "let's get on with it."

She sat back down at the scope and quickly located the fertilized egg. In a moment, she had injected what she hoped would be the magic bullet into each of the nuclei. She carried the dish over to an incubator, where it would sit for four or five days before the developing embryo would be transplanted into a recipient female cat.

Kal returned to the scope to look for more fertilized eggs. In the course of the next four hours, he and Vera found eighteen more and processed them in the same manner. Out of twenty-four oocytes, nineteen had become fertilized. Vera was not discouraged. She knew the success rate for IVF in cats was often lower.

For five days one or the other of the vets drove up to the institute to check on the developing embryos, to change the culture medium, and to inject the four future-recipient females with FSH. Vera was comforted by the fact that most of the eggs exhibited the expected cell division. Only four of the nineteen turned out to be non-viable. Meanwhile, Angelo sent daily e-mail messages relaying news from the CDC, as well as from France and Russia.

By Tuesday, three of the four recipient queens at the institute were showing signs of estrus. "Time to inject the gonadotropin," said Vera. "Will you take care of that, Kal?"

"Sure. Looks like the embryos are about ready for transplanting. We have three new morulas today. I think we should start tomorrow and continue on Thursday, if necessary."

"Tomorrow it is."

Vera, Kal and Jane prepared for another day of surgery. With Noah watching from the observation room, the trio set up equipment for the next series of operations. Each of the queens would receive either three or four viable embryos.

Vera opened the door to the cage of the black-and-white female they had named Gertrude. The cat hissed briefly, but, as Vera stroked her back and plied her with catnip, she calmed down.

"That's an appropriate name for a queen," Jane remarked.

Vera nodded. "There, there, milady," she said softly as she continued petting the animal. "We won't hurt you much. Wouldn't you like to be a savior of your species?"

The procedure for implanting the embryos was similar to that used to harvest the egg cells, but this time embryos were going in rather than eggs coming out. Vera manned the laparoscope, Kal again served as anesthesiologist, and Jane acted as surgical nurse. Vera deftly placed four embryos in Gertrude's left uterine horn.

"Wouldn't it be better to put two in one horn and two in the other?" asked Jane.

"You want to answer that, Kal?" Vera looked up from the cat at her colleague.

Kal grinned under his mask. "The reason is, Jane, that the embryos don't get implanted right away. They move around quite a bit for several days, and some will migrate to the other horn. It'll be several more days before the embryos finally settle down and become fixed to the uterine wall."

When they'd finished with Gertrude, and Kal had closed the incision, the three continued with Juliet, a rather small, jet-black cat, and then two tabbies, Miranda and Jessica.

"Nothing to do now but wait," offered Vera.

Jane began cleaning the surgical equipment. "How long before we know if the cats are pregnant?" she asked.

"We'll start weighing them twice a week, starting tomorrow," replied Vera. "Just like human mothers, cats gain weight almost from the beginning of implantation. Then, in about two weeks or so, we can do ultrasound."

"Oh," remarked Jane, "I didn't realize that ultrasound was used on cats. I thought it was just for humans."

"Nope. We've got a portable ultrasound unit back at the clinic. It's about the size of a laptop computer, so we can bring it over. Of course, we'll have to disinfect it if we're to use it here. Anyway, that's several weeks off."

Vera and Kal again took turns driving up to the institute each day to feed and water the kings and queens, clean their cages, and weigh the queens. On the Saturday following the embryo implantation, Kal noticed small weight gains in all four of the females.

On Tuesday, Vera again put the cats on the scale. "Kal, look at this." She handed him the tablet in which they kept their records.

Kal took one look at it and smiled. "That's it, then. All four are pregnant. We're going to have kittens."

August gave way to September. A high-pressure system over the Mojave Desert had warmed Camarillo to eighty-four degrees by mid-morning, as hot air rushed from the desert to the sea. Inside the air-conditioned rooms of the institute, nobody minded as the temperature was a comfortable seventy-four degrees. Vera prepared to perform the first ultrasound check of the pregnant queens, beginning with Miranda. Word had spread, and, outside the observation window of the BSL-3 cat lab, a small crowd had gathered, consisting mostly of technicians from elsewhere in the building and a few students. Noah too was a spectator. Lilith lay nestled in his arms. *The Star* had sent a reporter and photographer.

Jane held Miranda on the table. Vera booted the ultrasound computer.

She looked up at Jane. "Ready?" At Jane's nod, she held the wand over the cat's abdomen. She had positioned the monitor so that it was visible by the visitors, enabling all to see what she saw. "Here we go." In a moment she found it—a minute, rapid movement. Vera took a deep breath. *I can't let those lookie-loos see me cry.* She held up her two thumbs and forefingers toward the window and formed a heart symbol. She could barely hear the cheer from the spectators through the thick glass, but when she looked up, they were applauding. She moved the wand further down the abdomen. There was another tiny beater. The group needed no prompt this time and cheered again. Vera positioned the wand on the other side of the cat's belly. There she found a third beating heart. Miranda had received only three embryos. All had implanted successfully.

"Looking good," Vera said, hoarsely. "Jane! Keep the cat still!" Vera looked up to see Jane had let go, her hands groping for a tissue to wipe the tears streaming down her face. Vera laughed, and then she cried. The women hugged each other. Miranda lay quietly.

"Oh shit!" said Vera. "I forgot. We have an audience." She glanced at the visitors. They were still clapping; some were laughing, some crying.

Ophelia carried three viable fetuses also; one of the four she had received had not survived. Juliet and Jessica showed only two each.

"Ten out of fifteen," noted Vera. "That's better than I hoped for."

Jane said, "Oh? I was hoping for 100 percent."

"No, the success rate for embryo transplantation in cats generally runs around 50 percent. We got two-thirds."

"In that case, congratulations." She pointed at the cages. "Should we check the second batch?"

"No, it's a little too early for them. Remember, they received embryos a few days after the first group."

The crowd outside drifted away, but Noah remained. When Vera emerged from the lab, he gave her a hug.

"Watch out," she grunted. "You'll crush Lilith."

"Nah. I've got her."

"Here, let me hold her." Vera took the sleeping bundle. "You know," she remarked, "about eleven months ago, our little girl didn't look much different than those cat embryos."

Noah nodded. "This is a major milestone, isn't it? Nothing to do now but wait for the mothers to give birth."

"Yes. We're almost there. If the CDC manages to locate more feral cats, we could doctor some more embryos, but I understand that they've not been finding anymore."

A week later, Vera examined the first gravid queens for the second time. A smaller group of observers was assembled outside the window. As she moved the wand over Jessica's belly, Vera said, "There. See? Now there's a head."

Jane scanned the monitor. "I don't see ... oh, that round thing." She pointed at the monitor and then at her own head. The spectators saw it too. Jane and Vera could barely hear their applause through the wall.

All ten of the embryos were viable and developing as they should. Now it was time to check the second group. Jane retrieved a gray tabby named Helena from its cage and placed it on the table. The feral cats were still somewhat resistant to human handling, but could be calmed by constant petting and soothing talk. After a few minutes, Helena had stopped struggling and actually began to purr as Jane stroked her belly. "Must have been someone's pet cat at one time," Vera observed. She scanned the abdomen and shortly detected a diminutive beating heart, followed by another.

"Looks like only two viable embryos in this one," Vera remarked. "Let's check the rest." The other three queens, Diana,

Hermione, and a part-tabby, part-spotted female they had named Lady Macbeth—they called her Lady M—harbored six among them. Vera could find only one living embryo in Lady M. All in all there were now eighteen feline embryos in the BSL-3 cat lab at the institute.

Angelo, was in constant contact with the Paris and Russian groups. He kept Noah and Vera informed by e-mail. The Paris group now had thirty-seven viable embryos. They had lost one queen, carrying two embryos, to an unknown disease. She had just sickened and died. A necropsy failed to reveal the reason. The remaining twelve surrogate mothers were healthy, however. Several were already exhibiting nest-building behavior and were given piles of sterile cheesecloth to use at will.

The Moscow group had not received any additional feral cats after the first batch, but their fourteen embryos were developing normally. The CDC facility had received two more vanloads and was now host to sixteen gestating queens.

On Labor Day, Vera invited Jane and Gary over for barbeque. Vera propped Lilith against a cushion, and they enjoyed the shade by the pines. Noah manned the grill, while Gary and Jane tossed a Frisbee back and forth. Vera was exhausted. *Magic bullets, two-month-old baby girl, vet practice ... what was I thinking?* She noticed that Lilith's eyes followed the Frisbee whenever either Gary or Jane launched the disk.

Vera called, "Noah!" When he looked her way, she pointed at Lilith.

He came running over. "Son of a gun! That's new, right?"

"It's new." Vera was captivated by Noah's reaction to each new advance by their daughter.

"I wish it was time for the kittens to be born," Jane called. "The suspense is unbearable."

Gary walked over to Jane and put his hands on her shoulders. "You know," he said, "this whole idea is a long shot. It might well be a complete failure. Maybe the bullet didn't get incorporated into any of the embryonic DNA. Or, maybe some of the cats did get it, but it might not be oriented properly. There are a million things that can go wrong."

Jane put her finger to Gary's mouth. "Don't be such a pessimist. Can't you look on the positive side for once?"

"Sorry. I just don't want you to be crushed if none of the kittens survive."

"Is there any way to tell, after the kittens are born, if they have picked up the bullet?"

Noah called, "That's an interesting question, Jane. Gary, come over here a minute. Let's talk about that."

"What's on your mind?" asked Gary.

Noah was silent a moment. "Suppose we took some cells from the mouths of the kittens. We could use our RNA copy of the bullet to locate any DNA copies. We could either amplify them with PCR or confirm the bullet genes with pyrosequencing."

Gary nodded. "Right. If they're there, we should be able to find the sequences. Then we could at least predict which kittens will not be resistant to FHF."

"Yes, but finding a DNA copy of the bullet wouldn't guarantee that a kitten would be resistant."

Gary thought a moment. "Yeah, but if we could divide the kittens into two groups, one not likely to be resistant and the other possibly resistant, then, if, in fact, some of the possible group were resistant, that would be proof that our bullet worked."

"I wish you'd get out of the habit of using the word *proof* when you mean *confirmation*. But you're right. I think we should get set up to look at that." He turned toward the kitchen where Vera had gone to fix the salad. "Vera, did you hear that?"

"No," she called. "What is it?"

Noah described the plan to test the kittens for the presence of the bullet. "Can you get cells from a newborn kitten? Say, epithelia from inside the mouth?"

"Sure I can. That's a great idea." She paused. "Of course we may have a huge letdown. What if none of the cats has it? Then it's game over."

"Of course that's possible. But does it matter if we know that sooner rather than later?"

"I guess not. Oh, God, I'm scared. I thought I could take my mind off the cat thing for at least one day."

"I seem to recall," he replied with humor, "you chastising me once for saying something to that effect. You said that caring people were talking of little else these days. Remember that?"

"Yes. I guess the foot's in the other shoe."

"These patties are about done," said Noah, changing the subject. "Who wanted medium?"

The four sat down at the picnic table and did, somehow, manage to avoid the topic of FHF and the cats for the rest of the afternoon.

25

The fall Santa Ana winds wailed. In the BSL-3 cat lab, deep within the molecular-biology building, Vera and Kal could hear the shriek of moving air as it whipped around the building's corners.

"I think Miranda's going to have her kittens tonight," Vera mentioned. "She's been pacing back and forth in her cage and rearranging the bedding."

Kal nodded. "If I were the praying sort, I guess this would be the time."

When Vera arrived at the lab the next day, there they were—three tiny newborns. Vera approached Miranda softly. The three wee kittens were nursing. Miranda, eyes closed, was purring softly. *And they say that feral cats don't purr. Hah!* Vera examined the other gravid queens, and, by the time she returned to Miranda, the neonates were asleep. *I've got to sit down … I haven't seen a litter of kittens in two years.* She held her breath and drank in the sight. *Are these tiny creatures the last of their species? Or its resurrection?* One at a time she removed the kittens from the cage, weighed them, and, with a sterile cotton swab, brushed the sides of their mouths to obtain cells that Noah and Gary would use to find if the kittens had acquired the bullet genes.

Vera phoned Noah to tell him the news. He soon appeared, along with Gary and a few biochemistry students, and shortly, a small crowd had gathered outside the observation window. Vera dutifully held up the kittens for the onlookers' benefit, and, as she knew they would, the group applauded.

Later, when Vera brought the three vials containing the kittens' cells to Noah's lab, she said, "It's time for your part, my dear."

"Great! I'm glad to finally play a role in this drama."

"How long will it take to find out if these cats have the bullet?" she asked.

"Just a day or so. It's really not that much work. Gary, you want to get started on these?"

"Sure thing, Doc."

"It won't be too many days before we have more of these to process," Vera observed. I expect Gertrude is going to give birth any day."

"That's fine. Once we're set up to do these tests, it's pretty simple to do repeated runs. By the way," he added, "how are you going to name the kittens? I see you've labeled these tubes *A*, *B* and *C*. Can't we be more imaginative than that?"

"Hmmm. If we continue the Shakespearian theme, we may run out of names. Besides, I'm not sure of the sex of these kittens yet. I think we have two females and one male. It's hard to tell when they're just born. Let's wait until they are a few days old at least."

"*A*, *B* and *C* it is, then." He started to join Gary, and then turned abruptly. "Hey! Let's name the kittens after famous scientists!"

"I don't know if we could come up with enough female names," noted Vera.

"Sure we could: Marie Curie, Barbara McClintock, Grace Hopper, Ada Lovelace …" Noah paused for breath "Madame Lavoisier, Lise Meitner, Mary Leakey, Roz Franklin, Lynn Margulis, Vera Barnett-Chamberlin. There're lots of them."

"Oh, please. That last one doesn't belong."

Noah replied, "Oh, I don't know. History may decide otherwise."

"You're very kind, sir," she said, feigning a mock curtsey. "Anyway, as for the names, I'd rather stick to literature. Perhaps famous characters from novels." She laughed. "Can you imagine a cat saying 'Call me Ishmael'?"

Noah laughed. "Listen to us. As if choosing names for the kittens was at all important. What matters is if they survive FHF."

Tuesday morning of the following week, Vera relaxed at the clinic, reading the newspaper and sipping coffee, when a familiar figure entered. "Hello, Dr. Barnett, I hope I'm not disturbing you."

"No, I'm just taking a break. Uh, I know you, but I can't recall where from."

"Sorry. I'm Sandra McNally from *The Atlanta Journal-Constitution.*"

"Of course. Now I remember. You were here with Dr. Kraakmo last year."

"That's right. I'm still the lead reporter for FHF at *The J-C,* and I'd like to ask you a few questions, if you have the time. I've visited the CDC from time to time, and I'm pretty much up to date on their efforts, but I thought I might acquire a different perspective from you." She pulled out her small recorder and, when Vera nodded her assent, turned it on. "After all," she continued, "this thing with using the leukemia virus to carry FHF genes into eggs is your idea."

"Well, mine and Dr. Chamberlin's and his associate, Gary McKeever."

At that moment, Vera's phone chimed. It was Kal from the cat lab. "Gertrude has given birth to three kittens," he said, "*D, E,* and *F* have joined us."

"That's great," Vera exclaimed. "How do they look? Just a minute, Kal, I'm putting you on speaker. Sandra McNally from Atlanta is here."

"Hi, Ms. McNally."

"Sandra, please," she called out.

"Sandra, I phoned to tell Vera that we have our second litter. Three more kittens were born last night. They seem to be in good shape. I'll weigh them before I leave."

Vera said, "Don't forget to take mouth swabs for Noah."

"Right. The swabs are right here. By the way, Naomi, Adam, and Eve have opened their eyes, and Naomi is exploring the cage." In the end, they had decided to use biblical names for the kittens.

Vera laughed. "That's wonderful."

After Vera hung up the phone, McNally remarked, "Well, it seems I arrived at a propitious time."

Vera nodded. "Everything is going as well as we could have hoped. I understand that the other labs—Moscow, Paris, as well as the CDC—are making similar progress."

"I guess the big question on everyone's mind is what are the chances for success … for survival of the domestic cat?"

Vera shrugged. "As you know, nothing like this has ever been done before. We can only hope that we've got the science right … and that Mother Nature will give us a break."

McNally raised her eyebrows. "Do you believe in God, Vera? Is it okay if I call you Vera?"

"That's my name." Vera pursed her lips and pondered the question. "I guess I believe in some kind of God. Not the old bearded guy up in the sky, but a creative force that … oh, how can I put it … that started the big bang or something.

"In any case, whether our efforts to save the cats are successful or not, will depend not on any supernatural force, but on the validity of our ideas and on our laboratory and veterinary skills."

McNally's thumbs raced as she typed into her PDA. Vera stared. "Why all the typing?" she asked. "You're recording our talk, aren't you?"

"Yes, but I'm adding ideas for a column. You know, I'm not the only reporter here in Camarillo. I ran into several reporter friends, one from *The New York Times* and one from Fox News."

Vera chuckled. "Don't I know it! Almost every day, I have several show up, either here at my practice or over at the institute. I have to take time out to answer questions. I'm not complaining. The public has a right and a need to know what we're doing."

"You sound like a journalist."

Vera shrugged. "Fortunately, Lowell Stanaland has hired a PR pro to deal with the press so Noah and I aren't tied up. The guy puts out daily press releases on the institute's letterhead describing the previous day's developments, if there are any."

McNally nodded. "I'd like to see some of them."

"Sure," Vera said, "I'll transfer the entire batch to your PDA right now." She opened her laptop and hit a few buttons. "Done."

"Thank you so much," uttered McNally. She eyed the small screen in her hand. "Nineteen of them. This is great!"

Vera was pensive. "There's a huge amount of interest worldwide in the cat crisis. These press releases let everyone know when Adam the kitten opened his eyes, when Naomi could walk three feet without collapsing into a tiny ball of fur—every milestone."

"Now you sound like a poet," McNally said.

Vera was taken aback. "It's interesting," she observed, "that in the last fifty years we've had other calamitous declines in populations—some bat species, the Tasmanian devil, honeybee colonies—but in none of these did most people take such a keen interest. What's different this time?" She answered her own question. "It's obvious, isn't it? Cats aren't only our pets, they're … they're family."

Noah was feeding baby Lilith mashed peas, managing to get about a third of the green pulp into her mouth. "We finished the DNA work on the first three kittens today," he said.

Vera rushed in from the kitchen. "Why didn't you tell me? What did you find?"

"It seems that two of them have the bullet, but we couldn't find any evidence for it in the third. I think that *A* and *C* might survive FHF but I don't think that *B* will."

"They have names, now. Let me see … *A* is Naomi and *C* is Eve. Oh. The two females have the bullet, but the male doesn't. I wonder if that's significant. It would be ironic, in a horrific way, if only female zygotes were able to take up the bullet. All our work would be for nothing."

"Three cats is hardly a statistically significant sample. Let's wait until the other cats are tested. I understand that the group at the Pasteur Institute is doing the same tests, and we should hear from them in a day or two."

"You're right, of course. I guess I'm a bit anxious."

"Aren't we all? Incidentally, I don't see the point of keeping the kittens in the cages any longer. Either they are resistant to FHF, or they aren't. What's the point of continuing to protect them?"

"Yes, you're right, in a sense. However, I want to keep them secluded until they're old enough to immunize with the routine agents such as panleukopenia and calicivirus. It would be a terrible joke if we succeeded in protecting the cats against FHF with the bullet, only to have them die of some ordinary virus for which we have vaccines."

Noah wiped Lilith's mouth for the tenth time. "Hadn't thought of that."

The next day, Angelo sent Noah and Vera an e-mail summarizing the progress at the CDC, the Pasteur Institute, and the Moscow Veterinary Institute. Vera read aloud to Kal and Jane from her computer screen. "Four kittens have been delivered to date at the CDC. All are healthy."

"Hey, that's great!" Kal declared.

Vera read on. "Six kittens so far in Paris, but one died during delivery. André Fidèle suspects a congenital defect of some sort. The Moscow Veterinary Institute has five healthy kittens."

"Well," Jane remarked, "it's a start."

Over the next month, all the queens gave birth to their kittens. All were viable, except a few that had died during birthing—one at the institute and two at the CDC. In Paris, one of the queens died during parturition, and the three fetuses she was carrying were lost. All the kittens at the Moscow Institute for Veterinary Medicine had survived and were thriving. By November 18, there was a total of eighty-seven kittens housed in all four labs.

On Monday, November 22, Vera was sitting in Noah's office when his computer signaled a new e-mail. "It's from Angelo," Noah announced. He read the message aloud:

> *Noah and Vera*
> *I have heard from André Fidèle at L'Institute Pasteur regarding their tests for incorporation of the FeLV-FHF vector into DNA of the kittens. He reports that of the 33 kittens surviving so far, 27 test positive for the vector. Of these, twelve are males and the rest are females.*
> *Congratulations!*
> *Now only one question remains. Will the incorporated vector protect the kittens against FHF?*
>
> *Angelo*

Noah looked up at Vera, and she at him. Her eyes became glazed. "Hold me!"

"Don't cry," Noah whispered. "I feel the same way. This is what we hoped for ... It's great news."

"Just one tear?"

Noah pulled away to see she sported a big grin.

"Obviously, both sexes are equally likely to incorporate the bullet," Vera noted.

By the end of November, technicians in the four labs had learned that, of the eighty-seven surviving kittens, twenty had not acquired the bullet genes. Those that had were about equally divided between males and females. Although the search went on for additional feral cats, no more were found in North America. A few were found in Norway, and five in North Africa, but all were already dying from FHF.

"It looks like we got started on this enterprise just in time," muttered Vera one morning while scanning the newspaper.

"What?" called Noah from the kitchen.

"I said, I think we began the work with the feral cats just in time. They're not finding any more uninfected cats anywhere."

Noah came out of the kitchen. "None at all? Nowhere on earth? Unbelievable!"

Vera took a deep breath. "When I read stuff like this, I'm petrified," she said. "Sixty-seven kittens on this planet capable of ensuring the survival of the species. Sixty-seven! I wonder what kind of odds the population biologists are giving *Felis catus* for survival. Of course, we don't even know if the bullet will work."

"I read a blog the other day on that very topic. Sixty-seven is right on the edge of the critical size for a population of small mammals to survive. Fortunately, the feral parents were acquired from different areas, and, therefore, have different gene mixes. We'll have heterogeneity on our side. Also, there's no doubt that these cats are going to receive the best possible care, and that will help ensure their survival."

"Always assuming of course," added Vera, "that the bullet actually protects them against FHF."

"Well, yes, I have to assume that. If the four populations of cats survive, it will be important to get them interbreeding as soon as we can in order to keep the gene pool as varied as possible."

Vera nodded. "Yes. I think we should start planning for that right away."

"Whoa! Don't you think we should wait until the big challenge?"

Vera stifled a sob. She rose and wrapped her arms around Noah. "I've got to believe that the bullet will be effective," she said softly.

"Yes. Yes, of course." Noah said nothing for a time. Finally, he asked, "When do you think we can expose the kittens to FHF?"

Vera thought a moment. "Well, first we've got to immunize the kittens against the other routine viruses. I figure we can start that on the oldest of the kittens in late December."

"Sheesh. That's a month off!"

"Uh huh. We'll just have to take it easy until then."

The day after Christmas, Vera immunized the kittens in the first batch, nine in all, against those feline viruses for which she had vaccines. She excluded FeLV, however, as this was the vector they had used to get the FHF genes into the fertilized eggs.

By the first week in January, all the kittens had received their shots. "Time to hurry up and wait," muttered Vera.

"How long before we can let the cats out of the lab?" asked Noah.

Vera closed her eyes and rubbed her forehead with one hand. "I think we should wait at least a month for the vaccines to take effect, then we can let the cats out of the bag, so to speak. I understand that the other labs are planning to wait that long."

"Whew! If patience is a virtue, we qualify as saints."

On Valentine's Day, the first three kittens had been weaned, and Vera announced that it was time to release them to the outside world. There was no fanfare, no press—no formal ceremony of any kind.

"Let's do it," she said to Noah and Kal.

"Of course, we're probably putting Adam to his death," Noah pointed out.

"I know. I know," Vera responded. "That's the point, isn't it? Adam lacks the bullet. Eve and Naomi have it. If Adam dies and the other two live, we'll know the experiment was successful."

"They should be separated," Noah said. "We could take one home ..."

"Yes," Vera agreed, "it will be a great playmate for Lilith. Besides, there should be plenty of FHF around from when Bastette had the virus. I'll take one to the clinic. We know that the place is full of FHF, so that'll be a good exposure. Kal, could you take the third home with you?"

"Sure. I used to have a cat before ..." He shrugged. "Which kitten goes where?"

Noah said, "Let's randomize the decision." He grabbed a pocket calculator. "I'll generate a random number from one to three. One is for Adam, two is for Eve, and three is for Naomi. Then I'll do the same thing again for the chosen kitten's destination. Okay?"

Vera and Kal nodded. Noah punched a few keys. "Adam goes with Kal," he pronounced, "Eve comes home with us, and Naomi gets to reside at the clinic."

Vera scooped up the two females and placed them in carriers. At the clinic, she decided not to house Naomi in a cage, but would let the kitten enjoy the run of the place. There was no point in protecting Naomi from FHF; she was either protected, or she was going to die anyway. After she prepared a soft bed of clean rags near the litter box, Vera grabbed a few cans of cat food left from a time when there were feline patients at the clinic.

When she arrived home with Eve, she put the pet carrier on the floor and opened its door. The kitten looked out with fearful eyes. Cringing, she then edged to the back of the carrier. Vera reached in, picked her up, and held her close to her chest.

"Doris," she called, "would you bring Lilith in here please?"

The nanny came in, cradling Lilith in her arms.

"Oh! Oh my goodness," she exclaimed, "I never thought I'd see a living cat again!"

Vera smiled. "With luck, in time, there may be many more. Well, here goes. Set Lilith down on the floor, please."

Doris did so, propping up the infant with a few pillows. Vera put the kitten down in front of her daughter. Lilith's eyes opened wide. She reached out toward the cat and started giggling.

Vera grinned. "Well, well," she said, "I guess this is going to work out." She put the kitten closer to her baby and placed one of Lilith's hands on her back. Vera then moved the child's hands back and forth in a stroking motion. Lilith's giggle broke into a hearty laugh. Eve purred loudly.

A few days later, Angelo arranged a teleconference among scientists working out of the four labs caring for bullet cats.

"We have two options," declared Angelo. "We can begin releasing kittens to the public right away, or we can keep them sequestered until they are old enough to breed. Then we will be able to release the kittens from the next generation."

André Fidèle said, "I don't see any reason to wait. The cats are either resistant to FHF, or they are not. If they are, then there is no reason not to release them right away. I think we would be wise to get the new generation as geographically spread out as possible."

"I don't agree," countered Vera. "At this stage of the program, there are still very few cats. They are precious. If something were to happen to even a few of them, this could reduce the breeding population below the critical size necessary to perpetuate the species. It is … or was common, before FHF, for cats to be run over by cars, or to be mauled by dogs or to die from infections. I feel strongly that we should breed the cats ourselves and only release them when we have, say, a couple of hundred worldwide."

"Yes," offered Professor Yuri Mishkin from Moscow, "Dr. Barnett is right. We must protect the first few generations until we are absolutely certain that the animals are resistant to FHF and that their numbers are over the hump, as the Americans say."

"Ah, *oui*," replied Fidèle, "I see that you two have a compelling argument."

"That's convincing," Angelo agreed. "Then we must set up breeding programs in each of our centers."

That evening, Kal was entertaining a lady friend named Karen, who was delighted with the kitten dozing in a corner of the sofa. "What's her name?" she asked.

Kal replied, "It's a he. His name is Adam."

"I think this is the first cat I've seen in a year. Do you really think the cats from the university will make it?"

Kal sat down beside Karen, handing her a bottle of Hefweizen. "We hope that many will, but I don't think Adam will be one of the survivors."

"Why?" Karen put down her drink. "Is he sick? He looks okay."

"I'm sorry. I didn't mean to upset you. It's just that Adam is kind of an experimental control. He didn't get the protective genes that are supposed to guard the cats against the FHF virus. I expect he'll start to show signs of the disease within a few days."

"Oh, that is so sad." She took the kitten in her lap and began stroking it tenderly. Adam, eyes still closed, purred. "Maybe you're wrong. Maybe he'll survive anyway." Kal said nothing.

The next day, as expected, Adam was unsteady on his feet and would take no food. The kitten expired eighteen hours later.

In the months that followed, Vera and Noah kept in touch with the centers in Atlanta, Paris, and Moscow. "Look," said Vera, pointing to the image on her laptop, "they're building special enclosures at the CDC." Noah peered over her shoulder. "Angelo says the compounds are large enough to accommodate up to a hundred cats each." She scrolled down.

"Whoa!" cried Noah as he read aloud. "The cats are sealed off from the public by concrete block walls. Spectators can observe the colonies through thick, double-paned windows."

Vera stood and put her arms around Noah. "There is so much effort, so much expense going into this. What if it's all for nothing?"

Noah pulled back. "Vera, c'mon! We've done all we can. Our ideas are sound. As far as we know, we've made no mistakes. It's up to nature—God, if you prefer."

Vera stared into his eyes without speaking. Finally, with a raspy voice, "Right." She pushed away. "Thank goodness we don't have to worry about protecting the cats from FHF."

By October, there were fifty-eight surviving sexually mature cats housed in the four centers. Those lacking the bullet had been removed from the colonies and died soon after. A few of the remaining animals had expired from causes unrelated to FHF.

Vera paced the room, Lilith in her arms. "It's time, Noah. Starting today we can let the cats mate. "

Noah looked up from his reading. "I know. Think about it. Half the human population knows."

Vera stopped pacing. She nodded, her face beaming. "Thank you. I'm so absorbed in the project, I guess I forget that much of the world is following it too … Oh Noah, I'm so scared."

Noah rose and enfolded mother and daughter. The three remained still for several minutes.

Vera placed Lilith in her playpen. "We haven't forgotten anything, have we?"

Noah wrinkled his brow. "Like what?"

Vera sat down beside him; she took his hand in hers. "Let's go over it one more time," she said. "In order to keep the gene pool as diversified as possible, we'll ship several of our cats of each sex to Atlanta for breeding. Likewise, cats from the CDC will be flown to the institute."

"Right. And the same exchange will be done with bullet cats from Paris and Moscow.

"I'm sorry, Noah. I keep expecting something to go wrong …"

"Vera! I'm the nervous Nellie, here. One of us has to be calm. You're appointed."

"Thank you," she whispered. "Maybe we can both relax." She kissed him warmly.

In November, just before Thanksgiving, Vera was checking her inbox. "Look, Noah, we got a break. Angelo writes that the mated females in all four labs are fertile. They're all pregnant." She yelled out, "Whoopee!"

Lilith began bawling. Noah picked up his daughter. "It's all right, sweetheart. That's just your mommy when she's incredibly excited."

By the end of the year, queens in Camarillo, Atlanta, and the two European cities were giving birth to litters of three or four second-generation bullet kittens.

In mid-March, Vera and Noah received an e-mail from Angelo, reporting that the French, and Russian groups had begun releasing cats from the labs.

In Paris, kittens were given to individual families. *Le Monde*, in cooperation with the Pasteur Institute, conducted an essay contest. In five hundred words or fewer, the writers had to explain why they wanted to care for one of the experimental cats. Three scientists from the institute, as well as several university professors, artists, and political personages served as judges. The winners each received a kitten provided, they could demonstrate they knew how care for the animal.

"We need to discuss this," Vera remarked after she read Angelo's message. How are we going to distribute the rest of the Camarillo kittens?"

"We could contact *The Star*," said Noah. "I'll bet that editor, Kohut, would love to get in on it."

Vera nodded. "Good idea. I don't want to have a contest like the French are doing, however. Reading essays would take too much time. Nevertheless, we do have to be sure that whoever takes a kitten knows how to care for it."

Vera phoned Douglas Kohut. As expected, he was pleased to have *The Star* help with distributing the cats. The next day on the front page, *The Star* announced a lottery. Winners would be given one of the kittens to take care of. Entrants had to demonstrate that they had the physical and financial means to take care of a cat. They were also warned that there was no guarantee that the pet would survive. An entry slip was printed right on the page. A drawing would be held for every kitten that was ready to be taken out of the lab. Within a week, the paper had received over four thousand entry slips, some from as far away as San Francisco.

By the following Tuesday, Vera was ready to release the first of the newly weaned kittens: two males and two females. The drawing was held at *The Star's* offices in Camarillo. Several hundred people had gathered for the event. A huge, wire-mesh drum held the entry slips. Mayor Yoshino was on hand to officiate. He turned a large crank to rotate it, and picked out the first winner.

The mayor read from the slip. "Lorena Menendez of Oxnard." He waited. No one came forward. "I guess she's not present. It's okay. Being here isn't a requirement. We'll phone her later."

Douglas Kohut stepped forward. "Here, we can call her right now on my phone." He dialed and, after a moment, handed the phone to the Mayor.

"Hello," said Yoshino, "is this Lorena Menendez?" He looked at the crowd. "I think it's her daughter. She's going to get her mother." A moment later he said, "Hello, Mrs. Menendez? Are you the Lorena Menendez who entered the drawing for a kitten?" He nodded vigorously toward the gathering. "I'm happy to tell you that you are the first winner." He addressed the people in front of him. "She seems to be rather excited." Back into the phone he added, "I'm going to let Dr. Barnett talk to you. She'll arrange how you can pick up the kitten." He handed the phone to Vera.

Two of the remaining three winners were present and were able to take their prizes home with them. The fourth was a man who lived in Simi Valley and could not be reached at first.

During the weeks that followed, more kittens were released in Paris and its suburbs, in Moscow, and in Atlanta. One April afternoon, Angelo arrived home early, carrying a cardboard carton. He could hear the faint strains of a Bach prelude through the thick door and smiled.

He put the carton down on the porch and let himself in. He sat down in an armchair just out of Dorothy's sight. When she finished the piece, she started to rise and spotted him. Dorothy screamed. "Angelo! You scared the daylights out of me."

He rose and took her in his arms. "I'm sorry, sweetheart. I didn't want you to stop playing just because I was here."

"Is something wrong? Why are you home early?" She was breathing hard.

"No, nothing is wrong at all. In fact, I have a surprise for you."

"What?" Her eyes widened.

"Just wait right here." He went back to the door and retrieved the carton. He set it on a table next to Dorothy.

"What is it?"

"Open it."

Dorothy pulled open the cardboard flaps. She gasped. "Oh. Oh, Angelo. I can't believe it!" In the box were two barely weaned kittens, one all black, and the other white. "I never thought ..." She started to sob. Tears streaming down her cheeks, she took both of them up in her arms and snuggled them to her breast.

Angelo nodded with satisfaction. "Dorothy, you must understand that it is possible that one or both of these cats may die. We don't know yet whether Chamberlin's vector will work."

Dorothy nodded. "Yes, I know. I've been following all the developments in the news, and you've been telling me about the project at the CDC. Why did you choose me to take two cats?"

"Why not? Who is more worthy or more capable? You helped fund Dr. Barnett's original experiments in California. You have more experience in taking care of cats than most people. Besides, it wasn't just I who chose you; it was unanimous by the committee overseeing the project."

"We'll have to pick up some items for the cats: food, litter box, bedding."

Angelo smiled. "Wait right here, please." He went back out to his car and soon returned with boxes of stuff—canned and dry cat food, small cat beds, a scratching post, two litter boxes, and cat litter—in short, just about anything and everything one might need to care for cats.

Dorothy shook her head. "Oh my. You are so thoughtful." She put the kittens back in the carton and put her arms around Angelo. "You will never know how much I love you."

"Maybe not. But if you love me as I love you, then ... I don't know how to finish the thought."

Dorothy grinned. "I think I get the idea." She began bustling about, setting out a water dish in the kitchen, preparing their bed, putting out food, and performing all the little chores she used to when she had a houseful of cats. "Do the kittens have names?" she called to Angelo in the next room.

"Yes. Let me see. I think the black one is called Hermione and the white one, Engelbert."

"Oh for goodness sake. Those are terrible names. Who named them, anyway?"

"It was the lab techs on the project. One day at lunch, they tried to think of the most outrageous names they could for the cats. They even made a list."

"Well, I'm just going to rename them. So the black one is female and the white is male?"

"Yes."

She thought a moment. "I'm going to name the female Nora and the male Torvald."

Angelo laughed heartily. "My dear, you recall that their marriage didn't end up so well."

"I know. But *A Doll's House* was our first evening out together, and if I name the kittens after the couple in the play, they will always remind me of that night."

26

By mid-summer of 2023, the second-generation kittens from the four centers had been released to the public in areas in and around Moscow, Paris, Atlanta, and Camarillo.

In mid-July, Noah received an e-mail from Angelo reporting that a cat known to be carrying the bullet had died of FHF in Moscow.

"Uh-oh," said Noah.

"What is it?" asked Vera. She walked over and looked over Noah's shoulder at the screen. "Uh-oh is right." She laid her hands on his shoulders. "That's the end of it, isn't it?" She sat down on the couch, her head in her hands. Her body sagged, as if devoid of energy.

Noah came over, sat beside her, and took her hand in his. "Look, it's quite possible that some of the cats didn't get all of the genes in the bullet. Don't overlook the fact that a large number of cats that acquired all the genes are still running around, while those that did not are all dead."

"But ... well, yeah, that's true."

At the CDC, Angelo barged into Bronkowski's office. "I have a thought," he proclaimed.

Bronkowski glared at Angelo. "Oh yeah? What is it now?"

"I think we should sponsor an international conference on FHF."

The director regarded his star epidemiologist. Angelo tried not to smile as Bronkowski's expression evolved from a scowl to neutral, and then to a nod.

Finally, Bronkowski spoke. "Say, that's not a bad idea. We could have different sessions for the molecular biology, epidemiology, pathology ..."

Angelo had expected an argument. For once he and his boss were in agreement at the outset. "I was thinking mid-September, perhaps the thirteenth and fourteenth."

"Sounds good. I don't think we've got anything else going on at that time. Whom would you invite?"

"I'll have to think about it. Certainly the groups in Paris and Moscow ... and Chamberlin and his wife. I can make a list."

Vera and Noah arrived in Atlanta on the twelfth of September and took a cab to the CDC. There they met Angelo, and, as Vera had never been to the campus, he gave them a guided tour. Later that day, Angelo drove Vera and Noah to his home. They would stay with the Kraakmos for the three days of the conference.

Dorothy heard their approach and opened the door. The two women hugged. "Oh, it's so good to see you again," Dorothy gushed. "Come in. Come in. Oh, Noah. I wish I understood more about how your bullet thing works. All I know is that it seems to have the ability to protect cats from the virus."

Noah, rather self-consciously, gave her a hug. "Yes, it looks that way. It's still too soon to declare victory. We'll know for sure in another six months."

Dorothy showed them to the guest bedroom. "You can leave your bags here. Angelo, dear, how about fixing our guests a drink."

"Absolut! What can I get for you, Vera?"

"Scotch over ice if you have it."

Noah said, "Do you have any of that Danish beer I drank on my last trip?"

"Yes. There's a deli not far from here that stocks it." After he filled a stein for Noah, he said, "Too bad all that work came to nothing."

"Yeah. That's for sure. If I had only had this RNA interference idea first, we could have saved a lot of time …"

"And a lot of cats," Vera interjected.

When they had settled in the living room, Vera noticed the two kittens playing with a cloth ball in a corner.

"Oh my goodness, I had forgotten that you had taken two of the CDC cats. What are their names?"

"The little girl cat is Nora, the little boy is Torvald," Dorothy replied.

"Those names sound familiar," Vera observed.

"They're the names of the main characters in the Ibsen play, *A Doll's House*," Angelo replied.

"Right. I remember now." She walked over to the kittens. "It's something of a pleasant shock to go into someone's house and find kittens playing. It's been a while. In time, I guess the novelty will wear off."

"We can only hope," offered Noah.

Dorothy set out a plate of sliced veggies and a dip. "You two have become world famous," Dorothy remarked. "I see your names in the paper all the time."

"If the experimental cats start dying, that fame will turn to notoriety," said Noah.

"Don't be so pessimistic," scolded Vera.

Noah shrugged. "Sorry. Just being realistic."

Vera had been apprehensive when Angelo asked her to open the conference, but she'd gamely agreed. She spent hours preparing a thirty-minute lecture on the history, pathology, and epidemiology of FHF. By Thursday afternoon, the invitees, eighty-seven in all, began arriving. After Angelo's glowing introduction, and short speech in which he referred to the veterinarian as the "savior of the species *Felis catus*, Vera bounded up to the microphone. As she did so, the assembled scientists began applauding and rising. Vera stood on the podium in shock. She spied Noah, a wide grin on his face, clapping with the others, and she gave him a slight nod. The standing ovation went on for two minutes before Vera motioned for the group to be seated. It took her another minute to regain her composure.

"Thank you so much," she began. "I … I don't deserve all that. There are many, many people involved in this project—many of you, in fact—and I am happy to have played a part." She went on to deliver her prepared speech, detailing Angelo's role in determining the origin of FHF, the early failed attempts at growing the virus in cell culture, and the failures of the immunization trials. She ended with a brief description of the bullet and of the search for unexposed feral cats.

Bronkowski had decided that only three separate sessions were needed—one dealing with the epidemiology of FHF, another devoted to its molecular biology, and the third for FHF pathology. After the opening speeches, the scientists, veterinarians, and molecular biologists split into three groups, where most of the knowledge-sharing occurred.

Noah chaired the session on molecular biology of FHF. It was the most crowded of the three. When he entered the room, the forty or so scientists gave Noah a standing ovation. Noah nodded to Nicky Brown, who applauded with the others. Brown returned the nod. Noah reflected, *Three years … has it really been three years since my futile trip to the CDC?*

"Thank you. Thank you," said Noah. "Please understand that my colleague, Gary McKeever, was equally responsible for the FHF-FeLV construct. Stand up, Gary." He stood hesitantly, his face flushed. He too received standing applause.

Noah described the construction of the FeLV vector and his choice of FHF genes. Angelo's friend André Fidèle reported on a simplified technique for manufacturing the vector, a procedure that cut hours off the time needed for the process. Other papers were primarily speculative and covered such arcana as a fourteen-amino-acid sequence in the Ebola region of the genome that the author believed was involved with the notorious hemorrhagic aspect of the virus. Another report described a matching sequence of the FIV and Ebola genomes that might have allowed them to recombine. One researcher proposed a hypothetical explanation for the attachment of the Ebola-like filaments to the spherical portion of the virus.

Most of the attendees at the pathology session were veterinarians. All had observed the same pattern—rapid onset, loss of muscular function, hemorrhage, and quick death.

The session on epidemiology was the most sparsely attended. Angelo described his discovery of the Seattle connection. Scientists from Europe, Asia, and South America described transmission patterns of FHF in their respective regions of the globe. One German epidemiologist provided a detailed statistical summary of FHF in the new generation of cats carrying the bullet, and of the control group that had not incorporated the vector. As all knew, every cat lacking the bullet had succumbed to the virus. However, about 15 percent of cats that had the FHF-FeLV genes incorporated, nine cats in all, also died. There was considerable speculation as to why that might be. It was generally assumed that those cats failed to incorporate some essential part of the vector. The upside, of course, was that 85 percent of the new kittens were apparently completely free of susceptibility to FHF.

The conference was a huge success. Months later, after the papers had been published in a slim volume, the first printing sold out within a week. The publisher went through seven before demand ebbed.

A few days later, back in Camarillo, Noah was going over a draft of a paper he was co-authoring with Gary for *The Journal of Molecular Biology* on the FHF-FeLV vector when Gary appeared in the office doorway.

"Hey, Doc, got a minute?"

"Sure, come on in. I'm going over our paper. Looks like it's about ready to send off."

"Yeah. I think so too," replied the young man. "The graph in the second figure may need reworking." The two men discussed the details of the figure. Gary then said, "Say, Doc, I want to thank you for acknowledging my assistance with the bullet at the conference the other day. You called me your colleague. That really got to me. I've always thought of myself as your student."

Two years after the first bullet-carrying kittens were born, 348 domestic cats were known to be alive worldwide. All of these carried the bullet genes. Very few cats from the first bullet litters had died from FHF.

The National Zoo in Washington had set up an intensive breeding program at their Front Royal campus in Virginia. Zoo personnel acquired three male cats and four females from the CDC, two males and a female from the French group, and a single female from the Russians.

In the heart of California's Mojave Desert, at a town named Rosamond, the Exotic Feline Breeding Compound had been established in 1977 to propagate, and thereby preserve, endangered cat species. There, one could find tigers, jaguars, ocelots, and a variety of other species. The common house cat was not one of their priorities—until now, when the species was close to extinction. After the bullet cats were released to the public, the EFBC acquired three males and three females and began a breeding program for *Felis catus*. Visitors, who were formerly attracted to the more exotic cats were now enthralled once again to have even brief contact with their onetime companion animal. The EFBC allowed children to pet them in a fenced-in enclosure. Many adults, who formerly kept a cat or two, were as eager as the children to approach and handle the felines.

The old Torre Argentina cat sanctuary in Rome was reopened as a breeding center and cat hospital. Similar programs were initiated at the Moscow Zoo, the Zoo de Vincennes in Paris, and the Shanghai Zoo.

Even the Melbourne Zoo began a breeding effort, ironic, considering the love/hate relationship the Australians previously had regarding domestic cats. In an odd turn of events, the head keeper of the Seattle Zoo decided that it would be a great public relations coup if it started breeding domestic cats. Their reputation had been unjustly besmirched by the fact that FHF had originated there.

Many of these programs were funded, wholly or in part, by donations from Feline Phoenix, which now served as the clearinghouse for all donations for the preservation of *Felis catus*. Although Vera's organization had paid out over seven million dollars in aid, it was still receiving donations from animal lovers. She had finally rented an office in Camarillo, hired three paid personnel, and appointed a board of directors, consisting of veterinarians and individuals from animal-welfare groups.

At Adolfo Camarillo High School, in the very city where Vera and Noah had brought about their miracle, Roberto Ruiz, a biology teacher, phoned his friend and fellow biologist, Booker T. Wilson, at Jordan High located in the South-Central area of Los Angeles. They exchanged small talk for a minute or two. Finally, Wilson asked, "So, Roberto, to what do I owe this call? You didn't phone me just to talk about the Dodgers."

Ruiz laughed. "No, no, Book. I wanted to discuss something with you. I have a crazy idea."

"You always had crazy ideas back in the day. So what else is new?"

"This one might have legs. You know that there's a huge movement to get people to breed cats, right?"

"Yeah. In fact, the cat thing and FHF have been a popular discussion topic in my biology classes for several years now. Even the inner-city kids at Jordan are into it. It's given me a great lead-in to population dynamics, ecology, disease, and a bunch of other subjects."

"Precisely," replied Ruiz. "Here's my idea. You and I, we apply for a grant from the National Science Foundation. The idea is that we acquire a couple of breeding pairs of cats for both our schools. We include a request for funds to build large enclosures on the school grounds. Then we let the students tend the cats, keep careful records of their health, growth rates, that sort of thing." He was speaking rapidly, now. "When kittens are born, the students record their phenotypes—hair color, size, sex, all the usual stuff. That way, we tie in basic genetics."

"And when the semester ends, then what?"

"Well, that's the beauty of it. The project gets passed on to the next class. This goes on for several years. When there's a surplus of cats, we give them away."

"Sounds good, but why do you need me? Why don't you just apply for the grant on your own?"

"Well, my friend, you already said it. I think the grant application might have more of a hook if it involved 'inner-city kids' as you call them."

"Aahh. I see. Yes, I see your point." He was silent a moment. "Let's do it!"

Four months later, their grant made headlines when the NSF awarded the two schools $50,000 each toward student-run cat-breeding programs. Within months, schools across the country, and then across the world, had adopted such programs.

Another year passed. The nine bullet cats that had died of FHF proved to be the exception. All the other bullet-carrying cats were completely resistant to the virus. The Cat Preservation Coalition was now sponsoring public service spots on television and radio encouraging families to adopt breeding pairs of cats.

Vera noticed one of these while watching the evening news. "Look at that, Noah," she remarked. "A few years back, those animal groups were advocating that people have their cats spayed or neutered. Now they're saying let 'em have babies."

"I think it won't be long before they go back to their earlier position. I read that there are now an estimated two thousand cats on Earth."

"I saw that article. That's from just sixty-seven kittens in the first litters."

"No, it was eighty-seven," countered Noah. "I remember that number." Vera grinned. Noah knotted his brow. "What? ... Oh. Right. Twenty of those didn't get the bullet. You got me."

"Yep. It's two thousand from sixty-seven," Vera said triumphantly. "By the way, I read something else today in a vet journal."

"Oh?"

"It seems that feline panleukopenia is gone."

Noah frowned. "What do you mean, gone?"

"Gone. As in wiped off the face of the earth. All of the feral cats that were picked up for the project happened to be free of the virus. Destroy the host and destroy the parasite."

"I'll be damned. It's an ill wind that has a silver lining ... or some such adage."

Vera laughed. "No, I think you mean 'Every cloud blows no good.'"

In time, the many breeding programs across the planet successfully brought the species *Felis catus* back from the brink of extinction. The domestic cat was removed from the endangered species list.

One day, at breakfast, Vera said, "Noah, why don't we invite Dorothy and Angelo to spend a few days with us? We haven't seen them since the conference two years ago."

Noah looked up from the paper, put down his coffee, and rubbed his chin. "Do you think they'd come all the way from Atlanta?"

"You won't know until you ask them."

"Okay, sounds good to me. I'd like to see them."

"We might spend a day at the beach, have a barbeque on the weekend. We could invite Gary and Jane. You think they'd make the trip from Los Angeles?"

"Sure they would. It's not that long a drive. I can send Angelo an e-mail right now. When do you want to have them here?"

"How about late June?" She glanced at a calendar. "We don't have anything scheduled for the week of the twenty-fourth. Is that okay with you?"

Noah nodded.

Noah and Vera picked up Angelo and Dorothy at LAX. The ride back to Camarillo gave them a chance to catch up on their comings and goings.

"How's your little girl?" asked Dorothy.

"Oh, she's great. She's learning the alphabet, and she loves playing with the kittens."

"But aren't they fully grown now?" asked Angelo.

Vera laughed. "The first pair are fully grown. I'm talking about their kittens—their first litter."

"Of course," he said. "I should have realized."

On the day of the barbeque, Noah puttered with the grill. Vera was in the kitchen, cutting up vegetables for the salad. Dorothy set out paper plates and condiments. Angelo sat in a lawn chair nearby, watching Lilith playing with four kittens on the deck.

Vera had taken a male kitten from the second litter of bullet cats so that she could breed it with Eve. She had called it Luke after adding New Testament figures to the list of biblical names. When the two cats reached sexual maturity, they soon generated their first litter. Now there were six cats at the Chamberlin home, and visitors had to watch where they stepped, lest they squash one of the animals. Three-year-old Lilith delighted in the cats, bringing Vera and Noah considerable amusement.

Gary and Jane arrived at noon.

"Hello, Dr. Kraakmo," Gary said when he saw Angelo.

"Ah, hello Gary. It's been quite a while, hasn't it? Please, call me Angelo. I think we've known each other long enough to drop the formalities, no? I won't call you Dr. McKeever if you don't call me Dr. Kraakmo, okay?"

Gary grinned. "Fair enough," he replied.

In the kitchen Vera wondered why Kal was late. *He's usually quite prompt,* she recalled.

On cue, the doorbell chimed. Vera shepherded Kal to the backyard. "Noah," she called, "Everyone is here. I think you can load up the barbeque now."

"Will do," said Noah. Soon the guests and their hosts were relaxing in the shade of the trees, sipping drinks.

"Tell me, Gary," said Angelo, "what are you working on at UCLA?"

"I'm looking at controlling elements in hemoglobin synthesis. Fudderman has a large grant for sickle-cell work, and I'm working on a small piece of the project."

"Are you able to use the skills you picked up from the FHF work?"

"Not really. However, I am drawing on the earlier work I did with Noah on MEFA, a disease that has a lot in common with sickle-cell."

Dorothy asked, "And you, Jane; how are you spending your time?"

"Well, I guess you could call me a freelance writer. I've been writing essays and articles for magazines. I've had two published so far."

"Really? Where?"

"The first one was a short essay on the importance of domestic animals to us humans. It appeared in *Reader's Page* on the web this February. The other one just came out in *Newstime.* It's a kind of first-person account of the bullet work we did with the cats—an 'I-was-there' description. It's rather long, so they're publishing it in three installments."

"Why that's just wonderful," Dorothy enthused. "I'll pick up a copy of the magazine. Do you have a copy of the first article?"

"You can read it on their website, if you're interested."

Vera said, "I have a copy. You can read it today, if you like. I'll get it for you after we eat."

"How about that novel you were always talking about?" asked Vera.

"Ah, yes," answered Jane, "the novel. Well, I've been keeping a computer file with ideas. I'm homing in on a plot that concerns a veterinarian who gets involved with the personal lives of many of her patients—or rather the companions of her patients. You'll never guess who the model for my protagonist is." She smiled smugly. "Hint: it's a female vet."

Vera reddened. "I never got involved in the personal lives of my patients," she protested.

"Oh?" chuckled Jane. "And how is it that Dorothy is here with us today?"

"That's different … I think." Now all present were laughing.

Jane added, "I'm also working on an expository article on the growing cat population for a veterinary magazine."

"That's great," said Vera, happy to change the subject. "Would you like me to look it over when it's finished?"

"Oh, thanks so much. That would be wonderful. I was going to ask you."

"Look at the child," said Angelo, pointing at Lilith. "Look how she enjoys playing with the kittens. Think about it. All over the world, there are children playing with cats. Adults too. We came so close to losing the species …

The others were silent, contemplating Angelo's remark. Finally, Noah rose. "Got to check on the goodies." He walked over to the barbeque and picked up the tongs. Gary and Kal soon followed.

"Looks like a stag party over there," Vera observed. Let's join them." The women went with the men, but Angelo strolled over to where Lilith was amusing herself with the kittens.

The child looked up at Angelo and smiled. "Kittekat," she said, pointing to the frolicking animals.

"Yes, kitty cat. In Norwegian, that's *katte*. It is spelled *K-A-T-T-E*."

Lilith cocked her head and stared at Angelo. *"Katte,"* she said, pronouncing it perfectly.

"Yes!" Angelo cried out, *"Katte*. You can speak Norwegian!" The group chatting at the barbeque looked over at Angelo's outburst.

"Looks like those two have struck up a friendship," Vera remarked.

They watched as Angelo picked up one of the kittens. He nestled the tiny cat in the palm of one hand, on its back. With his other hand, he began stroking its belly. "Nice kitty," he said. "Pretty poossy cat ... *pen katte ... nydelig katte.*"

Vera raised her eyebrows.

"Norwegian for *pretty kitty* and *beautiful kitty*," Dorothy whispered. "He's always saying that to our cats."

"This is the guy who used to say that he didn't like cats," Noah pointed out in a hushed voice.

Meanwhile, Angelo, oblivious to the others, continued to stroke the kitten that was now lying back, eyes closed and purring so loudly that Lilith could hear it.

"Katte purring," she said.

Angelo smiled. "Yes, the cat is purring. You have quite a vocabulary, little one." He continued petting the creature in his hand, murmuring to it all the while. All at once, he became aware of the crowd over by the barbeque. He looked up to find their eyes were on him. "Scandaloose," he muttered, just loud enough that the group heard him. They burst out laughing. Angelo shrugged, and then he smiled.

For *Felis catus* it was not ...

The end

Epilogue

Fifteen years after the first litters of bullet-carrying kittens were born, the domestic cat had regained its status as a common household pet.

One fall morning, an hour before sunrise, Lilith, now in her second year of high school, was already up completing a homework assignment she had been too tired to finish the night before. Vera and Noah were still sound asleep. Noah was jarred awake by the ringing of his phone.

He glanced at the clock by the bed. *Six thirty. Who calls at such an hour?* Suddenly, he was wide-awake. He recalled the time many years before when Gary McKeever had phoned him early in the morning to tell him of the theft of his research cats.

Vera too was now awake. Noah put the phone to his ear. "Yes," he said. "Who is it?"

A voice answered, "This is Dr. Lars Sundstrom calling from Stockholm on behalf of the Alfred Nobel Foundation. May I speak with Dr. Noah Chamberlin or Dr. Vera Barnett, please?"

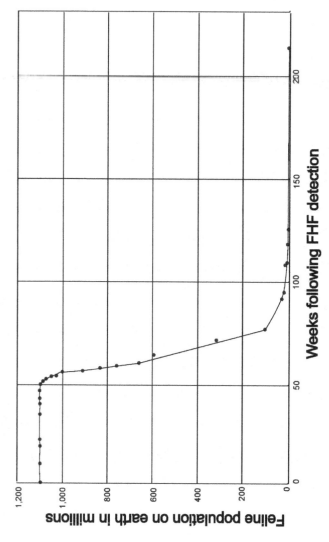

Weeks following FHF detection

Feline population on earth in millions

Reprinted from Jour. Epizool. 348: 344-53, June 14, 2029.
Courtesy of the authors, A. Kraakmo, V. Barnett and W. Bronkoweld

Author's Note

This tale is fiction, of course. Nevertheless, the actuality of emerging viruses is well documented. Ebola appeared on the epidemiological scene only about forty years ago. We are still attempting to understand where such "new" viruses come from—where they hide in nature.

Australia's island state of Tasmania is home to the world's largest living carnivorous marsupial, the Tasmanian devil (*Sarcophilus harrisii*). In the late 1990s a mysterious cancer appeared in these animals, whose population then numbered about one hundred fifty thousand. Devil Facial Tumor Disease (DFTD), as the cancer is called, may be caused by a virus or it may be a DNA defect; we don't yet know. The disease gives rise to tumors that develop around the faces and mouths of the creatures, hampering their ability to catch prey and feed. Once a devil shows signs of the disease, death by starvation is inevitable. To date, over 90 percent of the animals have died. Some biologists fear that the species may become extinct. It took over ten years for DFTD to become widely known, presumably because the Tasmanian devil is not part of our everyday experience or economy.

Throughout the United States, a mysterious disease named Colony Collapse Disorder is wiping out entire bee colonies. Beekeepers in several states first observed this phenomenon in 2006. The bee decline appears to be associated with the bite of a tiny parasitic fly. In addition to honey production, bees are important pollinators of a variety of agricultural crops; the economic consequences of a major die-off of our bees would be devastating. Unlike DFTD, Colony Collapse Disorder, however, is frequently in the news, because, of course, honeybees play a major economic role.

The idea that new viruses might appear by the linking of genes from other viruses, as occurred in this story at the Seattle Zoo, is not far-fetched. Mutation of viral genes is common. Recombination of genes from different viral strains is well established.

A scenario such as I've presented here is a nightmare that health professionals fear. The worldwide epidemic of influenza caused by a strain of virus known as H1N1 gave rise to the fear that this virus could give rise to a pandemic reminiscent of the 1918 disaster. A decade ago, Severe Acute Respiratory Syndrome (SARS) virus elicited similar fears. Avian forms of influenza are also a constant threat.

If an FHF-like virus were to appear in cats, cattle, swine, or, dare I suggest, in humans, would we be able to control it?

Currently the United States spends billions a year fighting real or imagined human foes. Perhaps we should provide support to further the goal of understanding viruses found in humans and in wild and domestic animal populations. The threat is decidedly greater than that of any human enemy.

Bonham Richards
May 31, 2012

Acknowledgments

I received invaluable technical information from many individuals. Nevertheless, it is quite possible—even probable—that errors have made their way into the story. Any such mistakes are solely mine.

My thanks to veterinarians Dr. Edgar M. Church and Dr. Karen Anderson Moore for information on veterinary practice and surgery as it pertains to cats.

Dr. Pierre Comizzoli, Reproductive Physiologist with the National Zoological Park, Washington, DC, provided essential technical details pertaining to feline surgery and artificial insemination, as well as feline gestation.

I am also grateful to Dr. Randall Singer, veterinary epidemiologist at the University of Minnesota, for his help with the technical literature.

The Feral Cat Foundation and Feral Cat Coalition supplied information on feral cats and their habitats.

The following careful readers looked over all or portions of the manuscript and provided invaluable criticism: Jody Avery-Smith, Eugenie Cansler, Ruth Carlson, Liz Ellenberger, Margie Hanft, Pepper Heimowitz, Anita Hunter, Shlomo Kreitzer, Margaret Goodman (whom I also credit for turning me into a cat person), Bob McCampbell, Kathy Merry, Alice Rene, Ida Robbins, Ruth Sherman, Barbara Speiser, Mario Speiser, Jeanie Tufts, Doris

Vernon, Jim Vernon, Barbara Wagner, Beverly Warren, Josette Wingo, and Lowdon Wingo.

Tasha Wisniewski furnished superb editorial assistance. Hugh Kramer also provided comments on the first six chapters.

Thanks to Ted Goodman for alerting me to Steinbeck's use of intercalary chapters in *The Grapes of Wrath.*

A huge thank-you to the many at iUniverse who contributed to the various phases of this book's development

Cover design by Andrew Healy.

Thank you, Joelle Steele of Feline Insights, for the feline image heading the intercalary chapters.

Finally, I affectionately acknowledge my two former feline friends, Lilith and Bastette, who, over the years, provided me not only companionship but a profound appreciation of the bond that can form between man and animal.

Selected Annotated References

Butler, Kiera. "Faster, Pussycat! Kill! Kill!" *Mother Jones,* June 2011, 72.
   Anti-feral article demonstrating how feral cats devastate bird populations.

Driscoll, C. A., et al. "The Taming of the Cat" *Scientific American,* June 2009, 68.
   Recent archeological findings regarding the history of feline domestication.

Garrett, Laurie. *The Coming Plague: Newly Emerging Diseases in a World Out of Balance.* New York: Farrar, Straus and Giroux, 1994.
   A compendium of information about the history, and future, of emerging viruses.

Jones, Menna E. and H. McCallum. "The Devil's Cancer." *Scientific American,* June 2011, 72.
   Discussion of Devil Facial Tumor Disease.

Lau, N. C. and D. P. Bartel. "Censors of the Genome." *Scientific American,* August 2003, 34.
   An introduction to RNA interference.

McKenna, Maryn. *Beating Back the Devil: On the Front Lines With the Disease Detectives of the Epidemic Intelligence Service.* Free Press, 2004.

Pendergrast, Mark. *Inside the Outbreaks: The Elite Medical Detectives of the Epidemic Intelligence Service.* Boston: Houghton Mifflin Harcourt, 2010.
A recent history of the EIS.

Rudacille, Deborah. *The Scalpel and the Butterfly. The War Between Animal Research and Animal Protection.* New York: Farrar, Straus and Giroux, 2000.
A review of the animal rights movement and related topics.

Singer, Peter. *Animal Liberation.* New York: Avon Books, 1975.
A philosophical underpinning for those opposing the use of animals for research.

Glossary

Alpha globin: A type of polypeptide chain found in hemoglobin.

Amino acid: A nitrogen-containing organic acid essential for life. Polypeptide chains are made up of specific sequences of amino acids linked end to end.

Antibody: (Immunoglobulin) A type of protein found in higher organisms, whose function is to bind to invading agents such as viruses and destroy them.

Autoclave: A type of sterilizer that kills microbes using steam under pressure.

B-cells: (Also called B-lymphocytes.) Lymphocytes which, when properly stimulated, manufacture antibodies that enter the blood.

BSL-1, 2, 3, & 4: Biosafety levels. Each designation refers to specifications for laboratory design in which microorganisms of potential danger are to be investigated:

a) BSL-1 labs—Those where any microbes to be investigated are considered not dangerous. Access to the labs is not limited to trained personnel. A high-school science lab is an example.

b) BSL-2 labs—Those where potentially dangerous organisms might be investigated. Example: a clinical microbiology laboratory in a hospital. Access to the lab is limited to trained personnel. Protective clothing, such as laboratory coats, are worn by lab personnel. Many procedures are carried out in biological safety cabinets equipped with HEPA filters.

c) BSL-3 labs—Labs where dangerous pathogens, such as the tuberculosis bacterium, pose a danger to others if spread through the air or by objects. Access to the lab is limited to highly trained personnel. Protective clothing, such as smocks, scrub suits, or coveralls, is worn by the lab personnel. Almost all work is conducted in biological safety cabinets.

d) BSL-4 labs—Labs where the most dangerous pathogens (Ebola, anthrax, etc.) are investigated. All air leaving the lab is HEPA-filtered. Entry to the lab is by means of an airlock. The lab is maintained under negative air pressure so that when a portal is opened, air does not readily leave the lab. Access to the lab is limited to highly trained personnel. Street clothing is removed in a changing room. Personnel wear special protective clothing. They decontaminate the protective clothing on exiting the lab and shower before donning their street clothes. All work is done in biological safety cabinets. These labs are generally in separate buildings dedicated to their use.

Bacterium: A type of microbe whose cells lack most of the membranous structures found in cells of higher organisms. Examples: *E. coli; Staphylococcus aureus.*

Buffer: An aqueous solution that resists changes in acidity. Example: human plasma.

Calicivirus: A type of virus responsible for upper respiratory infections and mouth ulcers in cats.

Capacitation: Changes in spermatozoa by which they become capable of fertilizing ova.

cDNA: Single-stranded DNA complementary to a sequence of RNA. cDNA is a normal intermediate in the replication of retroviruses. It is also commonly synthesized in the laboratory as a research tool.

Clone: A group of cells descended from a single ancestral cell.

DNA (deoxyribonucleic acid): A polynucleotide having a specific sequence of nucleotides that, when decoded by cellular machinery, determines all the hereditary traits of an organism.

dsRNA (double-stranded RNA): Most RNA in the cell is single-stranded. Most DNA is double-stranded. However, a small amount of dsRNA is found in cells, where it acts as a regulator of gene function. It is also produced by many, perhaps all, retroviruses. dsRNA plays an important role in RNA interference (RNAi).

Ebola: A virus causing a severe, generally fatal, hemorrhagic disease (Ebola hemorrhagic fever—EHF) of primates, including humans.

Electrophoresis: A lab technique by which dissimilar substances can be separated from one another by the different rates of movement of their molecules in an electric field.

Endemic: Of a disease that is always found in a distinct geographical area. For example, malaria is endemic in Kenya.

ELISA (Enzyme-linked immunosorbent assay): A sensitive immunological test for identifying antigens or antibodies. Its many uses include identification of viruses (HIV, Ebola, etc.) in human or animal fluids.

Envelope: Outer membranous capsule surrounding some viruses. The membrane is acquired during development of the virus when it exits the host cell and a portion of that cell is budded off, enclosing the viral particle.

Enzyme: A protein capable of speeding up a specific biochemical reaction. There are thousands of different enzymes in living organisms.

Epidemic: An outbreak of a disease in a human population characterized by a significant increase in the number of cases over the normal (endemic) level.

epithelium (plural: epithelia): A type of tissue forming the lining of all body surfaces. examples: cells comprising the skin or lining the mouth and digestive tract.

Epizootic: An outbreak of a disease in an animal population characterized by a significant increase in the number of cases over the normal level.

Escherichia coli (E. coli): A common intestinal bacterium. Often used as a research tool because it's genome has long been known. This microbe has occasionally achieved notoriety owing to the fact that some strains are pathogenic and can cause food poisoning.

Feline AIDS: An AIDS-like disease of cats caused by the Feline Immunodeficiency Virus (FIV)

Feline hemorrhagic fever (FHF): A fictional infectious hemorrhagic disease of cats characterized by sudden onset, rapid progression and death within hours or days.

Feline leukemia: A contagious viral disease of cats clinically similar to leukemia (a cancerous proliferation of leukocytes) in other animals and characterized by gradual loss of weight, malaise, and, eventually, death.

Feline Leukemia virus (FeLV): The causative agent of feline leukemia.

Felis catus: The scientific name of the domestic cat.

Fermentor: A vat capable of providing optimal conditions for the growth of industrial microbes used for producing vitamins, antibiotics, and other biochemical compounds.

FIV: See Feline AIDS.

Follicle-stimulating hormone (FSH): A pituitary hormone that stimulates egg maturation in females.

Gene: A portion of DNA responsible for a single (or closely related group of) function(s).

Genome: The entire complement of genes of an organism.

Globin: Any of several polypeptide chains that make up hemoglobin. In the adult mammal, hemoglobin contains two alpha-globin and two beta-globin subunits.

Gonadotropin: Name given to several hormones secreted by the anterior lobe of the pituitary gland. These hormones play a vital role in coordinating functions of the reproductive organs.

Granulocytes: White blood cells containing intracellular granules.

Hemoglobin: The protein found in red blood cells responsible for binding to oxygen and transporting it to all parts of the body. Adult hemoglobin is made up of four polypeptide chains, two of alpha-globin and two of beta-globin, as well as four iron-containing heme units.

HEPA filter (High Efficiency Particulate Air filter): An extremely efficient air filter capable of removing particles no smaller than 0.3 μm in diameter. This includes almost all bacteria, many viruses, as well as pollen, mold spores, and other particles found in dust.

Heterozygous: The state of having two different alleles (forms) of a given gene, one of which came from the male, and the other from the female parent.

In vitro: From Latin meaning *in glass*. Any process or experiment that is performed outside the living organism, such as DNA synthesis in a test tube.

Laparoscope: A surgical instrument allowing the observation and manipulation of structures inside the abdomen. A small surgical incision is made in the abdominal wall and the laparoscope, and a thin fiber-optic viewing device, is inserted through the hole. Additional surgical probes and instruments can be inserted through the same opening. In this way, surgical procedures are carried out inside the body without the necessity of a large incision.

Leukocytes: White blood cells.

Lymphocytes: Small white blood cells that play a key role in immunity by reacting to foreign substances in the body. There are two broad classes:

B-lymphocytes—Cells that secrete antibodies into body fluids.

T-lymphocytes—Cells that attack other cells infected with a microbe, and which interact with B-lymphocytes, modulating their activity.

Macroerythrocytic feline anemia (MEFA): A fictional hereditary disease of cats caused by a mutation in the alpha-globin gene and characterized by swollen red blood cells.

Messenger RNA (mRNA): A class of specific RNA molecules, each of which is coded for by a specific gene. mRNA functions to carry genetic information from DNA to the sites where proteins are synthesized.

Micromanipulator: A mechanical device consisting of motors and controls used to position tiny tools and pipettes extremely precisely as the user peers through a microscope.

Morula: An early stage in embryonic development consisting of a ball of cells.

Nucleotide: The basic subunit of DNA and RNA. A nucleotide is made up of a sugar molecule (ribose in RNA and deoxyribose in DNA), a phosphate molecule, and a nitrogen-containing organic base. DNA contains the four bases adenine, guanine, cytosine, and thymine. RNA contains the first three, but has uracil instead of thymine.

Oocyte (pronounced *oh-oh-cyte*): immature egg cell.

Panleukopenia (feline): A contagious disease of cats characterized by sudden onset, lack of appetite, and vomiting, generally resulting in death of the cat.

Plasmids: Small, circular, replicating pieces of DNA found in bacteria and in the nuclei of some higher organisms. They are separate from the organism's chromosome and carry a limited number of genes.

Polymerase chain reaction (PCR) A laboratory procedure for replicating DNA. It is commonly used with tiny quantities of DNA samples (such as might be found at a crime scene) to amplify the samples, allowing them to be analyzed and subjected to further experimentation that would be impossible with the original, minute quantities of DNA.

Polynucleotide: A chain of nucleotides in a specific order. The two important polynucleotides, DNA and RNA, carry information in the sequence of the bases in their nucleotides. That sequence in DNA comprises the genetic information passed from generation to generation. RNA obtains its base sequence as it is copied off of a DNA template and is the means by which the information in genes is used to carry out cellular functions such as protein synthesis.

Polypeptide chain: A chain of amino acids bonded to each other in a unique sequence. A protein molecule is made up of one or more such chains.

Promoter: A sequence of nucleotides on DNA that signals where the copying of a molecule of RNA is to start.

Pronucleus: A fertilized ovum has two nuclei, one from the ovum itself, and the other from the spermatozoon that fertilized it. These two nuclei are referred to as pronuclei at this stage. After they fuse and the DNA of the pronuclei undergo recombination, the resulting zygote contains only one nucleus.

Provirus: A viral genome integrated into the host chromosome and passed on to succeeding cell generations as the chromosome is replicated. Example: FeLV in cats is often present as a provirus.

Protein: A molecule consisting of one or more polypeptide chains. Proteins have diverse, important functions in living organisms. Most enzymes are made of protein as are muscle fibers, antibodies, and many structural components of skin, connective tissue, and many other components of the organism.

Recombinant DNA: DNA formed by the breaking of DNA strands from different sources (such as different chromosomes or different parents), and their reconnection into new sequences. Formed naturally in the process of fertilization or artificially in the laboratory.

Retrovirus: A virus with an RNA genome. In the course of their reproduction such viruses use this RNA to make DNA copies (cDNA) using an enzyme called *reverse transcriptase.*

Reverse transcriptase: An enzyme found in retroviruses that catalyzes the synthesis of cDNA from an RNA template.

Rhinotracheitis (feline): An infectious upper-respiratory-tract disease, not unlike a severe cold in humans. Caused by a variety of viruses, including caliciviruses and Feline Viral Rhinotracheitis Virus (FVR).

RNA: (ribonucleic acid) A polynucleotide having a specific sequence of nucleotides, whose sequence of bases is copied from a DNA template.

RNA interference (RNAi): The destruction of messenger RNA (mRNA) by a complex process that involves small-interfering RNA (siRNA), double-stranded RNA (dsRNA), and several enzymes. RNAi is thought to play an important role in regulation of cellular function as well as in defense against retroviruses.

Small interfering RNA (siRNA): Short segments of RNA about 22 nucleotides long. The siRNA is derived from partial digestion of dsRNA by an enzyme named *dicer*. It is an intermediate in the process known as RNA interference (see above).

Stem cells: Certain undifferentiated cells found in multicellular organisms having the potential to differentiate into any of a wide variety of cells. Two broad categories of stem cells are *embryonic stem cells* and *adult stem cells*. In the course of embryonic development, stem cells play a seminal role, as they differentiate into the various types of cells comprising the organism—muscle, epithelia, nerve cells, etc. In the adult (here, meaning the organism at any age after birth), the primary function of stem cells is to replace cells that die and to repair damaged tissue.

T-cells: (Also called T-lymphocytes.) See lymphocyte.

Transfer RNA (tRNA): A class of specific RNA molecules, each of which binds to a specific amino acid and, by pairing with three bases on mRNA, brings the amino acid to its correct position in a growing polypeptide chain.

Vector: In the context of molecular biology, any agent that can carry a piece of DNA into a cell. It can function in either of two ways:

a) Cloning vector—used for reproducing the DNA fragment.

b) Expression vector—used for making a gene product (e.g. a polypeptide chain) from the imported gene. Examples: plasmids, bacterial viruses, and retroviruses.

Virogene: One or more genes found on the host's chromosome with the information to synthesize a virus or its components.

Virus: A particle composed of nucleic acid and protein (and, for some viruses, lipid), capable of infecting a cell and using the cell's biochemical apparatus to reproduce itself. A virus is incapable of reproduction in the absence of a host cell.

Wright's stain: A staining procedure used to help distinguish different parts of a cell and to differentiate diverse types of cells. It is commonly used to stain blood smears, allowing the observer to make out the various types of white blood cells.